Man of War

Man of War

Alexander Kent

arrow books

Published in the United Kingdom in 2004 by Arrow Books

1 3 5 7 9 10 8 6 4 2

Copyright © Bolitho Maritime Productions 2003

Alexander Kent has asserted his right under the Copyright, Designs
and Patents Act, 1988 to be identified as the author of this work

First published in the United Kingdom in 2003 by William Heinemann

Arrow Books
The Random House Group Limited
20 Vauxhall Bridge Road, London SW1V 2SA

Random House Australia (Pty) Limited
20 Alfred Street, Milsons Point, Sydney,
New South Wales 2061, Australia

Random House New Zealand Limited
18 Poland Road, Glenfield,
Auckland 10, New Zealand

Random House (Pty) Limited
Endulini, 5a Jubilee Road, Parktown 2193, South Africa

The Random House Group Limited Reg. No. 954009

www.randomhouse.co.uk

A CIP catalogue record for this book
is available from the British Library

Papers used by Random House are natural, recyclable products made from
wood grown in sustainable forests. The manufacturing processes conform to
the environmental regulations of the country of origin

ISBN 0 09 943628 0

Typeset by
Palimpsest Book Production Limited,
Polmont, Stirlingshire
Printed and bound in Great Britain by
Cox & Wyman Ltd, Reading, Berks.

For you, Kim, With all my love.
The *Revenge* comes out of the squall!

To every thing there is a season, and a time to every
 purpose under the heaven:
A time to be born, and a time to die; a time to plant,
 and a time to pluck up that which is planted;
A time to kill, and a time to heal; a time to break down,
 and a time to build up;
A time to weep, and a time to laugh; a time to mourn,
 and a time to dance . . .
A time to love, and a time to hate; a time of war, and
 a time of peace.

Ecclesiastes 3:1–8

CONTENTS

New Horizon

Eight bells had chimed out from the forecastle and the lower deck was cleared while the ship moved steadily, purposefully some would say, toward the widening span of land, which seemed to reach out on either bow. The moment every sailor carried in his thoughts. The landfall. *This* landfall. Home.

The sails, already reduced to topsails and jibs, were hardly filling, the tough canvas still shedding moisture like rain from the final, overnight approach.

Hills and cliffs, at first in shadow and then opening up to the watery sunshine. Landmarks, familiar to some of the older hands, the names of others called down by the masthead lookouts while the land gained shape and colour, dark green in some places, but the brown of winter still clinging elsewhere. For it was early March, 1817, and the air was as keen as a knife.

Eight days out of Gibraltar, a fair passage when set against the adverse winds which had challenged every mile as they had skirted the Bay of Biscay, up and around the well-remembered names of Ushant and Brest, the enemy coast for so long. It was still hard to believe that those days had changed. As had the life of every man aboard this graceful, slow-moving frigate, His Britannic Majesty's ship *Unrivalled* of forty-six guns, and a complement of two hundred and fifty sailors and Royal Marines.

Or so it had been when they had left this same port of Plymouth. Now there was a sense of contained excitement, and uncertainty. There were boys who had become men while the ship had been away. They would find a different life waiting upon their return. And the older ones, like Joshua Cristie, the sailing master, and Stranace the gunner, would be thinking of the many ships which had been paid off, hulked, or even sold to those same enemies from the past.

For this was all they had. They knew no other life.

The long masthead pendant lifted and held in a sudden flurry of wind. Partridge, the burly boatswain, as rotund as his namesake, called, 'Lee braces there! Stand by, lads!' But even he, whose thick voice had contested the heaviest gales and crashing broadsides, seemed unwilling to break the silence.

There were now only shipboard noises, the creak of spars and rigging, the occasional thud of the tiller head, their constant companions over the months, the years since *Unrivalled*'s keel had first tasted salt water; that, too, right here in Plymouth.

And nobody alive this day would be more aware of the challenge which might now be confronting him.

Captain Adam Bolitho stood by the quarterdeck rail and watched the land edging out in a slow and final embrace. Buildings, even a church, were taking shape, and he saw a fishing lugger on a converging tack, a man climbing into the rigging to wave as the frigate's shadow passed over him. How many hundreds of times had he stood in this place? As many hours as he had walked the deck, or been called from his cot for some emergency or other.

Like the last time in Biscay, when a seaman had been lost overboard. It was nothing new. A familiar face, a cry in the night, then oblivion. Perhaps he, too, had been thinking of going home. Or leaving the ship. It only took a second; a ship had no forgiveness for carelessness or that one treacherous lapse of attention.

He shook himself and gripped the scabbard of the old sword beneath his coat, something else he did without noticing it. He glanced along his command, the neat batteries of eighteen-pounders, each muzzle exactly in line with the gangway above it. The decks clean and uncluttered, each unwanted piece of cordage flaked down, while sheets and braces were loosened in readiness. The scars of that last savage battle at Algiers, a lifetime ago or so it felt sometimes, had been carefully repaired, painted or tarred, hidden except to the eye of the true sailor.

A block squeaked and without turning his head he knew that the signals party had hoisted *Unrivalled*'s number. Not that many people would need telling.

It was only then that you remembered. Roger Cousens had been the signals midshipman. Keen, caring, likeable. Another missing face. He felt the northwesterly wind on his cheek, like a cold hand.

A voice said quietly, 'Guardboat, sir.' No excitement. More like two men exchanging a casual remark in a country lane.

Adam Bolitho took a telescope from another midshipman, his eyes passing over familiar figures and groups which were like part of himself. The helmsmen, three in case of any last second's trick by the wind or tide; the master, one hand on a chart but his eyes on the land. A squad of marines paraded, ready if needed to support the afterguard at the mizzen braces. The first lieutenant; a boatswain's mate; and two marine drummer boys who seemed to have grown since they had last seen Plymouth.

He steadied the glass and saw the guardboat, oars tossed, quite motionless at this distance. His jaw tightened. It was what his uncle had called *marking the chart for us*.

It was time.

Not too soon, and never too late. He said, 'Hands wear ship, Mr Galbraith!'

He could almost feel the first lieutenant's eyes. Surprise? Acceptance? The danger was past. Formality had taken over.

'Lee braces there! *Hands wear ship!*'

'*Tops'l sheets!*' Seamen strained back on braces and halliards. A boatswain's mate pushed two extra hands to add their strength as *Unrivalled* continued toward her allotted anchorage.

'*Helm a-lee!*' The slightest hesitation, and the big

4

double wheel began to swing over, helmsmen moving like a single body.

Adam Bolitho shaded his eyes as the sunlight lanced between the shrouds and flapping canvas, as the ship, his ship, turned steadily into the wind.

He saw his coxswain watching across the busy deck, waiting to call away the gig, ready for the unexpected.

'*Let go!*'

The great anchor dropped from the cathead, spray bursting up and over the beautiful figurehead.

After all the miles, the pain and the triumph, for better or worse, *Unrivalled* had come home.

Lieutenant Leigh Galbraith looked aloft to make certain that the excitement of returning to England had not allowed slackness to mar the sail drill.

Each sail was neatly furled, the masthead pendant curling in the offshore wind, the ensign streaming above the taffrail, bright against the land, hoisted to replace a well-worn and ragged one before the dawn had broken. Marine sentries were posted to prevent unlawful visitors, traders, even some of the local whores, coming aboard when they realized that *Unrivalled*'s company had had little to spend their pay on over the past months. And there was talk of slave bounty, and prize money, too.

He watched the guardboat approaching, an officer standing in the sternsheets shading his eyes. Their first contact with authority since leaving the Rock. *Unrivalled* would probably be invaded now by riggers and carpenters, some of whom might have helped to build her more than two years ago.

He shivered again. But it was not the bite of the March wind.

He had seen the ranks of laid-up ships, large and small, as *Unrivalled* had tacked slowly toward the anchorage. Proud ships, famous names. Some had already been here when they had last left Plymouth for the Mediterranean and Algiers, eight months ago.

Who would be next?

He confronted it, as a senior officer might examine a subordinate's chances. His record was good. He had taken part in every action at Algiers and before. Captain Bolitho had already recommended him for a command of his own, had put it in writing to the Flag Officer here in Plymouth before they had sailed. Suppose there was nothing? He might remain first lieutenant for yet another commission, until he was passed over altogether.

He dismissed it angrily. He had a ship, and a fine one, more than many could claim.

He walked to the entry port and touched his hat as the officer of the guard clambered aboard.

The visitor glanced around the upper deck and said, 'Heard all about it, your part at Algiers! Lord Exmouth was full of praise in the *Gazette*!' He handed Galbraith a thick, sealed envelope. 'For the captain.' He inclined his head toward the shore. 'From the admiral.' He looked over at some of the bustling seamen, disappointed perhaps that there were no wounded on view, no shot holes in the freshly painted black and white hull. 'Another boat is coming out to collect the despatches, and any mail you have to go.'

He reached for the guard ropes and added with a grin, 'Welcome home, by the way!'

Galbraith saw him over the side, and the oars were thrashing at the water almost before he had taken his seat.

Galbraith made his way aft, ducking without thought beneath the overhanging poop.

Past the wardroom, empty but for a messman; every one else would be on deck, sharing it.

The marine at the cabin door stamped his foot and bawled, 'First lieutenant, *sir*!'

It was something you never got used to, he thought. Every Royal Marine seemed to act as if he were on a parade ground, and not within the close confines of a ship.

The screen door opened and young Napier, the captain's servant, in his best blue coat, stood before him.

Galbraith took it all in at a glance. The great cabin which he had come to know so well, where they had talked, and shared their thoughts as much as any captain and first lieutenant could; and it was rare in many cases he had known. Times of anxiety and doubt. And of pride.

Some clothing was scattered across the stern bench, the captain's patched and faded seagoing gear, while his best frock coat hung swaying from the skylight.

Bolitho glanced at Galbraith and smiled. 'Is my gig

called away?' Then, half turned, 'Here, David, help me with this sleeve – a few more minutes won't matter. The admiral will know we are anchored.'

Galbraith hesitated, and held out the envelope. 'This is *from* the admiral, sir.'

Bolitho took it and turned it over in sun-browned hands.

'The ink is scarce dry, Leigh.' But the smile had gone, and the cabin could have been empty as he picked up a knife and slit it open.

Feet pounded overhead and blocks squealed as the boatswain's party made ready to hoist out the gig. The required formality of a ship's return from active service. Galbraith heard none of it, watching the captain's fingers curl around the envelope, its broken seal shining like blood from a sharpshooter's musket. He said, 'Is something wrong, sir?'

Adam Bolitho turned sharply, his face hidden in shadow. 'I just told you . . .' He checked himself with obvious effort, as Galbraith had seen many times when they had been coming to know one another. 'Forgive me.'

He looked at Napier. 'Never mind about the sleeve. They can take me as they find me.' He touched the boy's shoulder. 'And rest that leg. Remember what the surgeon told you.'

Napier shook his head, but said nothing.

'The ship will be moved. Repairs and general overhaul . . . as you were doubtless expecting.' He reached out as if to touch the white-painted timber, but dropped his hand to his side. 'She can certainly do with it, after

8

the battering she took at Algiers.' As if he were speaking to the ship and nobody else.

He brushed against the hanging coat and added, 'Tomorrow you will receive orders from the flag captain. We can discuss it when I return aboard.'

He stared at the envelope still crumpled in his hand. He must think clearly. Empty his mind, as he had forced himself to do when everything had seemed finished. Lost. Two people he had come to know so well since he had taken command of *Unrivalled*, just over two years ago here in Plymouth: he had been her first captain. Galbraith, strong, reliable, concerned. And the boy David Napier who had almost died, the great, jagged splinter jutting from his leg like some obscene weapon. He had been so brave, then and again later under the surgeon's knife when the wound had become poisoned. Perhaps like himself at that age . . .

His hands felt as though they were shaking, and the clamour in his mind seemed loud enough to fill the cabin.

When he spoke, his voice was very calm. 'I am losing *Unrivalled*. I am being relieved of command.'

So quietly said, while that same voice within screamed, *It can't be true! Not this ship! Not yet!*

Galbraith took a pace toward him, the strong features laid bare with disbelief and then anger, feeling the hurt like his own.

'It must be wrong, sir. Some fool of a clerk at the Admiralty!' He spread his hands. 'After everything you've done? Even the officer of the guard was full

9

of it, all about Lord Exmouth's praise for *Unrivalled* in the *Gazette*!'

Adam reached for his coat but Napier was already holding it, troubled, but still unable to understand what it would mean. Somehow it helped to steady him.

'Stay with me, David. There are things I must do.' He recalled suddenly what Napier had said when Rear-Admiral Thomas Herrick had asked him if he took care of his captain. *We take care of each other.* So simply said, yet in this impossible, reeling daze it was something to cling to. Little enough.

He said, 'Tell the others, Leigh. I'll speak to them later, perhaps in here.' His dark eyes flashed, revealing real pain for the first time. 'While I still can.'

Galbraith said, 'The gig will be alongside, sir.'

They paused, and abruptly shook hands. No words, and beyond thoughts. The Royal Marine stamped his boots together as they passed him and walked to the companion ladder; in an hour it would be all over the ship. But all the sentry saw was his captain and the first lieutenant, with the youth in the proud blue coat walking a pace or two behind them.

Galbraith took a deep breath as the companion opened to the clear, bright sky, feeling his shirt drag against the wound where a musket ball had scored his shoulders that day amid the burning madness of Algiers. Another inch, maybe less, and he would not be alive now.

He saw the captain turn to nod to somebody on the quarterdeck; he even smiled.

Another command, maybe. Something bigger,

grander, as a reward for his actions under Lord
Exmouth. In these times, it seemed unlikely.

Unrivalled was his ship. They had become one. *We
all did*.

He recalled the officer of the guard's cheerful words,
less than an hour ago.

Welcome home, by the way!

When he looked again, Bolitho was standing alone
by the entry port; Napier had already gone down into
the gig which was waiting alongside, oars tossed and
steady like white bones.

Luke Jago, the captain's coxswain, would be there,
vigilant, as Galbraith had seen even in the midst of a
sea fight. He probably knew or guessed, the navy's
way, *the family* as the old Jacks termed it.

The marines presented arms, and the calls trilled in
salute. When Galbraith replaced his hat the entry port
was empty.

Welcome home.

The admiral's flag lieutenant was tense, even embar-
rassed.

'Sir Robert requests that you wait a few moments,
Captain Bolitho.' His hand rested on the adjoining door.
'An unexpected visitor . . . you understand, sir.'

Adam walked into the other room, light and
spacious, as he remembered it from previous visits.
When he had been given *Unrivalled*, fresh from the
builder's yard, the first to carry her name on the Navy
List. And later, meeting Vice-Admiral Valentine Keen,
when Keen had held this command. And last year, in

July, when he had joined Lord Exmouth's fleet for the inevitable attack on Algiers. In those eight months so much had happened, while here in Plymouth there was yet another admiral, Sir Robert Burch, probably in his last appointment.

The lieutenant was saying, 'We all watched you arrive, sir. It is some time since I have witnessed such crowds. Some must have been awake before dawn.'

Adam laid his hat on a chair and walked to a window. It was not the flag lieutenant's fault; it rarely was. He had been one himself. He bit his lip. Under his uncle. Another world, it seemed now. And his uncle. . .

Sir Richard Bolitho had died nearly two years ago, killed on the deck of his flagship *Frobisher*, cut down by a single shot. The memory still burned as if it were yesterday.

The other man watched his face closely, trying to miss nothing. The young frigate captain whose name had appeared in the *Gazette* so many times, fighting hand to hand against any foe which had offered itself, before the war had ended and the sworn enemies had moved into an uneasy alliance. How long might it last? And for what reason? Perhaps the battle of Algiers would come to be remembered as the last great battle under sail. Lord Exmouth had been a frigate captain, probably the most famous and successful to emerge from that everlasting war. He must have put all doubts aside to break the unwritten rule he had always followed: never force an action where ships are pitted against sited shore batteries, and in his case a thousand enemy guns.

But the gamble and the skill had prevailed, and the battle had raged for most of the day. Ships had exploded and burned, men had fought to the death. He thought of the smartly handled frigate he had watched only this morning, shining in the early sunlight, and of Lord Exmouth's words.

I want you in the van. The same ship. He glanced again at the slim figure by the window, the black hair, the fine, sensitive features. The same captain.

Adam could feel the scrutiny. He was used to it. The frigate captain: dashing, uncaring, not tied to the fleet's apron strings. He knew well enough what they thought. Imagined.

He opened the window slightly and looked down at a squad of Royal Marines paraded in the square below. New recruits from the local barracks, very stiff and aware of their scarlet uniforms. A sergeant, rocking back slightly on his heels, was saying, 'You obey orders without question, *see*? When the time comes you will be sent to a ship of the line, or a frigate maybe, like the one that came in this morning.' He had turned slightly to display the three bright chevrons on his sleeve. 'But remember this, it's not the Colonel, or even the adjutant, who will decide.' He lifted his elbow a fraction. 'It will be me, see?'

Adam closed the window, the cold air still on his lips.

He thought of Corporal Bloxham, who was now a sergeant, a crack shot even with his 'Bess', as he had affectionately called his musket that day. When he had fired one shot and had saved his captain's life, and that of the boy who had lain helpless, his leg pinioned by the splinter. Another face he had come to know so well.

The flag lieutenant said quickly, 'I think the visitor is leaving, sir.' They faced each other, and he added, 'It has been an honour to meet you, sir.'

Adam heard voices, doors slamming, some one half-running, perhaps to summon a carriage for the departing visitor.

He picked up his hat. 'I would that it were under better circumstances.' He thrust out his hand. 'But thank you. Yours is no easy role. I know from experience.'

A bell tinkled somewhere, and the flag lieutenant seemed to make up his mind.

'*Unrivalled* will be docked, sir. But the reports have made it very clear that it will not be a quick overhaul like the last one.'

Adam almost smiled. 'The last *two*.' He touched his arm as they walked to the door; it reminded him of the court-martial after *Anemone* had been sunk. *Prisoner and escort*.

'Then I am not being replaced?'

The lieutenant swallowed hard. He had already gone too far.

He answered, 'My late father had a saying, sir, when things seemed against him. "Look to a new horizon".' He flushed as Adam turned to face him. He would never forget that expression.

He called, 'Captain Adam Bolitho, Sir Robert!'

Adam gripped the old sword and pressed it against his thigh. The reminder. He was not alone.

* * *

Luke Jago, the captain's coxswain, walked to the edge of the jetty and kicked a pebble into the water.

He was restless, unsure of his feelings and unable to think clearly, which was almost unknown for him. He was the captain's right-hand man, trusted by him, a position he had come to value more than he would ever have believed. It was sometimes hard to recall how it had been before that day, the handshake which had changed everything. The anger and bitterness were part of another life. He had been unjustly flogged at the order of a very different captain; even though an officer had spoken up for him and proved his innocence, it had been too late to prevent the punishment. There had been apologies, but the stripes of the 'cat' would remain on his back until the day he died. It was Jago's nature to mistrust officers, and the younger they were the harder it became to overcome it. Green young midshipmen who might listen to his advice, tricks learned after his years at sea in one kind of ship or another, could suddenly turn and snap like spoiled puppies when they found their feet.

He shaded his eyes and stared across at the anchored frigate. His ship, his home for just over two years. He should be used to it. There had been other days like this one.

He had listened to it all the way from Gibraltar. Hard men and young hopefuls alike, going home, getting the prize money and slave bounty they knew was their due. In the navy it was always dangerous to hope too much, or take things for granted. When they had left Plymouth eight months back, he had seen all the laid-up ships, the hulks, once the pride of a great fleet. When *Unrivalled* had anchored yesterday they had still been here.

He heard the boy Napier moving restlessly on the pile of baggage they had brought ashore less than an hour ago. His portly, round-shouldered companion was Daniel Yovell, who had volunteered to join the ship as captain's clerk when he had heard that the previous one had died. Or so Yovell had claimed. Jago knew differently now. Yovell had been clerk to Sir Richard Bolitho, then secretary aboard his flagship. And his friend, an unlikely one to find in a man-of-war. Stooped, gentle and devout, he had been given his own cottage next to the old Bolitho house in Falmouth where he had helped in estate matters, things Jago could not begin to guess at. But something had drawn Yovell back to the sea, and he had brought with him volunteers when Captain Adam had been short of trained hands. Men from Sir Richard's last ship, and some who had served him earlier during the wars. Jago kicked another pebble into the water. All those bloody enemies who were now supposed to be treated as allies.

And the boy, Napier, what must he be thinking, he wondered. Like many before him, he had been signed into the navy by his mother. She had remarried, and was now in America with her new husband, if that was what he was; Jago knew of plenty such cases. With the offspring safely signed on, the interest faded. Napier was devoted to the captain, and Bolitho never seemed too busy to explain things to him. Whatever

16

the fools on the messdeck believed, there was nobody in a King's ship who was as lonely as her captain.

Napier said suddenly, 'Boat's casting off!' He sounded tense, anxious. He was always a serious sort of youth. Jago, who went where he chose as the captain's coxswain, had seen life in the great cabin, beyond the screen doors and the scarlet-coated 'bullock'. It had made him feel a part of it.

He heard the distant splash of oars and the familiar creak of looms and found that he was clenching his fists. His mouth was very dry.

What about me? Yovell would go to his cottage. The boy was staying with the captain. He stared at the anchored frigate again. And *Unrivalled* was going into the yard, as he had known she would. All those engagements, when she had shuddered and lurched to the enemy's iron as it had smashed into the hull, often below the waterline.

And that last time at Algiers, when so many had fallen, while the air quivered to cannon fire and splintering timbers – had the fools forgotten that too? Or that on this last passage home, the pumps had been going throughout every watch?

Unrivalled would be paid off. After that . . . It would be decided by those who had never heard a full broadside, or risked everything just to hold a mate's hand when his life was being torn from him.

He would collect his pay and his bounty and take some time for himself. Some company maybe. A woman if she came his way. Captain Bolitho might not get another ship. He would not need a coxswain.

17

He was sharply reminded of the captain's face when he had returned from seeing the port admiral. He frowned. That had been yesterday. Jago had had the gig at this same jetty, the boat's crew in their smartest rig, as always. *A ship is always judged by her boats*, some one had once said. He was right, whoever he was. And a captain's crew had to be the best of all. It was not even *Unrivalled*'s proper gig; that had been too badly smashed by canister and musket fire to warrant repair. Like some of her original crew.

It suddenly hit him. Captain Bolitho had walked down those same stone stairs. Millions of sea officers must have come and gone that way, to promotion, a new ship, to accept orders or face a court-martial. It was easy to imagine. But yesterday the captain had called him aside on this jetty, to tell him that he was being relieved of his command, and was awaiting fresh orders. Not the first lieutenant, or any of the other officers. *He told me first*.

He said abruptly, 'How's the leg, David?'

The boy looked at him, surprised by the use of his name. Like the captain.

'It's getting better.' He walked carefully to the edge of the jetty, his eyes on the gig, the same one which had brought them and their kit ashore.

Yovell was on his feet too, watching Jago, remembering their first meeting last year, when Jago had suggested that he was too old for a seagoing job of any kind. They had become friends since then, although neither would ever understand the other. Except today.

Yovell had been there as Captain Adam Bolitho had

18

gone through the final tasks before departure. Papers to be signed and witnessed by Lieutenant Galbraith before he assumed temporary command, probably the only command he would ever hold, although Yovell knew from the dictated letters that the captain had never stopped requesting it on Galbraith's behalf.

He had seen the other side of things when some post had been brought aboard from a courier brig, letters they might have missed several times in the Mediterranean. But not letters he had been expecting, hoping for. Like the small scrap of paper he kept in his personal log book, from the girl he had met on that last visit to Plymouth.

He had never spoken her name. But Yovell had seen her just once, when he had been at the old Bolitho house in Falmouth, and a courier had come with orders for *Unrivalled* and her captain. In a little pony-drawn trap, side by side before she had driven away alone. He had seen him kiss his own wrist, where some tears had splashed down. Like lovers, he had thought. Perhaps another dream?

He put his hand on Napier's shoulder and said, 'The hardest part.'

Who was he speaking to?

He saw the gig turning slowly toward the jetty steps. At another time it might have been manned entirely by captains of the fleet or squadron. But today, only the abandoned hulks were the spectators.

Jago's lip curled. 'What a crew!' He almost spat on the cobbles. '*Officers!*'

The lieutenants Galbraith, Varlo, and young Bellairs,

who had been a midshipman when *Unrivalled* had first commissioned. Luxmore, the captain of marines, Partridge the boatswain, even Old Blane the carpenter. Midshipmen too, with Deighton at the tiller by the captain's shoulder.

The bowman, another midshipman, shipped his oar and scrambled into the bows with his boathook, but almost pitched headlong.

'Toss your oars!'

In the sudden silence there was cheering, unbroken but faint in the cold offshore breeze.

Yovell felt the boy's shoulder shiver under his hand. He was an imaginative youth; perhaps he was thinking the same. That the cheers might have come from those listless, empty ships.

Captain Adam Bolitho stood up carefully and waited for the gig to come fast against the stairs.

He heard and saw none of it. It was like a confused dream, and yet each phase stood out as a separate picture. Handshakes, faces thrusting through a mist to speak, to call something, a fist reaching out as he had found his way to the entry port. Even the shrill of calls had sounded different, as if he were an onlooker, somewhere else.

If he had given in . . . He gripped his sword more tightly. He had seen it happen to others, and it had happened to him.

He glanced through the tossed oars and saw the ship. His ship.

The cheering did not stop. All those faces. But this was not the moment. *Turn away. Do not look*

20

back. How it was. Had to be in the navy, if you wanted to survive. And now emotion was the greatest enemy.

He stepped on to the jetty. Nobody spoke. The boat cast off.

Never look back. But he did, then he raised his hat, not soon enough to shield his eyes from the hard glare. They were smarting anyway. *Do not look back*. He should have known.

Jago was here. 'You decided then, Luke?'

Jago watched him impassively, then thrust out his hand. 'Like before, eh, Cap'n?'

Adam nodded to the others. The carriage would be here from Falmouth; the admiral had made the arrangements, barely able to conceal his relief that their brief meeting was over.

He looked again, but the gig was hidden by the jetty wall. Tonight Galbraith would sit in the great cabin and drink alone.

In the same breath, he knew he would not.

He looked at Napier and was moved by his obvious distress.

He gripped his shoulder. 'Get some hands to carry our gear, eh?'

He saw Yovell half lift one hand, as he usually did when he wanted to remind him of something.

He shook Napier's shoulder and said, 'I had not forgotten.'

Had he really expected that the lovely girl called Lowenna would somehow be here to see the ship come to anchor, as she had watched them leave? After

21

all the months, and the news of the battles, had he still believed in miracles?

He realized that Napier was looking at him, and had asked him something. He tried again, but all he could hear were the flag lieutenant's words.

He said quietly, 'We must look to a new horizon together.'

They began to climb the stairs. Jago waited until some seamen ran down to collect the baggage and the captain's sea-chest. Only then did he turn his back on the sea. And the ship.

2

Their Lordships' Command

Nancy, Lady Roxby, stood very still by the open door of the study, wanting to go to him, but afraid to move or touch him.

She had forgotten how long it had been since the coach had rattled around the drive, the horses steaming after their journey from Plymouth. Now the coach stood as if abandoned in the stable yard, the horses gone to the comfort of their stalls. It was raining, the sky beyond the familiar line of bare trees dull and threatening. And yet her nephew was still wearing his coat, the shoulders black with rain, his boots muddy. He was even still holding his hat, as if he were unprepared to stay, to accept what had happened.

She waited while he strode to the portrait, which was hanging in its new place by the window opposite the broad staircase. It would catch the light there, but be sheltered from glare and damp. She doubted if he had seen it.

He said suddenly, 'Tell me again, Aunt Nancy. I had no news, no letters at all except yours. You never forget, no matter how it may damage your peace of mind.'

Then she saw him reach up and touch the portrait, his fingers gently tracing the single yellow rose which the painter had added after the girl Lowenna had pinned it on his coat. She moved closer and studied him. The same restlessness, which her brother Richard had likened to that of a young colt. The youth was still there, the ghost of the midshipman, and the young sea officer who had gained his first command, a brig, at the age of twenty-three. But there were lines, too. Strain, authority, danger, perhaps fear also. Nancy was a sailor's daughter, and the sister of one of England's most famous. *Loved*. Without turning or breaking this precious contact, she could feel all the familiar faces, paintings, watching from the stairwell and the dark landing. As if to judge this latest portrait of the last Bolitho.

She said, 'It was a month ago, Adam. I wrote to you when I had found out all I could. We all knew what had happened, Algiers, and before that. I wanted everything to be better for you.'

He turned and looked at her, his eyes very dark. Pleading. 'There was a fire at the Old Glebe House. Was she . . . ?'

She held up her hand. 'I saw her. I had already told her that I wanted her to come to me whenever she felt she needed . . . a friend.' She calmed herself. 'Sir Gregory had ordered some work done on the old building, and the roof over his studios. It was a foul day, a squall off the bay . . . They were melting lead, for the guttering, I was told. Then the fire started. In that wind it spread like a wildfire in summer.'

Adam imagined it yet again. The Old Glebe House had been abandoned, then sold by the church authority at Truro; most of the locals had thought Sir Gregory Montagu mad when he had bought it. He had visited the place only occasionally, having property in both London and Winchester. Adam could see it as if it were yesterday: the famous painter guiding him through one of the many gaunt, littered rooms to avoid another visitor, his nephew. When he had seen the girl poised and motionless, her naked body chained to an improvised rock constructed of crumpled sheets draped over a trestle. Andromeda, held captive as sacrifice to the sea monster. Like a perfect statue, she had not even appeared to be breathing. Her eyes had met his, then dismissed him.

Lowenna.

He had written to her, hoping the letters would find her. That she would feel something, some emotion or memory, the yellow rose, or the time he had been thrown from his horse and his wound had burst open. She had come to him, and something had broken down the barrier. Perhaps she had written; it was common for letters to go astray, ships missing one another, others wrongly directed.

He had laughed at himself for keeping the fragment of paper she had sent over to *Unrivalled* when they had sailed from Plymouth to join Lord Exmouth's squadron.

I was here. I saw you. God be with you.

Nancy was saying, 'Sir Gregory was a stubborn man. None more so. You saw that for yourself. He insisted on being taken to London.'

'Was he badly injured?'

'He was burned, trying to help Lowenna. There was a lot of smoke. She did not stay for long. She wanted to be with him for the journey to London.'

Adam put his arms around her, moved by the familiar way she had used the girl's name. *All those years*, since the day he had walked from Penzance armed only with Nancy's address and a letter written by his dying mother. All those years, and Nancy was still like a haven.

They walked arm in arm into the study, where there was a good fire blazing, making the shadows dance across the paintings and the floor-to-ceiling book-shelves. She noticed that everything was clean and polished, even the ranks of old books, shining from some housemaid's duster rather than use. But a room so well-known to her, and lovingly remembered, in this house where she and her two brothers and sister had first drawn breath.

She heard the rain, louder now, pattering against the windows.

She often thought of this room, and the women who had stood here and waited for a ship, the ship, which one day would not return.

The grave, watching faces lining the stairway told the full story.

Adam took her hands in his. 'You see, Aunt Nancy, I am in love with that girl.'

She waited, her inner voice whispering, *don't be hurt again, Adam*.

There were sounds on the stairs now. The youth, David Napier, who had come with Adam as on his previous visit, excited despite the loss of *Unrivalled*. His hero worship had moved her more than anything. Especially when the portly Daniel Yovell had whispered like a conspirator when Adam had gone out of the house, striding almost blindly, as if he had been searching, unable to accept what she had told him.

It had been before the Bolitho coach, with Young Matthew on the box, had even left Plymouth.

Yovell had described it, squinting, his gold-rimmed spectacles pushed up on to his forehead as she had seen them so often. 'It was a tailor's shop in Fore Street, for naval and military gentlemen. Captain Adam bought that fine coat for the boy . . . Sir Richard had an account there also.' He had overcome a sudden, poignant sadness. 'The tailor comes out, rubbing his hands, m' lady, sharp as you please, and asks, "What will you be wanting this time, Captain Bolitho?" And then the Captain puts a hand on the lad's shoulder and says calmly, "Your services for this young gentleman. Measure him for a midshipman's uniform." And the lad staring at him, eyes filling his face, unable to believe what the Captain had done, been scheming, indeed, for months.'

Nancy had understood immediately but had said nothing to Napier. Adam had acted despite what had awaited *Unrivalled*'s return. It was what Richard might have done. The very thought made her eyes fill with tears.

She asked quickly, 'When will you hear about a new appointment?'

Adam smiled, glad to break the uncertainty. 'I was told that word will be sent from the Admiralty, direct to this house.' He looked around the study again, and at the portrait near the window. All the Bolithos, except Hugh, his own father.

He put it from his thoughts. 'It means there will be a ship.'

'A frigate?'

'I am a frigate captain.'

She turned away and adjusted a small vase of primroses. Dear Grace always managed to brighten the house with some sort of blossom, even in March, when a Bolitho was coming home from the sea.

She hung on Adam's words. They were what Richard had said when he had returned from the Great South Sea with the fever which had almost killed him.

And their lordships had given him, not a frigate, but the old *Hyperion*.

Adam picked up a sketch from the desk, a mermaid and a passing ship. He felt a chill, like the whispered betrayal of a secret. *Zenoria*, who had flung herself to her death from the cliffs . . . like the little sketch his cousin Elizabeth had sent him. Richard's daughter. Tragic even to think of what had happened. The love and the hatred, a child in the middle of it.

He asked abruptly, 'How is Elizabeth? Happy enough with you, I'll wager.'

Nancy did not answer. Adam and the young daughter of the country's hero, *my admiral of*

England, as Catherine had called him, had one thing in common.

They were quite alone.

On the opposite side of the house, by the stable yard, Bryan Ferguson stood at the window and watched Daniel Yovell finishing a bowl of soup which Grace had prepared.

'That should keep the cold out, my friend. There's a good fire in your cottage, too . . . we've kept an eye on things for you since you "volunteered" for service!'

Yovell put down the spoon. 'That was a goodly welcome, Bryan.' He nodded toward a pile of estate ledgers. 'Perhaps I can give you some help with that?'

Ferguson sighed. 'I'd not say no to that.' He changed the subject. 'We knew you were on your way home some days ago. The courier brig brought word. News travels fast around here.'

Yovell loosened his coat and felt for his watch.

'We saw her leave when we were still at Gibraltar.' He frowned. 'She was bringing the reports of *Unrivalled*'s damage to Plymouth. I think the Captain knew then, in his heart. He tried to shut it from his mind. *Unrivalled* meant so much to him. In my poor way I strive to understand, but a captain of any ship must see things quite differently.'

Ferguson looked at the ledgers. As steward of the estate he tried to be meticulous, to miss nothing. But he was not a young man any more. He did not even glance at his pinned-up sleeve, nor consciously recall

29

the Battle of the Saintes, where he had lost his arm thirty-five years ago. Grace had nursed him back to health and Captain Richard Bolitho had offered him the post of steward.

As if reading his thoughts, Yovell said, 'D'you still see much of John Allday?'

'He comes over from Fallowfield for a wet every week. We go down to the harbour sometimes. He likes to watch the ships. He still feels it, very badly.' He walked to the fire and poked it; it was spitting in the rain lancing down the squat chimney.

He paused to pat the cat, dozing as usual by the hob, and added, 'Captain Adam's coxswain . . . he looks a hard one.' It was a question.

Yovell smiled, his glasses slipping down again. 'Chalk and cheese, some might say, but they hit it off from from the start. Not another Allday, though!'

They both laughed.

Outside, sheltering beneath the overhanging stable roof, David Napier turned his head to listen. It was getting dark already. He knew he should be tired after the drive from Plymouth. Drained. But he could not throw off the feeling of confused disbelief. The welcome had been genuine and overwhelming. Grace Ferguson had almost smothered him, demanding to know about his wounded leg; she had shown even more concern than on the occasion of his previous visit. *At the request of his captain*. He had gone over it again and again. Like the second operation on his leg, which the Irish surgeon O' Beirne had carried out at sea just before the bloody battle at Algiers. The wound had become poisoned, and the alternative was death. He could not believe that he had not been afraid. The sudden agony of the knife, hands pinning him down on the table, the pain mounting to match the screams he knew had been his own; he had nearly choked on the strap between his teeth until merciful darkness had saved him.

And then, through it all, he had remembered the Captain's arm on his bare, sweat-soaked shoulder. And his voice, saying something about a pony ride. He turned and peered into the stable at Jupiter, the pony, high-spirited and contemptuous of his untrained efforts to ride him on that first visit to this great house, which he dared now to think of as a home.

Jupiter snorted and stamped, and Napier withdrew his hand. The coachman they all called Young Matthew, although he must be years older than the captain, had told him about the pony's habit of biting whenever he saw the opportunity. What would his mother think if she could see him here? He shut his mind. She would not care.

The rain was stopping. He would find the kitchen and see if he could help the cook with something.

He licked his lips. *It would not go away*. That moment when the coach had swayed to a halt outside a shop and the Captain had said, almost sharply, 'Come with me. This won't take long.'

Even then he had believed the Captain was in distress about the ship, still suffering those last moments which he had endured alone, with the final handshake and the gig bearing off from the jetty. He would have understood that well enough.

But when the Captain had said to the beaming tailor with his gaudy waistcoat and dangling tape measure, *for this young gentleman*, he had not been joking. He had known that, seeing Yovell's obvious delight. *A midshipman's uniform*.

Part of a dream. Unreal. He might change his mind. *This young gentleman*.

And why did he believe he could rise to the incredible offer of a new life?

'You there – is anybody about today?'

Napier swung round, shading his eyes with his wrist in a shaft of watery sunshine. He had not even heard the approaching horse, he had been so deep in his thoughts.

It was a young woman, riding side-saddle and dressed all in red, the habit the colour of some of the wine he sometimes served his captain. She had dark hair, tied back with a scarf, and was soaked with rain.

She tossed her head. 'Are you going to help me, or are you just going to stare?'

A door banged open and old Jeb Trinnick, who, Napier had been told, had been in charge of the stables since any one could remember, limped on to the cobbles. A giant of a man, his appearance was made more fearsome by his solitary eye, the other having been lost in a carriage accident so long ago that the story had grown into legend.

He glared at the mounted girl and said, 'Lady Roxby

won't be none too pleased about you comin' 'ere all alone, Missy. What's become of young 'Arry?'

Again the scornful toss of the head. 'He couldn't keep up.' She gestured to a mounting block. 'Help me down, will you?'

Napier reached up as she slid from the saddle, and old Jeb Trinnick led the horse away, still muttering to himself.

She stepped down to the ground and glanced at him. 'New here, aren't you?'

Not a woman after all. No more than a girl. Napier was not a good judge of ages, especially of her sex, but he guessed she was, like himself, fifteen or close enough. She was very pretty, and her hair, which he had thought dark, was drying to the colour of chestnuts in the fading light.

'I'm with Captain Bolitho, miss.'

He noticed the way she stood and moved, confident, impatient. He did not see her start at the sound of the Captain's name.

'His servant.' She nodded. 'Yes, I think I heard something about a visit. Last year? You fell off a donkey.'

'I can take you to him, if you wish, miss?'

She watched the stalls being opened.

'I think I can find my way.' But she was staring at the nearest loose box, at the powerful horse shaking its head in the direction of an approaching stable boy.

She was about to leave. Napier said, 'A fine mare, miss. She's called Tamara.'

The girl stopped on the steps and looked directly

into his face. It was the first time he had seen her eyes. Grey-blue, like the sea.

She said, 'I know. It killed my mother.'

Old Jeb Trinnick came past and watched her walk up to the house.

'Stay clear of that one, my son. Too good for the likes of us, or so she thinks, I daresay.'

Napier was looking at the big mare, which was watching the boy with the bucket.

'Was that true about her mother?'

'*Her* fault.' The eye swivelled round to another boy forking scattered straw. 'Lady Bolitho, Sir Richard's widow, she was.' His rugged features creased into a smile. 'Good to have the young Cap'n here again. But I suppose you'll be off soon? The way of sailormen?' He turned away as some one called his name.

It was then that it hit Napier, like opening a door and coming face to face with a nightmare. On board *Unrivalled* he had seen several midshipmen join for the first time. Young, eager, some completely inexperienced. He had heard them meeting the Captain. He gripped the stable door tightly.

If he was to become a midshipman, he would be facing it alone.

They would *not* be sailing together. Not this time. Perhaps never.

His own words came back to mock him. *We take care of each other*.

'Still on yer feet, then? I'd have thought you'd be tucked up in a nice soft cot somewheres, while you've still got the chance!'

Napier swung round guiltily, wondering if he had spoken his thoughts aloud.

But it was Luke Jago, a heavy chest over one shoulder as if it weighed nothing, and in contrast holding a long, delicate clay pipe in his other hand.

Jago did not wait for an answer. 'They've fixed me up with a room in Bryan Ferguson's cottage. Grace is goin' to bake somethin' special tonight, just for me.'

Napier was always surprised that Jago could accept or overcome almost anything. He spoke of the steward and his wife as if he had known them for years. A hard man, dangerous if crossed, but always fair. A man without fear, and, he thought, a man you would never really know.

Napier said, 'I'm looking at the horses.'

Jago peered at his pipe. 'Bryan an' me will take a walk down to a little inn he's told me about. Might get Mr Yovell to toddle along too.' It seemed to amuse him. 'Though the Bible's probably more to his taste!'

They both turned as another horse was led out of the stables.

Jago remarked, 'Dirty weather for somebody to be out on the roads.'

Napier saw the groom adjust the reins, and test the girth straps while the horse stamped impatiently on the cobbles. Even in the dying light he could see the dark blue saddle cloth, the gold wire crest in one corner.

'The Captain's horse.' He thought of the girl in the wine-red habit. It was a strange time to go out riding, with his aunt and his young cousin to welcome him home.

Napier said softly, 'He's badly troubled. Losing the ship . . .'

Jago was watching him curiously. 'Not all he's bothered about from what I've heard, my lad.' He grinned. 'Sorry. Before too long now I'll have to call you "mister", 'ow about that, eh?'

Napier did not respond to his raillery. 'But we'll work somethin' out, *if* you does as I tells you!'

Napier looked at him.

'I want to do the right thing, you see . . .' and Jago knew it was serious. The danger, his wound, which should have cost him a leg, would have with most seagoing sawbones he had known, were nothing compared with this next challenge.

He put one hand on the boy's shoulder, and said, 'Keep yer nose clean, an' do right by the lads who will have to look up to you, God 'elp 'em.' He shook him gently and added, 'You'll be on the quarterdeck afore you knows it!'

They heard boots on the cobbles and Adam Bolitho paused to look at them, walking toward the restive horse.

The groom called, 'Keep an eye open on them roads, Cap'n Adam, zur. War or no war, there still be footpads about!'

Adam showed his teeth in a smile, but Napier recognized the anger in his eyes.

To Napier he said, 'Feel like testing Jupiter, David? Tomorrow, perhaps? I thought I might ride over to Fallowfield, see John Allday and his family.'

'I could ride Jupiter *now*, sir.' But he knew that the

Captain was not hearing him; his mind was elsewhere.

Then he was up and mounted, an old boatcloak flapping like a banner in the wet breeze. He swung round and looked up at a window, Napier could not see which one, and shouted, 'I shall be back in time – tell the kitchen!' Then he was away, the hooves striking sparks from the worn cobbles.

Jeb Trinnick had joined them, soundlessly for a big man with a limp. When he saw Jago's pipe he pulled a pouch from beneath his leather apron.

'Try some o' this. Got it off a Dutchie trader last week. Seems fair enough.'

Jago brightened. Another bridge crossed.

'That's matey of you!'

Napier asked, 'Is the Captain going far?' He wiped some droplets of rain from his face, like tears. Like that day, all those months ago, when he had seen him with that beautiful woman, driving a smart little pony and trap.

He heard Jeb Trinnick say dourly, 'If I'm any judge he'll be makin' for the Old Glebe House.' He nodded, the single eye gauging the trail of smoke rising from Jago's pipe. 'Evil it is, or was. My youngest brother used to live over Truro way, afore he went over the side after Camperdown. Full o' spirits, he said. Even the Church was glad to rid itself of the place to the first buyer it could get. Old Sir Montagu, that was.'

Jago puffed out more smoke. 'Good baccy, Jeb.'

Somehow, Napier knew it was because of that same woman; he remembered the Captain's face when he

37

had read the little note she had sent out to *Unrivalled* before they had sailed to join the admiral.

Jeb Trinnick made up his mind. 'All the same, I'll send one of my lads after 'im.' He grinned. 'Just to be on the safe side!'

Napier watched him limp into the shadows. A man who could deal with everything that came his way. He felt despair closing around him again. Better to be like Trinnick, or Jago. Not to care . . .

Suddenly he heard the snap of Jago's delicate-looking pipe, which he had carried so carefully and filled for the first time with Trinnick's Dutch tobacco. It lay in fragments on the ground, rain splashing over it, dousing the smoking ash.

It mattered to Jago too, more than he would ever allow himself to show. He had hardened himself against it, perhaps because of other captains he had served. Looked up to, admired, hated; and one he had described as second only to God.

But this one mattered. And to David Napier, who was all but fifteen years old, it was a lifeline.

The courier arrived at the old grey house around noon, a week almost to the hour since *Unrivalled* had dropped anchor in Plymouth.

Ferguson had been in the stable yard, watching Napier riding the pony Jupiter slowly but confidently, back and forth, 'gaining an understanding' as Grace had put it.

The courier was known to Ferguson, as he was to many sea officers who lived around Falmouth.

Ferguson had reached out to sign for the canvas envelope, but the courier had said almost curtly, 'Not this one. Captain Bolitho himself, or I shall have to wait until he returns.'

Ferguson heard his wife call, 'Tell the captain, Mary!' She would stay with him until they all knew. She never changed; nor would she.

The courier relaxed and climbed down from his mud-spattered horse. All the way from Plymouth, and before that; how far had that envelope travelled, Ferguson wondered?

The wheels had probably started to turn when a guardship or keen-eyed coastguard had reported *Unrivalled* beating her way upChannel. A sight of home.

Grace Ferguson said, 'You've time for a glass, or a hot posset afore you leave?'

The courier shook his head. 'No, ma'am, but thank you. I've another call yet. Old Cap'n Masterman's place at Penryn. Bad news, I'm afraid. His son is reported missing. His ship foundered on a reef, I'm told.'

Ferguson turned, hearing the step on the cobbles. It was a familiar enough story in Cornwall.

Adam Bolitho took it in at a glance: the courier standing with his mount, Young Matthew who had been supervising Napier with the pony, Ferguson and Grace the housekeeper, and Yovell who had stopped in his tracks by the gate to the rose garden. Catherine's roses, or soon would be again.

Like badly rehearsed players, but joined by something which none of them properly understood.

The courier had produced a small writing tablet from beneath his stained cloak, the pen already dipped. What Lowenna must have used that day when she had been there to see *Unrivalled* weigh and stand out to sea.

He thought of the Old Glebe House, how it had looked that night when he had ridden over to see it. How the horse had whinnied and shied, perhaps because of the stench of sodden ashes and charred timbers. Or because of something more sinister. The burned-out windows, stark and empty against the racing clouds, of the room where she had kept her harp, next to the roofless studio where he had first seen her chained to the imaginary rock. The sacrifice . . .

He had gone back again in daylight. It had been even worse. He had wanted to go alone but Nancy had accompanied him, had insisted, as if she needed to share it.

The main part of the house was too unsafe to explore. Ashes, blackened glass from those tall windows he remembered so vividly, broken beams jutting like savage teeth. A few charred canvases. Impossible to tell if they had been empty or partially finished when the fire had raged into the studio.

Or being repaired. Like the one of Catherine, which she herself had commissioned to hang beside Sir Richard's portrait, in 'their room' as most of the household still called it. Dressed in a seaman's smock and little else, what she had been wearing in the open boat when she and her Richard had been shipwrecked.

Allday, when he could be persuaded to speak of it, had painted his own picture of Catherine and Bolitho, who had won the heart of the country when they had endured the open boat which might have ended everything. Her courage, her example, a woman amongst desperate men in fear of their lives, had left an indelible impression on Sir Richard's old coxswain. 'She even got me to sing a ballad or two!' He had laughed about it, proudly.

He had never known Nancy to hide her thoughts from him. She had suddenly faced him in the overgrown drive, the blackened building and chapel a grim backdrop, with the sea beyond. Always waiting. *Perhaps a new horizon.*

'It was Mary, the upstairs maid, who found it, Adam.' She always added a title, like a label, to any member of the household, in case he should forget between visits. Like the lesson which had been handed down to him over the years, when speaking of his sailors, the people, as Richard Bolitho called them. *Remember their names, Adam, and use them. A name is sometimes all they can call their own.*

Mary had run screaming to the kitchen. The portrait of Catherine had been slashed, again and again. Only the face had been left intact. As if that some one had wanted the world to know who it was.

Sir Gregory Montagu had not been optimistic, but he had taken the damaged canvas to his studio. Now they would never know.

Adam had thought about it ever since. There had been gypsies in the area, more of them than usual, but

41

it was not their way of things. Food, money, some-thing to sell; those were different. He had hated himself for even considering Belinda's daughter Elizabeth. She would see Catherine as the enemy, the marriage wrecker, but she had been visiting a friend over the border in Devon at the time.

He realized that he had signed for the envelope and that the courier was climbing into his saddle again.

He knew that Yovell and Ferguson had followed him into the house, wanting to help, yet keeping their distance.

He entered the study and picked up the knife that lay beside Elizabeth's sketch of the mermaid, think-ing of the watch which had once stopped a musket ball, and the little mermaid engraved on its case. Just a shell now, and he knew that the boy Napier still carried it like a talisman.

For a moment longer the knife hesitated, the seal and Admiralty stamp blurred in the thin sunlight. The knife had belonged to Captain James Bolitho. Sir Gregory Montagu had been here then, asked to paint an empty sleeve on the portrait over the stairs, after Captain James had lost an arm in India. Perhaps he was watching the last Bolitho from that portrait now, the son of the man who had betrayed his father's trust. And his country.

He heard the envelope fall to the floor, although it must have opened itself; he did not remember return-ing the knife to the desk.

The beautiful handwriting, so familiar and precise in its terms. And without heart.

42

Addressed to *Adam Bolitho, Esq. On receipt of these orders, will proceed with all despatch* . . . His eyes hurried on. But no ship's name or title leaped out at him like a voice, like a picture. Like that first command, the little brig *Firefly*. Or *Anemone*. He tried again. Or *Unrivalled* . . .

To place yourself at the convenience and service of Sir Graham Bethune, Knight of the Bath, Vice-Admiral of the Blue, and to await further instructions. There was more, and a smaller note with details of travel, lodgings, and other matters which seemed meaningless.

Yovell was the first to speak.

'Is it good, sir?'

Ferguson was pouring something into a glass. His hand was shaking. *Something else I should have noticed.*

'The Admiralty, Daniel. Their lordships wish to see me. It is a command, not a request.' He added with sudden bitterness, 'Nor a ship!'

The heavy document had fallen beside its envelope. Despite his girth, Yovell picked it up and said quickly, 'Do you see, sir? There is writing on the reverse.'

Adam took it. A captain without a ship. God alone knew there were so many like him. *No ship.*

He stared at the writing, but saw only the face. Vice-Admiral Bethune. He had met him several times, lastly at Malta. Bethune had begun his service as a young midshipman in the little sloop-of-war *Sparrow*, Sir Richard Bolitho's first command. A man easy to like, and to follow, and, in his day, the

43

youngest vice-admiral since Nelson. Once a frigate captain himself, then promotion, and lastly the Admiralty.

I am sending you a letter very shortly; it concerns some proposals which were brought to my notice. You will treat all instructions with utmost secrecy. On that, I am depending. Then his signature. Adam turned the sheet to the light. Bethune had written, almost like an afterthought, *Trust me.*

He replaced the glass on the desk. Claret or cognac? It could have been anything.

Yovell said, 'London, sir.' He shook his head and smiled sadly. 'Sir Richard never cared for the place. Not until . . .'

Adam walked past him, but briefly touched his plump arm. 'Until, Daniel. What a span that one word covers.'

He left the study and found himself staring into another log fire. Unseen hands always seemed to keep them blazing.

'I shall need Young Matthew for the first leg to Plymouth. After that . . .' He moved to the fire and held out his hands. 'It will all be laid down in the instructions.' A long, tiring and uncomfortable journey. And at the end of it? It might be nothing. Or perhaps he would merely be required to describe *Unrivalled*'s part in the attack and final victory at Algiers. 'I shall need more kit than usual. I must tell Napier . . .'

He broke off abruptly. Napier would not be going to London. Bethune's innocent enough note had been added for a reason. He looked directly at the round-shouldered figure of Yovell across the hall. 'Send word to the tailor for me, will you?' He saw Napier watching him from the passage which led to the kitchen. He knew. His eyes said it all.

Adam thought of Bethune again. It was all he had. *Trust me*.

Vice-Admiral Sir Graham Bethune moved some papers on his broad desk and stared at the ornate clock on the opposite wall, with its wind indicator and simpering cherubs.

He had walked to the Admiralty, across the park for some of the way, declining the offer of a carriage or, as was sometimes his habit, riding his own horse. It was not conceit, but a sense of purpose which carried him through each day.

He stood up, surprised that the exercise had not calmed his nerves. It was absurd; he had nothing to worry about.

He walked across the room and paused to study the painting of a frigate in action. It was his own, pitted against two big Spanish frigates. Bad odds even for a daring young captain, as he had been then. He had nevertheless run one of them aground and taken the other. Unconsciously, his hand touched the gold lace on his sleeve. Flag rank had followed almost immediately, and then the Admiralty. Routine, lengthy meetings, conferences with his superiors and sometimes the First Lord; he had even been called to elaborate upon various plans and operations to the Prince Regent.

And it had suited him, like the uniform, and the respect which went with it.

It had been wet in the park, but there had been all the usual horsemen and women about. He often expected to see Catherine there, riding herself, or in the carriage with the Sillitoe crest emblazoned on it. Like that last, arranged meeting. He bit his lip. The final one.

He stood by a window and looked down at the jostling carriages, carriers' carts and horses, always alive, moving.

It was a life he had grown used to, accepted, and one he lived with a zeal which often surprised his contemporaries. He took care of himself; although he enjoyed good wine with the company to match it, he was always careful not to slide into overindulgence. He had seen too many senior officers deteriorate and age before their time. It was sometimes impossible to imagine them, sword in hand, walking their own decks while death whined and stung all around them. He moved to the desk again, the restlessness stronger than before.

And what of me?

Some chose to ignore it, imagined perhaps that rank and seniority were everlasting. He touched the folder uppermost on the desk. And upon his mind.

At the close of the previous year the Navy List had carried two hundred admirals, and eight hundred and fifty captains. Commanders and mere lieutenants added up to another five thousand. The great fleet and all the squadrons, even those commanded by highly successful or famous officers, had been cut to the bone. Whole forests had been felled to build those ships, and now every anchorage and waterway had its sad reminders.

And what of me?

There was not an admiral left under the age of sixty, so that all promotion was at a standstill. A captain, if he was lucky enough still to be employed, could remain thirty years in that rank without moving.

He grimaced. Or survive on half-pay, shadowy figures who walked the seafront, watching. Remembering. Dreading.

He thought of his wife. *Lady Bethune*. It was hard now to think of her any other way. *'You can retire when you wish it, Graham. You're not a pauper. You can see more of the children.'* Their two 'children' were adults, and they met like pleasant strangers. His wife was in control. Like the night at that reception when she had smiled while Catherine Somervell had been humiliated. The night Catherine might have been raped, even killed, but for the intervention of Sillitoe and some of his men.

Bethune still relived it, again and again. He had entertained her here in this opulent room in the seat of Admiralty. The youngest vice-admiral on the Navy List since Nelson. And might remain so if things got even worse.

And she, the woman who had outraged society when she and Sir Richard Bolitho had lived openly together.

He looked at the chair where she had been seated, remembering her scent of jasmine. Her eyes when she smiled. Laughed, then . . .

Maybe he could obtain an appointment in one of the dockyards, like Valentine Keen. He had also served under Richard as a midshipman; now his flag flew over the Nore. But a navy without ships was no inspiration. The old, eternal enemies were uneasy allies now, in name anyway.

Like the anti-slavery campaign, which many had believed over after Exmouth's victory at Algiers.

He walked past the chair and tried again to shut it, and her, from his mind. Sillitoe was her protector, although many hinted that they were lovers also. He, too, had made a fool of himself when he had expressed his feelings and his fears for her.

He recalled the meetings he had had with the First Lord.

'Slavery will not go just go away because of an Act of Parliament, Graham. Too many fortunes have been made from it, and survive on it still . . . Their lordships and I have considered it deeply and often. A new command, entrusted with a difficult and possibly dangerous task. A show of force, enough to make plain our determination, but fluid enough not to antagonize or disrupt our "allies" in this matter.

'You will know, Graham, that there is no shortage of applicants.' He had let the words hang in the air. 'But I would prefer *you* to take it.'

Bethune was at the window again, looking down at the endless movement. People and the din of traffic, horses and iron-shod wheels. Another world, in which he would be a stranger; and some one else would be sitting here in this room.

He liked the company of women, and they his. But a risk was a risk all the same. And in any case, he might retain this present position for months. He sighed. Years.

He tugged down the front of his waistcoat and stared at his reflection in the rain-dappled glass, and thought of Richard Bolitho again. As if it were yesterday. His eyes as he had watched an oncoming enemy, the pain there when he considered the cost in lives. His decision, and a voice very level. *So be it, then.*

There was a tap at the ornate doors, timed to the minute.

'Well, Tolan?'

'Captain Adam Bolitho is here, Sir Graham.'

The shadow moved over the rich carpet, his face as Bethune remembered it. Like a younger version of Richard; even then, people had often taken them for brothers.

The same firm handshake; the elusive smile. And something else, desperation. It would have been uppermost in his thoughts all the way from Cornwall. The journey would have taken almost five days, changing horses, sharing a carriage with strangers, and, all the time, wondering . . .

Adam Bolitho had more than proved his worth, his skill, and his courage. The armchair strategists at the Admiralty had described him as reckless. But then, they would.

He recalled his own uncertainty, which had made him write *Trust me* on the back of the orders to this dark, youthful man. *I was like him. The frigate captain. That was then.*

To prolong this meeting which could be the start of many, or the last, would be insulting to both of them.

He said, more abruptly than he had intended, 'I have been given a new appointment, Adam, and I want you for my flag captain.' He held up his hand as Adam seemed about to speak. 'You have done a great deal, and you have won the approval of my senior officers, as well as the unstinting praise of Lord Exmouth. I, too, have seen you in action, which is why I want . . .' He reconsidered. 'I *need* you as my flag captain.'

Adam realized that the elderly servant had dragged up a chair for him and vanished into an adjoining room.

It was all he could do to put events into some kind of order. The endless journey, his arrival here at the Admiralty. Blank faces, and heads bowed to listen, as if he were speaking a foreign language.

He looked up at the gilded ceiling as somewhere high in the roof a clock began to chime, and he was aware of birds flapping in alarm, although they must hear the same sound at every half-hour.

He massaged his eyes and tried to clear his mind, but the images remained. He had told Young Matthew to take a different route into Plymouth, where he had been instructed to change carriages.

He could see the words like blood. *Never look back*.

With a telescope he had eventually found *Unrivalled*, not far from her previous anchorage. In a week she had changed almost beyond recognition, topmasts and standing rigging gone, her decks littered with discarded cordage and spars, crates and casks piled where the eighteen-pounders had once been ranged like marines at their sealed ports. The ports empty. Dead.

Only the figurehead remained intact and unchanged. Head flung back, breasts outthrust, proud and defiant. And, like the girl in the studio, helpless.

Never look back. He should have known.

Bethune was saying in his quiet, even voice, 'You have been in commission for a long time without much rest, Adam. But time is not on my side. Your appointment will take effect as soon as convenient to their lordships.'

Adam was on his feet, as if invisible hands were forcing him to leave.

Instead he asked, equally quietly, 'What ship, sir?'

Bethune breathed out slowly, half-smiling. 'She's the *Athena*, seventy-four. She is completing fitting-out at Portsmouth.' He glanced at the painting of the embattled ships, a flicker of regret crossing his features. 'Not a frigate, I'm afraid.'

Adam reached out and clasped his hand. Was it said so easily, the most important moment for any captain? He looked at Bethune and thought he understood.

For both of us.

He said, 'Perhaps not a frigate, sir. But a *ship*.'

A goblet, chilled in readiness, was put into his hand.

Her name meant nothing to him. Probably an old two-decker, perhaps like the one where it had all begun for him. *But a ship*.

He touched the sword at his thigh.

He was not alone.

3

Absent Friends

The coach jerked violently as the brake was applied and came to a swaying halt, the horses stamping on cobbles, very aware that their journey to Portsmouth was ended. Adam Bolitho eased forward on the seat, every muscle and bone offering a protest. He had only himself to blame; he had insisted on leaving his temporary lodgings the previous evening, at an hour when most people would have been thinking of a late supper or bed.

But the coachmen employed by the Admiralty were accustomed to it. Driving at night, the wheels dipping and grinding in deep ruts, or through rain-flooded stretches of the long Portsmouth Road, two stops to change horses, another to wait for a farm wagon to be moved after it had cast a wheel. They had paused at a small inn in a place called Liphook, to drink tea by candlelight before starting on the final leg of the journey.

He lowered the window and shivered as the bitter air fanned across his face. First light, or soon would be, and he felt like death.

He heard his companion twist round beside him and say cheerfully, 'They're ready for us, it seems, sir!'

Lieutenant Francis Troubridge showed no trace of fatigue. A youthful, alert man, ever ready to answer Adam's many questions, he had displayed no resentment or surprise at the call for a coach ride through the night. As Vice-Admiral Bethune's flag lieutenant, the most recent of several to all accounts, it was something he probably took for granted.

Adam looked toward the tall gates, which were wide open. Two Royal Marine orderlies were nearby with a porter's trolley, and an officer in a boatcloak was observing the coach without impatience.

Even that was hard to accept. On the roof of the Admiralty above Bethune's handsome room was the first link in a chain of telegraph stations which could pass a signal from London to the tower over the church of St Thomas almost before a courier could find, saddle and mount a horse. News, good or bad, had always moved with the speed of the fastest rider. Not any more, and provided visibility was good the eight or so telegraph stations could send word well ahead of any traveller.

Adam climbed down on to hard ground, and felt it rise to meet him. Like a sailor too long in an open boat in a lively sea, he thought. He shivered again and tugged his own heavy cloak around him. He was tired, and throbbing from too much travel: Falmouth, Plymouth, London, and now Portsmouth.

He should have slept throughout the journey instead of trying to study his orders, or glean fragments of intelligence from his lively companion.

He had the feeling that the young lieutenant was watching him now, discovering something, for reasons of his own. He had certainly gone to a lot of trouble to find out about the officer put into his care. At one point, when they had stopped to change horses, Troubridge had remarked, 'I was forgetting, sir. You were flag lieutenant yourself some years ago.' Not a question; and Adam thought that he could have given the exact year when he had been his uncle's aide.

He saw that the other officer had thrown back his cloak to display the epaulettes of a post captain, like his own.

'Welcome, Bolitho!' His handshake was firm and hard. The dockyard captain, who probably knew more about ships and the demands of the fleet than any one.

They fell into step, while the marines began unloading chests and baggage from the carriage; they did not speak, nor so much as look at the new arrivals.

The dockyard captain was saying, '*Athena* is anchored, of course, but she's awaiting more ballast and stores. My clerk has left a full list for your attention.' He shot him a quick glance. 'Have you met up with *Athena* before?' A casual comment, but it was typical. In the 'family' of the navy it was common enough for a sailor to cross paths with the same ship throughout the years of his service at sea.

'No.' He pictured the spidery writing, which he had read by the light of a small lantern while the coach had juddered and rolled through the darkness.

Built at Chatham in 1803, just two years before Trafalgar; not an old ship by naval standards. He had found that he was able to smile. Maybe Troubridge had seen that too. 1803, the year he had been given his first command, the little fourteen-gun brig *Firefly*. He had been just twenty-three years old.

Laid down and completed as a third-rate, a seventy-four gun ship of the line, *Athena*'s role had changed several times, as had her station. She had served in the second American war and in the Mediterranean, in the Irish Sea, and then back to the Channel Fleet.

Now, out of nowhere, she was to be Sir Graham Bethune's flagship. Her artillery had been reduced from seventy-four to sixty-four, to allow more accommodation. No other reason was given.

Even Bethune had been vague about it. 'We shall be working with our "allies", Adam. My flagship is not to be seen as a threat, more as an example.' It had seemed to amuse him, although Adam suspected Bethune was almost as much in the dark as himself.

He said, 'She has a full ship's company?'

The other captain smiled. 'All but a few. But these days it's easier to find spare hands, with no war at the gates!'

Adam quickened his pace. Here there was activity, even at this ungodly hour. Heavy, horse-drawn wagons, filled with cordage and crates of every size. Dockyard workers being mustered for a new day's repairs, perhaps even building. Unlike the empty gunports at Plymouth. Unlike *Unrivalled*.

The other captain said suddenly, 'You'll be more used to a fifth-rate, Bolitho. *Athena*'s a good ship, in structure and condition. The best Kentish oak – maybe the last of it, from what I hear!'

They halted at the top of some stone stairs, and as if to a signal a boat began to pull away from a cluster of moored barges, the oars rising and falling with mist clinging to the blades like translucent weed.

Adam saw his own breath drifting away, hating the cold in his bones. Too long on the slave coast, or clawing up and down off the Algerian shoreline . . . It was neither. A new ship, and one already destined for some ill-defined task. The West Indies, with a vice-admiral's flag at the fore: probably Bethune's last appointment before he quit the navy to serve in some new capacity where there was no more war, no more danger. When they had stopped at Liphook to take tea Troubridge had mentioned his own father, an admiral at the end of his service, but now he had been given an important role in the growing ranks of the Honourable East India Company, where, no doubt, he would want his son to join him after this latest stepping-stone which might eventually lead to oblivion.

Easier to find spare hands. The dockyard captain's words seemed to hang in the air like his breath. Like many of *Unrivalled*'s people, those who had cursed the unyielding discipline, or simply the petty-mindedness of those who should have known better in the close confines of a King's ship. Those same men might now be seeking a ship, any vessel which would give them back the only life they fully understood.

'There have been one or two accidents, of course, quite common when refitting, and when every one wants it done in half the time.' He shrugged heavily. 'Men lost overboard, two falling from aloft, another rigger too drunk to save himself in the dark. It happens.'

Adam looked at him. 'Her captain was relieved of his command. He faces a court-martial, I'm told.'

'Yes.' They watched the boat come alongside, two young seamen leaping ashore to fend off the stairs.

He found himself holding his breath. His uncle had warned him about joining a new ship, especially as her captain. *They will be far more worried about you, Adam.* But he thought of the old clerk at the Admiralty, who had lingered in Bethune's room after the vice-admiral had gone to speak with one of his superiors.

'Your uncle, Sir Richard, was a fine man, sir. A great man, given the chance.' He had stared at the door, as if afraid of something, and blurted out, 'Take care, sir. *Athena*'s an unlucky ship!' He had scuttled away before Bethune had returned.

A lieutenant, impeccably turned out, eyes fixed on a point above Adam's left epaulette, raised his hat smartly and said, 'Barclay, second lieutenant, sir, at your service!'

An open face, but at this moment giving nothing away. One of many he would come to know, and know well if he had learned anything since *Firefly*, all those years ago.

He looked around, almost expecting to see Napier

57

hovering there in his blue coat and clicking shoes. Or Luke Jago, watchful and cynical, an eye on this boat's crew for instance, already judging the ship. His ship. Troubridge was climbing into the boat, preceeding Adam in the correct manner. The dockyard captain stepped back and touched his hat.

Adam returned the salute and nodded to the lieutenant . . . he frowned, and the name came to him. Barclay.

The boat's crew, smartly dressed in matching shirts and tarred hats, faced aft, eyes unmoving, but fixed on the new captain. Wondering. Assessing. Adam stepped into the sternsheets, the old sword pressed hard against his hip.

The ship, any ship, was only as good as her captain. No better. No worse.

He sat down. *So be it.*

'Cast off!'

He tugged his hat more firmly on to his head as the boat pulled away from the jetty, and into a cold breeze which he was beyond feeling. At any other time it was easy to lose yourself in your thoughts, allow the boat's crew and its routine carry on without you. This was different. Unlike *Unrivalled*, when he had commissioned her at Plymouth; he had been there when most of her company had arrived on board, while the builders and riggers were still putting the finishing touches to their new frigate. Or even *Anemone*, which had gone down after a bitter action against the Americans, and he had been wounded, and taken prisoner . . .

He saw a guardboat pulling between two moored transports, the oars tossed as a mark of respect, an officer standing in the sternsheets to raise his hat.

Adam reached up to drop the boatcloak from his shoulders, so that both epaulettes could be seen. The guardboat had known of his arrival; perhaps everybody did. Nothing remained confidential for very long in the 'family'.

The stroke oarsman's eyes had moved for the first time to watch what he had done, his loom rising and falling steadily, unhurriedly as before.

One of my men. What is he thinking at this very moment? Or young Troubridge, whose father had flown his own flag as an admiral; was he aware of the significance of this day and what it meant to the frigate captain at his side? The officer who had been singled out for praise for his behaviour at Algiers by Lord Exmouth himself?

He tensed, the sword gripped between his knees, cold and discomfort forgotten. As if he were some one else. A spectator.

Slowly at first, then more deliberately as the boat turned slightly into the first true daylight, the ship was already taking shape, her tracery of spars and black rigging rising above the indistinct shapes of other moored vessels. It might not have been *Athena*, but he knew that it was.

The bowman had boated his oar and was standing, facing forward with his boathook, and Adam had not seen him move.

The boat's coxswain swung the tiller bar, but

hesitated as the lieutenant held up his hand. Anxious, nervous of making the wrong impression on the new captain.

Adam found that he could spare a thought for the man he was relieving, a man he did not know, had never met. Stephen Ritchie, a senior captain on the Navy List, who had commanded *Athena* for three years, in war and in peace, was now 'awaiting the convenience of a court-martial' as it had been euphemistically described in the *Gazette*. Troubridge had been sparse with his information, but Ritchie had evidently been in serious debt, not unusual in the navy, and had made the grave mistake of falsifying accounts to obtain further credit. He must have been in very deep trouble to take such risks. He was paying for it now.

He glanced up as the bowsprit and long tapering jib boom reached up and over the boat like a lance. The figurehead, clad in armour, was still hidden in shadow.

Adam caught a slight movement above the beakhead, a face withdrawing, some one posted to give the first warning.

It came immediately.

'*Boat ahoy!*'

The lieutenant was on his feet again, hands cupped.

'*Athena!*' The waiting was over.

Adam felt the ship rising over him, the fresh paint reflected on the sluggish current like white and black bars, with the gunports creating their own checkered pattern. Masts and standing rigging, hammock nettings all neatly packed and covered; they must have piped all hands long before dawn. As a midshipman he had done it himself, going without breakfast in order that some great man would find all to his liking when he stepped aboard.

The boat was coming alongside, oars tossed and dripping, while the bowman and some figures clinging beneath the ship's entry port eased the hull into the remaining shadows.

Not much longer than *Unrivalled*, but she was a two-decker and seemed to tower above him like a cliff.

He had crammed his mind with the basic details. Now they seemed to revolve in confusion. One hundred and sixty feet in length, and of one thousand four hundred tons. A frigate was always busy, always crowded. It was hard to accept that *Athena*, when fully manned, would carry five hundred souls, officers, seamen, and a contingent of Royal Marines for good measure.

There was a sudden silence, or so it seemed. The lieutenant was facing him, pleased, worried, or merely relieved that his part was over; it was hard to tell.

Adam looked up at the ship's side, the tumblehome curving away to reveal the 'stairs', and the entry port which looked a cable's length away. He was reminded of his visit to Lord Exmouth's flagship *Queen Charlotte* at Plymouth, when the admiral, knowing he had been wounded, had ordered him to use a bosun's chair as he left, and the sailors had cheered him for it. As Exmouth had said, 'Pride is one thing, Bolitho, but conceit is an enemy!'

He reached out for the guide rope, but turned his

head as he did so, and stared over the brightening expanse of Portsmouth Harbour. Some moored ships, still merged together in the retreating shadows, and land beyond. That would be Gosport. The small note, still folded in his pocket. *I was here. I saw you. God be with you.*

He knew that one of the side-boys, sent down in his white gloves to offer a helping hand if need be, was staring at him, mouth half open.

Adam nodded to him and began to climb. *Lowenna. If only . . .*

He heard the slap of muskets being brought to the present, a far-off bark of commands.

Then the long, drawn-out trill of calls.

A salute to the captain, on this day.

The first few moments as he stepped through *Athena*'s entry port and raised his hat to the quarterdeck and the ensign lifting lazily above the taffrail were blurred, swift impressions. The marines stiffly paraded as if on a barrack square, the pipeclay from their slings still drifting above their leather hats, their officer with drawn sword at the present. The fading twitter of calls, Spithead Nightingales as sailors called them, and the rattle of a solitary drum.

A lieutenant, taller and older than Adam had expected, stepped from the rank of waiting officers and said, 'Stirling, sir. I am the senior here.' A hesitation. 'Welcome aboard *Athena*.'

They shook hands, pausing while the marines brought down their muskets in unison.

He walked slowly along the line of assembled officers, shaking hands with each one of them. *Athena* carried six lieutenants in all; Barclay had remained in the boat alongside, so the introductions did not take long. Young for the most part, and for the present merely faces. There were two scarlet-coated marine officers, a captain, and a lieutenant who was in charge of the guard of honour. The eight midshipmen were held at bay by a rank of senior warrant officers; as Adam had heard his uncle say more than once, the backbone of any ship.

He could feel Troubridge keeping close behind him, perhaps less assured hemmed in by this press of strangers.

Stirling, the big first lieutenant, watched each face as he made his introduction, with an occasional mention of a particular duty or part of ship.

Adam thought of Leigh Galbraith, *Unrivalled*'s first lieutenant. He had been a big man too, but light on his feet at sea or in action. *Never look back.* It seemed to mock him.

He knew something about Stirling. He had been in *Athena* for three years, like her disgraced captain. Old for his rank, passed over for promotion, partly because he had been a prisoner of war in Spanish hands until that country's change of fortune, but also because he apparently had made no effort to obtain it. Unlike Galbraith . . .

He realized that some one had spoken his name.

It was the sailing master, a man with such a weathered face that his eyes seemed snared by the crowsfeet and lines of many leagues in every kind of sea. A strong face, the eyes bright blue, the mouth breaking into a smile.

Adam gripped his hand, the years falling away.

'Fraser, isn't it?'

The smile widened into a grin. 'Fancy you rememberin', sir.' He almost glanced at the other warrant officers. Almost. 'Few years that goes back, when I was master's mate in the old *Achates*, sixty-four, Cap'n Valentine Keen, so it was!'

'You've done well, Mr Fraser.'

Fraser released his hand. 'I saw you leave *Achates* to take your first command, sir. I often think of them days.'

They moved on, but Adam could still feel the handshake. Was that all it took?

They had reached the quarterdeck rail; his shoes were clinging to fresh pitch, and he saw where tools and paint brushes had been hastily hidden under strips of old canvas. Paint, pitch and tar, spunyarn and hemp. The sailor's lot.

The big double wheel, motionless and unmanned, the compass box shining in the growing light. Marines, fifers and drummers, seamen and petty officers, midshipmen and ship's boys, all packed into this unfamiliar hull.

'Thank you, Mr Stirling. Have all hands lay aft, if you please.'

One of the young midshipmen sneezed and ducked his head to hide his embarrassment. Probably about Napier's age. He had a sudden flash of memory: the tailor's old-fashioned shop in Plymouth, Napier's face when the tape had been stretched across his slight shoulders for the first time, and the tailor had called measurements and meaningless advice to some hidden assistant. It was something he would never forget: it had been like seeing himself.

He looked up and around at the assembled ship's company. On the gangways on either side of the main-deck, above the batteries of black-muzzled eighteen-pounders, clinging to the ratlines and shrouds, some even standing on the boat tier and its newly painted hulls. It was hard to imagine how all these men and boys could find space to live and hope as individuals.

He stared along the length of the ship to the Union flag flying above the beakhead, and the armoured shoulder of the goddess Athena. Again he felt the prick of uncertainty, almost guilt. He could still see *Unrivalled*'s lovely figurehead, like the girl in the studio.

'Ship's company, *uncover*!'

Officers and seamen alike removed their hats, while others seemed to lean out and down from their various vantage points to watch each move, hear every word which would make this man their captain. The one man who held the power of life and death, misery and happiness, over every soul aboard.

Adam had removed his hat and tucked it beneath his arm. He took out the familiar roll of parchment and stared unseeingly at the beautiful copperplate script: some one else's words, somebody else's voice reading them.

It was addressed to Adam Bolitho, Esquire, the commission which appointed him to the *Athena, willing and requiring you forthwith to go on board and take upon you the charge and command of captain in her accordingly* . . .

Some he remembered from other ships. Some he knew almost by heart. Many of the men assembled here today would have heard the same words many times, if they had served long enough.

He cleared his throat, and knew that Stirling was gazing at him with scarcely a blink.

'. . . *hereof, nor you nor any of you may fail as you will answer the contrary at your peril.*'

Like *Unrivalled*, and *Anemone*. And like the little brig which had been his first command, and had been brought back to life by the hard handshake of *Athena*'s sailing master just minutes ago.

Stirling was nodding, but watching some of the assembled hands as if to discover the true feeling of the ship. His ship, for three years.

Troubridge murmured, 'I can take you to your quarters, sir. They are all but ready for use.' He was mentally ticking off his flag lieutenant's ever-present list. 'A cabin servant has been appointed. He served the previous captain.' He frowned as somebody gave a cheer. 'He requested to remain on board.'

Adam turned as the lines of seamen and marines began to break up and separate into groups.

He said, 'An issue of rum would not come amiss, Mr Stirling.'

Stirling bit his lip. 'I'm not sure that the purser has arranged it, sir.'

The purser. The man who usually counted every coffee bean and biscuit as if it were his own. He could vaguely recall a limp handshake, and an Irish name. It would come back to him.

He said, 'Then *tell* him, if you please.' He saw a barge full of dockyard workers poling abeam, some of the men giving another cheer as they passed.

A new beginning for the ship. He followed Troubridge aft and beneath the shadow of the poop. A bigger ship, but still he had to duck his head to avoid the first deckhead beam.

There was no sentry at the screen door, and the air was heavy with fresh shipboard smells. The cabin seemed larger, unlived in. When he made to open one of the sloping stern windows, there was wet paint on his fingers.

A captain's retreat. He looked at the new black and white checkered deck covering beneath his shoes. Except that Bethune and his staff would be right there, below him. A private ship no longer.

In a day or so Luke Jago would arrive with some of the things which had been taken to Falmouth. He eyed the space near the bench seat across the stern. The chair would be right there . . . He gazed at the harbour shimmering beyond the thick glass windows. Provided Jago had not changed his mind. Taken his bounty and prize money and swallowed the anchor.

He looked up at a skylight, then deliberately removed his dress coat and hung it from the latch, where it would swing to the harbour's easy motion. Like that day when he had received his orders. When he had been told he was losing *Unrivalled*. Just like that.

Defiance; anger; he found it was neither.

He said abruptly, 'I would like a shave, and a bath of some sort.'

Troubridge exclaimed, 'I doubt if the ship is quite ready, sir.' The flag lieutenant was never far away. 'I could call away a boat, and have you in the George at Portsmouth Point in no time.'

Adam moved to the opposite side, and the screen across the sleeping cabin.

'Too many ghosts.' He did not explain. 'Find that servant you mentioned, and then . . .'

Troubridge was opening a cupboard and taking out a finely cut goblet.

He smiled, almost shyly. 'I did arrange a small welcome for you, sir.'

Feet stamped beyond the screen door, and Adam heard a corporal reading out the standing orders to the marine sentry. More stamping, then silence.

He sat on the bench seat and looked around the bare cabin.

'Then you will join me, eh?'

There was a muffled burst of cheering and Troubridge could not contain a grin. 'Ahah. The rum has been issued, sir.'

Adam took a goblet and glanced at the breech of a twelve-pounder which shared his quarters, and would be one of the first in action if this ship was ever called upon to fight.

It was cognac. Probably some of Bethune's.

He stood, and raised the goblet. 'To the ship!'

Troubridge was young but he was quick to learn, and he felt that he knew this captain better than he had expected he would ever do after so brief an acquaintance.

He lifted his own goblet and said simply, 'And to absent friends, sir.'

It was done.

Bryan Ferguson stood by the window of his cramped estate office and watched the horses being manoeuvred toward the carriage in the centre of the stable yard. The sky was a clear, pale blue, the air like ice, but it was likely to remain dry for the journey to Plymouth. Young Matthew and his lads had made a fine show with the carriage, he thought. You could see your face in it; even the harness shone like black glass.

A special day, but he was also saddened by it. He heard Yovell speaking to somebody in the passageway and was suddenly grateful that the portly secretary was coming back here when he returned from Plymouth. From his mission, as he had put it. Yovell was good company, and a great help with the never-ending work connected with the estate, and anyway, Ferguson had told him frankly, was too old for a sea-going existence.

He glanced down at his empty sleeve. He was grateful, something he had not been able to admit before, not even to his beloved Grace. He was the one who was getting too old for this work, the estate, the tenant-farmers and stock holders who knew his shortcomings. Yovell was a kindly soul, but nobody's fool, and he had a mind like quicksilver. And in any case . . .

He turned as Yovell came in, carrying his heavy coat with its attached cape. He was rarely seen without it, and today he would need it.

'The tailor has gone, Daniel. At long last.'

Yovell studied him gravely. 'I shall deal with *him* when I'm in Plymouth. I have a few matters to attend to for Captain Adam. You have quite enough to do here.' He counted off points on his plump fingers. 'The Captain's personal baggage has gone ahead.' He smiled gently. 'The chair also. It might take the edge off his new responsibilities. But knowing him as I do, I doubt it.'

Ferguson looked out at the carriage again. The horses were standing peacefully in the traces, harness adjusted, a stable boy giving them a last currying before departure. Local people would see the carriage and its familiar crest, and maybe they would wonder. Not a Bolitho this time; the old grey house was empty again.

He saw Luke Jago crossing the yard and knew he would miss him also. Jago had a strange, blunt way of making friends. A bad enemy if you crossed him, he thought.

Every landsman's idea of the true sailor. In his fine jacket with its gilt buttons, flared neckerchief and nankeen breeches, he would give any one confidence. He thought of John Allday, and the moment

70

when the two coxswains had met for the first time.

Allday was his best friend, and they shared an inseparable past, even though Ferguson's seagoing life had ended when he had lost his arm in battle. Most people might envy the big, shambling man who had been Sir Richard's coxswain, who had been with him at the end, and had held him as he died. Now Allday was happily married to his pretty Unis, and together they managed a successful inn, The Old Hyperion, over in the village of Fallowfield. They had a little daughter named Kate. Not many Jacks who had stepped ashore had found such satisfaction.

But Ferguson had seen the truth in those blue, honest eyes which could rarely hide a secret.

Allday envied Jago, because of the other life which had been taken away.

Jago pushed noisily through the door and dropped his chest on the floor.

'Time to shove off, then?' He nodded to Yovell. 'Thanks for finding a place to lay my head.'

Ferguson swung round. 'Not visitors! Not now!'

Yovell patted his arm.

'Easy, Bryan. I think it's Lady Roxby. I rather thought she might call.'

The other carriage turned in the yard and a boy ran to calm the horses.

Grace was here now, hurrying to greet her as she was assisted down. Ferguson saw that the girl Elizabeth was with her.

He heard Jago remark, 'Break somebody's heart, that one will, if I'm any judge.'

71

Ferguson also noticed that his wife had been crying, as he had known she would.

But she was smiling now, gesturing to each of them in turn. 'Come into the house, will you? I only wish Captain Adam could be here!'

They walked up the broad steps and into the familiar hallway. The study door was open, a fire burning cheerfully. Almost as if one of those faces in the portraits would be there. Waiting.

They were a very mixed group, the one-armed steward and the plump Yovell, who had become so much a part of their lives. Jago, at ease but never relaxed, soon to join his captain, and questioning even that. The two women, and the slim, upright girl with the chestnut hair.

Nancy heard one of the servants give an excited handclap, and some one call out something from the broad landing. Very quickly, she made her decision.

She saw Jago turn and stare at her, his usual composure, sometimes hostility, gone as she grasped his hand in hers. It might be the worst thing she could do . . . But she said abruptly, 'I know you, Luke Jago. My nephew trusts you, and so must I.' She thrust an envelope into his fist and felt his fingers close round it like a trap. 'Give him this. Tell him . . .' She broke off as Ferguson called, 'Well done! *Well done!*'

Jago stared past the woman he knew to be Captain Bolitho's aunt. He knew, too, that she was more than merely that. It was enough. The envelope was in his jacket pocket.

'Good as done, m' lady.'

Nancy turned away, angry that tears might spoil this day.

She walked to the foot of the stairs and opened her arms, holding him as she had once held Adam, a lifetime ago.

The youth Elizabeth had described as 'the captain's servant' had gone. In his new midshipman's uniform, with the single-breasted tailed coat and white collar patches which still haunted her memory, he was some one else.

She embraced him and thought she heard Grace Ferguson sobbing, as if she, too, was losing somebody dear to her.

'He would be so proud of you, David.' His slight shoulders were rigid under the new blue coat, as if he were still trying to come to terms with it. 'It is what he wanted for you.'

David Napier swallowed hard and gazed past them at the big doors, standing open to the cold air. The wall, the curving drive, that line of trees. And the sea.

He was going to another ship; he could feel the stiff document folded inside the pocket of the coat. He stared at the gilt buttons on each sleeve and saw himself as he had just seen his reflection in the mirror on the landing.

He thought his hands were trembling, but when he held one out to the sunlight it was quite steady.

He had no right to think of this house as his home, but the feeling would not change, or go away. He looked at their faces, each one in turn, so that he should not forget: Grace, wiping her eyes and trying to smile, her husband, who had done all he could to make him feel welcome, and Yovell, the man who had shared so much with him in *Unrivalled*, and had taught him about things and deeds he would never otherwise have known. And the lady who had just hugged him. Part of a great family. *How can I leave them now?*

It was Luke Jago who cut the cable.

'Here now, *Mister* Napier, we'd better get a-moving if we're to get you on board today!'

As he climbed into the carriage Napier paused to look at the house, and to wave, although he could see very little in the hard light.

But he thought of his mother. Might she have been proud, too?

4

'The Higher We Climb . . .'

The small working party of seamen had retreated from the cabin, and the screen door was closed once more.

Adam Bolitho stood by the stern windows and felt the sun warming his shoulders through the thick glass, although he knew it was still very cold on deck.

He ignored the litter of cases and bags which had just been delivered, each seaman darting a quick glance around the cabin, and at the man who had been their captain for almost four days.

He hestitated, then walked slowly to the high-backed chair which had received the particular attention of the boatswain's mate in charge, a mahogany bergère upholstered in brass-nailed dark green leather. A chair you could doze, even sleep in, and be readily on call. Where you could plan and think, somehow separated from the ship and her routine. There were a few scratches and a dark stain on one arm rest, but it was the same chair, the one she had wanted him to have after Sir Richard had been killed in *Frobisher*.

He gripped it and moved it very slightly. He had sat here many times himself. Feeling it. Sharing it with his own command, *Unrivalled*.

'May I suggest something, sir?'

Adam turned sharply; he had forgotten that he was not alone.

John Bowles had been Captain Ritchie's servant for three years, and the previous captain's for a shorter period, until he had been killed in a sharp engagement with a French blockade-runner.

At first meeting Bowles seemed an unlikely candidate to fill the role of cabin servant. He was tall, slightly stooping because of the lack of headroom, with greying hair trained into an old-style queue, and long sideburns. His was a grave, rather melancholy face, dominated by a large, hooked nose, so that his surprisingly bright eyes seemed almost incidental.

Not a young man, and listed as forty years old on the ship's books, he was light-footed and unobtrusive, unusual for one so tall.

Adam said, 'Yes?' thinking again of Napier and his clicking shoes, his earnest and often deadly serious eagerness. *We take care of each other*.

Bowles moved around the chair, careful not to touch it, or so it appeared. He stopped suddenly and lifted up a small flap in the deck covering.

'Just 'ere, sir.' He indicated a brass ringbolt. 'The chair can be shackled, nice an' safe, if the sea gets up.' He looked directly at Adam for the first time.

76

Athena can be a lively lady in 'alf a gale if she feels like it.' He almost smiled.

He had a London accent, and Stirling the first lieutenant had told Adam that he had been working in a riverside tavern when he had become involved in some kind of brawl at the very moment that a press gang had been passing. The rest was a familiar story in those times; the lieutenant in command of the press gang had been thankful just to lay hands on a few more men, sailors or not.

It was strange that Bowles had apparently made no attempt to quit the navy when the war with France and her allies had at last come to an end. Adam found that he was touching the chair. *When my uncle was cut down.*

'That sounds a sensible plan.' He gestured to the other pieces of baggage but before he could speak Bowles said, 'I can 'ave it all stowed by the dog watches. I am instructed that you are dining with the wardroom, so I will make sure that everything is right, sir.'

Once Adam would have preferred a younger man, but it seemed unimportant now. Bowles belonged to the ship. A part of her. *And I am his third captain.*

Bowles said suddenly, 'That is a fine old sword, sir. I 'ave some special oil that might suit.' He was thinking aloud. 'Though I doubt we'll be doing much cut-an'-thrust on this commission.' He bared his uneven teeth in a grin. 'Us bein' a flagship an' all!'

Adam heard the sentry tap his musket on the grating outside the screen door.

'Midshipman o' the watch, *sir*!'

Bowles was across the cabin before Adam had seen him move, but he turned just briefly, like a conspirator, and said, 'Mr Vincent, sir.'

Adam faced the door. He had met Vincent, *Athena*'s senior 'young gentleman', but he doubted if he would have remembered his name after only four days. Almost due for examination for lieutenant. The first major step from warrant rank to quarterdeck. A King's officer.

The midshipman stepped smartly into the cabin, his hat beneath his arm. He was almost eighteen, but looked older, and very self-confident. He was in charge of *Athena*'s signals, and Adam had seen him shouting at one of his men only a few feet away, as if he were stone deaf or a complete fool. Stirling had been nearby but had said nothing. Adam thought of the much-hated midshipman in *Unrivalled,* Sandell, who had gone missing over the side one night.

'Yes, Mr Vincent, what is it?'

'There is a man who wishes to see you, sir.' He had narrow nostrils which were flared now with obvious anger. '*Insists*, sir!'

Adam looked past him and saw Jago waiting by an open gunport, a bag swinging back and forth in his hand.

'My coxswain, Mr Vincent. He has access to me whenever so required.'

Vincent was not the sort to make stupid mistakes. Jago's expected time of arrival had been in the order book almost since Adam had read himself in to the ship's company.

He said, 'But only officers were allowed free access, sir.'

Adam smiled, disliking him, and hoped it was convincing. 'That was then, Mr Vincent. You may return to your duties.'

The door was shut again and they stood facing one another, awkward despite what they had shared. Separated, perhaps, by the ship, a stranger to them both.

Adam gripped his hand. 'It is very good to see you, Luke.' He felt the smile breaking through and realized just how acute the loneliness had been. In the night watches, lying in his cot, staring into the darkness, listening to the occasional tread of a watchkeeper, the angle and bearing of each sound still unfamiliar. Or the movement of rigging, the slap of water alongside, two decks down now.

Jago grinned. 'You too, Cap'n. I see the chair got aboard safely?'

'Have a tot and tell me about everything. I want to hear it.' He sat down on the stern bench, his legs apart, his hands clasped, the young captain again.

Jago held up his fist. 'Two fingers of grog, an' one of water, if it's clean!'

Adam smiled. 'You will soon get used to my cox'n, Bowles.'

Bowles nodded doubtfully. 'And a cognac for you, sir.'

The door to the pantry clicked shut.

Jago glanced at the chair again, at the broad, curving deck beams and the glistening paintwork; felt the slow movement of the hull.

'No fifth-rate, sir. Bigger than we're used to.' He half-listened to the squeal of calls, and the clatter of tackle as more stores were hoisted inboard to be stowed away.

Then he said lightly, 'She'll suit, sir. 'Til something better is offered!'

Adam felt his muscles relax, and accepted, perhaps for the first time, how deeply the change had affected him.

'And what about young David? Did it go off all right? I wish I could have been there.'

Jago thought about it, recalling the final handshake, the sudden anxiety, the ship rising above the boat he had unofficially borrowed for the occasion. He still found it hard to believe that he had even cared. That he still did. It went against almost everything he knew.

The challenge yelled down from the ship's side, and his own firm and immediate response.

'*Mr Midshipman Napier, sir! Coming aboard to join!*'

Just another 'young gentleman'.

But he said, 'I was proud of him, an' that's a fact.'

He took the glass from Bowles as he stooped over them and added, 'An' he got his frigate, which is more than some can say!'

Bowles returned to his pantry as the cabin echoed with laughter.

Things might be very different, he thought as he polished glasses. They needed to be.

Jago wiped his mouth with the back of his hand.

'Almost forgot, sir.' He groped into his jacket. 'Lady, er, Roxby, give me a letter for you.'

Adam put down his glass, his bowels like ice.

Jago was saying, 'I've 'eard you'll be goin' up to London again . . . ?'

Adam flattened the paper on the bench and read it slowly. Some one had printed an address in large capitals. Almost a child's writing.

He heard himself answer, 'Yes. Two days' time. The Admiralty. Final instructions, I believe.' His brain refused to concentrate. Even Nancy's scribbled words made no sense.

It is all I was given. I am still not sure I should have told you.

Adam was on his feet without realizing it, one hand on the back of the chair.

'I am still a stranger to London. I marvel that people there can find their way from one street to another.' He was making a fool of himself. 'The place they call Southwark? All I know of it is an inn called the George – I took the coach from there to the George here in Portsmouth. That's all I can remember.'

Bowles walked from the little pantry, his head lowered as if he had been listening to something elsewhere in the poop. 'I knows Southwark, sir.' He pronounced it 'Sutherk'. 'I *knows* it, sir.' He moved one of the empty glasses, his mind far away. He was thinking of the tavern where he had once worked and had a room of his own. Of the din and upheavals when sailors came ashore from the ships moored on the great river, looking for drink and willing company.

81

And the crimes committed in those parts, the ragged corpses which dangled from the gibbets at Wapping and Greenwich as grim reminders. 'It is changing with the times, I believe, sir. Not always for the best.' Even the hated press gangs had trod warily where he had lived by the Thames. 'Some parts, sir . . .' He raised his eyes, gauging the captain's mood. 'It's not safe to walk alone or unarmed.'

Adam nodded slowly, moved by his cautious sincerity.

'Thank you, Bowles. That was well said.'

He walked to the stern windows and looked down into a lighter which was being warped beneath the counter. Faces peered up at him. There was a woman, her legs uncovered, displaying a basket of bright scarves, grinning broadly. They could have been invisible.

Nancy was afraid of offering him hope. But suppose her information held the truth? That for some reason Lowenna needed him?

Tonight he was being entertained by his officers, in his own ship, as was the time-honoured custom. Two days from now he would be in London, with Bethune. More secrets, although Jago had heard about the trip within an hour of stepping aboard.

He turned his back on the glittering water and overlapping masts and said, 'Can you read this, Bowles?' He held out the letter.

'Sir?' His eyes merely blinked, but it sounded like *of course*.

Adam cursed his own impatience. 'I meant no disrespect.'

The big nose trained round again. 'None taken, sir.' He almost smiled. 'In my old trade, the merchants I dealt with would rob you blind if you couldn't read and unravel their accounts!'

He held the letter to the reflected sunshine. 'I knows that street, sir. Some wealthy folk lived there, but they fell on hard times. I'm told that things is very different now. There was some talk that a new dock was to be built close by.' He handed back the letter and added apologetically, 'Unless you needs to go, sir . . .' He did not finish.

Adam moved restlessly across the cabin. Suppose he had not been going to London at Bethune's request? Nobody could say when *Athena* would be ready for her passage to the West Indies, or even if the orders had been changed by some higher authority.

There would be no other opportunity. No chance to discover the value of this small, crudely printed note.

He had a command, a ship when so many others had nothing. Not *Unrivalled*, but a ship . . .

He knew what Nancy feared most, about him and for him. To her, those brief meetings with Lowenna might not be enough. They would still be strangers, and his visit could do more harm than good. He touched his coat, as if to feel the yellow rose he had seen in the portrait at Falmouth. Bethune or not, he knew he would have gone.

Unless you needs to go . . .

Jago interrupted his thoughts. 'I'll be with you, Cap'n.' Suddenly alert, tense, like all those other times. But there was something else, almost a warning.

Adam looked at him, knowing he should refuse. It was something personal, not a reason to involve him in something unlawful, dangerous.

Jago, the man who hated officers and all those who abused authority, who had been wrongfully flogged, and, although declared innocent, would carry the scars of the cat until his dying day.

The same man had made certain that David Napier had been delivered safely to his new ship with the warrant of midshipman, a breed he had been known to dismiss with contempt on many occasions. And lastly, the man who had waved aside the chance of being paid off, the opportunity of living as he chose, and traded it for this.

He said, 'Can't be no worse than Algiers, sir!'

Adam smiled. 'I take too much for granted, Luke. Thank you.'

Bowles said, 'The first lieutenant will be here shortly, sir.'

Adam nodded. He had told Stirling that he wanted to go through the muster books and the watch bills, also the red punishment book, often the best gauge of any ship, and especially her officers.

Stirling would probably prepare him for the wardroom invitation to dinner, the individuals behind the uniforms he would be meeting.

He thought of the other note which was folded so carefully in his pocket. Almost falling apart now, but all that he had of hers. What might the formidable Stirling say if he knew his captain's secret fears?

84

He smiled a little. No wonder dear Nancy was troubled about him.

'First lieutenant, *sir!*'

Bolitho turned to face the screen door. The flag captain.

Lieutenant Francis Troubridge smiled regretfully, and said, 'You will not be kept longer than necessary, sir. I am afraid this room is in a state of chaos.'

Adam Bolitho tossed his hat on a vacant chair and looked around the big room he remembered so well from his previous visit. It looked as if it had been hit by a whirlwind. All the paintings, including Bethune's frigate engaging the two Spaniards, were arranged in a rank along one wall, numbered for removal to his house, or perhaps destined for another room in the Admiralty. Boxes and ledgers in other piles; even Bethune's handsome wine cooler was covered with a grubby sheet.

Troubridge was watching him, one hand still resting on the door handle.

'The higher we climb, the more precarious the perch, sir.'

Bethune was leaving, going to an important post in the West Indies. And already another was taking his place, like a door closing behind him.

Troubridge was in his element here, Adam thought. At ease with the senior officers they had met, always ready to remind Bethune of any small detail some one else had overlooked.

A civilian member of the Board of Admiralty, a

personal friend of the First Lord as Troubridge had recalled, had explained some of the complications which had followed the various acts of Parliament and treaties to control and then abolish the slave trade, once and for all. There had been an Anglo-Portuguese treaty which still allowed Portugal to continue loading slaves in her own ports, and another which made Portugal ban the trade north of the Equator, but allowed her the freedom to continue trading below it. And the same with Spain, which, to Adam, made a mockery of the original resolutions. Spain and Portugal were still able to trade freely south of the Equator, where even a simple sailorman could appreciate was the richest harvest both in the Indies and the Americas.

In Britain the slave trade was a felony. Elsewhere it was still able to make a fortune for those daring and ruthless enough to risk seizure and punishment.

Bethune's command was to be a fluid one. To cooperate with the ships of other nations, but to ensure that regular patrols continued on and around the most likely shipping routes so that any vessel carrying slaves, or fitted and equipped with the means of restraining them, could be arrested, and the owners or masters brought to trial.

Troubridge was followed by two clerks who were making copious notes about everything. They would find life aboard a King's ship very different when they joined *Athena* at Portsmouth.

Adam had also seen a file marked *Rear-Admiral Thomas Herrick*. His uncle's old friend. He recalled his visit to *Unrivalled* in Freetown, that melting pot of the anti-slavery patrols, where some terrible scenes had ensued when overloaded slavers had been escorted into harbour, their human cargoes more dead than alive after being crammed into conditions which were like vignettes of hell.

Maps, charts, signals, information; it would be easy to lose his way in minutiae. Adam kept his mental distance, or tried to. A captain's viewpoint had to take priority: time and distance, the most favourable routes, the anchorages and safest channels, and the reliability or otherwise of charts where an unmarked reef could rip out a ship's timbers like a knife through butter. Fresh water, stores, medical supplies, and a routine which kept men fit and ready to fight if the need arose.

It was difficult to see those aspects clearly in the Admiralty's map room, impressive though it was.

If Bethune had any doubts he did not show them; he was easy-mannered, almost casual at times. Maybe that came with flag rank, too.

Another door opened and two workmen entered, an oil painting held carefully between them. Bethune and another officer, a rear-admiral, followed them.

Adam had already been introduced to the rear-admiral, Philip Lancaster, whose exploits during the second American war had brought him to their lordships' notice.

Bethune said, 'I hope you'll be comfortable here, Philip.' He was looking at the picture of his frigate, and it was then that Adam saw the first hint of uncertainty, perhaps dismay. He was leaving this secure world for the unknown. A ship instead of power, strategy, and ambition. Lancaster pointed to the opposite wall, by accident or choice, Adam wondered. It was where the frigate had hung, guns blazing, colours streaming above the smoke of battle.

'There, I think.'

It was a full-length portrait of the man who had just spoken. It was a good likeness, a quietly determined face, with an anonymous sea as a background.

Bethune licked his lips, and smiled. 'You must get it brought up to date, eh, Philip?'

In the portrait, Lancaster wore the uniform of a post captain.

It was something to say, to break the silence.

'I intended to, Sir Graham. It was all arranged.' He stopped, frowning, as a servant came to stand just inside the doors, and announced, 'The First Sea Lord is ready to receive you now, sir.'

Bethune relaxed slowly. In charge again. 'Well, what happened?'

They were picking up their hats, looking around the disturbed room; only the ornate clock had not been moved.

Lancaster adjusted his dress coat and shrugged. 'It was in the *Times*. The artist I intended fell down dead the other day.' He strode past the servant, adding, 'Most inconsiderate, don't you know!' He laughed.

Troubridge waited. 'Are you ready, sir?'

But Adam scarcely heard him. He wanted to go closer to the portrait, but could not. Dared not.

He did not need to examine the artist's signature. It would be the same hand which had painted the empty sleeve on the portrait of Captain James Bolitho, and the portrait of Sir Richard. He was touching his lapel. *And the yellow rose on mine.*

He thought suddenly of *Athena*'s wardroom, brightly lit by candles and shining with the mess silver. The faces, some sweating badly by the end of the evening, the loud laughter at some joke made by Tarrant, the young third lieutenant. A ponderous speech by Stirling. Looking back, it seemed more a homage to the previous captain than one of welcome.

And the long journey from Portsmouth to the Admiralty, Jago sitting with him in the coach, more ill at ease than he could ever recall.

Now here. And now this.

Troubridge had moved and was facing him.

'If I may help in any way, sir?' The admiral had already been dismissed from his thoughts. This, the present moment, was suddenly important, although he could not determine why.

Adam said, 'The artist he mentioned. Do you know his name?'

'Yes, sir. He once did a portrait of my father. It was Montagu . . . Sir Gregory. It was very sudden, I believe, sir.'

The Admiralty servant coughed politely and Troubridge said, 'We *must* go, sir. The First Lord dislikes being delayed.'

Their feet made the only sound in the long corridor. Occasionally they passed a window, where carriages in the distance and, once, a troop of dragoons gave a touch of normality.

She was in that house. Like Andromeda. Helpless and alone.

The tall doors were just a few paces away: the room where the great news had broken. Trafalgar. Waterloo. And Algiers.

Troubridge said suddenly, 'You can trust me, sir.'

Afterwards he knew he would never be able to forget Captain Bolitho's expression. His eyes. Nor want to.

The great doors had opened as though to some signal, but Adam turned abruptly and gripped the flag lieutenant's arm as if nothing else mattered.

'I am not sure I can trust myself!'

The journey seemed endless, and Adam had lost count of the streets and squares, the gleam of water whenever the coach drove close to the river. It was late, and pitch dark, and yet there seemed to be people everywhere, and when he lowered a window he could hear the clatter of wheels and horses, smell woodsmoke and the occasional aroma of cooking whenever they passed yet another tavern. Did nobody ever sleep in the capital?

The coachman showed no uncertainty, and Adam guessed he was used to these journeys with little notice or none at all; Troubridge had said as much. He was often employed by senior officers not wishing to draw attention to themselves. Troubridge had learned fast since his appointment as Bethune's aide.

Adam wished he knew what Jago was thinking, up

there beside the coachman, probably wondering what had made him insist on joining them.

Troubridge was thinking aloud.

'Getting close.' He was peering through the opposite window. 'That looks like the church.' He hesitated. 'I was here once before.'

Adam saw some glowing braziers beside the road, dark figures crowded around them for warmth and companionship. Coachmen, grooms, servants, it was hard to tell. Waiting for their masters to become tired or bored with whatever pastime or indulgence had brought them here.

The houses were higher now, several storeys, some with windows lighted, chandeliers giving a hint of the district's original luxury. Much as the solemn Bowles had described. Other houses were in total darkness, shutters closed, walls neglected and flaking in the carriage lanterns.

Troubridge murmured, 'Number Eighteen, sir. We're passing it now.'

Adam felt even more uneasy. Cheated. It was no different from all the others.

Troubridge said doubtfully, 'Looks deserted.' He leaned out of the window. 'Some lights up there, sir.'

The coachman said nothing, and had climbed down to attend to his horses.

'What kind of people, I wonder . . .'

Troubridge shrugged, and Adam thought he heard the clink of steel.

'Gaming rooms.' Again the hesitation. 'Brothels. I did hear that artists come here to earn their keep.'

Jago was by the door, although he had made no sound. He said, 'Some one comin' now, sir.'

A group of men, perhaps six in all, one calling back to a coachman, telling him to wait *without fail*. A loud, slurred voice. One used to being obeyed.

They were going toward the house, Number Eighteen. One of them was laughing; another called, 'Put it away, John, you can have all you want to drink inside!'

They heard the crash of the knocker, enough to wake the street.

The door was partly open, more voices, angry this time, one harsher than all the others.

'So I'm a trifle late, man! What is that to you? Just do as you're damn well told by your betters and be sharp about it!'

The door opened wider, and there was more laughter. Then silence again, and the street was empty.

Adam said, 'I am going inside.' *Suppose I am wrong?* 'Stay here.'

He was on the road, the horses turning their heads to watch him.

Without looking, he knew that Troubridge was following him, while Jago had moved away to their left, almost as if he had changed his mind.

Troubridge said, 'I think you should consider . . .'

Adam had already seized the knocker. 'I *must* find out,' and the crash froze Troubridge into silence.

The door opened a few inches; Adam heard voices, muffled, deep inside the building.

'What do you want —' The shadowy figure seemed

to glide backwards, the door opening completely, the voice suddenly changed, all hostility gone.

Instead he said brokenly, 'Thank God. You got the message!'

The door had closed behind them; the high-ceilinged entrance was lit by only two candles and Adam could see the stains on the floor, the lighter patches on the walls where pictures had once hung, like a travesty of Bethune's room at the Admiralty.

He swung round and stared with disbelief. His first visit to the Old Glebe House; being met by the dour-faced figure, who had looked more like a priest than a servant. This same man.

Adam seized his arm; it felt like a bone through his coat.

'Tell me what is happening. Take your time.' He tried to keep the urgency out of his voice, willing the other man to stay calm.

The house was suddenly silent, and very still. He could hear Troubridge's breathing, fast, unsteady. Or was it his own?

The other man said slowly, 'Sir Gregory died, sir. He lost the will to live. His injury, after the fire . . . but for her I'm not sure what . . .'

Somewhere above them a door banged open and there were more shouts and laughter, one of them a woman's voice, hysterical. The door slammed and there was silence again. The late arrivals had reached their destination.

Adam's eyes were becoming accustomed to the feeble lighting. When he leaned forward he could just discern a spiral staircase rising overhead, a gilt banister, lit here and there by candle sconces, or perhaps an open door. An even larger house than it had seemed. He thought of Troubridge's comment. Gaming rooms. Brothels.

He seized the servant's arm again. 'She is still up there?'

'First landing, sir. She was just about to leave when . . .'

The scream broke the stillness, locking mind and movement, making thought impossible.

He was running up the stairs, heedless of uneven and torn carpet snaring his shoes, guided only by the scream although it had ended as abruptly. There was a sudden crash, like some one falling, and the sound of breaking glass. On the landing above, more doors had opened and voices made an insane chorus, like the climax to a nightmare.

Adam saw the gleam of light under a door and flung his shoulder against it. After the dark stairway the glare almost blinded him, but he took it in at a glance. Like the moment of close action. The first fall of shot. The carnage, and the wild disbelief that you had lived through it.

A studio, the same soiled and paint-daubed sheets, mock pillars and classical busts, one crowned with real laurels. And a long couch like the one he had seen at the Old Glebe House, where Lowenna had sat for Montagu's most promising students.

A tall looking-glass which he had seen used to direct light on to a subject lay in fragments, and a man was clutching a bloodied sheet to his face even as he tried to stagger to his feet.

Adam said, '*Stay where you are!*' He did not raise his voice, or did not think he had, but the other man fell back against the couch as if he had struck him. Some one about his own age, and vaguely familiar; he did not know or care. If he had moved, he would have killed him.

The girl stood facing him, quite still, as if posing for an artist. Only the painful thrust of her breast made a lie of her composure. She had one hand to her shoulder, where there was a tear in her gown which would become a bruise on the bare skin. In the other she was holding a brass candlestick.

She said quietly, 'Adam.' She repeated his name as if she believed she were mistaken. 'How did you *know*?'

The man on the couch exclaimed, 'She might have killed me!' He broke off and cringed as she raised the candlestick again.

But she tossed it under one of the sheets and said, 'I was leaving. He tried to stop me. Then he tried to . . .'

She would have fallen if Adam had not seized her, held her, soothed her with words he scarcely understood, and did not remember. Behind him he heard the soft click of a pistol being uncocked. Troubridge had been ready.

He stroked her back, holding her without looking at her, feeling the resistance, the nearness of a complete breakdown. Remembering the secrets Montagu had told him, and what Nancy had discovered for herself. The nightmare, the brutal, lusting figures. The suffering and the shame.

He held his cheek close to the long, silky hair, his voice low, so that no one else existed.

'I wrote to you, Lowenna. I wanted you to know, to believe . . .'

For a moment he thought she had not heard, but felt her nod very slowly, her dark hair clinging to his face.

'I dared not. I was not sure. About myself. What I might do. It did not seem fair to you. To us . . .'

The man on the couch stirred, his shoes scraping on broken glass. Adam heard Troubridge say, almost gently, 'Easy, now, be still, eh?' The hammer clicked again and there was silence. Even the sounds from the other rooms had faded or gone completely.

He said quietly, 'I only heard about the fire when I returned to Falmouth.' He held her more closely as she began to shiver. 'I'll take you where you'll be safe.'

'I have some friends, not far from here.' She winced as the man shouted, '*Whores!*'

She said, 'Of your making. As you would have used me!'

Then she stood back a little, his hands still around her waist, and added, 'This is Sir Gregory's nephew. I think you may have seen him at one time.'

Calmly said, but he could feel through his hands what it was costing her.

'I had my belongings packed, ready to go.' She

shook her head, trying to shut it out. 'He said terrible things, taunted me, tried . . .' She shut her eyes. 'I wanted to stop him . . . kill him.'

A tall, painted screen shuddered to one side and Jago appeared in the room.

He said, 'Found another door, Cap'n. Thought it might be a bolt-hole.' He reached out casually and gripped the other man by the arm. 'Stay anchored, matey. I don't like surprises, especially from your sort of filth.' He did not even raise his voice. He did not need to.

Adam guided her to the empty fireplace, suddenly conscious of the cold. Hating the place, the smell of paint and oil.

She was gazing at him, her eyes unmoving, like the moment he had first seen her. On that day, Montagu's nephew had just arrived, and the bearded painter had taken him through another room to avoid a meeting. But for that . . .

'Take this.' He unclipped his cloak and folded it around her. 'I have a carriage downstairs.'

She had not heard him. She said, 'Sir Gregory's house is locked up until legal matters have been settled. His brother is a lawyer, you see.'

Adam did not see, but he could well imagine the complications Montagu's sudden death would create. And Lowenna would be completely alone.

Troubridge said, 'I know a place where she can stay a while, sir. There must be some one . . .'

She had turned to study him, as if she had not realized any one else was there, and attempted to smile. But the nightmare was returning.

Instead, she looked very directly at Adam's face, as if to memorize each detail, as Montagu might have done before starting to paint.

She nodded again, very slowly.

'Walk with me.'

Like that day in the garden, or that other day, when she had given him the rose.

Then, with her arm through his, she left the deserted studio, her head erect, her hair falling around her shoulders, even darker as they moved out on to the landing.

Troubridge followed, the pistol still dangling from his hand. He had learned a lot today in a very short while. About his captain, and about himself.

He heard Jago slam the door, and thought he called something to the man who still sat on the studio couch, the bloodied sheet pressed to his face.

Things could have gone very wrong. He might have been killed, or been forced to kill some one else. It would have meant ruin, and shame for his father, the admiral. *And I was not afraid. Not once.*

He also noticed that neither the captain nor the lovely woman wrapped in the boatcloak once looked back.

He thought of her voice when she had said, *walk with me.*

All he could feel was envy.

5

A Last Resort

'*Oars!*'

One more pull, and then the cutter's twelve blades rose, dripping from the murky water, to rest motionless on either beam like spread wings. It was bright and cold, the oarsmen's breath combined like steam as the cutter lost way, rocking gently in the current.

Adam Bolitho stood in the sternsheets and watched the moored two-decker rising above him, the newly gilded beakhead and bowsprit swing across the boat as if *Athena*, and not the cutter, was moving.

The figurehead, too, was freshly painted, the eyes set in a grey stare, the face beneath the plumed helmet handsome rather than beautiful, as the Greek myths would have insisted.

He sensed that the others were watching him. Stirling, the first lieutenant, slumped by the coxswain, breathing heavily, and the midshipman in charge, one hand almost touching the tiller bar as if he were afraid the coxswain might make a mistake in front of their captain. Sitting more comfortably on the opposite side was Fraser the sailing master, his bright blue eyes missing nothing as the current carried them slowly into *Athena*'s shadow.

They had already circled the ship twice, Stirling occasionally indicating the recent work carried out by dockyard people or the ship's own company. Factual and to the point, but seldom offering an opinion.

Fraser, on the other hand, had rarely stopped talking about the ship. *His* ship, how she would behave at sea now that some of the ballast had been moved aft to make her stand more trim 'in the deep water', as he put it. It should have been obvious to the dockyard, and also to Stirling, he thought. With half her twenty-four pounders removed, replaced now by painted wooden 'quakers', *Athena*'s ability to sail close to the wind might have been seriously impaired.

Fraser said, 'She looks right, sir! Feels it too, I'll wager!' A fellow Cornishman, and from Penzance, where Adam had first drawn breath, he did not care to hide his enthusiasm, or his eagerness to get to sea again. 'A fine sailer, sir! Close-hauled, even under storm stays'ls she can hold her own with a frigate, beggin' your pardon, sir!'

Stirling had remained silent.

He shaded his eyes and looked across at the battery and the town beyond. They would be leaving Portsmouth within the week, and there were still important matters to be checked, and if necessary questioned. Changed . . . like this forenoon. A seaman was to be punished for insubordination, insolence to an officer.

Adam had seen more floggings than he could recall, some deserved, some not, and more usually brought about by the qualities of the officer involved. He had even witnessed a flogging around the fleet, the most barbarous display that could be instigated by the Articles of War, every captain's guide and final defence. The prisoner had been taken from ship to ship, to receive so many lashes at each one, while all hands were mustered to watch, and to take warning. Bound as if crucified to a capstan bar across the boat used for punishment, the flogging was carried out to the beat of the Rogue's March, a portion of the total lashes awarded at each rated ship. No longer human, just a torn, bloodied thing, the blackened flesh burned by the lash, the bones laid bare. Very few lived through such brutal punishment.

Only once had Jago spoken of his own unjust flogging. Almost as if the humiliation were worse than the agony.

It was never a comfortable thing to carry out in harbour, surrounded by other ships and watching eyes.

If an officer tried to be popular he would lose respect. If he used any pretext to enforce his will, he was not fit to hold his commission.

It was a captain's final decision.

He said, 'Return alongside, if you please.' He could not remember the midshipman's name. But next time . . .

Perhaps if he had not remained for an extra day in London, it would not have happened. He was angry just thinking about it. *Athena*'s punishment book told its own story: too many punishments awarded for the most trivial reasons. Two dozen for skylarking on deck after being reprimanded by a warrant officer. Drunk and disorderly when sharing hoarded rum for somebody's birthday or a rare promotion, three dozen lashes.

The last captain, Ritchie, had apparently never questioned the cause, rather than the actual deed. Three years in command, but he had left no impression, no example others could copy or avoid. And now he was under arrest, awaiting a court-martial. With his quarters emptied and repainted, it was as if he had never been aboard.

He looked up at the starboard gangway and saw some seamen busy splicing, new hands who had volunteered to one of the recruiting parties. Almost unheard of a year ago.

Stirling said, 'You've not forgotten the man for punishment, sir?'

Adam saw the stroke oarsman's eyes flicker quickly between them even as he laid back on his loom. Ready gossip for the messdeck.

The Captain didn't give a damn!

Adam nodded toward the new hands as they passed abeam.

'I hope they won't, either, Mr Stirling.'

A few faces had already made their mark, but the majority were still strangers.

Athena would be putting into Plymouth. He had confronted that. But he knew he had not accepted it.

He had told Lowenna as much as he could. The ship was under confidential orders, but her going to Plymouth had been in the *Times* for all to see. Troubridge had found him a copy to show him the item about Sir Gregory Montagu.

Adam had tried to make her accept his aunt's open invitation, and her friendship, and go to Cornwall, and wait there until he could visit her. He felt the familiar despair. And why should she? *Athena* might be away for months. Years, if their lordships thought it necessary, or prudent.

In the end they had been together for less than an hour, at the house where she had friends, in a part of London called Whitechapel. A house which was owned by the most formidable woman he had ever seen. And she was quite adamant.

'You'll stay where you are, Lieutenant, or whatever post you hold, and you will behave yourself.' She had stood with her brawny arms folded. 'Or I shall know the reason, *sir!*'

He had embraced Lowenna, while Troubridge and Jago had carried in her few pieces of baggage.

Then she had followed him to the door and had gripped his hands in hers.

'Take your cloak, Adam.'

She had watched him while he released her hands to unfasten the cloak.

'I love you, Lowenna. I have to see you. To tell you, to share . . .' He got no further.

She had smiled, but he had seen that she was trembling, and not because he had removed the cloak.

She had touched his lips, with fingers like ice.

'I want to love you.' She had stepped back into the hall light, and raised one hand to her own lips. She might have said something more, but the door was shut, the others already in the coach.

'*Man the side! Cap'n comin' aboard!*'

Stirling was on his feet, his hat doffed as Adam began to climb. The boat's crew, oars tossed, stared fixedly astern, the water running down the looms and over their legs.

Adam glanced down at the midshipman. Vicary. That was his name.

Even if she visited Nancy, he might not see her. Vice-Admiral Bethune was hoisting his flag in Plymouth. Because it was convenient? Or was there another, private reason? Troubridge did not know, or would not say. Adam remembered his voice. *You can trust me.* And the sound of his pistol being cocked in that terrible room. He knew Troubridge better than that now.

The calls shrilled, and a lieutenant stepped forward to greet him. Stirling was climbing up behind him, treading heavily as he raised his hat to the quarter-deck, and the flag.

Their eyes met. Strangers.

'Very well, Mr Stirling. Pipe all hands.'

He walked to the hammock nettings and looked across at the other ships lying nearby.

Plymouth. They might see *Unrivalled*, if . . .

He swung round and faced the keen breeze as the boatswain's mates ran between decks, their Spithead

Nightingales reaching out like extensions of the figure by the nettings.

'*All hands! All hands lay aft to witness punishment!*'

He watched the seamen scrambling through hatchways and clawing down from their work high above the decks.

The master-at-arms, Scollay, his mates and the ship's corporal, the boatswain Henry Mudge, with the hated red baize bag which contained the 'cat', and the prisoner, a young seaman named Hudson. Lastly, George Crawford the surgeon.

There was silence, and Adam looked steadily at the crowded figures and faces, all waiting for him to read the words of his authority. His power. He saw a solitary gull circling around the Union flag, the spirit of some old Jack. He cleared his throat and began to read.

Once he paused as the shadow of a sail passed swiftly across the quarterdeck, a lugger loaded with casks of salted beef or pork making its way to another anchored two-decker. Some of the lugger's seamen were staring at *Athena*'s crowded upper deck, understanding exactly what was happening. *Getting a checkered shirt at the gangway,* as the old hands called it.

What would Lowenna think of him if she could see him now?

He closed the book with a snap. This was not a dream. This was now.

'Bosun's mate!' Like hearing some one else. 'Do your duty!'

* * *

Vice-Admiral Sir Graham Bethune put his signature on the last document and leaned back in the unfamiliar chair, looking around the room, which had been borrowed for the occasion.

He had been excited about this moment ever since the First Lord had proposed him for the West Indies appointment: a challenge, perhaps a risk, but going ahead, not remaining in the same post, waiting for the inevitable like so many of his colleagues here. There was always a last time for everything, and he was surprised at the sentiment which had prevented him from even looking into his old office at the other end of this floor. Surprised or guilty?

He had already said his farewells to those he had grown close to; it was an awkward experience, like leaving a ship. And tonight it would be worse, at his own house on the outskirts of London. Some senior officers, even the First Lord, would be coming to pay their respects, offer their good wishes, perhaps glad they were remaining under the Admiralty's protection in these difficult times.

He heard voices in the corridor, boxes being moved. His boxes. Even the sounds were different here. His new flag lieutenant, Francis Troubridge, would be dealing with the last rites of office. Very young, but already proving himself extremely capable. He half smiled. And discreet.

He found himself at a window although he did not recall leaving the chair. April was just a few days old. Like that other April, three years ago; could it be so long? Since the telegraph on the Admiralty roof had received the signal, the incredible news that Napoleon had surrendered and abdicated. The endless war had been over, or so they had thought.

This same carriageway had been alive with cheering and gaiety within the hour. Boys who had grown into men, or served with Nelson aboard *Victory* at Trafalgar, had brought about the impossible dream.

He watched the traffic and the groups of people, the occasional splash of colour from a passing uniform. The dream was over.

Bethune was not politically involved, but he could not help but be aware of the shortages and rising prices. Half the national income went on paying the war debt. The men who had saved their country from tyranny were coming home to unemployment, even poverty.

He thought of his wife. She would be in her element tonight, flattering the guests, and always in charge. How did she feel about his going back to sea at this stage of his service? One of the youngest flag officers on the Navy List. Or had been.

'You don't *need* to go, Graham. But if you must, then I suppose you must.'

Was that all it meant to her?

The elderly clerk was gathering up the papers. Bethune knew him better than some of tonight's guests.

Bent over, with watery eyes, soon due for retirement. Oblivion. Hard to believe he had served aboard Black Dick Howe's *Queen Charlotte* at that great victory still called 'The Glorious First of June'.

He paused now, and said, 'I'll lock up after you leave, Sir Graham.'

Bethune had never seen him at a loss before; it surprised him, and he was moved by it. Vice-Admiral of the Blue. Successful and safe, no matter what happened after this.

The door opened. It was Tolan, his servant.

'The carriage is here, Sir Graham. All stowed.' He must have sensed the atmosphere, the uncertainty between admiral and clerk. 'Mr Troubridge has gone on ahead.'

'Yes. I told him not to wait.' Tolan had been his servant, afloat and ashore, for as long as he could recall, and would be with him aboard *Athena*.

When he looked again, the clerk had vanished. Another ghost.

Bethune picked up the letter from the table. Perhaps this was the true moment of decision. He had made several attempts to write it, on Admiralty paper, so that it would not appear unseemly or too personal. In his old office it might have been easier. Where she had visited him, 'up the back stairs'; they had joked about it. He had pretended, not wanting to shatter a friendship which had existed even then, in his own heart, anyway.

Lady Catherine Somervell. Always so easy to see in his thoughts. Her smile, the touch of hands. His fury and despair when she had almost been raped in that little house at Chelsea. He had walked past it several times, or driven by, knowing it was impossible, dangerous too, for his own security and future in the only life he wanted or understood.

Their last arranged meeting was always there, fixed

in his mind. How she had called out to him, her eyes flashing with contempt as she had walked away from him toward her carriage.

'Are you in love with me, Graham?'

He could not remember his answer, shocked by the directness of the question. But he could still hear her response, her dismissal.

'Then you are a *fool!*'

It was madness, but he had thought of little else. As if it had given purpose and drive to the immediate future. Madness . . .

And yet when it came to him, he had not hesitated. No doubts.

My dear Catherine . . .

Regrets might come later.

'See to this, Tolan.'

Tolan took the letter and placed it in his pocket. Their eyes met only briefly.

'Good as done, Sir Graham.'

Together they walked out into the corridor. Mercifully, it was deserted, and unusually still. As if the whole building was holding its breath, listening.

Bethune was suddenly glad to be leaving.

Lieutenant Francis Troubridge jumped lightly from the carriage and peered up at the house. In broad daylight it was not what he had expected or remembered from that one visit with Captain Bolitho and his lovely companion.

He felt the coachman's eyes on him. A mere lieutenant, admiral's aide or not, did not, apparently, warrant the courtesy or effort of climbing down to open the carriage door. Or anything else.

Troubridge looked around at the other houses, all of which appeared to join or overlap, fronting a square, somehow apart from the crowded streets he had watched on his journey here.

Whitechapel was very different from what he had come to think of as his London. Thriving markets, streets alive with carriers' carts or hawkers pushing their barrows, bawling out their wares and swapping jokes with housemaids and passersby. You could still hear them in this quiet square, and see the church tower which the coachman had used like a beacon to steer himself through the bustle and noise.

'Be long, sir?'

Strange to think that after today there would be no more free Admiralty transport, coachmen who were used to taking senior officers and their aides to such outlandish places as Whitechapel.

'As long as it takes. Wait here.' He gazed up at him. 'Please.'

Troubridge was twenty-four years old, but already experienced enough to appreciate that but for his father's reputation and influence he would never have been offered the post of flag lieutenant. Bethune had wanted to rid himself of his previous aide, related in some way to Lady Bethune. He smiled. That had clinched it.

If he had left the Admiralty a few moments sooner he might have missed being passed the sealed note. Tolan, Bethune's servant, had somehow intercepted it.

Protecting his master, or making a new ally; it was not easy to tell with Tolan.

He faced the front door and examined his feelings. A ruse, or some kind of trap? He thought of the moment when Captain Bolitho had burst into the room with its mirrors and burning lights. The woman with the heavy candlestick in her hand, the sprawled, whimpering figure lying amongst the shattered glass. The bared skin where her gown had been torn from her shoulder. The captain's face when he had taken her into his arms. *And the cocked pistol in my hand. Was that really me?*

He almost jumped as the knocker echoed throughout the house. He had used it without knowing, without hesitation.

He could recall catching a glimpse of a fearsome woman, who had confronted them at this same door. Even the captain's coxswain had been impressed.

But it was a small, pale-faced maid who opened the door now.

'Who shall I say?' A local girl. He heard the same accent on the streets, and in some of the houses where he had left senior officers to enjoy themselves.

'Troubridge. I have come to . . .'

He got no further. The small person even executed a hasty curtsey.

'You are expected, sir!' She smiled, and it made her look younger still. 'This way, if you please.'

It was a room apparently on the other side of the house; there were windows from floor to ceiling, with some sort of garden beyond. Not normally in use. He

111

took it in quickly, the easel with what he thought was a canvas cover, what looked like a page of scribbled notes pinned to it. A dying fire in the grate, and chests lying in a corner with some of the baggage they had brought from Southwark, still packed.

The strangest thing of all was a harp, standing by an upturned stool. It was badly burned, blackened by smoke, and most of its strings were broken.

He heard the door close behind him. It was hard to imagine the noise of a few minutes ago; the house was very quiet, so still that he flinched as a dying log collapsed in the grate.

She had written to him. He was surprised she could remember his name; there had been no time. And yet . . .

He walked to the easel and lifted the cover. As if some one had burned away one side of the canvas, the wooden frame split and blackened. Like the harp.

But the painting itself was otherwise intact, or perhaps it had been carefully cleaned. He moved slightly to allow the filtered sunlight to bring it to life.

The lovely girl, head flung back, her face filled with terror and the pain of the chains which held her against the overhanging rock. Her taut breasts and naked limbs almost touching the sea and leaping spray, where the shadow of some monster merged with the charred canvas.

No wonder the captain was in love with her. Who would not be?

He covered the painting. *Lowenna*. She had signed her note simply that. He moved away from the easel, unnerved in some way, as if he had stumbled on some-body's secret. Like an intrusion. A breach of trust.

'I am glad that you could come, Lieutenant.'

He swung round and saw her watching him from that same door.

She was dressed from throat to toe in a loose blue-grey gown; when she moved it seemed to swirl around her, and she seemed insubstantial, unreachable. He noticed that her feet were bare on the thick rug, despite the coldness of the room. When she turned to glance at the ashes in the grate he saw her hair as if for the first time, falling to her waist, shining like glass in the April light. Like the hair in the painting, across the straining shoulders and bared breasts.

He heard himself exclaim, 'Andromeda!' and could feel himself flushing. 'I do beg your pardon. You see . . .'

She smiled, and reached out to take his hand, all tension gone.

'You saw the painting, Lieutenant? You are full of surprises!'

He said, 'My father is an admiral, but his brother chose the Church. My education, such as it was, bordered on the classical!'

He found it easy to laugh at the absurdity of his explanation, and his own confusion. He tried again. 'I came as soon as I was able.'

She looked at her hand on his. Surprised? No, deeper than that.

She said, 'I had a letter from Captain Bolitho.' Her chin lifted slightly. Defiance, a challenge. 'From . . .

113

Adam. I should have been brave, sensible. Or tried to explain.' She moved away, her hand lifting as if to pluck one of the twisted harp strings.

Then she faced him. 'His ship has left Portsmouth?'

Troubridge nodded, and found his lips were bone-dry; he wanted to lick them.

'*Athena* will arrive at Plymouth tomorrow, according to the telegraph.' He knew she did not understand, or perhaps want to, and hurried on. 'Sir Graham Bethune will hoist his flag in ten days' time, the roads permitting.' It was a little attempt to bring back her smile. It failed.

She said, 'I may not see him again. He could be away for a long time. He will forget . . .'

Troubridge had scant experience of women, and none with some one like this. But he knew she was going over and over the same arguments, fears even, which had caused her to send him the message. Before he could reply she said almost abruptly, 'Your captain is a man of war,' and shook her head, so that some of the hair spilled unheeded across her arm. 'At war with himself too, I think!'

He saw her hand on his cuff, gripping his wrist, as if it and not she were pleading.

'Now there is so little time.' Her eyes were dry, but her voice was full of tears. 'I wanted to tell him so much. So that he would not be hurt, not be damaged because of me.'

Troubridge put his hand reassuringly on hers and felt her stiffen immediately. Was that what had happened? Like the man on the studio floor, or others

114

before that? He recalled Adam Bolitho's face. He would have killed for her. He tried not to look at the baggage, the unopened boxes. She was Sir Gregory Montagu's ward, or had been. It seemed as if she had no one to watch over her now. Montagu's property was in the hands of lawyers, leeches, he had heard his father call them. Where would she go? Posing for some so-called artists, like the painting under the cover . . .

He said calmly, 'I could arrange a carriage for you. You can pay me back when you feel like it.' He saw the sudden anger fall away, like a cloud passing from calmer water. 'For the first part of the journey, at any rate.'

She put her hand to his face, and touched it very gently.

'Forgive me. I am not good company today.' She swung away from him. 'Sir Gregory left me well provided. With money.' She seemed to shiver, with either laughter or despair. 'To think that I dared to stand on the shore and watch his ship sail away. Say nothing, do nothing, let him fade out of reach!' She turned back, and her composure was gone, her body trembling within the loose gown. 'I want to stand beside him with pride, not endless guilt and the terror of what I might do to him. To us.'

Troubridge made up his mind. Stupidly, he remembered what a senior post captain had once told him. Warned him. 'A flag lieutenant does not make decisions. He merely acts on those determined by his betters!'

He said, '*Athena* cannot sail without her admiral. Sir Graham will not be joining her for ten days. Even then, there will be matters to deal with before we weigh anchor.'

Her eyes filled her face; she was close enough for him to feel her quick breathing, catch the scent of her body.

She said, 'What must I do?'

'I am going to Plymouth ahead of Sir Graham.' He swallowed. *What are you saying?* 'Three carriages and a wagon of some kind.' He was seeing it in his mind, and later he might see the risks even more clearly.

'You would do that for me?'

He felt the tension running out, like sand. 'For both of you.'

She walked back and forth across the room. 'And you ask and expect no reward?' She did not look at him. 'Sir Gregory would have approved of you.' She put her hand to her breast and held it there. Recovering herself, like preparing for a painter's pose, and beyond. *The enemy*.

Troubridge looked down at his sweating hands, surprised that they appeared normal. Relaxed. He said limply, 'It were better that you should have a maid for company.'

Afterwards, Lieutenant Francis Troubridge thought it was probably the first laughter that room had heard for a long time.

Adam Bolitho nodded in passing to the Royal Marine sentry and continued into his cabin. A cold, brilliant morning, everything familiar and yet at once so strange. It was always a demanding time, for captain or newly signed landman alike. The time to up-anchor, to bring the ship to life, so that every block and piece of cordage worked as one: the ship under command.

Bowles' tall, stooping shadow moved into the sunlight slanting from the stern windows.

'Somethin' to warm you, sir?'

Adam smiled, and could feel the tightness of his mouth and jaw. He had held a command since he was twenty-three. Surely there was nothing new to catch him unawares. He had seen many eyes darting glances at their new captain, a few threatening fists when this man or that was slow at the braces or running to lend his weight to a capstan bar. There was even a fiddler, although you could hardly pick out the tune above the bang and thunder of released canvas, the rigging creaking as the fresh northeasterly filled sails and heeled *Athena* hard over to lean above her own reflection.

The harbour mouth, always a challenge with no time for second thoughts. Even Fraser, the sailing master, had remarked, 'Don't look wide enough to drive a four-in-hand through it!' Outwardly calm, as Adam had always remembered him. Something to cling to when surrounded by faces still mostly unknown, unproved.

He cradled the mug in both hands, relaxing very slowly, his ear still tuned to the thud of the tiller head, the scamper of bare feet overhead and the occasional bark of commands.

It was strong coffee, some of his own stock which

Grace Ferguson had packed for him, in between her farewell sniffs and sobs, laced with something even stronger, and he saw Bowles' private smile when he nodded his approval.

He thought of Stirling, the first lieutenant. He had handled the chaos of weighing anchor and had directed the seamen to their immediate duties of making sail and then shortening it again in a sudden squall, with apparent ease and confidence. His powerful voice was quick to point out a clumsy mistake or lack of purpose. But rarely it seemed to offer encouragement or praise when they were equally deserved.

Barclay, the second lieutenant, who had first greeted Adam's arrival, was Stirling's opposite, never still. He was in charge of the foremast with all its complicated rigging and the ever-busy jib sails, a vital part of any ship's workings, leaving or entering harbour. Adam put down the mug and stared at it. *Or when called to fight*.

Athena, like most of the ships he had seen, might never stand in the line of battle again. But the Algiers campaign, and the events leading up to it, had taught him lessons he would, must, never forget. It took more than a flag to determine who was an enemy.

He thought of Plymouth again. How would he feel? What might he find there?

He pictured the chart in his mind. A hundred and fifty miles to go, provided the wind remained steady; 'trustworthy', another of the sailing master's descriptions. Once clear of Wight and the Needles they could . . .

He heard the sentry shout, 'First lieutenant, *sir!*'

Another thing he had learned about Stirling. Always on time. To the minute, no matter what was happening on deck.

He was here now, head bowed beneath the deckhead beams, his heavy features expressionless.

'I think we shall exercise the eighteen-pounder crews before we pipe a stand-easy.' He noticed that Stirling had the red-covered punishment book, and tried to accept it. He had called him to this very cabin after the flogging which had been ordered in his absence. Upholding discipline, as Stirling had insisted.

Adam had always hated it, had almost fainted when he had witnessed his first such punishment. It was necessary, as a final resort . . . He thought of that last flogging, for insolence to Blake, one of *Athena*'s eight midshipmen. The young seaman in question, Hudson, a maintopman, had been called on deck while he was off watch to stand in for another who had suddenly reported sick. Hudson had been in his hammock, the worse for drink after consuming some extra tots by way of celebration.

It happened; and as a maintopman Hudson was a trained seaman, not some loafer from the local petty sessions. Adam had discovered that Blake was generally unpopular, but was the son of a senior captain, and like most of the other 'young gentlemen' was overdue for his examination for lieutenant.

'What is it, Mr Stirling?' He thought of Galbraith in *Unrivalled*, their gradual understanding of one another despite differences and the barrier of rank.

The comparison caught him unprepared, like being stripped. Could he ever call Stirling by his first name, discuss and share their problems here in the great cabin?

Stirling pouted his lower lip.

'The master-at-arms has just reported a man dead, sir. Nothing any one could do. In the main hold, which is open as you know, sir, ready to take on fresh stores when we anchor.'

'It's Hudson, isn't it?' He saw the brief start of surprise. 'Tell me.'

Stirling shrugged. 'Hanged himself. I called the surgeon.'

Adam was on his feet again, and had moved to the leather chair, running his fingers along the back, like holding on to something.

'Hudson was twenty-two years old, a volunteer, and a trained seaman. He was about to be married, and then he was "awarded" punishment.' His voice was quiet, almost lost in the clatter of rigging and the sea alongside. But he saw Stirling flinch with each word, as if he had sworn at him.

'I was left in charge, sir. He was insolent to one of my midshipmen. He had been drinking, too.'

'And you ordered *two dozen lashes*. Was that not extreme for a normally well-behaved and disciplined hand?' He did not wait for an answer. 'You saw his back after the lash had done its work. He was to be married, God knows rare enough in this life we lead. Would any one want to lie with his new bride, with a back like that?'

Stirling tugged at his neckcloth as if it was suddenly too tight.

'You were in London, sir . . .' His voice trailed away.

'And I supported your decision, *Mister* Stirling, as is my duty.' He pushed himself away from the chair. 'In future, if in any further doubt, *ask me*!'

He walked to the stern windows, his body angled to the sloping deck.

'We will exercise the upper battery in ten minutes. I intend to time each drill.'

Stirling left the cabin without another word, and Adam knew he had failed. Stirling would never change. Perhaps he did not know how.

A man dead. Like the stroke of a pen in the log, and now in the muster book. *D.D. Discharged – Dead.* Was that all there was to a life?

He moved to the quarter gallery and let the wet breeze soak his hair and face.

A bad beginning.

The voice seemed to awaken a broken memory. Like a condemnation.

Athena, sir? An unlucky ship!

Calls shrilled and feet pounded on deck as the hands ran to prepare the eighteen-pounders on the lee side for drill.

But the voice remained.

6

Destiny

Captain Adam Bolitho stood by the quarterdeck rail, only his eyes moving to watch some landmark or another vessel on a converging tack, while all the time the land continued to reach out as if to engulf the whole ship. During the night and early morning the wind had backed a little, slowing their progress and *Athena*'s final approach to Plymouth. Adam had been on deck since before dawn, preparing himself for this moment. A captain's responsibility, when any oversight or impatience could cause a disaster.

He had thought about it even as he had been swallowing several mugs of Grace Ferguson's coffee. He had entered and left Plymouth many times, as a junior officer as well as in command of his own ship. And yet this time seemed completely different, even the widening span of the Sound unfamiliar. Hostile.

'Steady she goes, sir, nor' by west.'

That was Fraser the sailing master, standing by his

chart with one of his mates, ever watchful, one hand hooked into his coat, the fingers drumming soundlessly to show that he was anxious. For his ship or his captain? It was impossible to tell from his rugged features.

Adam had to stop himself from looking aloft as the main topsail flapped and banged noisily. They were losing the wind, the land acting like a shield.

He heard Mudge the boatswain bawling orders, and bare feet slithering across the damp planking to obey. Blocks squealed, and spray dripped from the braces as more men added their weight to haul round the great main yard. So close-hauled now that they would appear to be almost fore-and-aft to any observer on the land. Adam recalled Fraser's words when they had first spoken on this deck.

An excellent sailer, close to the wind even when under storm stays'ls.

Adam watched the pale sunlight flash from something ashore. That was less than two months ago, in this same harbour. When he had lost *Unrivalled*. How was that possible?

He said, 'Let her fall off a point, Mr Fraser.' He held out his hand and felt a midshipman lay a telescope across his palm.

As he raised it to train across the starboard bow he heard Fraser giving his orders, sensed his relief that the captain had noticed the stubborn drift as the wind spilled from the canvas above their heads. Adam steadied the glass and studied the big three-decker, in exactly the same anchorage as when he had first boarded her and had met the famous admiral, Lord Exmouth, in person. When he had told him that he had wanted *Unrivalled* to be ready to take her place in the van when he commanded the fleet attack on Algiers. That, too, seemed a lifetime ago. Now a rear-admiral's flag curled from *Queen Charlotte*'s mizzen, her moment of glory past. Like *Unrivalled*.

'Guardboat, sir!' A hoarse voice, one he had come to recognize among the many still unknown to him: Samuel Petch, *Athena*'s gunner, who had been at sea since he was nine years old. He talked about his various charges, from the twenty-four pounders to the lowly swivel guns as if they were alive, each with its own peculiarity or drawback. Petch had been a gun captain aboard the old *Bellerophon* in Collingwood's Lee Division at Trafalgar. That made him different. Special. The old Billy Ruffian, as she was affectionately known, was still with the fleet. A survivor, like Petch.

Adam trained his glass again, figures working on the forecastle leaping into focus for just a few seconds. Barclay the second lieutenant, with his anchor party, was shading his eyes to stare aft at the quarterdeck, waiting for the signal to drop the larboard anchor.

A good officer, Adam had decided, working both with the foremast and its complex spars and rigging, and his own battery of guns. More importantly, with his men.

He heard Stirling shout something to one of the midshipmen, who was hurrying along the starboard gangway. The first lieutenant never seemed to use a speaking trumpet, or even carry one, unlike most of his trade. He would use just one of his big hands held to his mouth, and his voice carried effortlessly like a fog horn.

Apart from matters of duty and routine they had spoken very little since the discovery of the body in one of the holds. To him it was in the past, no longer important. It was a common attitude among sailors; Adam had known that for a long time. A man existed as a shipmate from the moment he was signed on. When he left your ship, by choice or enforcement, or like the wretched seaman named Hudson, discharged dead, he was written off. Never look back. Never go back.

Adam looked up at the masthead pendant, gauging the wind, the strength of it under the lee of the land.

Sunlight lanced down through the overlapping web of black rigging and made his eye smart.

It is the ship. I am the stranger here.

A frigate was something alive. You could feel her every mood, match it with your ability.

He closed his mind to the doubt.

Any ship was only as good as her company. And her captain.

He heard Fraser say to one of his master's mates, 'About true, I'd say, eh, Simon?'

Adam glanced at him. No words were spoken. None were needed.

'Man the braces – hands wear ship, if you please!'

Stirling's voice broke the stillness.

'Tops'l clew lines! Take that man's name, Mr Manners!'

Adam raised the glass again, watching two slow-moving fishing craft, and a smart schooner spreading sail while she tacked toward the Point and the grey Channel beyond. Then he moved the glass toward the anchored flagship. Beyond her the land was shrouded in mist, where the other fleet still lay. Ghosts, some with great names, remembered for their valour in battle against a common enemy. Hulks now, gunports empty and blind, masts down, decks littered and neglected.

He thrust the telescope away and felt it taken by some one. It was all suddenly sharp and in focus, the faces real, waiting.

He lifted his hand and saw Lieutenant Barclay raise his own in acknowledgment.

'*Let go!*'

He saw the spray burst over the gilded beakhead as the anchor hit the water, and the cable was controlled by compressor under Barclay's vigilant eye.

He imagined he could feel *Athena* slowing, coming to rest, swinging above her own immense shadow.

Men pounded along the deck, hauling ropes or flaking them down in readiness for the next command from aft. High overhead, the big topsails had already been kicked and fisted into submission and were furled or loosely brailed to dry.

Soon boats of every kind would be heading out to meet the new arrival. More stores to be loaded, recruits to be found to fill gaps in the muster logs. To await orders, and their admiral.

Adam unconsciously glanced at the foremast truck

where Bethune's flag would soon be flying. No longer a private ship. How would it be?

He saw Jago standing down by the boat tier pointing out something to one of the midshipmen, probably thinking of young Napier, or wishing he had remained ashore when he had the chance.

He turned and looked across the water, the Hamoaze, where the river Tamar, his river, separated Cornwall from the rest of England.

It might as well be the moon. He shaded his eyes again. Where she had waited to watch *Unrivalled* weigh anchor and sail to join Lord Exmouth's fleet, when she had sent over the little note which was inside his coat at this moment. And that last embrace.

'Officer of the guard coming aboard, sir!'

'Very well, Mr Truscott, I'll see him in my quarters.'

He reached out and touched the big double wheel, now unmanned and motionless, but throbbing quietly to the thrust of the current far below. By keeping busy, things would fall into place. A captain had no choice; and he was lucky. There were many others who would be walking the shore and looking out at the ghost ships, and the sea which had rejected them. The only life they knew or wanted.

He glanced down at the boat tier and saw Jago looking up, somehow isolated from the bustle around him. Like those other times, when men had died, and their world had exploded about them. And they had come through it, together.

Jago nodded and then raised one hand slowly; a salute, a greeting, it was more than either.

The ship had reached out. For both of them.

Stirling strode aft and touched his hat. 'Ship secured, sir.'

'Thank you. It was well done.'

Stirling said nothing, but stood aside from the companion to allow him to pass.

Past the Royal Marine sentry and through the screen, shining in its new white paint, and into the great cabin.

Bowles was opening the quarter gallery to allow some air into the cabin, but turned and gave a sad smile. 'Last time we'll see old England for a while, sir.'

Adam nodded. 'So be it, then.'

As if his uncle had spoken for him.

George Tolan, personal servant to Vice-Admiral Sir Graham Bethune, stood in one corner of the inn's courtyard as the carriage was being moved nearer to the vaulted entrance. It was early morning; too early, he thought, after this long and almost leisurely journey from London.

Now it was over, with Plymouth only fifty miles away. He glanced up at the inn sign: The Royal George of Exeter, the county town of Devon. He had been given a comfortable room, as was the custom with an admiral's servant, good food, and a bed as big as a barn. He might even have been able to share it with some one, but for Bethune's sudden attack of urgency.

The last day on the road, but their journey would take them through country lanes for part of the way. It was Saturday too, and Exeter would be particularly busy, with a market fair at one end of the city and a public hanging at the other.

He adjusted his smart blue coat and stamped his booted feet to restore the circulation. Or perhaps, like his master, he was getting nervous, unsure of the change from land to ocean again.

He was safe, and he had no complaints about his work or the man he served. There was always the nagging thought. Not like fear; he had seen that over the past twenty years, knew all its faces, or had told himself often enough to believe it. Except . . . He looked toward the entrance, at the girl who was tipping water into a small garden. She noticed him and smiled. If Bethune had decided to prolong his stay at the Royal George, things might have been very different.

A few people who were crossing the yard glanced at the blue-coated figure. Tolan was used to it. Not tall, but very erect, shoulders squared, exuding a permanent alertness which he took for granted. Like a soldier, some might think. Which was indeed how George Tolan, aged thirty-nine, had started his adult life.

He had been born and raised in the old town of Kingston on the banks of the River Thames, the only son of a grocer who from the beginning he knew to be a drunken bully. His mother was cowed by his fits of rage, and the young George Tolan had been beaten often enough to know hatred as his only defence.

He could still remember the day it had all changed. His father had driven him out of the shop and sent him to get a particular ale from one of his drinking

129

cronies, with the inevitable threat of what he might expect if he took too long about it.

And there, in the market place, he had seen the army recruiting party. While a drummer boy rattled a slow tattoo, a burly sergeant had nailed up a poster on a stable door, and lastly a young officer had made a short speech about honour and duty, and England's need for her sons to step forward and volunteer to follow the drum.

His father never got his special brew, but on that day George Tolan, aged sixteen, had made his mark and been pounded on the back in congratulation by the officer and his sergeant together. He was their only volunteer that day.

And despite the drills and forced marches, the rough and often brutal humour, and the ritual of field punishment, young George Tolan had loved it.

As the war with the old enemies, France and her allies, had continued to spread and mount in ferocity, Tolan's life had changed yet again. As the fleet increased in strength there was a shortage of marines, the backbone of any fighting ship when it came to action at close quarters, both afloat and in forays ashore. They also acted as a disciplined force which could be called upon to maintain order among ships' companies which were largely comprised of pressed men, dragged aboard His Majesty's ships to fight and, when necessary, die without question or protest.

Some of Tolan's Surrey regiment were drafted to the Channel Fleet, in his case to an old two-decker, not so different, he supposed, from *Athena*, soon to be Bethune's flagship. After tented camps and austere barracks, the day to day experiences were at first a challenge, and then a contest between the marines and the overcrowded world of the messdecks.

It was the first time Tolan had ever seen the sea, but like the Corps itself he grew to accept it.

Perhaps even then he had been conscious of the invisible barriers which stood between the marines and the overwhelming mass of sailors, pressed or otherwise, and divided forecastle and quarterdeck. At divisions, or when hands were mustered to hear the captain read out the Articles of War while some poor devil was stripped and tied to a grating to receive a flogging, or when they were posted as sentries to stand guard over dwindling water supplies, or to prevent men from deserting when the ship was in harbour or close to the shore. Only in battle, when the enemy's flag flew high alongside and the air was choked with smoke, did those barriers fall, and they became of one company.

And then, just twenty years ago, the impossible had happened, and the entire country reeled in shock and fear. The fleet, which admirals and parsons alike had always described as *our sure shield against all peril*, had mutinied at the Nore and at Spithead. A French invasion was daily expected, and too late the Admiralty had been forced to accept what foul conditions, savage punishment, and in many cases tyrannical discipline had brought down upon their heads.

Tolan had been reminded of it when he had been listening to the old clerk at the Admiralty, the one who

131

had fought under Black Dick's command in the old *Queen Charlotte* at the Glorious First of June, just three years before the mutiny had broken out. Howe himself had been at the Admiralty, but his fairness and undoubted popularity were still remembered by those same men of his old flagship when mutiny had snared her with all the others. Howe and other senior officers were forced to swallow their pride and parley with the mutineers' delegates, and something far stronger than discipline and fleet orders had won the day. Many officers were removed from duty, some dismissed from the service. Mutineers who had used violence against officers and messmates alike were punished, even hanged. Order was restored, and the country turned to face the enemy across the Channel once again.

But aboard Tolan's ship it did not end without bloodshed. The captain was a disciplinarian of the old school, and when his company voted to follow the example of the fleet and refused to obey any further commands from aft, he had been beside himself with disbelief and fury.

The arms chest had been forced open, and the mutineers had driven most of the officers and the more trusted hands from the upper deck. Only the scarlet line had stood fast, muskets loaded, bayonets fixed.

The young officer, who had been from Tolan's own regiment, had raised his sword, and for an instant it seemed that the threat had passed. Then the captain had ordered him to fire on the mutineers. Tolan could remember the complete silence, as if it were yesterday.

132

Faces staring at one another across a few feet of decking. Seamen who had joked and chuckled when the soldiers, acting marines, had been forced to learn the crafts of seamanship and man the braces to alter course, amused by their attempts to cling to their army training and customs even at sea.

The sword had sliced down. *Fire!* Obey orders without question. All he knew.

The complete silence.

Then a young corporal on the right of the line, one of the only true marines aboard, half turned, smartly as if to an order, and called, 'Belay that! Ground your arms!'

Some laid down their muskets, others stared around, confused and overtaken by the swiftness of events, so that the crack of a pistol shot seemed like a broadside.

Tolan had got to know the young corporal, and had learned many things from him. How to keep a clean and smart kit in the close confines of a ship, how to cook, and what it took to prime and load a cannon. How to survive.

He still thought about it. The corporal lying on the deck, his eyes wide with shock as the shot had killed him.

Like a mad dream. His own musket pressed into his arm, the officer swinging round with the pistol still smoking in his hand. Then the jerk of the butt against his shoulder, the officer's hat flying into the air with the blood from his shattered face.

Like many others, Tolan had deserted that day, and

so it had continued, running and hiding, while a ruthless search for culprits spread across the country.

In desperation he had presented himself to a recruiting party put ashore from a frigate. Bethune had been her captain, his first command. It was the perfect disguise and the perfect place to lose himself. He had once served as an officer's orderly, and it was not long before he was selected to attend the captain.

There had been testing moments. Once in Portsmouth dockyard, he had come face to face with a tall lieutenant, whom he had recognized instantly despite the passing of the years. A midshipman aboard that same ship when he had shot down his own officer. Just a glance, nothing more. Another time when he had quit the sea to accompany Bethune on some mission or other he had met a man by the Thames in London, the same river which ran within half a mile of where he had been born. *Don't I know you?*

It had got no further. That time . . .

He straightened his back and plucked his coat away from his chest. He was sweating. Would he never be able to forget it?

He saw Bethune's minute secretary Edward Paget coming down the steps, an important-looking satchel under one arm. A worrier, Tolan had long ago decided, always asking questions and making notes. Good at his work, though. He almost smiled. Otherwise Bethune would have cast him adrift years ago. Others did not seem to notice. Bethune was always ready to listen and to discuss, if it suited him. Handsome, dashing, with an eye for pretty women; a man who looked after himself. Must be fifty or even over, but looked far younger. A man Tolan could understand, and like, but underneath it all he was steel, something Tolan had marked well.

He saw that the carriage was already loaded, and apparently ready. It was time. How strange that the flagship at Plymouth was named *Queen Charlotte*. Not the same ship which had been at the centre of the Great Mutiny, but her name had been carried on. The navy's way. It was like a reminder. A warning, if he needed one.

'Ah, there you are, Tolan!' Bethune peered up at the sky and then at the cathedral as the clock began to boom the hour. 'Good sleep?' He nodded. 'That's as well – I doubt it will be an easy ride.'

He had not waited for an answer; he rarely did.

They walked to the carriage together in silence.

It was only then that Tolan realized Bethune, always so buoyant and confident, was unwilling to leave.

She stood very still and upright by the opened gate, her body completely covered by a cloak. She had even pulled its hood over her head so that her long hair hung down her back, out of sight.

It was well past noon; she had heard a church clock strike somewhere. It seemed an eternity ago.

She shivered, glad of the cloak; there was a fresh southeasterly breeze blowing in from the sea. But she knew it was not that. She looked down the slope and saw the Tamar through the trees, some small craft tossing at their moorings as if they were in the Channel.

She thought of the note the post boy had brought to the house behind her. *Dearest Lowenna. Together at noon tomorrow*.

Today. Perhaps something had happened. Perhaps he had changed his mind. She had gone over it so many times since the earnest young lieutenant, her companion and guardian all the way from London, had described it all to his captain. Made light of it, perhaps joked with his fellow officers aboard the *Athena* about his exploits with the captain's 'friend'. In the same breath, she knew Francis Troubridge would not. Probably a couple of years her junior, but he had seemed from another generation, courteous, friendly, protective, not once attempting any intimacy.

At the inns where their little procession of coaches and carts had paused on the journey she had seen the curious stares, the nudges and the grins. But Troubridge had always been there, ready to ensure that she and her maid had all the privacy they could want.

She looked at the river again. The opposite bank was Cornwall, where she had been born. She closed her fists hard against her sides. She had never thought of it as home. It was merely a place where she had been forced to avoid faces she knew, places where she might be remembered. Montagu had changed that for her. She would have gone mad otherwise. She had once tried to kill herself.

She shivered once more, but not from cold, and pressed her hand to her breast, surprised that her breathing seemed so even. It brought Sir Gregory Montagu back to her thoughts, the day he had died, with the same dignity he had shown in life. He had tried to tell her something, but the two doctors, old friends of his, had insisted she leave the room for a few minutes. He had not recovered. She knew that he had started to die after the fire; he had been trying to save some paintings, in particular one which had brought Adam into her life. A blazing beam had fallen into the studio and smashed him to the floor, and his right hand had been broken and burned beyond recognition. The hand which had brought him fame, and fame to those he had captured on canvas. Which had rendered the elusive quality of Adam's smile, precisely as she had described it.

Almost the last words he had spoken to her were, *It's like destiny, my girl. Fate.*

What had he meant? Was she still deceiving herself?

She thought of the people who lived in the house behind her, a local boatbuilder and his wife. Montagu had stayed here several times in the past when he needed to work without interference or arousing local curosity. Perhaps she should not have accepted Troubridge's willing offer of help to come here. London, then? More studios, one pose after another, with her inviolable guard always intact.

She thought of that last time, when she had almost killed Montagu's nephew. *I wanted to kill him.* The rest was a mist. Adam holding her, the young lieutenant Troubridge suddenly transformed, dangerous, with a pistol in his hand. Others too, but mostly Adam's hands holding her. Like that day when his horse had thrown him and his wound had burst. Dazed and delirious, he had touched her, held her, and she had lain beside him, her body rigid, her mind screaming as the nightmare returned. Groping hands, pulling at her, forcing her to suffer unspeakable rape and violation. When it came to her now, it was endless. And always the pain . . . Her father's voice somewhere in the fog, pleading and sobbing.

She had fought against Adam's friendship, the growth of the one true feeling she had allowed to blossom. She remembered her own voice, calling out in the night. *It's love I want. Not pity. Can't you see that?*

She swung round. A horse. She pushed the hood back from her cheek. Two horses. She was breathless, as if she had been running. It had to be him. Nobody used the road at this time of day. Perhaps he was bringing Troubridge with him. To protect her good name. As a witness . . .

The horse came around the bend in the road, a second rider a few yards behind.

She wanted to run to him, to call his name, but she could not move. Adam was above her one moment, and the next she was in his arms, pressed against him, her arms trapped by the heavy cloak.

'I am so sorry for the delay, Lowenna. The flagship made a signal. I came as soon as I could. If only . . .' The rest was lost as he put his arm around her shoulders and held her face against his.

She murmured, 'You came.' She saw the uncertainty in his eyes. 'It's all I care about.'

She heard the other rider say, 'I'll wait at the forge,

zur. Just call when you needs me.' He sounded awkward but vaguely pleased.

Adam walked with her toward the white-painted house, seeing the river beyond. The girl's shoulders were firm under his arm, her dark hair streaming in the breeze like silk. He tried to piece it together. Troubridge's excitement when he had climbed aboard after his journey from London with Bethune's belongings. Happy that he had become a part of it, nervous that he had gone too far.

He had seen one of the boatswain's mates by the entry port turn and stare as he had seized Troubridge's hands and exclaimed, 'You have saved my *life*. Don't you know that?'

He hardly saw the room as she guided him to a tall, ladder-backed chair and watched him throw his hat and cloak on to another, the same cloak he had wrapped around her when he had smashed his way into the house in London. He reached for her hands and held them. They were very cold.

'Are we alone?' He did not hear her answer, but began to get up again.

She put her hands on his shoulders, repressing him a little. 'How long do you have? They are over the river, in Saltash. They'll not be back until sunset, I think.'

She touched his face, his cheek, and, gently, his lips. 'I was so afraid. I have thought about you so much, maybe too much.' She shook her head. 'I'm not making very much sense.'

He said, 'I have to rejoin *Athena* by the dog

watches.' He smiled, and the strain fell away from his face; he looked very young. 'That'll be around sunset, too!'

She stood back from him and unfastened the cloak, letting it fall, then she allowed herself to look at him again.

'Sir Gregory told you.' She held up her hand. 'He must have trusted you very much. Otherwise he would have said nothing.'

'I want you, Lowenna. That is all I know and care about. If it takes time, then we will *find* time. And I want you safe while I am away.'

'Safe?' She watched a gull drift past the window. 'You will be gone soon.'

'You can stay at the house in Falmouth as long as you care to. Grace and Bryan Ferguson will make you most welcome.'

'You know what people will say, and think, Adam. She shelters beneath the Bolitho roof – what does she offer in return?' She smiled, as if a cloud had passed away. 'I shall call upon your aunt. She was very kind to me. And she loves you greatly – I could feel it.'

He took her hand again but did not look at her.

'Will you give up the studio work?'

'Are you asking me to? Will you give up the sea for me?'

She returned the grip on his hand. 'That was unfair of me. I would never ask it of you.'

Adam saw her sudden anxiety and said, 'Next time we meet . . .'

He got no further.

'*No*. Not the next time, Adam. There may be no next time, who can tell?'

When she spoke again her voice was level, calm, only her eyes giving a hint of tension.

'The first time I saw you . . . It was something Sir Gregory taught me, made me put above and before all else. Forced me to find myself, maybe by losing myself in others, in the paintings. I gave myself to the work, and could hold all else at bay. Looks and stares, the thoughts too . . . they meant nothing. He taught me all that, but when you came into that room and looked at me, I felt something . . . very different.' She repeated, 'Not the next time, Adam. Otherwise we might wait in vain.' She turned her head slightly, as if she had heard something. 'Fate, perhaps?'

Adam said, 'I would never hurt you, Lowenna.'

She slipped from his hand and walked to the far corner of the room.

'It has to be now. *I must know*, for both our sakes.' Then she was gone, and Adam saw a shoe fall as she disappeared up a narrow staircase he had not seen before.

He stared at his hat and cloak, lying where he had tossed them.

Leave now before you destroy something that was never yours. Another voice persisted, *go, and you will never see her again*.

He did not remember climbing the unfamiliar staircase, but stooped to recover her other shoe, which had fallen just outside the door.

Perhaps more than anything else the shoe recalled

it to him, what Montagu had told him, and the fear and disgust he had seen for himself when he had smashed his way into that room.

He thrust open the door and saw her sitting on the bed, her hair spilling over her shoulders and the sheet which she had drawn across her body, one hand holding it close to her throat as if she were about to pose for another sketch, a new beginning.

The light was poor, but he could see her clothing where she must have thrown it, with the same quiet desperation she had used to kick off her shoes.

He heard himself say again, 'I would never hurt you, Lowenna.'

She nodded slowly, her eyes so dark that it was impossible to know her thoughts.

He began to unbutton his coat but she shook her head.

'No. As you are. Not the next time. It has to be now.'

Then she lay back and deliberately raised her hands above her head, crossing one wrist over the other, her hair wrapped around them as if she were tied like a captive.

He leaned down and cupped one shoulder in his hand. She did not flinch, but watched his hand as if unable to move. The captive again.

Then she looked up at him and whispered, 'Whatever I do or say, no matter how much I protest, take me. Teach me. *I must know*, for both our sakes!'

She cried out as he dragged the sheet away from her body, until she was naked, her arms straining as if they were, in truth, tightly held.

He felt himself soothing her, holding, stroking, exploring her until the blood pounded in his brain like a fever.

She gasped and opened her eyes very wide as his hand found her. How it must have been, again and again.

Compassion, love, need, it was all and none of them. He was kissing her, and her arms were free and clasped around his shoulders. There were tears too, like that day; he could taste them.

He felt her body arch beneath his hand, and her voice, small and far away.

'Now, Adam . . . dearest Adam. Take me.'

The same church clock broke the spell, but only partly.

She lay naked across the bed, resting on her elbows, while she watched him struggle into his uniform. It seemed darker but it was an illusion, born of joy and of guilt.

Then she stood and put her arms around him and he held and stroked her, kissed the bruises his buttons had left on her skin.

'You must go.' She tossed the hair from her face. 'The sea will always be a rival, but not my enemy.'

The two horses were standing by the gate, their handler no doubt nervous about the time. But he said nothing, and watched Adam climb up into the saddle. He saw the youthful post captain touch his side as he reached down for the reins; he was not to know that it was an old wound, making its presence felt once more.

Adam turned the horse toward the road, and paused to look back at the house. The windows were in shadow now, like eyes at rest, but he knew she was there, in that same quiet room where life, or fate, had changed them. He could still feel her, her fear and doubt giving way to frenzy and then submission. *I can still feel you.* There would be pain, too. But the fear was gone, perhaps forever.

He felt his crumpled shirt rubbing against the wound, and remembered her lips caressing it as they had lain together.

A woman passed him, carrying a bundle of wood. Without thinking, he raised his hat to her and smiled, felt her staring after them as the horses increased their pace.

He remembered suddenly and vividly a time when he had been a child, and he had been taught to swim in the sea. It had been on the north coast of Cornwall, where the sea is often moody, the breakers pounding the hard sand like thunder. His instructor had been a friend of his mother's. He allowed himself to confront it: one of her lovers.

Out of his depth, the current dragging at his body with sudden strength, he had heard the man calling to him to return to the beach. Instead, he had fought depth and breakers together. Somehow he had survived, his mind reeling from exhaustion and fright.

But above all, he remembered the sense of triumph and of joy.

He twisted round to look back at the house, but there were only trees, and the river.

He spoke her name aloud. And she would know it, hear it on the wind.

Like destiny. Like fate.

And the next horizon.

7

Under the Flag

John Bowles, the cabin servant, walked to the sloping
stern windows and opened the dress coat which he had
just finished pressing, held it carefully in the harsh
glare of reflected sunlight, and made sure that it was
perfect. Beyond the screen door and beneath his feet
the ship was unusually quiet. Sometimes it was hard
to believe that the hull held nearly five hundred human
beings. He gave a slow grin. *If you could call some of
them that*. It had been rather different earlier in the
day, since dawn when all hands had been piped to work
ship, and prepare for the arrival of the great man
himself. Extra care with the rigging, standing and
running alike, more hands sent aloft to check each
lashing, and no loose ends, 'Irish pennants', the Jacks
called them, to offend the vice-admiral's eye. There
was still a hint of cooking in the air, the heady aroma
of rum, Nelson's Blood, but the ship was ready.

He had glanced into the spacious cabin beneath this

one, and watched it being transformed into something almost palatial. Rich and very costly furniture had appeared as if by magic, even a few paintings in the admiral's sleeping quarters. If they ever had to clear for action some one would have to keep a close eye on those as everything was dragged below and the screens were torn down to strip *Athena* to her true identity, a fighting ship. He had seen the vice-admiral's servant supervising every aspect of the transformation, a smart-looking man, utterly unmoved by the bustle and confusion around him. Bowles had tried to make conversation, but the man, Tolan, had seemed withdrawn, disinterested in anything that might distract him from his purpose.

He gave the dress coat a final examination. *First impressions*. He almost smiled. It was something the previous captain, Ritchie, had often said. He had served him a long time, but looking back, it was as if he had never really known him. Now awaiting a court-martial. That, too, had surprised Bowles. It was said that Adam Bolitho had been court-martialled a year or so ago, after losing his ship to a Yankee and being taken prisoner. He gave the coat a quick shake. There was a lot he had yet to discover about his new master. Who, for instance, would gallop overland in his best uniform, as if he did not have a care in the world?

He peered across the cabin and saw him now at his desk, his chin resting on one hand, still writing. Today, of all days, when *Athena* was to become flagship to an admiral about whom most of them knew nothing, the captain could still find the time to put pen to paper.

In an opened shirt, dark hair dishevelled as he ran his fingers through it, as if it were an ordinary day. The small book he carried in his coat lay beside him on the desk, and the well-worn letter he always kept folded inside it. A dreamer one moment, restless and alert the next. Quick to intervene when he thought Stirling had overlooked something. Bowles nodded slowly to himself. In battle or a raging storm, Stirling was like a rock. Duty was duty; like the Articles of War, it was enough.

Adam Bolitho had been well known for his exploits as a frigate captain; a few of the ship's company had served with him in the past, some even under his famous uncle. Perhaps *Athena*'s next commission was not going to lead them to another backwater after all . . .

'*Boat ahoy?*'

The challenge was clear and loud, and Bowles could almost feel the panic it would cause the watchkeepers and, more especially, the first lieutenant. *The vice-admiral had changed his mind, and was already heading out to his flagship.* Catch every one unprepared. He had heard the flag lieutenant, Troubridge, discussing it with the captain. Sir Graham Bethune was to dine with the port admiral at his residence ashore; his host would have his own barge collect and bring him to *Athena* at four bells of the afternoon watch.

He cocked his head to listen as somebody replied to the challenge.

'*Aye! Aye!*' So, an officer on board, but nobody

important. Probably some mail for *Athena*, the boat coming early to avoid involvement with the admiral.

He realized with a start that the captain had turned in his chair.

'Nervous, Bowles?'

Bowles held out the coat. 'I did wonder, sir.' He looked at the desk again. Dark blue silk, shining in the filtered sunshine. He had had little to do with the quality, but he recognized a lady's garter. So that was where the captain had been, the sudden need for urgency.

Adam stood up. It was almost time. Pipe all hands, band and guard to man the side. The band would consist of small drummers and fifers; they had been drilling when he had returned aboard. He walked aft to the windows and rested his palms on the sill; it was warm from the deceptive sunlight. Yesterday. Was it only that? The ship had swung still further to her anchor, but he could imagine the road, the sloping hillside, the Tamar. He thought of those last minutes. Seconds. The final touch.

And tomorrow, or a few days at the most, this ship would weigh and put to sea, like all those other times. But so different.

'I'd better get ready, Bowles.' He wondered how Bethune was feeling about this day. No regrets? No doubts?

He heard the sentry tap his musket on the grating outside the screen door.

'Captain's cox'n, sir!'

Jago was exercising his privilege of coming and

going as he chose, no doubt to voice his resentment that *Athena*'s gig, *his* gig, was not being used today to collect the vice-admiral.

If we 'ad our own barge, I'd have 'em in shape in a week, sir!

It was the closest he would come to pride.

Jago stepped through the door, his hat in one hand, his tanned features unable to contain a grin.

'Visitor, sir.' He stepped briskly to one side. 'Special visitor!'

They stood facing one another, the captain in his shirtsleeves, with dishevelled hair, and the young midshipman, very erect, but all confidence gone now that his determination had deserted him.

'Good God, David, it *is* you! Come over here and let me look at you!'

Napier said, 'We anchored this morning, sir.' He gestured to the stern windows. 'The lower anchorage. I asked for permission . . .' His voice trailed away as Adam seized him by the shoulders and exclaimed, 'You'll never know . . .' He saw the gleaming midshipman's dirk. 'It suits you, David.' He shook him gently. 'It does indeed suit you!'

Napier nodded, his eyes very serious. 'For my fifteenth birthday. You remembered. I had no idea.'

Adam walked with him to the stern windows, his arm around his shoulders.

'Is everything all right, David? The ship? Everything?'

The youth turned and looked up at him. No words, just the look, then he said, 'I have settled in,' and

150

forced a smile. 'The captain remembers my name now.' He could not keep it up. 'I miss looking after you, sir.'

Jago said, 'I think the boat is waitin', sir.'

'I'll see you over the side, David.'

Napier shook his head. 'No, sir. You know what they would say. Favouritism.'

'So my uncle taught me.' They stood by the open door, Jago, Bowles, the ship, another world.

Adam said, 'If ever you need anything, write to me. One day we'll serve together again.'

Napier looked slowly around the great cabin, as if he wanted to forget nothing.

Jago cleared his throat. 'I'll take you on deck, *Mister* Napier, sir!'

But this time it did not work.

Bowles watched it all in silence. No matter what task they were called upon to perform, and how this unknown captain would deal with it, he knew that this was the man he would always see and hear.

He realized that the door was closed, and that his captain was by the desk again, fastening his shirt.

He said, 'A fine young man, sir.'

Adam did not hear him. It had been like seeing himself.

The admiral's barge pulled purposefully between the anchored ships, the oars rising and falling like polished bones. If any other boats or small craft appeared to be on a converging course, or about to cross her path, the sharp-eyed lieutenant who remained standing beside the coxswain would merely raise one hand in the air, and the tiller would stay where it was.

Seated in the sternsheets, Lieutenant Francis Troubridge felt the excitement running through him, and it was all he could do to contain it, sitting as he was within a few feet of his superior. It was like nothing he had experienced before. Even the barge crew was smartly turned out, matching shirts and tarred hats, lying back on their looms, eyes astern, but never on the admiral.

Occasionally they swept past a boat which had stopped to allow them to pass unimpeded. All oars tossed, an officer standing, hat raised in salute. Some of the local craft carrying passengers or working parties from the docks also showed their respect: cheers echoed across the choppy water, and aboard one harbour boat women waved scarves and aprons, their voices lost in the timed creak of oars.

Troubridge glanced covertly at Bethune. Not to be in an office or visiting some large man-of-war in one port or another, *but at sea*. What he had always wanted, and this time with the status and privilege of being the admiral's personal aide.

Bethune was sitting very upright on a cushion, one foot quietly tapping on the bottom boards, his handsome profile completely at ease, a slight smile never far away whenever another boat stood clear to allow the barge to pass.

That was something Troubridge had soon learned about his admiral. Unlike so many he had seen at the Admiralty or on ceremonial occasions, he had never allowed himself to be visibly drunk. He had seen the port admiral stagger as he had waited on the stone stairs, while Bethune stepped almost casually into the waiting barge. Self-discipline, or something even stronger.

'Ah, there she is!' Bethune had pulled out his beautiful watch. 'Right on time, eh, Flags?'

Troubridge flushed. He had intended to point out *Athena* for the admiral's benefit. Bethune had beaten him to it.

'She looks well, Sir Graham.' He saw the slight smile again. Like a rebuke.

Athena seemed to tower over them, as if they had covered the last cable in seconds. Rigging blacked down, each yard and spar perfectly set, White Ensign curling from her poop and the Union flag in the bows, her new paintwork shining in the sunlight like glass.

Troubridge thought suddenly of his father, how proud he would be of his youngest son, and felt some of the tension draining away. This was what he wanted.

'*Boat ahoy?*'

He smiled despite the solemnity of the occasion. Everybody in Plymouth would know this barge, and its purpose here today. The navy never changed.

The big coxswain looked swiftly at Bethune's shoulders and cupped his hands.

'*Flag! Athena!*'

Troubridge watched the scarlet line of Royal Marines, the blues and whites of the assembled officers and lesser ranks, warrant officers and the rest. The mass of the ship's company was crammed into

153

the main deck and between the gangways, others on the forecastle and aloft on the fighting tops where a man could find space to stand.

He saw faces duck down out of sight at one of the gunports as the barge altered course and headed for the main chains and the freshly gilded entry port.

The lieutenant in charge gave his orders, but Troubridge heard none of it, staring at the black and white hull rising above him. The bowmen had shipped their oars and were facing ahead, their boathooks held in readiness. Side-boys were already positioned on the bottom stairs, to take the lines, or fend off the barge to avoid an unseamanlike collision.

There was a bosun's chair just in sight above the nettings. The anchorage was choppy, and it was not unknown for a senior officer to escape falling over-board by that less dignified route.

Another order, and the oars were tossed and held steady in two dripping ranks; the barge had been made fast.

But Troubridge was remembering the tales he had heard as a boy, from his father or some of his friends. Of Nelson, 'Our Nel', leaving England in *Victory* for the last time; walking the deck of his flagship with his young flag lieutenant, Pasco, while the enemy had spread and filled the horizon, and together they had composed the signal every true Englishman still knew by heart.

'Are you ready, *Mister* Troubridge?' Bethune was standing upright, holding out his expensive boatcloak, not even using a seaman's shoulder to steady himself against the motion. 'They are waiting for us, as you see!' He was actually laughing.

Then he reached out, pausing only to add, 'You did as I asked?'

Troubridge swallowed. 'Aye, Sir Graham.' He should not have been staring aimlessly around. In a moment he would be sick.

Then the air quivered to the bark of commands, the crack and slap of muskets being brought to the present, pipeclay drifting above and around the twin ranks of gleaming bayonets.

Calls trilled, and to another shouted command the small section of fifers and drummers broke into *Heart of Oak*.

Troubridge scrambled up and over the steep tumble-home and almost pitched headlong through the finely carved entry port.

He recovered himself and dragged off his hat in salute. The din of fifes and drums stopped, and a solitary call shrilled loudly in the silence as Bethune's flag lifted and broke free at the mainmast truck.

He saw the captain step forward from among the other officers, the formality broken by a sudden handshake, and Bolitho's smile, which he felt he had come to know better than anything else about him.

Bethune had been about to receive the usual introductions before he was released to the peace and privacy of his new quarters, when he stopped and pointed at some seamen below the boat tier.

'That man! *You!*'

People swung round and stared, and a lieutenant

almost ran to seize the offender who had caught the admiral's eye.

Troubridge relaxed, muscle by muscle. He had been through the muster book and ship's records and had discovered one man who had actually served with Bethune when he had been a captain. The man in question was standing exactly where he had been told, still unaware of the reason.

Bethune swung round and exclaimed, 'Grundy? Tom Grundy, isn't it? In the old *Skirmisher*, remember?'

The man was grinning, as others craned forward to witness this extraordinary encounter.

'Yessir, that's me! God bless you, sir!'

Bethune patted his arm. 'Good to see you again, Grundy!' He strode on, smiling and nodding to the assembled officers.

Troubridge watched the ranks breaking up, crowding around the astonished Grundy to slap him on the back, or share a grin or a joke with the one seaman who had been recognized by the admiral.

Troubridge gazed up at the new flag whipping out at the fore. There was a lot they all had to learn about the man who flew it.

Vice-Admiral Sir Graham Bethune leaned back in his chair, his fingers interlocked behind his head while he surveyed the broad expanse of his day cabin. His secretary, Edward Paget, sat opposite him behind a little table, his pen poised by the pile of letters already completed.

Bethune said, 'The last is for the First Lord's eyes *only*, Paget. You know what to do.' He frowned as something clattered across the deck, accompanied by the squeal of a block as the unknown object was hauled away. It seemed to take a long time. He would have to get used to it. He glanced over his shoulder at the hazy green of the land, a sail passing between it and the anchored flagship like the fin of a shark.

His servant Tolan had entered by another door, a list in one hand.

'All the wine is stowed, Sir Graham. Separate from the special delivery which came aboard in Portsmouth.'

Paget looked up severely.

'All checked? Good wine can easily walk in a ship this size, you know!'

Tolan ignored him. Paget was good at his work; he would not still be serving Bethune otherwise. He was short and had a low forehead, and an unusually wide mouth; Tolan had long ago decided that he must have been a frog in a previous life.

He said, 'The captain is coming aft to see you, Sir Graham.'

'I know. I'm ready,' and to his secretary, 'I want all those sent ashore today, no matter what time you've finished them.'

Paget's wide mouth opened and closed without comment. He was used to it.

Bethune sighed and rubbed his stomach.

'Well, Tolan, any regrets?' He did not expect an answer. 'We sail tomorrow, come what may. The Indies again. Antigua.' Seeing it in his mind. No more walks in the park, or riding his favourite mount down to the river. Where he had last seen Catherine Somervell. Where he had felt like a conspirator. But he must be careful. Very careful.

The screen door was open and Captain Adam Bolitho was standing by an empty gunport where an eighteen-pounder had once been positioned. Much had changed during *Athena*'s last refit, less armament giving more room for storage. And additional space for an admiral's quarters.

'Ah, Adam. I trust you satisifed the curiosity of the wardroom? We shall weigh at high water. Your sailing master—' Impatiently, he snapped his fingers.

Adam said, 'Fraser, Sir Graham.'

'Of course.' He grinned at his flag lieutenant. 'Another Grundy, eh?'

Adam said, 'I just heard about Captain Ritchie. The verdict at his court-martial . . .'

'I intended to mention it, Adam. But things have been moving quickly since I came aboard yesterday.' He pressed his fingertips together, his head slightly on one side. 'Does it disturb you?'

'The verdict was *not proven*, Sir Graham. That means he may be entirely innocent of the charges.'

He saw Troubridge half raise a hand, as if to warn him. Bethune smiled.

'Equally, it might mean he was guilty as charged.'

Adam persisted, 'But he would still be in command of this ship!'

'While you, Adam, would be on the beach, with no ship at all.'

'That is not what I meant, Sir Graham.'

Bethune stood up without effort, his hair almost brushing the deckhead.

'When I was given this mission, for that is what it is fast becoming, I wanted a good flag captain. I can think of another one or two, but *I wanted you*, do you understand? Your record is enough, but there are other reasons, too. I will not insult you by parading them for inspection.' He had raised his voice slightly, but appeared calm, even relaxed. 'As far as I am concerned, Captain Ritchie can—'

He swung round as Tolan said, 'Beg pardon, Sir Graham, but there is a message for the captain.'

Bethune nodded slowly, in control again.

'Very well.'

It was Evelyn, the sixth and most junior lieutenant, his hat crushed under one arm, trying not to be seen staring at the admiral and the splendid cabin.

'I am s-sorry, sir.' He gulped. 'But I was told that you wanted to know immediately when *Audacity* was shortening her cable.'

Bethune remarked, 'The old frigate *Audacity* – I thought she was due for the ship breakers!' He chuckled, and added, 'Captain Munro. Friend of yours, is he?' And waved his hand. 'I was forgetting. You sponsored a midshipman for *Audacity*. Somebody's favourite son, was he?'

Adam said, equally casually, 'He served with me in *Unrivalled*.' Like walking into a trap. Bethune knew all about it, just as he knew about *Athena*'s last captain.

Bethune was opening another sheaf of papers.

'Carry on, Adam. You will be dining with me tonight, eh?'

'Thank you, Sir Graham.'

Troubridge followed him to the door and out.

'I am very sorry for that, sir.'

Adam touched his arm. 'Rest easy.'

On deck, it seemed cool after the admiral's cabin. He loosened his neckcloth and drew several deep breaths. This was a Bethune he did not recognize.

He glanced at the flag above the foremast and took a telescope from the midshipman of the watch.

For an instant their eyes met. A young, pouting face with an upturned nose . . . it fell into place. He was Blake, an admiral's grandson, who had been at the centre, if he was not the actual cause, of Hudson's flogging. And his death.

I should have known. Prevented it.

Lieutenant Evelyn called, 'Starboard quarter, sir!' He seemed quite recovered from his attack of nerves in the cabin.

Adam waited for his breathing to steady, and watched the other ships leap into focus as he trained the glass over and beyond the anchorage. No difference, and then the slightest movement, other masts turning, coming into line, yards and rigging suddenly hidden by clouds of filling canvas as *Audacity*, of twenty-four guns, broke out her anchor and gathered way. They would all be busy, too busy to stare around at the bigger ships of war as they tacked toward the open sea.

He said, 'Make to *Audacity*, *good luck*.' That would

set them guessing. But some one might tell David. It was a small ship. A frigate . . .

'From *Flag*, sir?'

Adam kept the glass to his eye. 'No. Make it from *Athena*.'

He heard the flags flap out from the yard and imagined some one calling *Audacity*'s captain, and the curiosity it would arouse.

The frigate had almost completed her manoeuvre when Lieutenant Evelyn shouted, '*Acknowledged*, sir!'

Adam returned the telescope, and walked to the opposite side of the quarterdeck.

He knew Stirling was observing him from beside the compass box, and said, 'I shall be doing Rounds in the first watch, Mr Stirling.' He saw the immediate caution. 'Last night in port. Captain's privilege, or should be.'

Stirling hesitated. 'I'd like to accompany you, sir.'

Adam smiled. 'Thank you. That suits me well.' He turned toward the anchorage again, but there was no more movement.

If I was wrong and he hates his new life, then he will come to hate me. He thought of the silk garter now locked in his cabin. *And if I have wronged her, I will never forgive myself.*

He could still feel Stirling watching him as he returned to the companion way.

A small step. But it was something.

Luke Jago held the razor up to the light and tested the blade with his thumb before folding it away in its worn case.

The captain never seemed to need much of a shave. If he left his own face unshaven for more than a day, it felt more like a piece of sword-matting than skin.

He looked over at him now, knowing him in almost every mood, something he had once thought he would never be able to do again. With an officer.

He saw all the signs. Only half of John Bowles' coffee was gone, and the breakfast remained untouched.

He tuned his ear to all the other sounds, men moving about the hull, wedges being tapped home, loose gear stowed away, all boats secure on their tier, except one which would tow astern once *Athena* was at sea. A last chance for any one who went overboard. It happened, although not as often as you might expect. Jago's mouth twisted into a smile. Especially after last night. The hoarded rum, and the unexpected issue of the coarse red wine the lower deck called Black Strap.

Sailing day.

He glanced again at the captain, still in a clean shirt and breeches, his coat hanging on the door of his sleeping quarters. Once at sea he would be changing into one of his weather-stained coats and the white trousers favoured by most officers. He thought of the admiral: it was hard to imagine Bethune ever having been other than what he was now. At least he spoke to the men who served him. Unlike some. Unlike most.

Jago thought of the days, and weeks, ahead. Antigua he knew well enough. A friendly place, but that was when it was threatened with war: the old enemies,

France and Spain, even the Dutch. It was a long haul, nearly four thousand miles to all accounts. It would sift out the seamen from the 'passengers', the braggarts from those with brains.

And he thought of Napier. *Mister* Napier. Make or break, they all said. He would be all right, if little pigs like Midshipman Blake and the haughty Vincent left him alone. There were Blakes and Vincents in every ship Jago had ever known. Napier was a good lad, but it took more than a fancy new uniform or a smart dirk to make an officer.

He heard voices, and then the sentry's call. 'Midshipman o' the watch, sir!'

Bowles was there, the door half open, as if he too was very aware of the captain's mood.

Jago sucked his teeth. Speak of the devil. It was Mister bloody Vincent.

'Guardboat alongside, sir. Request for last mail.' He stood very erect, only his eyes moving as he watched the captain, silhouetted now against the stern windows, one hand resting on the tall-backed chair.

'On the desk.' Adam turned to look at them, as if undecided. Now that it was too late. 'Just those. Thank you.'

He had already seen the guardboat pulling around the anchored *Athena*; even without a glass he had recognized the officer in charge. The same man who had come aboard *Unrivalled* and had brought his new orders, and told him that he was losing his ship.

Two letters, one to his Aunt Nancy; a proper epistle this time, he hoped. Usually when he wrote to her a single letter could take weeks to finish, with sea miles covered, interruptions of every kind, and war. But she understood. She had good cause.

And the other . . . He did not have the words. It was not like seeing her again. Holding her. Seeing her emotions, her fears. He was sailing in a few hours' time, and he would be away for months. Or longer. Who could tell?

He seemed to hear Bethune's words. *This mission, for that is what it is fast becoming*. What did he have to offer her? Why should she wait? She had lost enough of her life already.

He looked back at the desk. The letters and Vincent had gone.

He picked up his little book and glanced at the coat on the door; it was no longer still, but swaying slightly. The wind was back. He pictured the different faces he had come to know in so short a time, reacting. Fraser the sailing master watching the masthead pendant, getting the feel of the wind's power, how it would affect his calculations, and his captain. Stirling, eyes aloft on spars, yards, and rigging, all the possible dangers for the topmen, making sail, fisting hard canvas, careful of each hand and foothold. Old Sam Petch, the gunner; he would check each weapon and its breeching rope to make sure nothing would break adrift if the weather worsened in open water.

He heard Bowles refilling his coffee cup, reading the signs.

Too much brandy, perhaps? He thought of the contrasts when he had done Rounds the previous evening. From one end of the ship to the other, with Stirling thudding behind him and a midshipman preceding, without the usual formality of a ship's corporal or the master-at-arms. He had seen their expressions when he had removed his hat each time he had entered a mess or walked through one of the crowded gundecks. Surprise, appreciation, amusement, it was hard to tell. But it was always there, the lesson Richard Bolitho had drummed into his nephew when he had been new and green, as green as David Napier. *Show respect. It is their home too, remember that.* He had felt Stirling following his example, perhaps for the first time in his service.

The warrant officers in their own mess had been at ease, even with their captain. Ready to answer a casual question, and to offer one. *Do you miss Unrivalled, sir?* And without thinking, he had replied, *I miss a part of each ship I've ever served.* Curiously, it was the first time he had put it into words.

Then the Royal Marines' messdeck. The 'barracks'. Everything in its place, an air of soldierly camaraderie which marked them out from all those crowded around them.

The midshipmen's gunroom, untidy despite their hasty efforts to prepare for his visit. Living day to day like every midshipman, thinking only of reaching the final step in the ladder, the examination for lieutenant, and only then becoming a King's officer. Few ever considered that the step from gunroom to quarterdeck was merely the beginning.

Had Luke Jago been with him, he would have seen

it with different eyes, the potential tyrants and bullies, the toadies and the failures. And, just occasionally, the one who would listen and learn, and deserve his new authority. He had been more often right than wrong.

And Rounds had taken him to the sick bay on the orlop deck, below *Athena*'s waterline, where George Crawford the surgeon and his mates had to deal with every kind of ailment and injury from gunshot to a fall from aloft, fever to the aftermath of a flogging.

Crawford was a wiry, quietly spoken man, with very clear eyes and a voice which was neither incisive nor callous when he talked of his trade. A far cry from *Unrivalled*'s big, witty Irishman, Adam thought.

In an hour's time he would report to the vice-admiral. They had dined together; Troubridge and Henry Souter, the captain of the Royal Marines detachment, had also been there. The conversation had been light, and untainted by duty, or as much as it could be. And the wine, as Adam had guessed, was predictable. Too many glasses. Only the vice-admiral had seemed unimpaired. Adam had been almost grateful when he had been called away to carry out Captain's Rounds.

He wondered if Bethune had remained in his cot since the dinner.

He smiled. Jago probably had an answer to that, too.

The sentry shouted, 'Officer o' the watch, sir!'

It was Barclay, the second lieutenant.

'The officer of the guard has left a package for you, sir. There is no address or superscription. I am not certain I should have accepted it.'

'Who gave it to the guardboat, Mr Barclay?'

The lieutenant might have shrugged, but suppressed it. 'Somebody from a local boatyard . . .'

Adam saw the house, white against the trees and the Tamar. Empty, but for two people.

'Show me.'

Jago took it from the lieutenant and carried it into the main cabin.

'Down here, sir?'

It was square, and wrapped in pale canvas, like a tray. Adam shook his head. His mouth was dry.

'No, Luke. On the chair.'

Jago stood it upright against the chairback and regarded it suspiciously. Bowles bent as if to unfasten it but Adam said, 'I'll do it.'

It was a frame; it must have been freshly made, perhaps only a day or so ago, the wood smooth but unpainted. From the boatyard.

He did not recall unwrapping it, or how long it took. He stood back and looked at the portrait, hardly daring to breathe or move. He knew that Jago and Bowles had gone, and the screen door was shut.

It could have been that day. The eyes, and the arms pinioned to the rock. The hint of the monster about to break surface. He reached out to touch it, and saw that the smoke stains had been cleaned away.

He had written to her. She would not receive his letter until after *Athena* had set sail.

But she had already answered him.

Andromeda.

8

Storm Warning

Adam Bolitho leaned his hands on the chart table and looked down at the sailing master's log. Neat and observant, like the man, he thought. A pair of brass dividers began to slide across the uppermost chart and Adam put them in a small drawer. Around him the ship was coming to life again, timbers murmuring, loose gear clattering, while the sails filled and hardened. He had been on deck when both watches were called to make more sail, and had seen the sea break into long patterns of white horses, then into steep-sided crests, the canvas swelling, holding *Athena* hard over, the topmen skipping about the yards like monkeys, glad to be doing something after the periods of perverse breezes and torrential rain.

He thrust himself away from the table without another glance at Fraser's calculations; he knew them by heart. It was their ninth day at sea, and they had logged barely one thousand four hundred miles, without sighting another vessel of any kind after leaving the coastal waters of Cornwall. It made the Atlantic seem even vaster, and gave many of the younger hands a sense of loneliness they had never experienced before. The sun, when it appeared, was bright but without warmth; that and wet clothing did little for comfort or discipline.

He heard some Royal Marines clumping across the deck for another drill or inspection. Captain Souter, their commanding officer, had organized marksmanship contests with his men divided into squads, one competing against the other. They had lined a gangway and fired at pieces of driftwood thrown outboard from the bows. Apart from good training, it had provided a welcome distraction for seamen off watch, some of whom would doubtless have bets riding on the results. Sailors would bet on almost anything, lawful or not.

But it had not lasted for long. Vice-Admiral Bethune had sent a message requesting that the musketry cease forthwith. It had been disturbing his concentration.

He was about to look aft and changed his mind. He had no idea what Bethune did for most of the day, but he rarely appeared on deck. Adam made his daily reports on progress, and the ship's routine. Usually Bethune was reading his confidential papers, or dictating to his secretary. His smart, impassive servant was almost always present, as if Bethune could not bear solitude.

He walked to the weather side of the quarterdeck, Barclay, the lieutenant who had the watch, moving to the opposite side in the accepted fashion to allow his captain some pretence of privacy.

He looked along the main deck. It was nearly noon; the galley funnel was giving off its usual greasy plume of smoke. And there would be the customary issue of grog. He watched the shark-blue horizon sloping across the beakhead and jib sails: no sharp edge, but another hint of mist. He looked across at Fraser; he would have noted it. Rain again before the dog watches. Wet clothing, damp hammocks.

The midshipmen were grouped around the sailing master, each with his own sextant, ready to take the noon sights and check the ship's position. Again. He studied their faces, serious, intent, or anxious, the younger ones at least. Those who were expecting a summons to the examination for lieutenant were more confident, like Vincent, straight-backed, his sextant carelessly held in one hand. Probably very aware of his captain's presence on deck. And another, Rowley, who came from a long line of sailors, handsome until he smiled. He had lost two front teeth, knocked out by a block in a gale before Adam had assumed command.

He thought again of Napier; he had all this and much more to overcome.

Fraser said, 'Ready!' and all the sextants swivelled round as eight bells chimed out from the forecastle. The sun was being helpful today, but you could never be sure. It was not unknown for somebody to turn over the half-hour glass too early during each watch, so that a man's time on deck could be shortened with

170

the sand only partly filtered away. 'Warming the glass', as it was called, could make a mockery of any calculation.

Fraser and one of his mates were making notes, and one of the youngest midshipmen was holding his hand up to ask a question, as if he were still at school. The noon gun would crash out at Plymouth, and the gulls would rise from the water, screaming and squawking, as if it had never happened before. Adam walked to the hammock nettings and gripped a lashing as the deck tilted over again.

And she would hear it. Perhaps she would picture this ship, further and further away. Perhaps she was regretting it. And suppose . . .

'Excuse me, sir.'

Adam turned abruptly, and for a second imagined he had voiced his fears aloud.

It was Tolan, the admiral's servant, immaculately turned out as always, his calm features without expression.

He always had the feeling that Tolan missed nothing. Bethune relied on him completely. Always on call, Tolan even had a little cabin of his own, screened off from the admiral's pantry.

'Sir Graham sends his compliments, sir, and would you consider joining him in the last dog watch?'

It was not a request. It was an order.

They both turned as there was a sudden confusion on the main deck. A man Adam vaguely recognized as one of the cook's assistants was running wildly after a chicken which must have escaped from the pen on

171

the lower gun deck, 'the farmyard'. It had doubtless been selected for Bethune's table this evening.

There were jeers and hoots of laughter as the man ducked around the breech of an eighteen-pounder and sprawled headlong, his feet caught in his apron.

The luckless bird, unable to fly, seemed to bounce up the quarterdeck ladder in a last attempt to get away.

One of the Royal Marines in the afterguard who had just been dismissed from the drill tossed his musket against the hammock nettings and seized the chicken by its legs. To the cook's assistant he called, ''Ere, matey, you'll 'ave to do better next time!'

The watchkeepers were already being relieved, and Fitzroy, the fourth lieutenant, was about to take over from Barclay, but all Adam saw was Tolan as he reached out and caught the marine by the wrist, and swung him around as if he weighed nothing.

'Don't *ever* leave a musket like that, you bastard!' He thrust the man aside and snatched it up, turning it to hold it within inches of the marine's face. 'See that, damn your eyes? If it had fallen you could have killed somebody!'

Adam called sharply, 'Belay that!' He felt the pain in his side, the wound caused by a dying marine dropping his loaded musket. Another inch, the surgeon had said . . .

'Carry on, Tolan. Tell Sir Graham I shall be delighted.'

Strange that he could be so calm after that flash of anger. And something more.

'Everything all right, sir?' It was Stirling, striding

through the crowd of watching seamen as if they did not exist.

Adam shrugged. 'It passed over.' He saw the cook's assistant hurrying away with the chicken, pursued by ironic cheers, hoots and clucking from the remaining onlookers.

Lieutenant Fitzroy had taken over the watch; new lookouts were already perched high aloft. Viewed from the quarterdeck, they looked as if they were about to slide down the horizon.

Fitzroy said dutifully, 'Steady she goes, sir. Sou' west by west. Full and by.' He touched his hat. 'Permission for the cooper to bring new casks on deck?'

'Granted.' Adam turned away. Routine had taken over once more. Had saved him.

From what? He saw the sergeant of marines glaring at the man who had so carelessly discarded his firearm. But it was Tolan's anger and swift reaction that lingered in his mind.

Stirling was saying, 'That fellow had his wits about him, sir. Not what you'd expect.' He straightened up, as if he had gone too far. 'I keep thinking I've seen him before somewhere.'

Then something caught his eye and he shouted, 'Thompson, flake down that line and do your work smartly for a change!' The first lieutenant was back.

Dugald Fraser, the sailing master, folded his arms and stared into the hard glare as if to defy it. He had been at sea all his life and had served in almost every class

173

and size of ship. As master, he was at the top of his profession, something he rarely considered. He did not see the point.

He watched the sea boil along the weather side, bursting occasionally over the gangway, draining along the scuppers and making the guns shine above their buff-painted carriages.

The horizon was almost gone, the margin between sea and sky lost in mist and drifting spray.

'The wind's veered a piece, sir.' He glanced at Lieutenant Fitzroy by the rail, his body angled steeply against the tilt of the quarterdeck. The helmsmen, too, were clinging to the big spokes, taking the strain of sea and rudder. He tasted the salt hardening on his cracked lips. Fitzroy was young, but he was experienced. He should have acted before this.

Fitzroy looked over his shoulder as *Athena* gave a great shudder, and more water tumbled over the gangway and sluiced down among the men working on deck. The afternoon watch was not yet over, but it would soon be dark in this weather.

'The captain must be informed.' It sounded like a question.

Fraser said, 'Aye,' and winced as water splashed his face and neck. Nearly June, and it felt like winter. 'We should shorten sail an' let her fall off a point.'

He almost grinned at Fitzroy's expression of relief.

A boatswain's mate said, 'Cap'n's comin' up, sir.'

Fraser watched a working party reel and stagger on the forecastle, making something fast, bare feet slithering on the wet planking, bodies shining, soaked to the skin.

The captain was hatless, hair blowing unheeded in the wind and wearing one of his old seagoing coats, patched and stitched like any common seaman's. Fraser was satisfied. You would still know he was the captain no matter how he was dressed.

Adam was looking at the sky, the masthead pendant whipping out, bar-taut, like a spear. The ship was labouring heavily, but shaking off the crested rollers with each plunge.

'We will alter course two points. Steer west by south.' He wiped his face with his sleeve, and smiled. 'If we can't fight it, we may as well use it!' He touched Fraser's arm as he gazed at the sea, and waited for the right moment to move to the compass box. Then he said to the helmsmen, 'Are you holding her? Another hand on the helm, maybe?'

One of them tore his eyes from the flapping driver and shouted, 'Not yet, zur! She'm good as gold!' and they laughed as if it was a huge joke.

Fraser heard it, and inwardly noted it, as he might compose an entry in his log.

When Captain Ritchie had walked this quarterdeck it had been very different. Passing a casual moment with his sailors would have been unheard of. He had been respected, but Adam Bolitho had something Ritchie would never have recognized. The two helmsmen were tough and experienced, had seen it all, or thought they had. But off watch they would be telling their messmates how the captain had asked their opinion, even joked about it . . . Adam Bolitho did not appear to have changed since the old *Achates*.

He heard the captain call, 'Mr Fitzroy, you'll need more hands on deck, and lively too! I am not a mind reader, you know!'

Calls shrilled and seamen ran to their stations, ready to wear ship, and, when ordered, take in a reef and bring the canvas under control. 'And tell Mr Mudge to hoist the quarter boat aboard. It will be swamped otherwise.'

There was no edge to his tone, but Fitzroy exclaimed, 'I had it bailed an hour back, sir!'

Adam regarded him thoughtfully. 'Send another man down to bail it, and we will have a burial on our hands, I fear.'

The horizon had finally disappeared, a new darkness creeping beneath a bank of clouds like a cloak.

'Steady she goes, sir! West by south!'

A master's mate muttered, 'Bloody wind's droppin', Mr Fraser.'

Fraser tightened his coat about his throat. 'Rain's back too, I see!' Even above the din of sea and thrashing canvas he could hear the heavy drops, like shot being scattered from a gunner's pouch.

He saw the captain's dark eyes flash as he swung round and pushed the soaking hair from his forehead.

Some one shouted, 'Might blow itself out! I was in the Atlantic in ninety-nine when we had the worst storm—' The voice trailed away as Adam lurched to the rail again and waited for the deck to steady itself. He was drenched, the water like ice on his spine and running down his thighs.

The flashes had died in the mist and advancing rain, but the thunder still hung in the air. And in his memory.

He said, 'Pipe all hands. Fetch the first lieutenant directly.'

He knew they were staring at him, probably thinking he was losing his nerve.

Fraser saw it as if it was already written in the log. He was too old a hand to forget.

It was not just a storm, and if it was, it would not last.

It was gunfire.

The Royal Marine sentry outside the admiral's quarters brought his heels sharply together and as if by magic the screen door opened, one of Bethune's servants holding it, and bowing his head as Adam entered. Nothing was said. Perhaps Bethune found announcements unnecessary, distracting.

After the squeak of blocks, with seamen scrambling through and over lively halliards and braces, the admiral's quarters were like a sanctuary. It was impossible, but here even the motion seemed less, the shipboard noises subdued. Remote.

The dining space was in darkness, all the candles doused, if they had ever been alight in the first place.

Adam groped his way past unfamiliar furniture toward the day cabin, where Bethune was sitting at his desk, some dishes before him, a bottle of some kind propped upright in an opened drawer. His coat hung on the back of his chair, and his fine waistcoat was unbuttoned. Somehow, Adam thought, he still managed to look elegant and relaxed. Beyond the desk the stern windows were completely black, but in the reflected light he could see water running down the thick panes, rain or spray, probably both.

Bethune put his hand to his lips and pulled a chicken bone from his teeth before tossing it into a bowl at his elbow.

He looked at Adam while he dabbed his mouth with a napkin.

'Anything new to report, Adam?'

'The wind is steady. Fraser thinks it will hold. So do I. Not strong, but it will see us through the night.'

'That is not what I asked.' Bethune reached for the bottle, but it was empty. 'What do you think it was? Really think?'

A shadow emerged from the other cabin and a full bottle was placed in the drawer. It was Tolan, as quiet on his feet as he was quick.

'Gunfire, Sir Graham. Then an explosion.' He could feel the weariness closing around him again. What had taken him on deck without waiting for the officer of the watch to call him? Not the wind or sea. That was experience, standing hundreds of watches in every kind of weather, and almost every ocean.

He was still not used to this ship. It would take more time. Choose the right moment.

He thought of his uncle again. Instinct: if you had it, you had to trust in it.

Bethune was watching Tolan's hands come from the shadows and fill his goblet. 'An attack? Pirates? What other seafarers would be ready and eager to fight

178

in these conditions?' He tasted the wine without comment. 'They will be up and away by now, whoever they were.' Then he said curtly, 'I'm told that the galley fire is still alight?'

Adam contained his sudden anger. It sounded like an accusation.

'I knew we would not be going to quarters. Tomorrow?' He would have shrugged, but his shoulders ached too much. 'Things may have changed. I considered that the people should have a hot meal while they can.'

Bethune smiled. 'I was not questioning your judgment, Adam. Far from it.' Just as swiftly, he changed tack. 'When do you estimate we shall reach English Harbour?'

Adam caught sight of his reflection in the sloping windows. Moving slightly to the vibration of the tiller head, like a spectre looking inboard from this violent ocean.

'The north-east trades will give us a soldier's wind. I'd estimate two more weeks.'

'Or thereabouts. What I calculated myself. After that . . .' Bethune held the glass up to the faint light. 'We will discover the latest intelligence from the commodore at Antigua and, of course, the governor. I am sure that our "allies" will do all they can to assist!'

He held one hand to his ear as calls trilled, as if from another world. 'You can fill their bellies and warm their souls with rum, but it does not always win popularity.'

'They are cold, hungry, and tired, Sir Graham. I owe them that, at least.'

'As you say.'

Adam left the cabin, the door closing behind him as silently as it had opened.

He rubbed his eyes. Bethune had not offered him any wine. And he had not waited to share the unfortunate chicken.

He listened to the hiss of the sea beyond the sealed gunports, and imagined the watch on deck, peering into the darkness, thinking of the echoes of battle, or the death of a ship in distress. Their world.

Jago was lounging by the companion ladder, but straightened up as Adam seized the handrail.

He did not need to be told. It was still too close to Algiers and all those other times. When your mind and nerve could become blunted, like a badly used razor.

'All quiet on deck now, sir.'

Adam made to pass him. 'I'm just going to take a turn around, Luke. It does no harm.'

Jago did not budge. 'You've not eaten anythin', sir.' He saw the keen, warning eyes, but persisted, 'Bowles told me. Upset, he was, too.'

Adam reached out impetuously and gripped his arm. 'One day, you will go too far!' He shook him gently. 'Until then . . . I will go aft. And maybe . . .'

Jago stood back, and grinned. 'Aye, Cap'n. *Mebbee* – that's more like it!'

He watched him climb the companion. A good wet of brandy, or some of that fancy wine the officers gulped down, would do him more good than harm, the mood he was in.

He remembered the painting he had seen, carefully placed where it would be safe even if they ran into a hurricane. Only a picture, but the woman was real enough. Like *Unrivalled*, second to none . . .

A corporal of marines marched past him, another bullock close on his heels. Changing the sentries for the middle watch. For tomorrow . . . no, today.

He saw the white crossbelts crisp and clear against the shadows of the nearest twenty-four pounder. Always the reminder.

He thought suddenly of the vice-admiral: a good reputation, popular too, they said.

Jago walked away, humming silently to himself.

But not one you would ever turn your back on.

The relieved sentry and the corporal marched away to join their companions in the 'barracks'. A hot meal at this hour was unheard of, in the Corps or anywhere else, and a tot as well for good measure. It was not to be missed. Tomorrow could wait.

In the little pantry adjoining the admiral's quarters, George Tolan was standing with a glass in his hand, adjusting to the deck's slow roll and the solitary lantern's beam swinging across his face.

All this time. All those years. I should have been ready. He had trained himself to always be prepared. For the slightest hint, the weak moment which could still betray him.

Very deliberately he filled the glass with wine. He sensed the warning again, like a signal, or a flare in the night. He would have to be doubly careful, even to the amount of wine he drank. Something far stronger would be better, but Bethune would notice. It would destroy everything he had worked for.

His mind hesitated, like a keeper feeling for a trap, before he allowed himself to think it over again. The stupid marine who had tossed aside his musket just to make a fool out of the cook's assistant and his damned chicken. The musket had been at half-cock. Safe, or so the untrained idiot might think. Many had discovered otherwise to their cost; he had heard that the captain had been wounded by such a shot.

His guard must have been down, he thought. He had snatched up the heavy weapon, had caught it perfectly at the point of balance. Just like all those other times, all the drills and the bellowing sergeants. The skill, and eventually the pride at what he was doing. Only a second's carelessness, and he had acted as if he was back in the line. And like that day when he had killed his officer.

He had listened to Bethune talking with the captain. For a moment he had imagined that Bolitho had noticed his reaction, his ease with a musket. Twenty years ago. It could have been yesterday.

He wiped the glass and held it up to the swinging light.

Bethune would be calling him very soon now. His cot was ready, his heavy robe laid out on a chair. They would talk for a while as he helped him into the cot, and perhaps brought him another drink. He talked but never listened, unless he wanted to hear something.

Tolan heard the little bell tinkle from the admiral's quarters. He would not throw it all away now, after twenty years.

He picked up his tray and opened the door.

'Coming, Sir Graham!'

He was safe.

Adam awoke with a start, his eyes hot and sore, his mouth like dust. It was Jago, bending over the coat, one hand shielding the shuttered lantern while he waited for his senses to recover.

Adam struggled into a sitting position, his mind groping for details and sounds. He felt as if he had slept for only a few minutes.

'What's happening?'

Jago watched him impassively, eyes in shadow.

'Dawn comin' up, Cap'n. First light very soon.'

'Already?' The cabin seemed to be as dark as ever. Then he smelled fresh coffee, and thought he heard Bowles moving about in the pantry.

Jago added patiently, 'There may be trouble we have to deal with today. You said so yourself, Cap'n. They'll be lookin' to you. So I thought a shave might be in order, so to speak.'

Adam groaned and climbed out of the cot, feeling the deck, angled but steady. 'I've no time for that now, man!'

But the anger refused to come, and eventually he shrugged and said, 'I suppose it makes sense.'

He walked across the checkered deck covering and sat in the chair by his desk, thinking of Bethune somewhere beneath his feet. As refreshed as ever, no doubt. He smiled. What made him a flag officer, far removed from the day to day problems and discomforts of ordinary sailors. The smile grew. *Or captains . . .*

Feet thudded overhead and some one shouted. He felt Jago's hand on his shoulder, like a groom quieting a restless horse.

'Easy, Cap'n.' The razor glinted in the solitary light. 'I'll not be long. You take some coffee first.'

Adam leaned back in the chair and thought of the painting in his sleeping cabin. He had been looking at it, at her, when he had fallen asleep, the spiralling lantern keeping watch over both of them.

Where was she now? What was she doing, thinking?

Now that she had had time to consider and remember, how would she see that moment, when they had become one?

Bowles was here, head bowed beneath the deck-head beams. 'Clean shirt, sir, and another coat.' He glanced at Jago; he might have winked.

Adam stood up and touched his face. Like the hot coffee, the shave had pushed the tiredness aside.

Jago remarked, 'Lighter already, Cap'n.'

Adam fastened the shirt and tugged the neckcloth into place. He was ready.

'The picture – put it somewhere safe, Bowles.'

'All done, sir.'

Adam walked to the chair and touched it. They would never discover the reason for the gunfire and the flashes in those black clouds; this was a vast ocean, with ships tiny by comparison, like drifting leaves on a mill-race.

'I'm going on deck.'

Bowles nodded gravely. Jago waited, seeing the indecision, the doubts.

He left the cabin and walked past the chart room and into the fading shadows. Anonymous shapes moved aside, faces and voices becoming people he had come to know: the morning watch, four o'clock until eight, when the ship, any ship, awoke.

Stirling, as first lieutenant, had the watch, and was already facing aft, as if he had known the captain would choose this moment to come on deck. Instinct . . .

Adam said, 'A quiet watch, Mr Stirling.' He moved to the compass box and glanced at the card swaying easily in the small light. West by south. Nothing had changed. He peered up at the topsails, pale but still indistinct, moving occasionally to the thrust of the wind. 'A good man aloft?'

'Sir. I've two up, sir. Although . . .'

Adam turned to stare out at the sea. '*Although* you think there'll be nothing for them to see.'

Stirling stood his ground. 'It's been a while, sir.'

'Yes.' He was right. Any pirate or unlawful trader would have spread every inch of canvas if they thought a King's ship was close by.

He walked to the lee side of the quarterdeck and saw a long feather of spray burst from a patch of dark water. Like a fall of shot. A fish of some kind, a large one too.

He heard the hoarse voice of Henry Mudge, the

boatswain. 'Put two good 'ands on this splicin' as soon as it's light, Mr Quinlan. I shouldn't 'ave to tell *you* these glarin' faults, eh? If you wants to sit that exam one day, an' Gawd 'elp the rest of us if you does . . .' His voice faded on the sudden boom of canvas as the driver filled in a gust.

Another face. Quinlan was one of the youngest midshipmen. Feeling his way. Like David Napier.

The two helmsmen pulled down on the big double wheel, one leaning round to watch the compass card, the other staring aloft at the peak of the driver to gauge the wind's strength, and that of the sea against the rudder far below his feet. He had a vivid tattoo on his muscular arm, a wild bird with spread wings, and what looked like a human skull beneath it.

Adam was suddenly alert, and wide awake. Just moments earlier, the sailor had been in complete darkness.

He strode to the rail and watched the sea gaining colour, light spilling from the horizon far astern, giving life to the topsails and driver, shining on spray-dappled planks and gangways. On upturned faces and those working on the yards, and a man in an apron carrying a bucket, pausing to note the wind's direction before heaving its contents over the lee side.

Adam shaded his eyes and looked at the masthead pendant, licking out from the truck, brightly coloured as it caught the dawn and held it. The galley fire was rekindled and there was smoke in the air. The men of the forenoon watch would be going to breakfast, such as it was, probably some of the leavings from the unexpected supper their captain had arranged in a moment of kindness – or madness, as the word had it on the messdecks.

He walked slowly to the rail again and felt salt like dried sand under his fingers.

And down in his quarters Bethune would be smiling to himself. Shaking his head, wondering if he had made the right choice for his flag captain.

'*Deck there!*'

All caught like unfinished sketches. The man in his apron, his empty bucket poised in mid air. Two seamen listening to the young midshipman named Quinlan, others frozen as they stared up and through the mesh of rigging, to the invisible lookout in the crosstrees.

Stirling's voice echoed above all other sounds.

'I hear you. *Where away?*'

It seemed an age before the lookout called down again.

'Fine on th' starboard bow, sir! Wreckage!'

Adam snatched up a telescope and trained it beyond the forecastle, to a dark horizon still unwilling to cast the night aside.

'A good lookout indeed, Mr Stirling. We could have missed it altogether in this light.'

He realized that Troubridge was beside him, wide-eyed, as if he had just been dragged out of his cot.

'Sir Graham heard the noise, sir.' He was almost apologetic. 'He sends his compliments . . .'

'Tell Sir Graham that we have found wreckage. We were right.'

Troubridge paused at the top of the ladder and turned

to look back at him. Very young, like the night they had broken into the studio together.

'*You* were right, sir.' And he was gone.

Adam saw Jago watching from the poop ladder. At ease now. It was out of his hands.

The light was gaining strength every minute; faces became individuals and the sea on either beam reached away to its horizon. There were groups of seamen, jaws champing on the remains of their breakfast, when normally men strung it out until the last possible moment. Something different. Anything to break the monotony of routine and trimming sails.

The sea was still lively, something that had to be considered from *Athena*'s poop, high compared with that of a frigate.

He raised the telescope which had appeared as if by magic at his elbow. Another midshipman . . . his mind faltered . . . Vicary, had been observing him and was ready.

Clearer this time. He squinted and tried again. A living, working ship. Was that all that remained of her?

The lookout was a good one. High above the deck, he had the benefit of the changing colours on the sea's face in the first light of the dawn, and the unbroken crests and long, undulating troughs which were never completely absent in this great ocean.

'Have the jolly boat ready for lowering, Mr Stirling. Volunteers.'

He felt his fingers tighten on the telescope. Like dust scattered across the blue-grey water. Hundreds of fragments widely spread over a mile or so, maybe more.

He did not see Jago move but heard him murmur, 'I'll take the jolly boat, Cap'n. The gig's still on the tier.' Calm, almost matter-of-fact.

Mudge the boatswain was shouting orders to his men on the main deck, his voice louder than usual in the damp air.

Stirling said, 'Boat's crew mustered, sir.' No doubts this time. An order was an order, something he accepted without question.

He heard the young midshipman named Vicary suppress a gasp, and Adam saw that his eyes were wide and fixed, like saucers. And no wonder.

'What is all the excitement about?' It was Bethune, staring around the quarterdeck, then down toward the boat tier where tackles were already being manhandled into position. 'I see no need for further involvement.' The smile returned. 'We've both seen and weathered far worse, eh, Adam?'

Some of the watching seamen grinned like conspirators. They had not set eyes on their admiral since he had joined the ship at Plymouth.

Every available telescope was trained on the pathetic fragments which reached away on either bow, some with shape and meaning now. A mast, or part of it, with sodden canvas still attached, trailing cordage like weed, and a complete portion of grating drifting quite apart, clean in the hard light as if it had just been scrubbed.

'Well, if you need to discuss anything further . . .'

Bethune paused, one hand on the rail, his head half turned as a voice yelled, '*Deck there! Larboard bow!*' He seemed unable to continue, then, after a moment, shouted, '*Bodies, sir!*'

Adam strode to the nettings and trained the telescope with great care. It gave him time, allowed his anger to subside. He heard himself say, 'I'm lowering a boat, Sir Graham.' The glass steadied as *Athena*'s hull rode easily over another unending trough. Long enough to see it. Share it, before the picture dropped out of focus. A piece of timber, probably decking, blasted away by the explosion, with two figures clinging or stranded across it. One was all but naked, the other wore uniform, the same as some of those standing around him.

He heard Scollay, the master-at-arms, exclaim, 'Ours, by Jesus!'

He glanced across the deck. 'Heave to, Mr Stirling.' He sought out the boatswain's rotund figure. 'Lower the jolly boat as soon as we come about.' He saw Jago pause to stare up at him, then he was gone.

He realized that Bethune had not moved, and was standing with his hand still on the rail, his hair blowing in the wind, as if he could not grasp what was happening.

Adam raised the glass again, feeling the deeper pitch of the deck as, with sails thundering, *Athena* came heavily round and into the wind. Calls shrilled, and orders were yelled to topmen and those manning the braces, but Stirling's booming voice overrode them all.

Adam looked for the jolly boat. One moment it was being swayed up and over the larboard gangway, then it vanished, only to reappear well clear of the side, pulling strongly for the nearest cluster of flotsam and the two corpses.

He said, 'There are other bodies close by.' He pressed the glass hard against his eye, so that he would not forget. Corpses, pieces of men, rising and dipping as if in some obscene dance.

He said, 'Fetch the surgeon.'

'Comin', sir!'

Adam moved the glass very slightly and saw Jago's face loom into life, eyes nearly closed against the early sunshine.

'I'm here, sir.'

He held the glass steady, waiting for the deck to rise again. He did not turn his head, but knew it was Crawford.

'Have your people ready.' He lowered the glass and handed it to Midshipman Vicary, but Jago's face remained; he was standing in the tossing boat, managing to hold up and cross both hands above his head. 'There is a survivor. Warn the bosun to be ready. Use my quarters if you wish. It might save time, and a life.'

Bethune said, 'I should not have questioned your judgment, Adam.'

Adam had not even seen him move from the rail. 'I had a feeling.' He shrugged. 'I can't explain it, even to myself.' He watched the light returning to Bethune's eyes, some of the familiar confidence. But for just that

191

short while he had seen it broken down, as if he had lost control.

Bethune looked up, perhaps at his flag, streaming from the fore.

'Call me if you discover anything. But get under way as soon as possible.' Again the slight hesitation. 'When you think fit.' He strode to the companion without another look at the sea, or the pitching jolly boat floating amongst the thinning carpet of flotsam and death.

Lieutenant Francis Troubridge held the screen door open and tried to summon a smile of greeting as *Athena*'s captain walked into the admiral's day cabin. As the door closed he heard the bell chime briefly before it separated this world from the rest of the ship.

'Sir Graham is waiting for you, sir.' He wanted to say so much more, to share some small part of what had happened. The ship hove to, the tension on deck, all eyes on the jolly boat and the captain's coxswain giving his signals, then returning on board with the one survivor.

And all the while, Captain Bolitho had been on deck, watching, passing orders while he brought the ship under command again, his voice calm enough, but his eyes telling a different story.

Adam glanced around the cabin, with its elegant furniture and fittings. It seemed unreal, but in some peculiar way it helped to steady his nerves. In a ship it was always a matter of time and distance: it began with those simple lessons, grouped around the sailing

master; he had seen the midshipmen listening to Fraser.
He rubbed his forehead. Only yesterday? How could
that be? Shooting the sun, and later, much later, perhaps
a star in the heavens. Fixing a ship's position by taking
a compass bearing of a landmark, a church tower
perhaps. He let his mind wander. Or perhaps St
Anthony's light at Falmouth . . .

Yesterday. And now it was the last dog watch again,
when Bethune had been eating his chicken at that
desk.

The servant Tolan appeared out of the shadows, a
tray with one goblet balanced on it.

'Cognac, sir.'

Troubridge said quickly, 'I hope you don't mind,
sir. I thought you might care for it.'

Adam felt the strain draining away, like sand from
the glass.

'Thank you.' And to Tolan, 'And you, too.'

Then he sat down in a chair which had already been
prepared for him, like the mariner's eternal puzzle.
Time and distance. Bethune was offering him both.

Darkness was already falling over the heaving water,
with a few stars pale and clear now that the clouds
had dispersed. *Athena* was on course once more,
making good the time lost in their rescue attempt.

The cognac was good. Very good. Probably from
that shop in St James's Street in London where his
uncle had often bought wine, and his Catherine had
ordered it for him when he was away at sea. *And for
me* . . . He rubbed his eyes again, trying to clear his
thoughts, to see the events in order, neat and helpful.

He felt his mouth crack. Like Fraser's log book and his careful notes, day by day. Hour by hour.

The vessel was, had been, the *Celeste*, a naval courier brig, one of the many which served every fleet and base wherever the Union flag was flown. Overworked and taken very much for granted, these small vessels were the vital link between their lordships at the Admiralty and virtually every captain afloat.

Adam had seen *Celeste* mentioned several times, in despatches and once or twice in the *Gazette*. The fleet's apron strings, but never in the vanguard of battle, amid the seeds of glory.

The survivor was the *Celeste*'s acting master, a prime seaman named William Rose, who had come originally from the seaport of Hull. Not young, and he had served at sea most of his life, first in a merchantman, but mainly in the navy.

Adam could still hear his hoarse voice, recounting vague fragments about himself. Up there in his own cabin hours ago, watching, listening. The surgeon had been doubtful; he had seen too many men go under. But Rose had great strength, and a determination to match it.

Adam had known sailors plead to be left to die after being wounded in a sea fight, anything but be taken below to the dreaded orlop and the surgeon's saw and knife. He himself had grown to hate the very smell of a sick bay, and the terrors it could hold, even for the bravest. Which was why he had told the surgeon to have Rose taken to his own quarters.

He raised the goblet, and stared at it. It had been refilled; he had not even noticed.

The *Celeste* had been on the same route as *Athena*, to Antigua; she had even sailed from Plymouth, two whole days before *Athena* had weighed. No wonder Bethune had become so agitated when he had been told the vessel's name. She had sailed under his orders, confident that she would reach English Harbour far ahead of any two-decker.

It was like hearing Rose speak again, one strong, rough hand grasped around his own. Describing it. Recalling it, piece by piece. He would occasionally stray from the exact sequence of things, speaking of Hull, and of his father, who had been a sailmaker. Then the hand had tightened, as he had described the sudden squall which had hit them without warning. *I told the captain what I thought about it, but he wouldn't listen. Knew it all, he did. Anyways, he was under strict orders to complete a fast passage.* Adam had seen a tear at the corner of his eye; pain or despair, who could say? *Y'see, our old Celeste could always do better than any other courier!*

And pride was there, too.

They had lost the fore topmast, and had been drifting to sea and wind while they had fought to carry out repairs. And then another sail had come in sight. A big barque, and she had stood off the disabled *Celeste* until they were close enough to exchange signals. *A Yankee, she was. Our captain asked if she had a doctor on board, as one of our lads was badly injured by a falling spar.*

Adam stared through the salt-caked stern windows. No courier brig should ever heave to or converse with a stranger. It had all been planned, although how and when was impossible to imagine at this stage.

The barque had drawn closer to *Celeste* and all pretence had ended. He could still feel the grip around his fingers, losing its strength as Rose had gasped, *They ran out their guns and fired into us at point-blank range, double-shotted by th' feel of it.* His voice had cracked with disbelief, reliving the moment. *Our captain was the first to fall, damn his eyes!* There had been another tear. *But it weren't his fault. They boarded us and cut down every man-jack they could find. The rest of us was driven below while the bastards ransacked the captain's cabin.*

There had been a long pause, the silence broken only by Rose's laboured breathing.

Crawford had whispered, 'Severe stab wounds. Poisoned, but I can do nothing. He's going.'

Rose had spoken once more, his voice easier, perhaps beyond pain.

There was an explosion, sir. A magazine. Don't remember any more. Until . . . He had stared suddenly at Adam. *Tell 'em* . . .

It was over for the only survivor.

He looked up as Bethune entered the cabin and stood, seeming to study him for several seconds.

'So you see, Adam, it was no accidental skirmish. It was prearranged. Some one knew full well what *Celeste* was carrying: my orders and Admiralty instructions which were to be acted upon without delay. Her commander should have known, damn him!' The mood changed again, and he half smiled. 'But you know what they say about the ones who command brigs, like frigates, eh? Faster than anything bigger. Bigger than anything faster!'

He looked around the cabin, as if he were remembering something. 'In a moment we shall have a meal together. Just the two of us. The ship can manage her own affairs, for a while, anyway.' He seemed to come to a decision. 'I wanted this appointment, and I intend to make it succeed to good purpose, come what may.' He eyed him calmly. 'I have no intention of becoming a scapegoat because of others at this point in my life. We are *committed*, Adam. Together – remember that!'

Tolan and the two cabin servants pulled a screen aside to reveal a candlelit table and two chairs.

Bethune was speaking to Tolan, smiling and gesturing. But his words still hung in the air.

Like a threat.

9

A Death in the Family

Nancy, Lady Roxby, leaned forward in her seat and reached up to tap the carriage window with her parasol.

'This is far enough, Francis. You may wait here for us.' She did not turn to look at the girl beside her. 'It will do us good to stretch our legs now that the rain has passed over.' Something to say, to break the tension. She looked across the lane, past the overgrown and untended shrubs, to the Old Glebe House, occasional home of Sir Gregory Montagu, the great painter. She rested her hand on the door. 'If you change your mind, Lowenna, we can leave right now. Go back to Falmouth . . .' Then she turned to her companion, feeling her uncertainty, the sudden distress. 'I just want you to be happy, with *me*.'

Lowenna stared past her. All those months ago, but she could still feel it. The fire raging through the building, driven by the wind, roaring like something alive with a malignant will of its own.

She climbed down from the landau and looked along the rutted lane. The wall where she had found Adam lying in his blood after being thrown from his horse, when his wound had burst open. And she had been the only one there to help him.

She walked slowly toward the house. She could smell the charred timbers, wet and shining from the brief, heavy rain. Fallen bricks and masonry, broken glass glinting now in the returning sunlight. Exactly as she had last seen it. Avoided by people from the village; haunted, some said. A place used by smugglers, others claimed.

They had thought Montagu mad when he had bought it and converted it into a studio, several studios eventually, where he had worked and had trained others to follow his profession, spurred on by his fame and his genius. And now he was dead. Had begun to die that very day when the fire had broken out.

The doors were open or hanging charred from their hinges. Sunlight played through a great hole in the roof, so that the old stairway seemed to come alive again as her shoes crackled on fragments and scattered ash.

She knew Lady Roxby was following her. Wanting to help. And caring, as she had that time when they had first met, here in this house, when she had come to see Adam's portrait.

She heard a bird fluttering through the main studio, nesting perhaps. The same studio where Adam had stood looking at her. Andromeda . . . she felt it like pain. He was gone. The rest was like a dream . . . something she was terrified of losing.

Why I came back here.

She quickened her pace and came into the old garden. Overgrown, a wasteland, but the roses were still here, clustered by the wall, holding the sunshine, as fresh and yellow as they had been that day. Like the rose on his coat in the finished portrait.

She stooped to pick one, twisting the stem, and saw blood on her finger. She could almost hear his voice.

Nancy watched her, without speech or movement: the figure in the flowing blue-grey gown, a wide-brimmed straw hat hanging from her shoulders. Lowenna . . . 'joy' in the old Cornish tongue. After what she had suffered, perhaps the fates were repaying what they owed this dark-eyed girl.

She crossed the moss-covered cobbles. 'Here, let me. I'm more used to it than you are.' She felt the girl stiffen, the old barrier rising between them, like those first meetings; it was her only defence. She added simply, 'I've not much else to do these days, y' see!'

She felt the girl's arms around her, the dark hair against her face.

'Don't ever say that, dear Nancy. You are always busy, always helping others. It's why I love you so much.'

They gathered roses in silence. Then Lowenna said, 'We shall leave the rest. It is our place.'

They walked slowly back to the lane, where Francis was fastening the two hoods, which he had lowered in their absence. The landau's hoods were made of greased leather, which had to be constantly rubbed with oil and blacking to keep them pliable and waterproof. Lowenna noticed that the coachman, ex-cavalryman that he was, was wearing white gloves, without a single mark or smear.

'Thought it would be nice an' easy for the ride back, m' lady.'

Nancy smiled and touched his arm. 'Where would I be without you?'

Lowenna climbed up into the landau and tightened the ribbons of the hat beneath her chin. Nancy must have been lovely as a young girl. Now Roxby, her husband, 'The King of Cornwall', was dead. Lowenna recalled their first meeting, when Nancy had said openly that she had had two lovers in her life. Now she was nearly sixty, but the light was still there, in her eyes and in her manner.

And she had not questioned her. Why had she come? How long might she stay? But this was the West Country and news rode a fast horse. Nancy knew all about her brief stay at the Plymouth boatbuilder's house. She had asked once about the painting, and how it had survived the fire.

Lowenna had told her that she had sent it out to Adam's ship before he had sailed.

Nancy had gripped both her hands and had looked straight into her eyes.

'I will not ask if that was all you gave him, dear Lowenna. I can see it in your face.'

No rebuke or warning. That was Nancy.

The carriage clattered on to the main road, the horses glad to be on the move again, away from the lingering smell of fire. Past wild countryside made beautiful by great patterns of purple foxglove, and wild roses amid the hedgerows and slate walls.

At one point they passed parties of labourers clearing the way for a new road. Mostly young men, stripped to the waist, looking up as the carriage moved by. A sign of the times: men who such a short time ago had been in the uniforms of troopers or seamen. A new and unfamiliar life, but at least they had work to pay and feed them. Lowenna had seen too many of the other kind. Men along the pier or dock wall, watching the ships, even the lifeless ones. Like Adam's *Unrivalled*. Staring and remembering. But never the bad times, the harsh discipline and the ever-present nearness of danger and death. Only the comradeship, something she had felt and understood, like love.

'I have to go to Bodmin shortly.' Nancy reached out and folded the girl's hand in her own. 'The lawyers have arranged a meeting. Will you stay at the house until I come back? Longer, if you can.' She patted the hand as if to soothe it, like a startled creature. 'I would not ask you to accompany me, my dear.'

There would be too many bitter memories in Bodmin. Not least, members of her family who had turned their backs when she most needed their help and support. *No smoke without fire*. How could they even think it?

'Lawyers? Is it trouble, Nancy?'

'Always that, my dear.' She shrugged, glad that the

hurdle was past. 'But we do need them. Tenant farmers, repairs to cottages and barns . . . it never stops. I had hoped . . .'

She did not continue.

Lowenna remembered that she had two grown children, both of whom preferred London to Cornwall.

Nancy shaded her eyes as the roof of her own house showed above the familiar bank of trees.

'It's Elizabeth, you see. She has her own governess, of course, but she's growing up. Fast. Too fast, I think sometimes. She likes you. Admires you. I would feel less troubled if you were with her.'

'I've little experience, but I shall do my best.'

The grip tightened over her hand. 'Just be yourself. It will be good for her.'

Francis wheeled the horses through the gates, but heard them both laugh as Lowenna retorted, 'For *both* of us!'

A stable boy was already running to greet them, and Francis knew the exact moment when to apply the brake.

But his mind was still back on the new road, and the men who had paused in their work to watch this fine carriage sweep past. Glad to have employment when so many had come back from the war to find nothing; envious, too, maybe, at the sight of the lovely girl in the straw hat.

His boots hit the ground and he had the door open, and the step lowered without even noticing what he was doing.

But of course you never forgot. On the right of the

line, the spurs digging in, the sabres all coming down in one shimmering rank, then the piercing blare of the cornet. Charge! Of course you never forgot.

'I shall be ready if you need me, m' lady.'

But Nancy was staring past him, as if she had heard something.

'Take the roses, Lowenna.'

'What is it, Nancy?'

She shook her head. 'I'm not sure.' She climbed down carefully, one hand on her coachman's arm. 'Something has happened. If only Lewis were here . . .'

It was the first time she had spoken her husband's name.

John Allday walked carefully across the parlour floor, avoiding the parts recently waxed and polished. A plank creaked under his heavy tread and he glanced down at it. Something he could fix himself, play his part in running the inn. Belonging, being useful. Like the handsome inn sign, The Old Hyperion; it had been swinging in the fresh breeze from the Helford River, and it had squeaked with each move. A touch of grease would fix it. He had been in the yard, watching his friend Bryan Ferguson moor his plump little pony Poppy where she would be comfortable during his visit. Allday frowned. The visits had been getting fewer over the months; this was his first since young Captain Adam had set sail yet again, in a different ship, a third-rate no less, with a vice-admiral's flag above his head. As if he didn't have enough troubles . . .

He looked at his friend now, seated at one of the parlour tables, his head resting in his hand. Older, strained; it seemed to have happened so suddenly. Allday tried not to think of it too often. They *were* older. Thirty-five years ago they had been pressed together and put aboard the frigate *Phalarope* and taken off to war. Their captain had been Richard Bolitho. In Cornwall it was almost a legend. Ferguson had lost an arm at the Saintes, and had returned to Falmouth a sick man. His wife Grace had done everything to restore him, to give him back his confidence and his health, and he had become steward of the Bolitho estate, with the same Richard Bolitho who was to become a Knight of the Bath, and an admiral of England. *And I was his coxswain. And his friend.* He had called them and a few others 'my little crew'. And now he was gone, with all those other misty faces.

He put down two glasses and said, 'Have your wet, Bryan, an' tell me all the news. You're becoming a stranger here.'

Bryan looked up at him.

'Sorry, old friend. I'm getting past it. Time moves at a faster pace these days.'

Allday grinned, and said, 'Bilge! The whole estate would fall apart without you.' He winked. 'An' your Grace, o' course! All them good meals, a soft bed an' servants to wait on you hand an' foot – you should be on top o' the world.'

He sat down and looked around the parlour, the home Unis had made for them and their daughter Katie. The old life would never leave him, nor his desire for it, but he was grateful, and it troubled him to see his friend so dispirited.

Ferguson said, 'It used to be simpler . . . when *he* was alive. Now there are so many things . . . Grace does more than enough, and always has, as you well know, but there's no hand on the helm, too many outsiders to deal with . . .' He listed them on his fingertips. 'The tenants always need something, and the land does not bring in the returns it should. The new road won't help, not us anyway. Sheep to be moved, new walls to be built when the slate can be quarried. It takes me ten times as long to get around the estate and see every one.' He seemed to hesitate. 'I'm too old for it, and that's all there is to it.'

Allday took a swallow of rum to give himself time. The estate, but more importantly the Bolitho house, had always been there. One Bolitho after another, every kind of ship and campaign you could think of. You didn't question it; it was a part of their lives. Allday considered it. He lived with Unis here, in the little village of Fallowfield on the Helford River, not in Falmouth at all. But his heart was still there. *The Admiral's coxswain.*

He tried again. 'What about Dan Yovell? He was helping with the books, an' that. When he came ashore he said it was for the last time.'

Ferguson smiled sadly.

'What *you* once said, old friend, remember?'

Allday slammed down the glass. 'That was different. I was *somebody* in them days, an' that's no error!'

Ferguson reached for his own glass, as if he had only just seen it.

'The times we've had together, old friend.' He drank slowly.

There were voices in the adjoining Long Room, as it was known. Two salesmen had spent most of the morning in there. Ale, cognac, and some of Unis's beef. Money to burn. He did not need to look at the clock. Some of the workers from the road would be arriving soon. They could eat like horses, but their money was good, as Unis had often reminded him.

Dear Unis, so small and pretty; some of the customers got too stroppy when they had a few tankards of ale under their belts, and they thought it entitled them to take liberties with her.

He sighed. They only tried it once with Unis.

He said, 'Young Cap'n Adam will be well on his way to the Indies by this time, eh, Bryan? Brings it back when I think on it. Not the same for him, with a vice-admiral breathing down his neck, I'll wager!' He heard Unis's voice outside. He had not even noticed the sound of the carrier's cart coming into the yard. Unis had been into the market; he frowned; he could not recall what for. Then he swung round and exclaimed, 'You're not *leaving*, man? You only just came alongside!'

Ferguson drained the last of his rum.

'I have some things to do. They won't wait. Give my warmest regards to your dear Unis. She will understand. It's just that they won't wait.'

He hurried to the door and dragged it open as Allday

had seen him do so many times, swinging it to avoid catching his empty sleeve.

Unis came into the parlour, the child Katie pulling behind her with a huge basket she could barely carry. She liked to be a part of everything.

Unis put a parcel down on the table and said, 'That was Bryan, was it? Did he leave because of me?'

The child called, 'Uncle Bryan – where is he?' She always called him that.

Allday held Unis with one hand on either shoulder. As if he was afraid of breaking her, as she had sometimes told him.

'He had to get back. I think he's doing too much.'

She brushed some hair from her forehead and walked to the other door.

'The road workers will be here any minute.' She was dragging on her apron. 'Is the food ready? I asked if Nessa would see to that bread. And another thing . . .' She turned. 'What is it, John? I wasn't thinking . . .'

Dick, the local carter, came into the parlour, his arms full of parcels and a sack of turnips.

He grinned. 'You good folk talking about Mr Ferguson? He's not gone far – I think his pony has stopped for a quick nibble!'

Little Katie shouted, 'Uncle Bryan! I'm going to see him!'

Unis smiled. 'Forgotten something, I expect.'

Allday barely heard her. Poppy the little pony was always greedy, and Bryan often remarked on it.

He said, 'Stay here,' and it was as if he had uttered

some terrible oath. The carter had dropped one of the parcels on the floor, and the child was staring at him with disbelief, as if she was about to burst into tears.

Only Unis was calm, too calm.

'What is it, John? Tell me.'

Allday looked at her and repeated, 'Stay here,' then, 'Please.'

She nodded, all else unimportant. She had seen his face, his hand as it moved to his chest and the terrible wound from the Spanish blade.

The door closed and she walked numbly to the window. *All as normal*.

The two salesmen were about to leave, a group of road workers by the pump, one dousing his bare arms in water.

Ferguson's little trap was standing out on the road, the pony munching long grass by the stile. All as normal.

She saw Allday, her John, her man, walk slowly up to the little trap and stare into it. She did not hear him call out, but two of the road workers had run to his side, looking around as if uncertain what to do. Allday was not supposed to lift anything heavy because of the wound, although it was often pointless to try and prevent him.

She wanted to cry out, to run to him, but could not move.

The big, shambling figure, whose scarred hands could create delicate and finely detailed ship models, like the one of *Hyperion*, here in the parlour. The ship which had taken one husband from her, and given her another. The man she loved beyond anything had stooped over the little trap, and was lifting Bryan Ferguson with such care that he could have been quite alone.

She heard herself say quietly, 'Fetch my brother. Bryan Ferguson is dead.' She looked at the two empty glasses. 'We must send word to the house at once.' She thought of Grace Ferguson, but then she touched one of the glasses and murmured only, 'Poor John.'

Lowenna paused on the staircase where it turned to the right, and led to the landing and the main bedrooms which she knew instinctively faced the sea. She wondered what had made her hesitate, when Nancy had insisted that she should feel welcome here.

She rested her spine against the rail and looked at the portrait opposite her. A dark painting, partly because it hung in shadow, but also because of its age. Sir Gregory Montagu had taught her much in his almost off-hand fashion. Only the main subject stood out, a telescope cradled in one arm, a ship or ships burning in the background. Nancy had told her that it was Rear-Admiral Denziel Bolitho, the only one of the family to have reached flag rank until Sir Richard, with Wolfe at Quebec. She almost touched it: the sword he was wearing was the same one she had seen in other portraits in the stairwell, the same sword she had helped fasten to Adam's belt before he had left her. On that day . . .

She had been in other houses, larger and grander

than this. Montagu's residence in London, sealed by his lawyers after his death, was one of them.

She turned and looked down at the entrance hall, the cut flowers, and the most recent portrait by the tall window: Adam with his yellow rose. But none with such a sense of belonging, and the weight of history. Now the house was completely still, listening, holding its breath.

She had walked through the stable yard, the horses tossing their heads as she passed.

Nancy had said, 'If you need anything, the cook can help you.'

She had only met Bryan Ferguson twice, perhaps three times. A quiet, serious face. He had made her feel welcome, not a stranger.

She had seen his wife Grace before she had left here for the funeral. It would be over by now, or very soon, and life would return to this old house and the surrounding countryside.

She stroked the banister with her palm. What made this house so different from all those she had known or visited?

She had heard that Bryan Ferguson had no children; he and Grace had lived and served this house and all those who depended upon it. *They* were the family.

And now more responsibility would rest upon Nancy. Ever since they had returned from the Old Glebe House and received the news of Ferguson's sudden death, she had not stopped. Now she was at the funeral, separate, but very much a part of it and the world they all shared.

Like this house. The same family, six generations, and now in the stillness she could imagine any one of those faces alive, perhaps on this staircase, or down in the study with its well-worn books and old carvings. And Adam. She glanced up into the shadows. Would he ever leave the sea? When would they be together again? Lie together?

'Is some one looking after you?'

Lowenna turned and saw the other woman halfway up the stairs. She had seen her only once before, at a distance, pointed out by Nancy: the girl Elizabeth's governess, Beatrix Tresidder. She could even recall her brief description. Her father was a clergyman over Redruth way, Nancy had said, a poor parish, barely earning his keep. She was educated, and had been glad of the opportunity to put it to good use.

Lowenna looked down at her, dressed all in grey, her hair tied back severely with a black ribbon. Her own age, perhaps a year older or younger, it was hard to tell.

She said, 'Nancy said I should wait here,' and was surprised that she should feel almost guilty. 'You are Elizabeth's governess.'

'I do recall now – Lady Roxby mentioned it to me. But I've had so much to do over the last few days . . . Miss Elizabeth is with me.'

'She did not go with Nancy?'

'She was upset. It is her birthday tomorrow.'

'I know.' She came to a decision. 'May I call you Beatrix? We shall know each other faster and better if so,' and smiled. 'My name is Lowenna.'

'Well, as you say.' She seemed taken off guard. 'Shall you be staying long? I understood that you might be returning to London.'

Lowenna descended, knowing the other woman was watching every move. She had blue eyes, like the sea, and clear, pale skin; she could have been pretty if she had allowed herself to be. A defence, a barrier; perhaps she saw her as an intruder, like others she would have to meet if she remained here. She clenched her fist behind her back. *Where my heart wants to be.*

Beatrix said, 'Is there anything I can show you? I come here quite often; Miss Elizabeth likes to visit. It was her father's house after all. She has the right.'

They had reached the study, and Lowenna paused as she looked at the portrait again. The elusive smile. The young boy looking out, as Nancy had described it, and that she would know better than any one.

'Of course, you were employed by the late Sir Gregory Montagu, when he painted this portrait of Captain Bolitho?'

'We worked together, yes. I was his ward.' She stifled her sudden resentment, anger, at the remark. The hostility. *No smoke without fire.* She should be used to it. Ought to have outgrown it. 'He was a fine man. He saved my life. I shall never forget what he did for me.'

Beatrix nodded slowly, as if in thought. 'I understand. I was so thankful to be given this appointment. My father was glad for me, too.' Only for an instant, her eyes clouded. 'He could have been here in Falmouth today, with a good living, receiving the respect he deserves.' The outspoken resentment was gone as quickly as it had ignited. 'Just rewards do not always go to those who have earned them.'

Lowenna allowed her muscles to relax, very slowly. Like finding and holding a pose while the initial sketches took shape.

She said, 'Did you know Elizabeth's mother?'

'Of her. A fine woman too, to all accounts. Killed when she was thrown from a horse. I have tried to shield the child from that, and other memories and implications.'

There were sounds in the yard, a carriage, dogs barking. Nancy was back. They would leave here soon.

Her nails were biting into her palm; she had clenched her fist without realizing it.

I walked here with Adam. I was a part of it. Of him.

The doors were open; a breeze moved a bell-pull by the great fireplace, as if some phantom hand had called for attention.

Elizabeth walked across the polished floor, the sound of her riding boots sharp and clear.

She said, 'I am going for a ride, now that they're all coming back.' She looked directly at the tall, dark-haired girl with her governess. 'Will you go with me?'

'I don't ride, I'm afraid.' Lowenna could feel the other woman watching her, judging her. 'Perhaps I will learn some day.'

Elizabeth smiled, for the first time since she had come in.

Lowenna had seen the entry of her birth in the Bible in the study. Tomorrow she would be fifteen years old.

Had nobody else noticed it? She was no longer a child, but a young woman.

Beatrix said quickly, 'I think we should speak with Lady Roxby first, my dear!'

Elizabeth ignored her, and said, 'I can teach you, Lowenna.' Her smile broadened. 'It is a nice name. I shall soon show you the rules.' She glanced at her tutor. 'Easy!'

Beatrix persisted, 'I think we should wait until Lady Roxby . . .'

'I'm not having my birthday spoiled because of the funeral, miss! I am a Bolitho – I will not be treated like some of those people out there!'

Nancy walked up the steps, and said, 'Enough of that, *Miss* Elizabeth. I'll not have any showing off, today of all days.'

Lowenna could not see her expression, as the sunlight was streaming in behind her. But there was no mistaking her tone, and she was suddenly sorry for her. Her children, grown up long since and in London, and nobody to make the decisions but herself. And she owned one of the largest estates in the county.

She stood in the sunlight, her face quite composed.

'Furthermore, my child, I'm glad you remembered that you *are* a Bolitho. Now try to behave like one!'

She turned to Lowenna, seeing what many would miss. 'Hard, was it?' She slipped her hand through Lowenna's arm. 'The others will be here presently. I want you to stay.'

Lowenna thought of the stares and the unspoken comments.

'You mean it, don't you.' She felt the pressure of the hand again. 'Then I shall stay.'

Nancy turned her easily toward the newest portrait again, her grip surprisingly strong.

'I know love when I see it, Lowenna. Cherish it, and this sweet sorrow will soon pass.'

They were all arriving now, Daniel Yovell, his round shoulders stooped, his gold spectacles perched on top of his head. Young Matthew, the coachman, unsmiling, shocked by the death of his friend. Servants, estate workers somehow unfamiliar in their best clothes, and old Jeb Trinnick, his one eye averted to avoid unnecessary conversation. Nancy introduced her to only a few. The rest could draw their own conclusions.

And there was one who stood out, big, broad, and shaggy-haired. Nancy introduced him quietly as John Allday, Sir Richard's friend and seagoing companion. She remembered seeing him the day Adam had been recalled to duty.

Allday took her hand; it seemed to disappear into his powerful grip, and she felt defenceless under his steady gaze.

'I served with young Cap'n Adam as well, Missy, when he was just a lad. I heard about you an' him, o' course.' He touched her cheek momentarily with his free hand, and she could feel the strength of the man, and something deeper. She shivered as if she stood in a chill wind, but she remained very still, her hand in his, her skin alive to the roughness and the gentleness, and the years which had left this man so loyal.

She heard herself ask softly, 'How is it, John Allday? Do I measure up?'

For a moment she imagined he had not heard, or that he would resent her directness.

Then he nodded very slowly. 'If I was a much younger fellow, Cap'n Adam wouldn't get a chance in hell, Missy!' Then the grin came through, as if he had no control over it. 'As it is, I'd say you'll be flying with the wind afore you knows it! An' that's no error, neither!'

He looked at the open doors. 'Old Bryan said as much, bless 'im. An' he was right.'

She kissed his cheek, and said, 'And bless you, too.'

She knew that Nancy was smiling, saying something unheard, and that conversation had broken out again on every side.

And here was Grace Ferguson, very straight, her emotion contained, perhaps until she was alone and realized that it would be forever.

She did not resist when Lowenna hugged her, and said steadily, 'John speaks the truth and always did. You'll be right for young Captain Adam. After this, you come back to us. You belong here, and that's all about it.' She returned the embrace, suddenly unable to go on. 'You take care, y' hear?'

Nancy had called it sweet sorrow. It was far more than that.

It was nearly dawn when, in a strange bed, Lowenna finally fell asleep.

Perhaps then, in fantasy, he would come again to her.

217

10

Chasing Shadows

Adam Bolitho moved his shoulders very slightly and
winced as the heat seared his skin, as though he were
naked, or his coat had been hanging on the door of a
furnace. He had been on deck since first light, when
the sun had found them and pinned the ship down as
if motionless. It was now almost noon and he felt he
had scarcely moved from his place by the quarterdeck
rail, watching the land, which never seemed to draw
any nearer.

A landfall was always exciting, to landman and old
Jack alike. Few sailors ever questioned how or why
it was achieved, or even the reason for arriving in a
different place or harbour.

Adam glanced up at the topsails, barely filling with
wind, and flattened occasionally against stays and yards,
the flags all but unmoving. English Harbour, Antigua,
was the most important headquarters for the fleet which
served the Caribbean far beyond these Leeward Islands,

a fine, sheltered harbour with a dockyard which could accommodate even the larger men-of-war like *Athena*.

Adam shaded his eyes and studied the white buildings beneath the shadow of Monk's Hill, all shimmering in a heat haze, and small local craft, like insects on the milky blue water.

June was almost gone, and this was now the hurricane season: old Caribbean hands would know it well. Becalmed one minute and then caught in a roaring gale, with waves which could swamp any lesser vessels or run them ashore.

Both of *Athena*'s cutters were in the water, one on either bow, ready to take their parent ship under tow, if only to maintain steerage way should the wind desert them altogether. As it was, she was scarcely moving.

Adam plucked at his shirt. Like another skin. A good landfall, nevertheless.

He saw the officer in the starboard cutter stand to peer at the land as it moved out on either beam. It was Tarrant, the third lieutenant. Stirling had detailed him for the task, just in case something had gone amiss on their final approach. He had put an experienced leadsman in the chains for the same reason. *Athena* might be taken by a freak wind where she was denied the room to manoeuvre or change tack. It would not look well if Bethune's flagship ran into shallow water within sight of the anchorage.

Stirling had even checked each flag before dawn had opened up the horizon, fresh and clean to replace the ones worn by weather which they had hoisted the first day out of Plymouth.

Details, great or small, made up the first lieutenant's life. Caution, perhaps, was his true strength.

Adam said, 'My respects to Sir Graham, and please inform him that we are about to begin the salute.'

He heard the midshipman mumble something and rush away to the ladder, and imagined Troubridge bearing the news to his lord and master. He studied the land again and saw tiny, blinking lights on the foreshore and near some of the buildings, like fireflies braving the harsh glare: sunlight reflected from a dozen or more telescopes. *Athena*'s arrival would not be unexpected, but her timing would cause some confusion. He thought of the courier brig *Celeste*, which had blown to pieces, and her sole survivor, the acting sailing master named Rose, who had come from Hull. They had buried him at sea. Adam had never known *Athena* so quiet; every man in her company had been present. On gangways and in the shrouds, shoulder to shoulder on the main deck. Perhaps the closest in spirit they had yet been.

Celeste would have been carrying all the details of Bethune's arrival, both for the governor and the commodore in charge.

Adam touched the rail, like heated shot, his mind lingering on the burial. He wondered why he had never become used to it. Hardened. He had seen plenty of them, and as captain had committed more men to the deep than he could name or remember. But he was always moved by it, by the sense of community. *Of one company*.

'Ready, sir!'

He came out of his thoughts, irritated at being caught unaware. All the forenoon they had been creeping toward this mark on Fraser's chart, and when he should be at his most alert he had allowed his mind to drift. He had been sleeping badly, or not at all.

He saw Sam Petch, the gunner, staring up at him, his eyes slits against the relentless sunshine.

Another voice murmured, 'Sir Graham's comin' up, sir!'

Adam turned and touched his hat.

Bethune looked around casually. 'Nothing changes, does it?' He walked to the opposite side of the deck. 'Carry on, then, Captain Bolitho.' It sounded like, *if you must*.

Adam turned his back and gestured to the patient gunner.

The bang of the first shot sounded like a clap of thunder in the broad harbour. Gulls and other birds rose screaming and flapping across the smooth water, the smoke hanging almost motionless below the gangway. He pictured the people ashore seeing this ship, his ship, probably wondering what had brought her to Antigua. Trouble with slavers, pirates . . . Perhaps war had broken out again and this was the first they would know of it. Or, more likely, they would regard her with more than a touch of warmth, even sadness. *A ship from England*. England . . . for some of them it would seem almost an alien land by now. For some . . .

Petch walked slowly along the deck, measuring the interval between each shot in the salute, pausing briefly inboard of each gun. 'Number Three gun, *fire!*' and doubtless muttering to himself the old trick of timing of his trade. *If I wasn't a gunner I wouldn't be here.* 'Number Four gun, *fire!*' *If I wasn't a gunner I wouldn't be here.* 'Number Five gun, *fire!*'

Each shot echoed across and back over the placid water, so that it was almost impossible to distinguish the salute from the response of the battery ashore.

Adam thought again of the *Celeste*. Bethune had made a point of reading his report of the unprovoked attack on the brig, and had remarked, 'You must emphasize that every effort was made to intercept the vessel described by the one survivor. We had only his word for the description.'

Adam remembered the man's hard grip on his hand, his mute stare as he died. His last words, most of all. *Tell 'em how it was.*

He had left the log entry unchanged, and wondered why Bethune had not mentioned it.

He was here now, beside him, composed and apparently untroubled by the heat and the blinding reflections from the harbour.

'Not much of a show of force here today, eh, Adam? Three frigates all told, I am informed. And a whole collection of smaller vessels. Well, we'll soon change things.' His tone hardened slightly. 'Or I shall know the reason!'

He walked toward the ladder, dismissing it from his mind. 'I shall want the gig as soon as we're anchored.' He glanced around the figures on the quarterdeck. 'Your fellow – Jago, isn't it?' He did not wait for a reply.

Adam saw Stirling watching him. 'We will anchor directly. Recall the boats but hold them alongside. We can rig winds'ls as soon as the ship is secure.' Stirling looked as if he were about to protest. 'It will be foul enough between decks in this heat, Mr Stirling. Our people need some air to breathe in.' He smiled, but the barrier remained, like a breakwater.

Stirling strode away, his heavy voice dropping orders and calling names as he went.

Adam saw the various groups of seamen and marines, waiting, as if *Athena* herself would decide the time and place to drop anchor.

The starboard anchor was already swaying gently at its cathead, ready to fall, the forecastle party appearing to watch a loitering guardboat, but more likely their eyes were on the land. Different colours and smells, new faces, not those you were forced to look at every day and throughout each watch. And women, too.

Adam tried to imagine it as it must have been for his uncle when he had anchored here in the old *Hyperion*. Like this ship, she had worn a vice-admiral's flag. Sir Richard's own.

When he had met Catherine again, after losing her. It must have looked very much the same then, that year before Trafalgar . . . How could it be so long ago?

'*Standing by, sir!*'

Adam glanced up at the loosely flapping topsails, and right forward to the jib sails with Lieutenant Barclay's anchor party waiting, looking aft at their captain.

He thought, too, of his uncle's medal, for his part in the Battle of the Nile. Catherine had sent it to him, given it to him, perhaps because it reminded her too much of the man she had loved, and had lost forever.

He looked over at the nearest helmsman, the one with the strange tattoo. Never look back, they always said. That was the oddest part. When he thought of all the faces he had known so well in *Unrivalled*, most of them had already lost substance, except for the few. They would never leave him.

He stared up through the shrouds and beyond the maintop to the curling pendant.

'Hands wear ship, Mr Stirling.'

Calls trilled and bare feet pounded across the hot planking and the melting tar of the deck seams. The helm was going over, spokes creaking, the seaman with the tattoo very aware of his captain only a few feet away. Who wanted for nothing . . .

Landfall. If only she were here to greet me.

The sun moved across his face, then his shoulder. '*Let go!*'

Boats were putting off from the shore now, visitors, sightseers, traders; it was all beginning.

Adam nodded to the sailing master and walked aft toward the poop. For a moment longer he paused and stared at and beyond the headland. But there was no horizon. Sea and sky were merged in bright blue haze.

England seemed a very long way astern.

Jago brought the gig smartly alongside the jetty's worn stone stairs and watched the bowman leap ashore to fend off and make the boat fast. Not too bad a gig's crew, although he would never say as much. Not yet, anyway.

There were soldiers on the jetty, and a tall major waiting to greet the vice-admiral and his aide. Behind the soldiers and some kind of barrier he could see crowds of people, all eager to greet the newcomers. Like any port, when you thought about it.

The midshipman, Mister bloody Vincent, was on his feet, bobbing and raising his hat while the admiral and flag lieutenant stepped ashore. Jago heard Bethune say, 'The boat can remain here. This shouldn't take too long.'

Jago scowled. The captain never told him what to do. He trusted him. No good officer would leave a boat's crew sitting here in the heat, sweating it out, while he downed a few wets with the governor or whoever it was.

The major saluted, and Bethune shook his hand, putting him at his ease. Jago swore under his breath. *Never volunteer*. It was too late now.

He swung round, surprised that he had forgotten the other passenger, the admiral's servant, Tolan. One who caught your attention, made you wonder. Sharp, and always in control of things. Jago had tried to yarn with him but had got nowhere. Bowles had said as much himself, and *he* could talk the hind leg off a mule if he wanted to.

'Going on an errand, eh?'

Tolan stepped over the gunwale on to the worn stones. He gave Jago a brief, piercing look.

'You might say as much, yes.'

Vincent snapped, 'No gossiping in the boat, there!'

Jago contained his anger, and across the midshipman's shoulder saw the stroke oarsman mouth an unspoken obscenity. It helped.

Tolan reached the top of the stairs and turned to look down at the moored gig; it gave him time to settle his nerves. He could not fathom what had got into him lately, suspicious of the most innocent remark, ever since the incident with the marine's musket. *So face up to it. It's all over and behind you now.* And he liked the captain's coxswain, what he had seen of him and had heard others say. Tough, competent, reliable. A man with a past; he had seen the savage scars on his back when he had been washing himself under a pump. No wonder he hated officers . . . except, apparently, the captain.

Some children ran up to him, hands out, all eyes and teeth. The same anywhere, he thought. He ignored them. One sign of weakness and you brought an avalanche down on your head.

In the shade of the first buildings, it seemed almost cool after the harbour and the open boat. He looked around as he walked; it had not changed much, although there were fewer ships and sailors than the last time he had been in Antigua. In the frigate *Skirmisher*, Bethune's final command before his promotion to flag rank. A lot of water since then.

A woman carrying a basket of fresh fish walked past him. Tall, dark-skinned, a half-caste of some sort. Probably born of a slave mother. Some traders and planters had the right idea, he thought. Better to breed slaves than run the risk of being caught smuggling them from the other side of the ocean.

He looked at the last house, painted white like the others, a short flight of steps leading up to a balcony which faced the harbour.

He took out the letter from his immaculate coat and studied it for a few seconds. Bethune was a powerful man, and a good one to serve. He had watched him over the years, taking on more authority, and using it without obvious strain or effort. But sometimes he left his guard down, wide open to enemies, and at the Admiralty there would be plenty of those. He knew about Catherine Somervell, had even seen them meet in the park, only a short ride from that elegant office. Beautiful, she was. Hard to accept that she had once been the toast of the country, Sir Richard Bolitho's mistress. People had short memories, when it suited them. He had seen the vicious cartoon of her in a well-known news sheet. After Sir Richard's death in action she had been depicted nude, staring out at ships of the fleet, eyes open for the next to share her bed. He could recall Bethune's fury and dismay, as if it were yesterday.

But mail took a long time to travel. Diverted, lost at sea; there were a thousand reasons. Or, like the brig *Celeste*, sunk by an unknown enemy. It was not the first letter he had carried for him, but maybe this time he had made a mistake.

He climbed the steps and felt the sun on his face again as he reached the balcony. He saw a telescope mounted on a tripod, an open fan lying on a cane chair. Sir Graham had not made a mistake after all.

She was standing inside an open doorway, her hair hanging down on her shoulders, as if it had just been brushed. Dressed in an ivory gown, her throat and arms bare, she showed no surprise, no emotion at all.

She said, 'I remember you. Mr Tolan, is it not?'

Exactly as he remembered her. Poised, striking, and something more. She led the way into a long room, shutters lowered against the glare, a ceiling fan swaying soundlessly from side to side adding to the feeling of seclusion. She gestured to the telescope.

'I saw the ship come in. I never grow tired of watching them come to anchor.' She looked directly at the letter in his hand. 'From Sir Graham, I trust?'

Tolan's eyes flickered to the ceiling as the fan faltered for a few seconds, as if the unseen hand was listening.

'He asked me to deliver it to you, m' lady, no one else. In case it got mislaid.'

She did not move. 'I destroyed the others. Please return it to your master. I don't have the time . . .'

Tolan stood fast. *Like a drill*. He knew enough about women to see past her composure. She had been watching *Athena*'s slow approach, and had found time to prepare herself. To dress, and be ready. Perhaps she had expected Bethune to come in person. That could be dangerous, for both of them.

He said, 'He ordered me not to return to the ship without giving you the letter, m' lady.'

'And he must be obeyed, is that it?' She put her

228

hand to her side as if to straighten her gown. 'I am not at all sure that I . . .'

Another door creaked open and Tolan felt every muscle stiffen. But it was a young girl, a servant, half Spanish at a guess.

He felt his breathing steady again. For a second he had imagined it would be a man, the protector he had heard some one mention.

She said, 'Later, Marquita. I shall not be long.' When she looked at him again she was different; the confidence was fading.

'You may leave it if you wish. But I do not promise to read it.' She relented immediately. 'That was unfair of me. It is not your place to intercede. Like a second in a duel!'

Tolan knew she was thinking of the clump of dead trees in the park, where so many duels had been fought, mostly by officers from the garrison nearby. Over money, or an insult, or because of a woman. Like this one.

She asked abruptly, 'Are you married, Mr Tolan?'

He shook his head. 'I've not been so fortunate, m' lady.'

She reached out and took the letter from his hand. Just the faintest hesitation, perhaps doubt, her fingers brushing his. 'Maybe it is not too late.' She smiled. 'For either of us.'

He turned to leave the room, and she said, 'A secret, then?'

He nodded, unusually moved. 'Safe with me, m' lady.'

Tolan had reached the bottom of the steps when it struck him. She had not even mentioned *Athena*'s captain, who bore the same name as her famous lover.

He looked up, but she had vanished. Maybe it was all in the letter.

He strode along the narrow street. She would not burn it. Nor had she destroyed the others.

A woman you would die for, or spill another man's blood. And she had treated him with respect, had called him 'mister', not like most of the others who looked right through you.

There was still a little crowd of people loitering above the jetty where the gig's crew wilted in the heat, watching the comings and goings of the many harbour craft around the anchored two-decker.

Tolan paused by the wall, thinking of the girl he had seen earlier with her basket of fish, the beautiful way she had walked. He was not required on board the ship until dusk, when Bethune was receiving guests.

He remembered a house he had once visited when he had been here before. Like escaping, being himself, without a false identity and the fear of being trapped by some careless remark or deed.

A woman like that would give far more than her body.

He turned as a group of soldiers walked past him. A couple of them glanced at his uniform, uncertain of his rank or status, and one of them, a burly, deeply tanned corporal, gave him a nod and a grin.

Tolan could scarcely breathe, and leaned against

the sun-baked wall, his mind reeling while he listened to the soldiers' boots until they were lost in the noise and movement of English Harbour.

It was not possible. Like the nightmare he had tried to forget. He had seen the polished helmet plates, the familiar Lamb and Star of the Seventieth Foot, known as the Surreys. His old regiment.

He was not free at all.

Commodore Sir Baldwin Swinburne, senior officer of the Leeward and Windward Islands, took a glass from the profferred tray and held it up against the light of the nearest lantern. His forehead was set in a crease which faded as he took a slow sip.

'An excellent Madeira, Sir Graham. It has a ready tongue indeed.' He smiled, and watched Tolan refill his glass. 'But then, you always did have the taste for a good wine!'

Adam Bolitho stood by the stern windows, apart from the commodore and the elegant vice-admiral. Swinburne was heavily built, even portly, with a face which was hard to imagine young. Troubridge had told him that Bethune and the commodore had been lieutenants together somewhere along the road to promotion. That was even harder to believe; but Troubridge was never wrong in such matters. Considering he had been Bethune's flag lieutenant for such a short time, he had certainly discovered a great deal about his superior.

Bethune had returned on board in a bad mood. The governor had not been there to receive him. An official had explained that he had been forced to keep an appointment with his opposite number in Jamaica. The despatch confirming the flagship's estimated time of arrival in Antigua must have been destroyed with the ill-fated *Celeste*, or was now in some one else's hands. Bethune obviously believed it was the latter.

Adam watched the cabin servants moving silently in the shadows, and was careful not to leave his own glass unguarded where it might be refilled without his noticing. Bethune was equally abstemious. He and Swinburne were probably the same age. That explained a lot.

Bethune was saying, 'Three frigates, and one of them laid up in overhaul, is simply not good enough. I want every patrol area covered, even if local craft have to be temporarily commissioned into the King's service. I am told that we will never destroy the slave trade – well, I intend to prove otherwise. It is ten years since Britain passed the Abolition Act, and made the slave trade a crime. Other nations have followed, albeit reluctantly. Our new *ally*, Spain, for instance, has prohibited it, but has left a gap in the net by insisting that the trade is only to be banned north of the Equator. And Portugal is the same.'

Adam watched him with new interest. This was a different side to Bethune, fully informed, and almost passionately concerned with every detail. All those hours, days, sealed up in this big cabin had armed him well. Swinburne looked surprised and off balance; uneasy, too.

Bethune paused to sip his wine. 'And where are

the biggest slave markets today?' He put down the glass. 'Cuba and Brazil, under the flags and protection of those very same countries.'

Swinburne said, 'All our patrols are under the strictest orders, Sir Graham. They have caught several slavers, some empty, some not. The commanding officers are very well aware of the importance of vigilance.'

Bethune smiled. 'As well they might be. With some eight hundred and fifty captains on the Navy List at last count, each one would be well advised to remember his chance of survival, let alone promotion!'

Adam saw a boat pulling slowly past *Athena*'s quarter. He could see the phosphorescence trailing from the oars, like serpents keeping pace in the calm water.

He had read enough of the Admiralty reports to know the hopelessness of any attempt to wipe out slavery altogether. Swinburne had spoken of successful interception and seizure by the patrolling ships, but in fact not one in twenty of the slavers was ever captured. No wonder there were men hard and desperate enough to take the risk. A slave bought for less than twenty dollars in Africa would sell for three hundred and more in Cuba. And there had to be big money behind it. To build and equip larger and faster ships, to supply a ready market which was never closed. Regulations and Acts of Parliament were only pieces of paper to the faceless men behind the trade.

He wanted to pinch himself to stay alert. It was dark beyond the tall windows, with just the lights from the houses on the shore and the moored vessels nearby.

Almost as dark as when he had been called to go on deck, only this morning . . .

Bethune must have made some sort of signal. Tolan and the cabin servants had disappeared, and Troubridge was standing, framed against the screen door, like a sentinel.

Bethune said quietly, 'Lord Sillitoe is here, in the Indies. Baron Sillitoe of Chiswick. Why was I not told?'

Swinburne stared at him. As if he were hearing a foreign language.

'I had no instructions, Sir Graham! He is a man of influence, once the Prince Regent's Inspector General.'

Bethune did not hide the sarcasm. 'And his good friend, too, as I recall.'

Swinburne made another attempt. 'He is here to conduct enquiries, matters which concern his business, and the City of London.' He ended lamely, 'The governor left no instructions.'

Bethune said, 'He is a very dangerous man, and his father was the most successful slaver on record.'

Swinburne picked up his glass. It was empty. 'I know that Lady Somervell was with him. But I thought . . .'

Bethune actually smiled. 'You hold a good appointment here. Others might be envious. Think on it, eh?' He snapped his fingers. 'Now we can sup in peace.'

Troubridge had left the screen door and stood right aft by the stern windows.

'Your first lieutenant wishes to speak with you, sir.' He glanced at the servants, who were arranging chairs

234

again, lighting candles on the table. In the flickering light his young features looked suddenly grave, angry. 'And, *no*, sir. I did not know that Lady Somervell was here in Antigua.'

Adam looked past him. 'I shall not be a moment, Sir Graham.' But Bethune was lifting the silver cover from the dish and gave no sign of having heard him. He touched Troubridge's sleeve. 'Thank you for that.' He saw Tolan bringing more wine from the pantry. 'I thought I was the only one who didn't know!'

He found Stirling waiting by the companion ladder, his head bowed beneath the deckhead beams. There was probably ample room to stand upright, Adam thought; it was merely habit, born of a lifetime at sea in every class of ship.

'I am sorry to disturb you, sir.' His eyes glinted in the swaying watch light as he glanced at the white-painted screen, and the Royal Marine sentry at the door to the admiral's quarters. In the dim light, the scarlet uniform looked black.

Stirling lowered his voice.

'The sloop *Lotus* anchored an hour or so back, sir. Her commander is come aboard to report an action with a slaver.'

'Why so long?' It gave him time to mark down the sloop, like an entry in the log. She was one of the commodore's chain of patrolling vessels. But that was all.

'He went to the commodore's residence first. Said he knew nothing about *Athena*'s arrival here. All aback, he was.' He turned again as the sentry shifted his boots. 'I put him in the chart room and told him to wait.'

'You did right. I'll see him now.' He thought he heard a glass shatter beyond the screen, and somebody laugh. It sounded like Swinburne.

They climbed the companion ladder together, Stirling breathing heavily, but, Adam felt, glad to have shifted the responsibility so quickly.

On the quarterdeck the air was cool, clean, after the admiral's cabin. A few figures stood grouped by the starboard nettings. Beyond and below them Adam could see a boat, almost motionless, hooked on to the main chains.

Stirling paused outside the chart room, one large hand on the clip.

'His name is Pointer, sir. First command, apparently, six months on this station.'

'Thank you. That's a big help, believe me.'

'Sir?' He could feel Stirling peering at him through the darkness, as if he was expecting or searching for a trap.

It seemed unusually bright in the chart room after the quarterdeck and its silent watchkeepers.

Pointer, *Lotus*'s commander, was tall and thin with a narrow, bony face and clear, intelligent eyes. Still only a lieutenant, but already after so short a spell of command he carried an air of quiet authority.

Adam held out his hand, and saw a brief start of surprise.

'I'm Bolitho. I command here. Flag captain.'

Pointer grasped his hand firmly; the grip was bony,

too. 'Yes, sir, I just heard.' He looked at the unsmiling first lieutenant. 'And about Sir Graham Bethune. I have been out of contact with the commodore, you see. We did not know.'

Stirling said impatiently, 'The courier was blown up.'

Adam gestured to the rack of charts, all neatly folded, numbered and in order: knowing Dugald Fraser, they would be. Like his notes and personal log, even the gleaming dividers and rules were each in its place.

'Show me.'

Pointer opened a chart and flattened it on the table.

'Two weeks ago, it was, sir.' His forefinger touched the chart. 'I was in my usual patrol sector. I've had it since I commissioned *Lotus*, so I think I have the feel of it by now.' The finger moved. 'The sector runs from the Bahama Bank, westward to the Florida Straits. A regular run for slavers if they can slip past us.'

Adam sensed his pride, in what he was doing, more so perhaps in his command. He could easily picture the small ship, quite alone in that great span of islands and the countless channels that separated them. You could hide a fleet there, if the need arose.

Pointer said, 'We had been working the Straits for some time. The bigger slavers cross from Cuba to Florida to unload their cargoes before heading out into the Atlantic again. Some of them are large vessels, new and fast. They can often outrun our patrols.' The pride again. 'But not *Lotus*.'

Pointer had pulled a ragged pad from his coat. This he laid on the chart. There were scribbled calculations and compass bearings, but Adam's gaze settled on the date, June sixth, the day after they had sifted through *Celeste*'s pathetic remains and had found her only survivor.

He stared at the chart and the outline of Cuba, but for only a few seconds he saw Falmouth. June the sixth was his birthday, and it had completely slipped his mind.

Pointer had not noticed his expression. 'A big barque, she was, standing out of Havana, probably heading for Florida, under a full press of canvas. Sighted us and broke out the American flag, so I ordered her to heave to and await a boarding party.' He smiled and the strain showed itself for the first time. He was speaking to himself, reliving it. As if there was nobody else here.

'They often do that. The Yankees make such a huff-and-puff about any foreign officers trying to board one of their ships, and it often works, so the slaver gets clean away.' He peered at the charts again. 'So I ran out my guns and fired a couple of shots to warn him that I meant business.' He nodded slowly. 'I was ready for him. I'd heard about the heavy pieces some of those slavers carry. He went about and ran for the shore, back to Havana. He had the wind under his coattails and I could scarcely keep pace with him, the crafty bastard!' He stared at Adam, and but for his tanned skin might have blushed. 'I beg your pardon, sir!'

The door opened two inches. It was Troubridge. 'I'm sorry, sir, but Sir Graham has asked me . . .' He fell silent, as if he were gripped by the tension and could not proceed.

Pointer said, 'I followed him into the harbour, and I anchored *Lotus* and was boarded by an army of officials. I insisted that the barque was a slaver, and that under the Agreement I wanted to search her and confirm this. It is well known amongst our patrols that the Spanish captain-general in Havana is quite prepared to accept false papers and offer clearance to a ship's master, even if he is a known slaver. A lot of money must change hands in the process.'

'But you found nothing?'

He shrugged. 'I was treated with every courtesy, but I was not allowed to search the ship. The captain-general's aide was surprised that I should imagine that in a civilized city like Havana slaves could be landed and moved elsewhere without the authorities knowing. A day later I was allowed to put a party on board. They found nothing, and the flag was Spanish by that time. I can still hear the jeers and the curses as we weighed and put to sea.'

'Perhaps you were lucky. An "accident" might have been arranged for you and your *Lotus*.'

Together they walked from the chart room, and into the shadows. Pointer stopped momentarily and looked up into the darker patterns of shrouds and stays.

'If this ship had been there, they would have sung a different tune!' Yet he said it without bitterness, as if it was he who had failed in some way.

Almost as an afterthought, he dragged a canvas

envelope from his coat. 'My full report, sir.' The smile returned. 'Addressed to the commodore, of course.'

He was almost asleep on his feet. He must have driven his ship without a break, a passage of some fourteen hundred miles. Adam could still recall when he had commanded a vessel not very different in size and performance, in which her captain was always the last to go off watch.

Troubridge took the envelope. 'I'll tell Sir Graham, sir.' But he was regarding the bony lieutenant with barely disguised awe.

He was back in a few minutes, or so it seemed.

'Sir Graham's compliments, and would you return to your ship and remain ready to proceed to sea . . .' He faltered, sharing Pointer's exhaustion. 'Tomorrow, before sunset, as ordered by the Flag.'

Adam walked with him to the entry port where *Lotus*'s boat was already preparing to cast off.

'I am glad we met. I shall *see* you now when I hear the name of your command.'

They shook hands, and Pointer said, 'I remember when I was chasing a slaver, months ago, just before all the new rules had been agreed upon. I was almost up to him when he began pitching his slaves over the side. He did not have many left, but there were enough. The sharks were in a frenzy, and I shall never forget those last screams, and the silence.'

Adam touched his hat and watched him clamber down the side and into his boat.

He walked aft again, shadowy figures turning to watch him as he passed.

He could even feel the sentry's eyes beneath his leather hat as the door was opened for him.

Bethune sat at the table, Lieutenant Pointer's report carelessly spread across his knees.

He gestured with a knife. 'Didn't wait for you. Sir Baldwin must return to his headquarters. He has a lot to do because of this.' His tone hardened slightly. 'Some of it won't wait until tomorrow.'

Adam looked at the empty dishes and patches of spilled wine, like blood. He thought of *Unrivalled*, and the long patrols off the slave coasts of Africa. Freetown, and the bodies packed so tightly in the holds of captured ships that they could scarcely move or breathe. Human cargo. Like Pointer, he would never forget either.

The commodore came through the other door, Tolan and one of the servants at his elbows.

Bethune smiled, but did not stand up. 'Go with Sir Baldwin, will you, Flags? Explain to his duty officer what is required for tomorrow.'

Troubridge snatched up his hat and followed the swaying trio from the cabin.

Jago was already there, a bosun's chair rigged and ready for lowering the commodore into the gig alongside. He glanced sharply at Adam.

'You all right, Cap'n?'

Adam said only, 'When you get back aboard, lay aft to my cabin and have a wet with your captain.'

Jago bared his teeth, but did not smile. 'O' course, Cap'n, if the tackle was to run free while the commodore was bein' swayed outboard, I could be there all the faster!'

It had been a close thing. Adam gripped his arm.

'This is not what we have learned to accept, Luke, or been trained to fight. It's like chasing shadows.' He half turned as if to listen to the *Lotus*'s boat pulling away from the side. 'I almost envied that officer just now, at least for his freedom to act as he thinks fit!'

Jago relaxed slightly as the mood changed.

Adam stifled a yawn and grinned. '*Almost*.'

11

Trick for Trick

Lieutenant Roger Pointer, *Lotus*'s gangling commanding officer, swung away from the rail, his weariness
giving way to a broad grin as Bolitho, the flag captain,
appeared on deck. In the navy it was amazing how
quickly sailors could adapt, adjust to any kind of
change unexpectedly thrown upon them.

Like Vice-Admiral Bethune's order to be ready for
sea by sunset the day after his fast passage from
Havana, the jeers still ringing in his ears after being
refused permission to board the ship he knew to be a
slaver. Hardly enough time to take on fresh water and
to snatch a few casks of fresh fruit from the market.
And even then they had been ordered to weigh at
noon, not wait until sunset.

The other surprise had been the arrival on board of
Bethune's flag captain, his emissary to be carried to
meet Havana's captain-general, with a protest or warning Pointer was not sure. He had expected to feel

resentment, but common sense made him realize the value of Bethune's decision. He was still not certain how Bolitho felt about it.

They were three days out of English Harbour, with favourable winds making *Lotus* lift and plunge through the blue water like a thoroughbred.

He knew Bolitho's record and reputation almost as well as that of his famous uncle. *Athena*'s captain was now probably completely out of his element, but rank was rank and the navy had its own firm divisions in any ship, two-decker or lowly sloop.

It came as a surprise that Bolitho seemed prepared to accept the role of passenger, keeping his distance from the watch-by-watch affairs of the ship, but approachable in a manner Pointer had never expected or experienced before.

Adam walked to the weather side, feeling the sting of spray as it drifted aft from the forecastle, the elation of the lively hull, the din of canvas and rigging.

He had known full well what Pointer must have thought when Bethune's unexpected orders had been issued; he had suffered it himself when he had first taken command of the brig *Firefly*. After three full days at sea the barriers had dropped. There were still stares and surreptitious nudges when he took his daily walks on deck, but he understood the strength and the camaraderie of a small ship, and was heartened by the sudden willingness to talk, or speak of their lives and homes without it seeming an interrogation at a court-martial.

He could even feel a certain envy of Pointer and

his command. *Lotus* was like a smaller version of a frigate, well armed for her size, with sixteen twelve-pounders and a pair of carronades, and a total complement of one hundred and fifteen souls, including her captain. And no marines to mark the unseen boundary between quarterdeck and common seaman.

He shaded his eyes to stare abeam, at the faint, darker blur on the horizon. Haiti, a place always hated and avoided by sailors, even in their search for fresh water. Superstition, strange and cruel rituals . . . there was many a messdeck yarn to frighten new hands on their first passage. Even under French rule it had been bad enough, but since the slave rebellion and the retreat of the colonial army it had become even more dangerous.

Cuba was close by, and Adam wondered if the captain-general might see Haiti's change of ownership as a grim warning, a threat to himself and Spanish rule altogether.

Or perhaps, like Commodore Swinburne, he only wanted an uneventful existence in which to finish his career?

He looked inboard again. A small ship, one hundred and ten feet on the gun deck, not much more than four hundred tons. No wonder he had felt unsteady on his first morning at sea, after *Athena*'s massive timbers and heavy artillery.

He smiled to himself. It was different now, after only three days.

He called, 'Good morning, Roger. The wind is still an ally – it does you credit!'

Pointer touched his battered hat. He was still unprepared for it, no matter what he told himself. The youthful-looking figure, hatless, dark hair blowing 'all anyhow', as his boatswain had put it, open shirt, and a coat which had lost most of its true colour along the way: the admiral's trusted flag captain, perhaps poised for that next step up the ladder. *Like all the rest of us.*

He said, 'We should be off the Iguanas tomorrow forenoon, sir.' The grin returned. 'I'd not care to run through them in the dark!'

Adam nodded agreement, pushing the hair from his eyes. 'Then Cuba. A fast run indeed.' He saw the unspoken questions on Pointer's face. What it might mean for his ship, and for his reputation. 'I shall deliver Sir Graham's despatch as instructed, so that the captain-general or his representative is informed of the change in command.' He thought of the scattered wreckage and added bitterly, 'If he is not already aware of it.'

Pointer said, 'I have heard, unofficially, you understand, sir, that the captain-general always speaks through an interpreter.' He spread his big, bony hands. 'But that he speaks perfect English, when he chooses.'

Adam smiled. 'Well said, Roger. I have walked into *that* trap before.'

He recalled Bethune's last words to him before he had been pulled across to the *Lotus*.

'I have decided that you should represent me in this matter of negotiation, and our right to search suspect vessels. A show of force would be pointless, even if I had the ships to do it. I shall send for reinforcements

246

to increase the patrols. A few captures, some rich prizes, and we'll soon see a change of heart where the money lies.' Then, at the last minute, he had touched Adam's arm. 'Watch out for Sillitoe. I think he's desperate. So be on your guard.'

Adam had not seen Troubridge again before leaving the flagship. Deliberate? Or was he, too, under strict orders?

Pointer excused himself and walked away to deal with his first lieutenant, who had been hovering nearby.

Again he felt the stab of envy. Simply being in command, without obligation . . .

He saw Jago by the main hatch, turning to talk with one of *Lotus*'s petty officers. They were laughing, and Jago was thumping his back. Adam remembered that Jago had told him that one of the carpenter's crew had been celebrating the birth of his first baby. A girl. *No salt pork an' ship's biscuit for her!* He had not noticed the sudden shadow in his captain's eyes.

That first night at sea, getting the feel of it as Pointer had called it. The heaving motion, the boom and slap of canvas, the sluice of water alongside, seemingly inches from the swaying cot. Finding time to think, to reproach himself.

Suppose that one precious hour had ruined her life: if Lowenna found herself with child because of his inability to hold back, and shared the despair and shame of his own mother. She would be alone, and might be left with only hate in her breast, like the terrible memories she had been taught to overcome, if not forget. But Sir Gregory Montagu was dead. There was nobody else.

He had thought of the tablet in the old church, which he had insisted on erecting all those years after his mother's death.

In loving memory of Kerenza Pascoe, who died in 1793.

Waiting for his ship.

As he had lain in the cot, feeling the ship moving around and beneath him, he had stared into the darkness, seeing those last words in his mind.

He had eventually fallen asleep, the unspoken words still there.

It must never happen to you, Lowenna.

He came out of his thoughts, as if he had heard some one call his name. But it was Pointer again, his features tense. Making a decision. Or requiring one.

'Mr Ellis has reported that the masthead lookout is certain we are being held under observation. To the nor' east.' He saw the question in Adam's eyes. 'She'll know we're a man-of-war. No reason to keep her distance.'

Adam glanced at the dazzling sky. 'Good lookout, is he?'

Pointer bobbed his head, puzzled. 'My best, sir. He or one other – I always use them on this run.'

No landsman would ever understand that, Adam thought, but he had known such a seaman in *Unrivalled*. The weatherbeaten face and clear, bright eyes came back to him instantly. Even his voice, when Adam had climbed up to his dizzy, swaying perch to consult him after one such sighting. Sullivan: the name leaped out of memory, like the face. He had never been wrong.

He said, 'What do you think?' and saw Pointer relax slightly.

'If I come about to give chase we could lose him amongst the islands. We'll be in the main channel again soon, but not before dusk. Too risky then.' He watched him, frowning. 'Unless you think . . .'

'Leave him as he is, Roger. You spoke earlier of the Iguanas.' He saw the tired face lightening. 'Wait until first light.' He banged one hand into the other. 'We'll go for him then!'

'But your orders, sir?'

Adam knew the feeling. Beyond measure or control. Dangerous.

He replied, 'Our old enemy John Paul Jones had the answer, Roger. *He who will not risk, cannot win!*'

Jago had stopped by the mizzen shrouds. He had heard none of it, but he recognized the signs only too well.

It went against all his rules, but he was almost relieved.

'Ship cleared for action, sir. Galley fire doused.'

That was Ellis, the first lieutenant, clipped and formal. Adam could scarcely distinguish him from the other shadowed figures, moving to a familiar pattern. A strange feeling, as if he himself were invisible, or imagining it. The same drill he had seen and been a part of so many times.

It was uncanny in small ships; sailors could feel their way about, above or below deck in a way which no landsman would ever understand. They were in

249

complete darkness, with only the broken water surging back from the stem and marking their wake astern to betray their progress. *Lotus* leaned over, close-hauled on the starboard tack, swinging her jib boom like a pointer toward the invisible horizon, and the unknown ship. Adam could sense the tension around him. *If* the stranger was still there when first light found them. She might be an innocent merchantman, staying near a man-of-war for her own security and to ensure a safe passage. It was probably common enough in these disputed waters. How different from all those years, of open warfare, when a merchant captain would go out of his way to avoid a King's ship, fearful that she might board him and press some of his most experienced hands before he could find any means of protesting.

People were taking shape now, a face here, an arm or a fist gesturing to some one in the shrouds, and another shadow sliding silently down a backstay, feet soundless as they hit the deck.

The first lieutenant was with Pointer, speaking quietly, while the sailing master showed his teeth in the gloom as one of them said something that amused him. *Lotus* carried one other lieutenant; the rest of the ship's backbone was comprised of warrant officers. And a solitary midshipman. A small, close-knit company.

Adam thought of David Napier, somewhere at sea in the frigate *Audacity*. Would he be able to cope with the brutal humour usual in most ships?

He remembered the shy pleasure when he had

thanked him for his gift, the shining new midshipman's dirk. Like a bond. A talisman.

Jago must have been standing very close. He said, 'Masthead, sir.' Even he was whispering.

Adam looked up and realized he could see the reefed topsail, and high above it the long pendant, red and white, streaming in the wind, somewhere above all the darkness, holding the frail light as if it were free and unattached.

Pointer was saying, 'There may be nothing in it. But we shall load all guns in good time.' Nobody spoke, as if he were talking to himself. Or to *Lotus*.

Adam heard the boatswain calling out names, telling some one to *shift yerself, like an old woman this morning!* Then another sound, and he remembered that most sloops carried sweeps, long oars which could be run outboard and manned by all spare hands to give the vessel steerage way if they were suddenly becalmed. They could give her one or two knots in a dead calm. Enough to save her in an emergency.

There was a small oar-port beside each gun, and Adam recalled the galleys they had fought at Algiers. He realized he was touching his side, the wound which she had tended when he had been thrown from his horse. Which she had kissed in that last embrace.

Pointer was beside him. 'The sweeps might help if I need to cross her stern.' He walked away again. He was obviously in little doubt of today's outcome.

Lotus's only midshipman hurried aft, his white collar patches very clear against the sea's dark backdrop.

He held out a telescope, and said, 'First lieutenant's respects, sir.'

Adam could feel the youth staring at him. It would probably go in his next letter home. Midshipmen wrote notoriously long letters, never knowing when they would be collected by some passing courier, or indeed if they would ever be finished.

He said quietly, 'When will you stand for lieutenant? Soon, I trust?'

He heard the quick intake of breath. *Today the admiral's flag captain spoke to me.*

'Two years, sir, perhaps less.' He turned his head this way and that, and faltered, 'But I don't want to leave this ship.'

Adam put his hand on his arm and felt him jump. 'I know the feeling. But look ahead. When the chance comes, *grasp* it!'

He saw the midshipman's eyes gleam in the growing light as he looked up as if to see the invisible lookout.

'Deck there! Sail, fine on th' starboard bow!'

Pointer exclaimed, 'Still there, same course, by God!' He swung round, his voice sharper now. 'More sail, Mr Ellis – get the t' gallants on her if she'll wear it!'

Calls shrilled, and figures scampered to halliards and braces while topmen like scurrying monkeys dashed up the ratlines, faintly visible at last as the first yellow edge ran along and over the horizon.

The lookout's voice again, rising without effort above the banging canvas and squealing blocks.

'Deck there! She's a barque!'

'Steady she goes, sir. Nor' east by north! Full an' by!'

Adam relaxed his body, sinew by sinew. A converging tack. Pointer had done well to bide his time. If the stranger went about and made a run for it, they might still outsail him.

'What's your lookout's name, Roger?'

Pointer stared at him, his mind grappling with several things at once.

'Er, Jenkins, sir.' It sounded like a question.

Adam slung the telescope over his shoulder. 'I'm going aloft.' He felt the smile on his lips, as if he had no control over it. 'I'll not cross *your* bows!'

Jago followed him to the weather shrouds. 'You sure about this, Cap'n?'

Adam climbed on to the ratlines, feeling the spray cold against his hands, his face.

'They want evidence – I intend to give it to them!'

Jago stood his ground. 'It's *your* neck, Cap'n.'

Adam lifted his foot to test the next ratline. All those years ago, running up the shrouds with other 'young gentlemen', sometimes barefoot; no fear of heights, or danger.

He recalled Pointer's expression when he had quoted John Paul Jones. But the words still made sense.

Jago took his silence for something else. 'We've a few leagues to sail yet, sir.'

Adam looked down at him. His face was still in shadow, but he did not need to see it.

He said, 'I've seen enough men killed for a flag,

Luke. I'll not stand by while more of them die simply because of greed!'

Ellis, the first lieutenant, commented, 'A man of strong beliefs, Cox'n.'

Jago shook his head, rarely at a loss except for certain moments.

He answered harshly, 'Second to none, sir!'

He peered up again and saw Bolitho's shadow swinging out and around the puttock shrouds. Like a true seaman. There were few officers who would or could do it.

Why do we do it, then? He thought of the painting in the captain's sleeping cabin, hundreds of miles astern by now, the lovely, half naked woman held captive above the sea. And of the reality in that shabby room when the captain and young Troubridge had smashed down the door. *And I was with them.*

The captain should be with her right now, not risking his life all over again for some poxy slaves.

He heard a voice shout, 'All guns load, but do not run out!' *Bloody officers.*

Jago stared up once more but the captain had vanished. Past the maintop and upwards to the topgallant yard. If the ship changed tack again, or even if he slipped, it would be over in seconds.

He readjusted the heavy blade at his belt and looked for the dawn.

The voice seemed to answer him. *It is what we are.*

Adam threw his leg over the lookout's dizzy perch on the crosstrees and seized a stay for support. A very long climb from *Lotus*'s main deck, and he could feel his heart pounding against his ribs like a hammer. He was pleased that he was not completely breathless.

It was a sight which had always impressed him. Midshipman to post captain, it made no difference. The hull heeling hard over to the thrust of topsails and topgallants, each section of mast quivering and jerking to the press of wind and rigging. From this, the highest point in the ship, the sea was directly below him, the glassy blue and rearing crests reflecting the sails, angled far beneath his dangling legs.

He wiped the spray from his face and mouth, tasting the raw salt, his skin tingling. He swallowed hard. A long climb indeed.

He glanced at the masthead lookout, surprised that he was much younger than he had expected. He had a powerful voice which carried easily above and through the busy shipboard noises, like Sullivan in *Unrivalled*, but in fact he seemed only in his late twenties, slightly built, with an open face, deeply tanned almost to the colour of the mast.

He had been watching him climbing from the deck far below with interest, and not a little curiosity, as had some seamen on the main top as Adam had climbed past them. They had been rigging a swivel gun on the top's barricade, but had turned to stare, and one of them had called, 'Bit *dangerous* up 'ere, sir!' They had all laughed.

Adam took another breath.

'Good morning – Jenkins, isn't it?'

'That's me, sir.' He was studying Adam's flapping

shirt and the well-worn, tarnished epaulettes on his seagoing coat.

Adam unslung the telescope and peered ahead and across the bow as the mast reeled over again, the mainsail cracking and thudding to the wind.

Then he saw the other ship, like a delicate model, sharp against a horizon which was sloping over and down as if to dislodge her and *Lotus* together.

'Is it the same barque which you chased into Havana?'

Jenkins frowned, and it made him look younger. 'No, sir, different.' There was no doubt or hesitation. 'Something *about* her, see?'

Adam caught the Welsh accent. He levelled the glass again, or tried to as *Lotus* altered course slightly. It made it seem that the barque was the only vessel moving.

He waited for the mast to steady, and concentrated on the other vessel's rig. A large barque, with the usual untidy appearance when seen on this bearing, square-rigged on fore and main, fore-and-aft rigged on the mizzen, which gave her a broken outline, as if some spars were missing. Big and powerful. But how could Jenkins be sure it was not the one Pointer had described?

The lookouts aboard the barque must have seen *Lotus* by now. Even with the night sky astern of her, she would be laid bare as daylight drove away the shadows and opened up the sea like burnished pewter.

The lookout was wrapping a piece of cloth expertly around his head, and remarked casually, 'Gets a bit like the bakery up here. I wouldn't stay too long, sir.'

Adam smiled, and handed him the telescope. 'Here – tell me what you see.'

Jenkins held the telescope as if he had never seen one in his life. As if it was not to be trusted.

But he trained it with great care and said, 'It's her driver, sir. When it takes the wind over the quarter it . . .' He paused. 'Well, the driver-boom looks higher than it should.' He offered the telescope, as if relieved. 'As if to make space for something.' He ended lamely, 'But then again . . .' He stared at Adam as he used the glass and said, 'Jenkins, where did you get those eyes?' He hardly knew what he was saying: even the most experienced seamen might not notice it. *The flaw in the picture*. Nothing much. But a skilled lookout knew every sort of tide and current, and the mood of each spar and sail in the ships they passed.

Jenkins said, 'My da was a shepherd, good one too, see? I used to help him as a boy, got used to searching for sheep, straining my eyes for the stragglers. No life for me, I thought.' He might have shrugged. 'So I volunteered. Not pressed, see.'

Adam leaned out as far as he dared and saw the small figures moving about the pale planking between his feet. The barque's big aftermost sail, the driver, was higher than normal, as if the poop had been raised in some way. A glance at the masthead pendant, taut in the wind and pointing toward the other vessel. He measured the distance and bearing almost without thought. *If I am wrong* . . . He thought of the figures on the deck below. If he was right, they would not stand a chance.

He swung himself over the crosstrees. 'Thank you, Jenkins. I'll see that this goes in the log!' Something to say, to prevent the conviction from wavering.

He paused, one foot feeling for the first ratline, and looked up, startled, as Jenkins said, 'I was serving in *Frobisher*, sir. I was there.' He looked away. 'When they told me your name, I was so proud . . .' He did not go on. Could not.

Adam said, 'When Sir Richard fell. My uncle.'

He began to clamber down the swaying, vibrating shrouds, his mind suddenly clear, free of doubt.

They were all waiting for him as his shoes hit the deck.

He said, 'Your man, Jenkins – you were right about him.' He pausing, wanting his breathing to steady. 'The barque is not all she seems, Roger. I believe she carries heavier artillery than is customary for an honest trader.'

They were crowding closer to hear him, maybe to consider their own fate. Excitement, doubt, anxiety, as if something inhuman had dropped amongst them. He found time to notice that Jago was the only one who seemed as usual. Arms folded, his fingers loosely on the hilt of the heavy blade he always carried.

Pointer rubbed his chin, with the habitual frown as he listened to Adam's description. He was *Lotus*'s commanding officer. If the other ship proved to be an enemy, no matter in what guise, he would be held responsible if anything went wrong. Adam Bolitho was a vice-admiral's flag captain, part of a legend. But a passenger.

In a matter of a few months Pointer's promotion

would be in orders: commander, the first real step toward post rank. One error or reckless action, and he would join the thousands of unemployed, half-pay officers.

He looked along his ship and at the men he had come to know so well during his six months in command. The good and the untrustworthy, the hard men, and the ordinary Jack who had no choice at all but to trust his captain. He faced Bolitho, his searching eyes taking in the faded coat and stained epaulettes. There was fresh tar now on his hands and breeches from the climb to the masthead, but, in any ship, you would know him instantly as the Captain.

He said, 'I'll be guided by you, sir.' He saw his first lieutenant nod, and nudge some one beside him.

Adam touched his arm and for an instant looked at his hand. Steady: no uncertainty. Like a drug or a breed of madness.

'I shall put it in the log, Roger.' He thought of Jago's remark. 'It will be my neck.'

He stared up through the rigging and pictured the keen-eyed Welshman, searching for lost sheep before volunteering. Who was there on that terrible, proud day when Richard Bolitho had fallen on the deck of his own flagship.

It was past. This was now.

'So let's be about it, shall we?'

Ellis, the first lieutenant, lowered his telescope and called, 'Spanish colours, sir! No tricks this time!' It was impossible to tell if he was disappointed or relieved.

Adam looked up at the topsails, writhing and cracking, with the yards braced round so tightly they would
appear to any outsider to be almost fore-and-aft.

He gritted his teeth. The only outsider was the
barque, so much bigger now and angled almost across
Lotus's bowsprit. Two miles? No more.

He heard one of the helmsmen shout something and
the sailing master's response. To Pointer he said, 'She's
as close to the wind as she'll come, sir. If the wind
backs we'll be in irons!'

Pointer's eyes flickered briefly to Adam. 'Let her
fall off a point.'

Adam walked to the nettings and clung to a lashing while the deck tilted over again. It was taking too
long. If the Spaniard held his course he would be in
safe waters, and any further action would be taken
very seriously when it reached Havana, and later
Madrid. The 'alliance' between the old enemies was
already fragile enough.

He glanced along the deck. The starboard guns
loaded and manned, their crews crouched and hidden
below the bulwarks. One of the cutters had been
swayed from the boat tier, its crew and lowering party
hauling on the tackle, supervised by the boatswain,
making it obvious that they were preparing a boarding party. He did not need a chart. Soon they would
be on a lee shore, with shallows for an added hazard.

He could feel the sailing master's anxiety like something physical. Pointer, he knew, would be equally
worried.

He looked over at Jago, who was standing near the

helmsmen, arms folded, feet well apart to accept the angle of the deck. What might he be thinking?

'Make the signal! *Heave to!*' Like hearing somebody else. He measured the bearing and the range with his eye until it smarted. But he could see every detail of the sails, comfortably filling in the wind across her quarter. A few tiny figures in the lower shrouds, a flash of light from a telescope. He wiped his eye and raised the glass again. There were more men on the Spaniard's deck. Not running about or pointing at the sloop as might be expected. It was as if . . . The picture seemed to freeze in the glass. Past a boat tier to the poop and the wheel. Except that there was no wheel, and the raised poop appeared to be deserted.

'They're not shortenin' sail, sir.'

Adam said, 'Fire the warning shot!' He held up one hand and sensed that Pointer had turned to watch him. 'Then we come about.' They had to know, be ready. There would be no second chance.

The crash of the foremost gun seemed muffled by the din of canvas overhead. He saw the gun's crew sponging out and ramming home another ball, like a drill, part of the routine.

'They're shortening sail, sir!' Somebody even laughed.

Adam's fingers throbbed from the force of his grip as he steadied the glass, his feet moving without thought as the hull lifted and dipped, while the sound of thrashing canvas was like that of giant sea birds, spreading their wings in flight.

He blinked, but it was no error, or the effect of

strain. The barque's poop was moving, even as he watched, folding like painted canvas, as if controlled by a single hand.

There were men in plenty now, in teams, bowed over as they hauled at invisible tackles, even as three gunports opened below her mizzen mast and the driver boom which had first troubled the keen-eyed lookout.

Adam yelled, '*Now, Roger! Show them your teeth!*'

With the helm hard over and every spare hand hauling on braces and halliards, *Lotus* began to swing wildly to larboard. Spray burst over the scrambling gun crews as the ports opened as one, and her broadside of eight twelve-pounders squealed into the sunlight.

'Steady she goes! West by south!'

Adam watched the other ship, now almost broadside on, near enough to mark every detail. He saw smoke fanning across the barque's ports and the spitting orange tongues from two of them, heard the smack of a ball punching through the main topsail, within feet of the fighting top where the swivel gun's crew had called out to him. A split second later he felt the sickening crash of a ball as it smashed into the lower hull. All in seconds, and yet in so short a space of time he heard the words of *Celeste*'s only survivor before he, too, paid the price.

Fired into us at point-blank range, double-shotted by the feel of it!

They had all felt it now.

Pointer was gripping the rail, his battered hat still in place, his voice strangely calm.

'As you bear, lads! On the uproll . . .' He glanced only briefly at two running seamen, or perhaps at the sound of pumps. '*Fire!*'

Adam saw the carefully prepared broadside smash into the barque's poop, double-shotted and with grape for good measure. Pointer's gun captains knew their work well. In small ships, you needed to.

He saw thin scarlet streaks running from the barque's scuppers, as if she and not her sailors was bleeding to death.

There was more smoke in the air now; men were yelling below decks, and there were sounds of axes, and the clank of pumps.

But at each gun nothing moved. Every twelve-pounder was loaded and run out again, each gun captain faced aft, his hand raised.

'Ready, sir!'

Adam watched the other vessel. Perhaps that carefully prepared broadside had damaged her steering; her topsails were in confusion and she was falling slightly downwind.

He could still feel the force and weight of the ball which had crashed into *Lotus*'s hull. Like the ones which had fired into *Celeste* when she had been asking for medical help.

And all those other pictures which came crowding into his mind. On the African patrols when they had found another survivor, from a prize crew put aboard a slaver. The slavers had somehow overpowered the prize crew, and with the slaves still on board threw them to the sharks. Pointer had seen it, too. A sea of blood.

What had warned him this time? Fate? Or was it part of the legend he had heard sailors talk of?

He made himself lift the glass to his eye again.

He saw the splintered timbers and torn sails, some corpses sprawled where they had fallen. But the third gun was still thrust through its port, manned or not he could not tell. A big gun. Perhaps a thirty-two pounder. Even *Athena* did not carry such massive weapons.

Pointer was still by the rail, waiting. Perhaps he thought he had not heard him. He said, 'Their flag still flies, sir.'

He turned as his first lieutenant appeared through the companion hatch.

'We're holding it, sir! She'll live to fight again!' He stared around at the silent gun crews.

Pointer asked sharply, 'What is the bill?'

Ellis spread his hands. 'We lost one killed, sir.' He looked at, and through, Adam as if he did not see him. 'Mr Bellamy, sir.'

The only midshipman, who had never wanted to leave this ship.

Adam shouted, '*Broadside!*'

It seemed louder than before, and the smoke less eager to clear. He gripped his hands behind his back to contain the anger and emotion. He stared at the other vessel, the poop clawed away as if by some giant.

'Their flag is down *now*, Roger.' Jago was beside him although he had not seen him move. 'Prepare to board. But have the guns loaded and be ready. If he attempts to trick us or resists us this time he will drown in his own sea of blood!'

Jago followed him to the main deck where the boatswain's party were once again preparing to sway out and lower boats for boarding.

He knew he had to stay close to the captain. They had shared and done far worse, but he could not recall seeing him so moved. He thought suddenly of the girl in the portrait and wondered what she would feel if she saw her man like this.

'Boats alongside, sir!'

Pointer was gazing at the starboard side gun crews. But for Bolitho's instinct, second sight, or whatever it was, *Lotus* and most of these men would be dead.

And he was going across in one of the boats. Again, as if something or somebody was driving him.

He realized that Bolitho had paused with his leg over the side, and was looking up at him.

'Take care, sir!'

Adam shaded his eyes. 'You will need a prize crew, Roger. They might listen to us in future!'

'*Cast off! Bear off forrard!*' The boats were moving away from the side, some of the seamen peering at their ship, looking for the hole where cannon had smashed through the hull, and had killed one of their own. Others gripped their cutlasses and boarding axes and stared ahead at the unexpected enemy, ready to fight and kill if any one opposed them.

The sailing master murmured, 'Close thing, sir.'

Pointer pulled his mind together. 'We were ready

for that scum.' He beckoned to a boatswain's mate, still hearing the inner voice. *But I was not.*

Both boats were pulling strongly so that within minutes the drifting barque seemed to tower over them like a cliff. Adam crouched beside Jago and the boat's coxswain, his sword pinned between his legs. Two of the seamen were armed with muskets which they held trained on the barque, ready for a last show of force. He found time to think it strange not to have Royal Marines in either boat, but *Lotus*'s men were experienced in this sort of work. Over the months since the anti-slavery laws had grudgingly been accepted, they must have stopped and boarded many suspected slavers, some without result, and others which had been allowed to go free because of slackness in the wording of some regulations. Adam had heard of a case where a ship had been seized with only one slave still on board. Enough evidence, any sane person might have thought. But the Act stated any vessel carrying *slaves*, in the plural, so the vessel was released without charge. That clause, at least, had now been changed.

He peered across at the other boat. *Lotus*'s second lieutenant, Jack Grimes, was in charge. He was an old hand at the work, who had come up the hard way to gain his commission, from the lower deck. As some one had once said of such promotions, if he was good there was none better. *And if not, then watch out!*

Faces had appeared on the barque's forecastle and above the creak of oars and the sluice of water he could hear some one screaming.

Jago loosened his blade and muttered, "Ere we go, lads!'

'*Grapnels!*'

The boat surged alongside, the oars vanishing as if by magic. Hands snatched up weapons. Todd, the boatswain's mate in charge, yelled, 'Ready, sir?'

Adam felt Jago's hand on his arm. 'I'll get no thanks from Sir Graham if I lets you get killed first, Cap'n!' He thrust past him and flung himself up into the fore chains before any one could stop him. The second boat was already grappling the main chains, and Adam managed to see Lieutenant Grimes, hanger in one hand as he shouted something to the men close behind him.

He did not recall climbing up and over the side. One shot was fired, and somewhere a man cried out in anguish. But suddenly the barque's broad deck was theirs . . . Individual seamen ran to their allotted tasks as if they knew the ship like their own. One was already at a swivel gun and training it aft toward the poop and the blood-spattered aftermath of *Lotus*'s second broadside, others were rounding up some of the barque's people, and weapons clattered on the deck or were pitched over the side. *Lotus*'s men were in no mood for argument, and those who had reached the poop and had found the powerful guns half buried by the false superstructure needed no words of command to keep them fully alert, and ready to hack down any opposition. Had *Lotus* not played trick-for-trick and been ready to open fire, their little sloop would now be lying fathoms deep.

Seven of the barque's company had been killed in the broadsides; several others had been badly cut and wounded by flying splinters. Lieutenant Grimes made the first discovery. With one of his men he brought the barque's master to Adam from his hiding place in a spirit store in the poop.

He said harshly, 'We must mount a guard there, sir. Enough grog stored to float the flagship!' He pushed the ship's master forward. 'His name's Cousens, sir. English, God help us!'

Adam said, 'We have already met, *Mister* Cousens, have we not?' Even the brig's name, *Albatroz*, was ice-clear in his mind. Like a storm passing: the madness of the attack, each second expecting the jarring agony of musket ball or the blade of a cutlass, then this. A sudden calm which was almost worse.

A year ago, *Unrivalled* had put a boarding party aboard a suspected slaver. No slaves were found, but his men had discovered chains and manacles slyly hidden in a cask of boiling pitch. Evidence enough, his boarding party had believed.

But once delivered in harbour to face charges, the brig's master, this same man, must have laughed at them, and had walked free.

Cousens looked him up and down. 'You look as if you've fallen on hard times, Captain. An' once again, you'll find nothing.'

The calmness remained, although something deep inside him wanted to cut this man down, here and now.

He said, 'You intended that we should reach Havana ahead of you. So that we might be "detained" long enough for you to land your cargo.'

'I don't have to say anything until . . .'

He gasped as Jago seized his arm and twisted it behind his back.

'*Sir*, when you speak to a King's officer, you scum!'

Todd, the boatswain's mate, was hurrying aft, his face split in a great grin despite the blood and corpses around him.

'Captain, sir! *Found the cargo!*' Somewhere along the way he had had his two front teeth knocked out. The grin made it worse. 'Can't get right into it, sir, more locks and bolts than a Chatham whorehouse, but it's gold right enough, tons of it!'

Grimes scowled. 'Something else we'll have to mount a guard on.'

Cousens exclaimed, 'Not my fault! I was under orders!'

Adam turned away and watched the *Lotus* slowly coming about, her gunports closed, and from this bearing only the spreading tear in her main topsail to mark what had happened.

And the midshipman, *I don't want to leave this ship*, had been killed.

It gave him time. But there was never enough when you needed it so badly.

He said, 'Put this man in irons, and prepare to get the ship under way. We will ask *Lotus* for some more hands. We are going to need them.'

Grimes turned his back on the man called Cousens.

'The steering is undamaged, sir. But what do you intend?'

Adam glanced at the carving on the poop, the barque's name in gilt lettering. *Villa de Bilbao*. It, too, was splashed with blood.

'We shall return to English Harbour. I think we have evidence enough. Sir Graham's message to the captain-general will have to wait a while longer.'

Grimes paused to listen to one of his men, and said, 'She's a slaver right enough, sir. All the usual fittings, no covers on the hatches, just bars to keep the poor devils penned up for the journey, the last for some of them, no doubt!'

'And the gold?'

Grimes studied him guardedly, not yet sure of the bridge that might exist between them. Then he said bluntly, 'Payment for the last few cargoes, I'd wager,' and seemed surprised when Adam grasped his arm and said, 'I am certain of it!'

Cousens tried to thrust past Jago, shouting, 'What about me, damn your eyes!'

Adam looked along the littered and scarred deck, at *Lotus*'s men leaning on their weapons, another bandaging the arm of one of the barque's sailors, and turned toward Cousens again, remembering the terrified faces he had seen in a slaver's hold, women too, some no older than Elizabeth. They all ended up as pieces of gold.

'*You*, Cousens, will be put ashore and hanged. You fired on a King's ship, one authorized by law to stop and search any suspected vessel, as well you know. Those who pay you will not save you.'

He felt sick, furious with himself for caring so much. They had captured a prize which, given time, would reveal names and places.

If Cousens lived or died the trade would still go on. But just this once they had made their mark.

He walked over to watch *Lotus*'s jolly boat pulling across the water toward the *Villa de Bilbao*.

He realized that he was still gripping the old sword in his hand, but could hardly remember drawing it. Another minute and Cousens would not have had to wait for the rope. He tried again to shake it off, the narrow margin of life and death.

He watched the jolly boat pulling closer.

Help was on its way. Very carefully, he sheathed the sword which had served other Bolithos.

Not a moment too soon.

12

Catherine

Vice-Admiral Sir Graham Bethune paused under a
low archway and gazed up at the house.

'This is the one?' He saw Tolan nod, but felt
compelled to insist, 'You're certain?'

It was a warm evening, humid, and Bethune was
feeling it. He was wearing a boatcloak to cover his
gold-laced uniform and held his hat concealed
beneath it. He was breathing heavily. Perhaps they
were in for a storm; but he knew he was already
missing the regular rides and walks across the park
in London.

'It's damned quiet.' Again, Tolan said nothing, and
Bethune knew he had been snapping at him and every
one else since news of the arrival of the sloop *Lotus*
and her impressive prize had been carried to him.
Even the boat's crew which had brought him ashore
had felt the rough edge of his tongue.

And now he was here, and all his original

confidence had deserted him. It could have been the first time. It might never have happened at all, except in his mind.

The narrow street was deserted. Everybody, it seemed, was still down at the harbour, watching the activity, sightseers in their small craft being held back or chased away by the guardboats.

He thought of Adam Bolitho, remembering his face when he had lost his temper, forgetting that the flag lieutenant and the secretary were still within earshot. And Tolan.

It had blown over, but Bethune still wondered if the air between them would clear.

And Bolitho had acted correctly. As Nelson had often proclaimed, the written order should never be a substitute for a captain's initiative. And he was right.

He calmed himself with effort and unfastened his cloak.

He looked up at the steps and beyond, at the clouds drifting past Monk's Hill and the lookout station which had first sighted the ill-matched vessels making their approach. That must have been ten hours ago. Things had moved very quickly after that. He relaxed a little and said, 'I'm not to be disturbed. By anybody.' He relented slightly. 'Good work, Tolan.'

He reached the top of the steps and saw her waiting for him, as he knew she would be. Exactly as he always saw her in his thoughts, composed, beautiful, unreachable. She was dressed in dark green, her neck and shoulders bare and browned by the sun, her dark hair loose and quite still in the heavy air.

She said, 'I received your message. You should not have come. Antigua is like a village. No secrets.'

He glanced at the telescope in its tripod and across the placid water of English Harbour. There were still crowds of small craft moving around the barque, and boats alongside her, tackles busily hoisting and lowering equipment and stores.

A great capture, was how the commodore had described it. The whole of the Caribbean probably knew about it by now.

She hesitated, then held out her hand. 'But you are welcome, Graham.' She watched him bow his head to kiss her fingers. 'What's done is done.'

He said, 'The barque is the *Villa de Bilbao*, first registered in Vigo.' She noticed, too, that he did not release her hand.

'I know.' She saw him start. 'I was there, a year or so ago, when she was completed.'

She withdrew her hand and walked to the end of the balcony. 'I was there.' She shrugged. 'And several places in Spain, when I was helping Lord Sillitoe with some business matters. I speak Spanish well, you see.'

She swung round suddenly, her back to the water, her eyes flashing. 'Why am I telling you, of all people? You know it already! Everywhere we have been, there have always been questions, and suspicions. Spain, Jamaica, even here in Antigua!'

'And what about Cuba . . . Havana?'

She turned again, slowly, as if the defiance and anger had drained her.

'I heard about the slaver, and the attack on one of

274

your ships.' She shrugged once more, and Bethune felt it like a pain.

She continued in the same unemotional tone, 'I shall return to England soon. But you know that too, I suppose?'

He stood beside her and caught the scent of jasmine. 'Captain Adam Bolitho is with me. He knows you are close by, Catherine.'

She hesitated, and said, 'Kate.'

He said, 'You see the little sloop, the *Lotus*?'

'I watched her come into the anchorage. Just as I saw her leave, nine, ten days ago. I forget.'

He pointed across the balustrade. 'My first ship was very like her. A sloop-of-war, they were called in those days. She was named *Sparrow*.'

He felt her nod, her voice husky as she murmured, 'Richard's first command. He often spoke of her.'

He said, 'This is not like the "back stairs" at the Admiralty, Kate.'

She did not turn or look at him. 'Or the park, by the dead trees where foolish young men fought one another, and often died because of a woman.'

'You've not forgotten.'

'Did you think I would?' Then she did face him, sharply. 'But I'm not young any more, not just a girl who wanted to love and be loved! An *affair* – is that what they call it? Something those deprived of affection would never understand. Like that night when I was nearly killed, when he was the only one who helped and protected me, did any one really care—'

'I did, Kate, and well you know it. I cursed myself

a million times for letting you go alone to your house.'

He watched her, surprised that she was suddenly calm again; or so she appeared. Only her breathing betrayed her.

'What are you saying to me, Graham? You are bored with your personal life as it is? Your wife and children, two, isn't it, no longer engage all your attention and energy?' She reached up and touched his mouth with her fingers. 'No, hear me. The darling of the nation, they called me. The beloved of England's hero. It soon changed when Richard was killed. You saw the cartoons? The clever cruelty of the news sheets?'

He gripped her hand, and when she tried to pull it away held it more tightly.

'I *want* you, Kate. I have never stopped wanting you since that very first meeting.'

He felt her fingers relax. 'I remember.'

They faced the harbour again, side by side. Then he said, 'I shall be leaving the navy soon. Vice-admiral is more than I ever expected to attain.' He laughed hollowly. 'But Our Nel rose no higher, so I am satisfied. I may be offered a post elsewhere, perhaps with the East India Company – my aide's father seems to think it might suit.'

He turned away from the sea, toward her. 'But I want it with you.'

She moved to the telescope and touched it uncertainly, her composure shaken.

'I thought you wanted me as something else. There was no hint in your letters . . . I had no real idea.'

Bethune smiled. 'So you did read them.'

She looked away, one hand playing with her hair. 'And destroyed them.'

He said, after a silence, 'Your friend, Sillitoe. He may well be in serious trouble.'

Her hand moved, dismissively.

'I know about the company he deals with in London. He has made no secret of it. He was the Prince Regent's Inspector-General, as you well know.' She added sharply, 'As was my late husband, you were no doubt about to remind me.'

'It goes far deeper than that.' Something seemed to move him. He gripped her shoulders and held her directly in front of him, feeling the surprise, the irritation. 'I want you to stay here until you leave for England. No matter what is suggested, remain here. I will take care of things.' At any second she would break away, or scream at him. He could feel the warm skin under his fingers, like silk. Once again he had ruined it. Like the stupid midshipman he had just described.

She said quietly, not looking at him, her dark eyes veiled by the lashes:

'Do you know what you have done, Graham?' She shook her head, and he saw the gold filigree earrings gleam through her hair, the ones she was almost always wearing when they had met; Richard had given them to her. 'You have laid yourself wide open to blame, and worse, if it becomes known that you have warned me. Don't you care?'

He answered evenly, 'When you see an enemy, and his gunports are staring at you like pitiless eyes, it is too late to bargain, or count the costs.' Then the smile came, easily. 'I want you, Kate. No bargains. I have always loved you.'

A door opened and slammed shut. She said, 'My maid, Marquita. I shall ask her to prepare some wine. Surely we can sit together now, and be friends, before you leave?'

Later the little maid Marquita carried a message down to George Tolan.

He was no longer required to stand watch.

He did not return to the ship. Neither did his admiral.

John Bowles, the cabin servant, held up the captain's discarded coat at arm's length and exclaimed, 'This will not tolerate many more days at sea, sir! It was a blessing you didn't go aloft in your best uniform—I'm not sure what we could 'ave done.'

Adam leaned back in the chair and allowed his mind to drift. After *Lotus*, everything seemed to have changed. As if he had been away from the flagship for months instead of days; or as if he had never taken command. *Athena* felt so heavy and secure. She could have been aground but for the shifting patterns of reflected sunlight on deckhead and screens as she nudged occasionally at her cable.

Troubridge was by the stern windows, watching the harbour and the anchored barque. A different Troubridge from the one in the cabin below when Bethune had lost his temper. That had changed, also, when Bethune had learned about the cargo of gold, and some consignment documents for delivery in Havana.

Adam was surprised that he was not exhausted; he had scarcely slept aboard the barque, even though *Lotus*'s tough and experienced second lieutenant had been ready and able for the passage to Antigua.

When he had left the little sloop to be pulled over to *Athena* it had been a moving and unexpected moment. It seemed that, without planning or prompting, *Lotus*'s company had manned the side and the yards to cheer him.

He had said to Pointer, 'The credit goes to your lookout. He had his suspicions from the very beginning. There are not many like that!'

Pointer had been grinning all over his face and had shouted above the wild cheering, 'With respect, sir, I don't know of any post captain who would shin up the shrouds to hear anybody's views!'

Troubridge was saying, 'You may not have seen her, but the frigate *Audacity* anchored an hour before you did.'

Adam stared at him.

'Any messages?'

Jago was standing by the screen, running a cloth up and down the old sword, and frowning as he rubbed. He said, 'Young Mister Napier'll still be finding his feet after the long haul from Plymouth.'

Troubridge clapped his hand across his mouth. 'I *forgot*, sir! There was a letter sent across with the despatches. I was kept so busy . . .'

Adam recalled Bethune's display of temper, and said dryly, 'I'm not surprised.'

Bowles gathered up some empty plates and, with

the tar-stained coat held at a distance, said, 'I'll see about some fresh shirts, sir.'

Troubridge said, 'I must have a word with Paget, just in case . . .'

Adam held the letter in both hands.

'You stay, Luke. Have another wet. The admiral's ashore, so you can rest easy.'

Jago opened, then closed his mouth again. The letter would be from her. She must have written it almost before *Athena*'s topsail yards had dipped over the horizon.

He thought about Bethune and a lower-deck rumour he had picked up about his unescorted trip ashore. Unescorted, that was, but for the efficient Tolan. But it was impossible to get anything out of *him*. Like trying to open an oyster with a feather.

Adam held the letter to a lantern; outside the stern windows it had become quite dark. Lights were already moving on the current, and somewhere on the main deck he could hear water being pumped into the boats on the tier. Heat and sun could open up a boat like a basket without regular soaking in this climate.

The harbour, the unexpected prize, the short, savage fight and the death of a young midshipman seemed to fade; he was with her again.

He recognized the paper, some of Nancy's, the old Roxby crest another poignant memory.

My dearest Adam, my love . . .

Jago poured himself another measure of cognac. In some ways it was better than grog, he decided. He sat in a chair and studied the old sword, back on its rack once more. So many sea fights, the names and the places too mingled for him to remember; but that sword must have seen ten times as many.

He thought of the slaver, the whining sailors who would now face trial, and very likely a Tyburn jig at the end of it. They were scum. But neither were they worth dying for. He looked across at the tall-backed chair which had some fancy foreign name he could not recall, where the captain sat re-reading his letter. He smiled to himself. *In case he missed something.*

'Good news, Cap'n?' He still found it hard to credit that he could speak to an officer in this fashion, let alone a captain. Pride was not a term he used easily. But there it was.

Adam said, 'She wrote from Falmouth, but she is going to London very soon.' He glanced at the letter. 'She will be back there by now, I expect. Some legal business.' He pushed his fingers through his unruly hair. 'She wishes us well.'

He could almost hear her. *I want you. I feel you. I reach out for you.*

Jago asked, 'What d' you reckon'll happen to that gold?'

He folded the letter carefully. 'All those slaves which have been shipped out to these waters. Hundreds, maybe thousands. Slavers like Cousens take all the risks, but their rewards are greater than anything they could earn in honest trade. And now, because of greed or mistrust, we have that gold under lock and key.' He remembered the boatswain's mate Todd's summing up, *like a Chatham whorehouse*, and found that he could smile. The tiredness was gone. He touched her letter.

And I reach out for you.

The captured barque and others which had been reported were fast and well armed, but to crew and run them without the promise of rich reward was impossible. Bethune and his advisers at the far-off Admiralty were convinced that, without payment, no one would risk mounting opposition and the chance of being captured.

The major slaving countries, the United States, Cuba and Brazil, would find it even harder to lure men like Cousens, or others willing to face death at the end of a halter.

Outside the screen door, in another world, the marine sentry brought his heels together with a click.

'First lieutenant, *sah!*'

Adam faced the door. Some one for promotion or two dozen lashes. Taking on stores or recaulking part of the deck. Routine. Maybe the Stirlings of this world were right. Carry out orders and do your duty; leave the risks and the dangerous decisions to others. Perhaps a lesson he had learned the hard way and could never forget.

He remembered Bethune's casual comment after *Celeste*'s sole survivor, the only witness to murder, had died.

Don't become too involved. You lead, they follow — there is no room for sentiment beyond that.

He examined his own immediate reaction. Like a witness at a court-martial. Pointer may have suspected it. Jago had known it when he had pushed his captain aside as they had boarded the barque. Duty had nothing to do with it. *I am involved. I wanted revenge.*

He realized that Bowles had quietly returned and was opening the screen door. Like the flag lieutenant, he had thought it important that he should be left in peace to read his letter.

Stirling waited for the door to close.

'The wardroom have asked you to be their guest tomorrow for dinner in the mess. With the garrison so near, the food might be better than usual.' He did not smile, concentrating, as if to ensure that he had forgotten nothing. 'The wardroom' made certain that this invitation was not too personal.

'I would like that very much. Please thank them.'

Stirling nodded and produced a sheaf of paper. 'Now, about Mr Midshipman Vincent's promotion . . .'

Adam felt the tension slipping away.

It was the closest they had been.

Bethune sat up in the chair and touched his face.

'A good shave, Tolan, as ever!'

There was a taste of fine coffee in his throat, an inner excitement which he was still unable to contain, or come to terms with.

He recalled the consternation on deck when he had returned on board the flagship. Royal Marines taking up their positions, boatswain's mates moistening their silver calls so as not to scramble the salute as the vice-admiral stepped aboard.

He had spoken only briefly with Captain Adam Bolitho, who had been there to greet him. Clear-eyed and alert, with nothing to show of the sea fight and the unexpected capture.

Now the ship was fully awake, hammers thudding somewhere, while the sailmaker and his mates squatted about the main deck, the 'market place' as it was termed on most working days, needles and palms going like Maltese tailors.

Tolan was saying, 'Mr Paget is waiting to see you, Sir Graham.' He was thinking about the quiet house overlooking the harbour, and the woman, and wondering just how much Frogface Paget knew.

Bethune picked up the cup. It was empty. Again.

He recalled the wine, the last glimpse of the harbour and the winking lights. She had known almost from the beginning. He had felt it, as if she had been fighting a battle, against herself, perhaps. And who else?

He had never really believed it would happen. A word or a glance, he never remembered.

She had said, 'You must leave, Graham.' Even his name on her tongue had excited him.

He had held her, like two people frozen in a waltz without music. He had tried to kiss her, but she had turned her face away, had pushed at his shoulders, shaking her head, words lost in her hair, body tensed as he held her, tightly and without pretence. Then she had said, 'I don't love you, Graham. You know what I said.'

Her arms had fallen to her sides, like that moment on the balcony.

'I have never stopped loving you, Kate!'

He had held her, her waist, her back, her shoulders, had felt her body trembling, as if she were going to break away and run from him.

The room had been almost in darkness, but he had seen her eyes, and her mouth, the lips parted as if she wanted to say something. To explain, to protest; he did not wait.

But she did not resist; her mouth met his. It seemed to be endless, uncovering her, touching her body, her skin, then finding her, taking her.

He was still not certain if he would have pulled away, if she had tried to stop him.

Afterwards they lay together in the humid room, the overhead fan unmoving.

There had been no words, as if each was afraid to shatter the moment.

Tolan said, 'Flag lieutenant, Sir Graham.'

Bethune stood up and faced him. 'Send them both in.' He regarded him for several seconds, lost for words, which was unusual. 'Thank you, Tolan.'

'Sir Graham?'

'I shall not forget.'

He walked to the quarter windows and shaded his eyes, the water hard and bright, unmoving.

And she was over there. And he had once described Adam Bolitho as reckless.

Catherine folded the letter with great care, but hesitated before sealing it.

The house seemed very still, only the fan swaying

slowly back and forth to stir the heavy air. The shutters were lowered so that the sunlight criss-crossed the room in fiery bars.

It was probably noon. She propped the letter against the inkstand and plucked at the loose robe which covered her body from throat to ankle. Beneath it she was naked, still damp from bathing herself, as if to wipe away the feel and touch of each vivid memory.

She could open the blinds and go out on the balcony, and the view would be the same. The ships, the harbour's unending panorama of coastal and local trading craft.

And yet everything was changed, and she could not believe it.

She ran her hand inside her robe, across her shoulder, then down and around her breast. Forcing herself to relive it, confront what she had allowed to happen.

I do not love him. She did not even know if she had spoken aloud. Nor did she care. Perhaps it had been inevitable, and yet she would never have believed it of herself. She had become used to it, the stares, the hints, the lingering grip on her hand. She was stronger than any of it. She believed.

She thought of Adam, out there in the flagship, doubtless fretting over his lost freedom as a frigate captain. As Richard had done, and had shared it with her.

How would Adam take it when he heard about Bethune, and their liaison?

She was on her feet, the tiles cool to her bare soles. *It was not like that . . .* She picked up the ring from the table, so brilliant even in this shadowed room, rubies and diamonds. She could remember the little church in Cornwall where Richard had slipped it on to her finger. All so clear despite the years, and the pain in between. Where Valentine Keen had married Zenoria. She could still hear his voice. *In the eyes of God, we are married*. And that other memory, of Adam's despair as he had watched Zenoria, whom he had loved, become the wife of another man.

Adam's heart had been broken; he more than any one would understand what had happened here, within a mile of that other, grander house where she had seen Richard's ship coming to anchor, when they had been reunited against all odds.

She had even pulled off this ring before Graham Bethune had arrived. Shame? Guilt? *I do not love him*.

She knew it was impossible. It would ruin Bethune. He was young for his Admiralty appointment, and she knew enough about the navy to realize what envy might create. His wife would do the rest, and destroy him.

She looked at herself in a tall glass. Heard herself say, *but I'm not young any more, not just a girl who wanted to love and be loved*. Even in the dim light she could see the mark on her shoulder, where he had pressed against her, and she had given in. Her eyes flashed. Willingly . . .

A door opened slightly; it was Marquita.

'You rang the bell, m' lady?'

Catherine had already forgotten.

'I want you to take this letter to Mr Jacob down by

the jetty.' She waited for the girl to hold it. 'Give it to nobody else, Marquita. You understand?'

Marquita nodded slowly. 'Mister Jacob, m' lady.' She looked around. 'You not eaten?'

Catherine put her arm around the girl's slender shoulders.

'Tell Cook to go home. I shall not need anything.'

She clasped her shoulder, taken off guard, as the noon gun crashed out across the harbour.

'Big trouble, m' lady?' The girl's eyes were studying her anxiously. Both her mother and father had been slaves. It reminded her of Sillitoe, and Bethune's warning. Sillitoe, the man of power, feared by almost every one, who had cherished and protected her ever since that hideous night in Chelsea. Who had never touched her. She would not desert him now.

Perhaps when they returned to England . . . But the picture refused to form.

All she could see was the door of that Chelsea house, and what some one had carved on it. *Whore!*

She called out, but the room was empty.

13

The Only Ally

After the oppressive heat in the harbour the commodore's headquarters seemed cool by comparison within its thick, white-painted walls, with commanding views across the anchorage and main channel, and out toward the hazy blue horizon. There were old cannon along the bastion, probably Spanish, a hundred years old or more, with Commodore Swinburne's broad pendant hanging limply overhead.

As the gig had pulled out from beneath *Athena*'s great shadow, Adam had felt the sun on his shoulder like something physical. He had seen Stirling on the forecastle, watching while the second anchor was swayed out to its cathead, ready to let go without a moment's notice if a storm should break over the island.

Fraser the sailing master had said cautiously, 'Glass is steady enough, sir. But out here . . . you know how it is.'

Troubridge had accompanied him, pleased, Adam

thought, to get away from Bethune and his mounting impatience.

The gig had passed abeam of the captured barque, and it was hard to believe she had ever been raked by *Lotus*'s broadside; the dockyard workers had patched and painted over most of the damage. Adam felt there was hardly a piece of the *Villa de Bilbao* he had not examined. The metal bars to keep the slaves secure, and long planks, like shelves, in the holds, so that more living bodies could be stored in ranks, one above the other, like books in a case with hardly room to breathe or move. A nightmare.

Cousens had said nothing, and was locked in solitary confinement under military guard. He would go to the gallows in silence, perhaps more afraid of his employers than the hangman. And there was always the chance he might escape the fate he justly deserved. He had not been carrying slaves, and he might claim that he fired his guns in self-defence, in the belief that *Lotus* was a pirate or privateer under false colours. It was not unknown.

He had destroyed his charts minutes before being boarded, or thrown them overboard in a weighted bag with any other evidence close to hand.

Bethune had sent despatches by courier to the Admiralty, insisting on more ships for his command, frigates most of all. Nothing changed. Adam had never forgotten how Lord Exmouth had wanted *Unrivalled* in the van for his attack on Algiers. There were never enough frigates, peace or war.

They had been ushered into a large room, fans

swinging busily overhead, long blinds extended to hold the glare and heat at bay.

There were several other commanding officers present, including Pointer; *Lotus* was in the dockyard for repairs to her hull. Another captain was from the frigate *Hostile*, which had been undergoing a complete overhaul and was soon to rejoin the scattered squadron.

And there was Captain Ian Munro, of the frigate *Audacity*, their newest arrival. Adam had met him when he had come aboard *Athena* to make his report to Bethune: a young, round face, scorched rather than tanned by the Caribbean sun, with bright ginger hair. Adam remembered Bethune's sarcastic comment on the little frigate's age. *Thought she was in the breaker's yard.* Munro had obviously become used to such remarks. He had said cheerfully, 'She was launched the same year I was born. A perfect match, don't you think?'

He was twenty-eight years old, and although not yet posted would be confirmed in that rank before the year ended. *Provided*. But, like any frigate captain, he would not need reminding of the pitfalls always in wait.

Adam saw the quick glances, and the occasional smiles, although after nearly a month at Antigua, with *Athena* 'taking root' as Jago had put it, most of them were still strangers.

A door opened and Commodore Sir Baldwin Swinburne entered the room. Despite the fans he looked hot and uncomfortable, but very sure of himself, a different man without Bethune's presence.

Adam looked over at Troubridge and wondered how much he knew about the rumours. It was none of any one's business if Bethune used his rank and authority to visit Catherine. She was a beautiful woman, and she was far more than that. She had helped him beyond belief when Zenoria had killed herself. She had understood, even though Zenoria had not been his to love. And she had comforted him, then, and after Richard had fallen on board *Frobisher*. He pushed the thoughts away. It was useless going back.

Swinburne said loudly, 'Now that we are all assembled.' He glanced at Adam, and beamed. 'I can explain the development of our strategy to date.' He was enjoying it.

'When my sloop *Lotus* stopped and seized the barque now lying under our guns, it was assumed that she was making for Havana. We have had, after all, some experience in the tactics of the Spanish captain-general, have we not?' There were several chuckles. 'But we can never assume too much.' Once again, briefly, his eyes settled on Adam and the flag lieutenant. 'The *Villa de Bilbao* did not in fact intend to enter Havana. Her master, Cousens, would have allowed *Lotus* to make for that port.' He looked around at their faces, like a showman with some secret trick still in hand. '*Lotus*'s change of tack in the darkness caught Cousens all aback.'

Adam curbed his impatience. The flaw in the picture. Some one had discovered something. Or some one had bartered the missing information, perhaps for his own life.

Troubridge leaned over and whispered, 'I hope there are not too many ears listening to this, sir.'

Swinburne said, 'San José, so near to that clever encounter some four hundred miles east of Havana. That, gentlemen, is the key!'

Adam tried to picture it in his mind while the room around him buzzed with excitement, and not a little disbelief. All the months, the thankless patrols, and fighting off attacks when every foreign flag was an enemy, and pain, fever and suffering in the most brutal trade of all; and it had been under their noses. It would not produce a miracle. But it was a beginning.

'My clerk will outline the details, all that we have so far. Tomorrow I shall pass instructions to the rest of the squadron.'

Pointer had moved over to sit beside him. 'I find it hard to accept.' He wiped his forehead with a hand-kerchief. 'San José is avoided when possible. Bad approaches, and a small anchorage. Used to be forti-fied – some slaves rebelled there years ago, before my time. A slaughter to all accounts.'

'But still large enough to land slaves?'

Somebody tapped a table. 'Pay attention now!'

Adam pressed his spine into the chair. *A journey in hell*.

Rounded up, beaten and shackled, sold by their own people or rival tribes to daring and unscrupulous men like Cousens. Crammed into small vessels, and even-tually transferred to the new craft of the trade. Larger, faster, and often better armed than the ships which searched an ocean for the chance of a prize.

He reached inside his coat and felt the letter folded with the other one in his pocket.

High summer in Cornwall, and Catherine's roses would still be blooming in the old garden; Lowenna's, too. Like the house overlooking the Bay, waiting.

The commodore's clerk was droning on about Spanish authority, civil and military. Population and local trade; further details would be provided for every captain without delay.

Swinburne was mopping his shining face; the show-man was almost bowing.

Adam asked abruptly, 'Does Sir Graham know about all this?'

Troubridge gave him a keen glance, wise for one so young.

'Sir Baldwin has agreed to take charge of the first part of this campaign, if that is what it will become.' He lowered his voice. 'So if anything misfired, he might also carry the blame, surely?'

Captain Munro pushed through the others and held out his hand.

'I'm going to my ship, sir.' He regarded him curiously. 'Letter for you. From one of my young gentlemen.'

'How is he? I know I should not ask.'

Munro turned as some one called his name.

'He's a good lad.' He nodded. 'Quiet, but good.' Then he grinned. 'Suits me anyway, sir!'

And he was gone.

Adam walked out on to a stone terrace, the heat bathing him like steam. He could still hear the commodore's voice, his thick laughter.

And suddenly he was sorry for him, and it troubled him. Like a warning.

Seven days out of English Harbour found His Britannic Majesty's frigate *Audacity* of twenty-four guns deep in the Caribbean, rarely in sight of land and only once close enough to another vessel to exchange greetings. She had been a small brigantine, one of the squadron's widely scattered patrols, and on her way back to Antigua to replenish stores.

Captain Ian Munro was proud of his command and made a point of demonstrating it to his people, wardroom or messdeck. He had served only once before in the Caribbean, and then as a very junior lieutenant. Most of his service had been in home waters and the Mediterranean, and for one commission in the second American war.

When he walked the quarterdeck or found a piece of shade by the nettings he often thought of all the other captains who had preceded him, as varied as the campaigns in which *Audacity* had taken part. Toulon, St Vincent, the Nile and Copenhagen were only a few of her exploits.

He had heard the boatswain, one of the oldest men in the ship, giving what sounded like a lecture to the new midshipmen who had been sent aboard at Plymouth.

'Now listen to me and listen good. You're lucky to

be serving in this ship, an' you've a lot to live up to, to ever pass muster in *my* book! *Audacity* was built in the days when men knew 'ow to give a ship life! Launched on the Medway, an' built of the best Kentish oak, when they still 'ad some seasoned trees standin'!' He had used his big red hands to sketch the shape of the hull. 'The frames was *grown* in them days, not cut from loose ends of timber, so she's got double the strength of some of them high-fliers!' He did not hide his contempt for the newer fifth-rates in the fleet.

Munro loitered by the quarterdeck rail, watching and listening to the early morning shipboard routine.

The decks had been washed down soon after dawn, and were already bone-dry in the hot southeasterly. A fair wind, enough to fill the sails, for most of the time at least; *Audacity* was leaning over to larboard, close-hauled as she lay on the starboard tack.

The sailing master was standing with one of his mates near the compass box, outwardly unconcerned, his jaw still working on a piece of pork left over from breakfast.

Munro smiled, feeling the same excitement, which he knew the motion of the man's jaw did not conceal. A week out of harbour, checking the log, the tide, the compass, using the sextant. All to find one tiny cross on the chart.

He saw the two new midshipmen with a boatswain's mate. More instruction. He watched, trying to remember his own first steps.

In one ear and out the other, had been one summing-up.

The younger of the two, David Napier, seemed quieter than most midshipmen, but even in so short a time he had heard well of him. Keen to learn, and ready to try again if something went wrong. Sponsored by his previous captain, a Bolitho. He had never met him before Antigua, but knew his background almost as well as *Audacity*'s. Napier had been 'volunteered' by his mother, who had remarried and gone to America. Not a unique story, but the one behind it would be much more interesting, he thought. A well-known frigate captain and the nephew of England's hero; it seemed strange that he should care so much.

The second newcomer had been foisted on him by another captain as an obligation to some one important. Probably glad to be rid of him. And yet Munro could not have explained why, unless he openly interfered with the routine of his officers. Again he smiled to himself. And the boatswain!

Midshipman Paul Boyce was thickset, heavily built for seventeen, which was unusual; most young gentlemen were always hungry, but the rigour of their duties pared away any surplus weight.

Munro had heard no adverse reports of his work or behaviour in the months since he had come aboard. He was never late on watch or relieving others for duty. The Atlantic had put gun and arms drill to one side, but all hands had been busy aloft and on deck, setting and trimming sails, splicing: those running repairs which made a sailor's lot.

They carried six midshipmen all told. With the fleet

cut to the bone and ships being laid up in every major port, they were lucky to get a berth at all.

He glanced at the sea alongside and saw the topgallants reflected on the gently heaving water, the masthead pendant a tiny stab of colour.

He recalled the flag captain he had met at the conference: the vice-admiral's right arm, and with every chance of a glowing future ahead of him. A face you would not forget. And yet during their brief conversations, he had gained the impression that the envy was on Bolitho's side.

He looked at the main deck again and saw Midshipman Boyce coming aft with a master's mate, probably to do some chart work. He remembered that Boyce had injured his wrist somehow and was ordered to stand clear of general seamanship duties. He frowned, trying to recall the details; he would ask the first lieutenant about it.

'*Deck there!*'

Every face peered up, and a seaman about to take another turn on a halliard shaded his eyes with one arm to look aloft.

Even the sailing master's jaw was motionless.

'Land on th' weather bow!'

There were cheers from the forecastle, and knowing grins from the older hands.

Munro touched the rail. *The cross on the chart*. All those miles.

In his mind he could see it. The Windward Passage, or soon would be, that fifty-mile channel which separated Haiti from Cuba. Hated and feared by some, with difficult currents and badly recorded soundings.

Tomorrow or the next day they would be near the place where the sloop *Lotus* had made her capture.

He felt the same chill of excitement. This was now. A perfect landfall.

'Mister Napier, come over here!'

The youth stood facing him. Open shirt, none too clean, his white trousers already touched with paint or tar. Tanned skin, a legacy of other seas, in Bolitho's last command.

The surgeon had told Munro about the scar on Napier's leg.

'A miracle he didn't lose it, sir. I've known many a butcher who would have lopped it off without blinking!'

Another story there, too.

'Sir?'

'Can you go aloft for me?'

'Aye, sir.' His feet were bare and he was rubbing one across the other while he stared at the masthead.

'Tell the lookout there's a tot waiting for him when he comes down.'

Napier hesitated by the nettings. 'They say Haiti is an evil place, sir?'

Munro grinned. 'Don't you listen to all those old women between decks! Away you go!'

Napier gripped the shrouds, testing the unyielding roughness. His hands were still not used to it. He thought he saw the midshipman named Boyce staring at him from the poop. Just for a second, and he was gone.

For now.

Napier began to climb, his gaze fixed on the quivering ratlines. It was something he took for granted, and even in his first race up the shrouds with other youngsters in *Unrivalled*, he had never been troubled by heights.

All in so short a time. He had known fear, and had endured pain; his wounded leg still troubled him, but he refused to admit it. And he had found the closest thing to having a real home, even love, which he had never believed possible.

In all his fifteen years, *this* was the first time he had been made to hate.

Audacity's midshipmen's berth was no better and no worse than most ships of her size. Situated on the orlop deck below the waterline, it was devoid of natural light, other than that which filtered through gratings in the deck above.

The smells were many and varied, stale or hoarded food, and from the bilges beneath. It was partitioned by midshipmen's chests and a scrubbed table, while hammocks were slung wherever there was a space.

Napier went down to the berth, the 'cockpit', to change into his seagoing uniform for the remainder of the day. Only then could you be certain of the rank and status of *Audacity*'s complement of two hundred.

He adjusted the solitary lantern and opened his chest. On top of the books and clothing, sewing and stitching gear and his best hat, lay the dirk. He had never quite got over it, or the quiet way Captain Bolitho had given it to him to begin his new life, and to mark his fifteenth birthday.

He gripped it and turned it toward the swaying light. It had all started when he had left the dirk lying on the mess table soon after sailing from Plymouth.

There had been two other midshipmen here that day, quietly superior and aloof toward the new arrivals, although they had all been about the same age; and there had been Paul Boyce.

Like a contest, something he should have ignored or accepted.

Boyce had picked up the dirk and exclaimed, 'Look at this! A fine piece of workmanship, and from Salters in the Strand of London indeed! What lowly midshipman can afford such luxury? He has a generous sponsor, this one. I must learn the secret!'

Napier could remember the sudden flash of anger when he had snatched the dirk from Boyce's grip.

One of the others had snapped, 'No arms in the mess, you should know that!'

Boyce had bowed gravely. 'I do not mean to offend. I merely wondered what was given in return?'

On another occasion when they had been working with a party of seamen, restowing the boats for the long Atlantic passage, Boyce had tried to trip him. But Napier was quick on his feet, and Boyce had fallen and injured his wrist.

I'll not forget! It had been like that ever since, although Boyce was always careful not to show his hostility in the presence of a lieutenant or warrant officer.

But sooner or later . . . Napier stiffened as he heard voices. One was Boyce, the other was that of Scully, the young mess boy who helped look after the berth and was always hurrying on one errand or another.

Boyce was working himself up into a rage, which seemed to come without effort.

'What do you call this? I told you I wanted two clean shirts! I can't imagine what hovel you were raised in, but it makes me sick!'

Then Scully, anxious. Worse, he was terrified. 'I pressed them like you said!'

Something hit the table. '*Sir!* Say *sir* to me, eh?'

The lid of Napier's sea chest was still raised. Neither of them had seen him.

Boyce seemed to be humming to himself.

Then he said quite calmly, 'You know what I told you before?' The sound again. 'Bend over that chest. *Do it!*'

Napier rose on one knee, the scene fixed in his mind. As if there was not another soul in the whole ship.

The mess boy was bending over the chest, unfastening and dragging down his breeches, sobbing or pleading it was impossible to tell.

Napier said, 'Stand up, Scully. Cover yourself!' He saw the rattan cane in Boyce's hand. He had also seen the purple weals across the boy's buttocks before he could hide them.

Boyce was staring at him, his heavy features contorted as if he was going to choke.

'Spying, were you? I'll make you regret the day

302

you ever . . .' He gaped, as Napier tore the cane from his hand. '*What are you doing?*'

'We are going on deck to see the first lieutenant.' He did not take his eyes off him, but said to the cowering mess boy, 'And you will tell him what happened, now and at any other time. I will stand by you!'

He felt numb, but able to grasp that his voice sounded steady, resolute. Like somebody else. And it mattered so much. Maybe too much. It was all here and now. The shop in Plymouth, the tailor peering through his spectacles, the same way that Daniel Yovell did. Looking at the captain and beaming. *Oh, not for you, sir? The young gentleman this time!*

It mattered. He himself had worked in *Unrivalled*'s cockpit and had seen the other side of her 'young gentlemen'. He had soon learned that there were bullies on every deck, but in a small ship it was rarely tolerated for long.

Boyce shrugged. 'I shall explain.'

They all looked up as calls trilled through the messdecks overhead.

'All hands! All hands to quarters and clear for action!'

Napier closed and locked his chest, still unable to believe that he was so calm.

He was vaguely aware of Boyce's face flashing in the reflected light as he clipped the dirk to his belt.

A surgeon's mate ran past and Napier recalled that the sick bay and surgeon's quarters were directly adjoining the berth.

When he turned again, Boyce had disappeared, and

the mess boy was gripping the offending shirts in both hands.

He pleaded, 'Don't tell anybody, sir. I don't want no more trouble!'

How often had he said that?

Screens were being pulled down and feet pounded loudly overhead. Exercise or false alarm, he found he did not care. He felt as if he had suddenly grown up.

Then he was running with all the others.

Captain Adam Bolitho sat in the tall-backed chair and folded the letter he had reread with such care. From Nancy, and it had been like hearing her voice, her quick laugh. All this time, and he had not known about it.

Even if I had . . . The courier, a brig from Plymouth, had brought more despatches for Bethune. Nancy's letter had eventually reached Antigua by a longer route, and two different vessels. The last mail bag had been stamped 'Gibraltar'. And there had been two letters from Lowenna.

Loud thuds sounded throughout the ship. Stores; and perhaps the purser had managed to obtain some more fruit.

He stared through the stern windows. A few local craft were skimming the flat water, so there had to be some kind of wind. Here in the cabin, even with skylight and quarter windows open, it was completely airless. And *Athena* was still at anchor, as if she would never move again. The strain on the sailors was showing itself in the punishment book, the first sign in any ship. Flogging never cured anything, but neither did boredom.

He looked at the sky; angry was the word for it. But this was the hurricane season, and September was always the worst month. How *could* it be September?

He opened Lowenna's letter again. She had included a sketch drawn by his cousin Elizabeth. They were seeing quite a lot of each other. He felt more than relief. He was strangely grateful.

More shouts: a boat coming alongside. But still no frigates had arrived to reinforce the squadron, and to give the commodore any extra resources for casting his net around the slave routes.

The screen door opened and closed: it was Luke Jago. He was no longer announced by the sentry, a privilege he never abused.

'You wanted me, Cap'n?' His eyes flicked to the open letters. He was ready.

'Bryan Ferguson – you remember him, don't you?'

Jago nodded, seeing the office, the stable yard, and Grace, always planning and arranging things.

'We got on well last time we was in port.'

'He died. Heart gave out. He was never all that strong, though he'd be the last to admit it.'

Jago said, 'He'll be sorely missed, I reckon.'

'I heard a boat alongside?'

Jago walked to the quarter windows and grimaced at the sky.

'In for a blow by the makin's of it.' He recalled what Adam had said. 'Sir Graham's servant, sir.'

Adam said, 'He's been ashore for a few hours.'

'On an errand, I believe.' His eyes creased in a smile. The Captain didn't miss much even if he was always busy as hell.

Adam looked at the little sketch. Two mermaids this time, waving to an incoming ship. *If only it were true*.

Jago gauged the moment. 'Strange when you thinks of it, Cap'n. Us stuck in harbour, while young Mister Napier is out there, showin' us all what to do!'

Bowles had appeared soundlessly from his pantry. 'May I pour something, sir?'

Adam shook his head. 'Not yet. Sir Graham has been sitting with all those official envelopes. I think I had best be ready.'

Somewhere a door slid shut and Bowles nodded gravely. He knew every sound in the poop like his own body.

'I think that is probably wise, sir.'

Adam glanced at his coat, hanging from a door. It was barely moving. Lowenna had been in London, and had seen some lawyer who was dealing with Montagu's affairs. It had been raining there. She had returned to Falmouth, to Nancy. He thought of Ferguson, who had lost an arm at the Saintes, a lifetime ago. The house would be missing him. So would poor Grace.

'Flag lieutenant, *sah!*'

Troubridge entered the cabin but shook his head when Bowles offered to take his hat. He looked strained, even irritated, and said, 'I can't stay.' He joined Adam, looking briefly at the letters on the table.

'Sir Graham is sending for the commodore. I'm off to fetch him. May I use the gig?'

Jago was already by the door. 'Ready when you needs me, sir.'

Adam asked quietly, 'Is it trouble?'

Troubridge did not answer directly. 'How soon can you get under way, sir? They say there's a storm in the offing.' He looked very young, and vulnerable.

Adam saw Bowles reaching for his coat. 'Tell me.' And all the while, like other times, different places, the mechanics of his mind were clicking into place. How many officers were ashore? Which working parties could be found and recalled to the ship; how long would it take?

Troubridge sighed. 'Sir Graham had his response from the Admiralty. No more frigates, not yet in any case. One will eventually be coming direct from Freetown, otherwise . . .' He shrugged. 'The other thing is that we received a report about San José. Most of it is owned by a renegade Portuguese named Miguel Carneiro. Came to Cuba from Brazil after causing some embarrassment to the government there, and to greater powers in Lisbon. Claims to have some connection with the Portuguese royal family. It's all getting rather beyond me.'

Adam looked past him at the harbour, and the threatening sky. 'Is he the missing name, Francis? The slavers' paymaster?' He crossed the cabin and gazed at the anchored barque.

He said, '*Athena* can be clear of English Harbour before nightfall.'

He watched Troubridge's uncertainty, like some one else, all confidence gone. Bethune must have given him a harder ride than usual. But why?

He tried to lighten it. 'I'll not be sorry to find some sea-room if it's to be a real storm.'

Troubridge turned toward the door. 'Sir Graham is certain that at least three of the big slave ships are hiding at San José, maybe waiting for settlement. For the *Villa de Bilbao*'s gold.'

'Then they'll *wait*. The weather gives them an even better reason.'

He saw the conflict on the young lieutenant's face. Loyalty and trust, friendship and something more.

Troubridge said flatly, 'This man, Carneiro, he has been warned, or soon will be.'

'Gig's alongside, sir!'

'How can Sir Graham be sure of this?' He thought of the servant, Tolan, his absence ashore, and Bethune's fury upon his return. He had heard his voice even up here until some one had closed a door.

Troubridge hesitated, and seemed to come to a decision. 'There was a lady, sir. Sir Graham intended to see her.' He swallowed. 'Again. But the house was empty. Everything gone.' He made a halfhearted attempt at a shrug, and tried to smile. 'So you see?'

Adam walked with him, out into the sunshine, the heat and the busy normality.

Troubridge added, 'Sir Graham sends his compliments and . . .'

He doffed his hat and hurried down to the entry port.

Adam watched the gig pull smartly away from the side, and saw Jago turn to shade his eyes and stare up at the poop. *At me*.

So it was Catherine. Perhaps it explained her failure to answer his letters, when he had told himself that they had gone astray, like Nancy's. The rest he could imagine for himself.

He saw Stirling waiting by the quarterdeck ladder, grim-faced. A man who never changed.

'I want all shore working parties recalled. How many are there?'

The response was instant. 'Only two, sir. The carpenter's crew and the purser's clerk with five seamen.'

He glanced at the masthead pendant. Hardly moving, but in no time it could become a screaming gale.

He looked across at the barque again. 'I want to see the sailmaker, as soon as I've left the admiral.' He saw each word hit its mark. 'No more visitors aboard, except for the commodore, of course.'

Stirling touched his hat, but did not smile.

As he walked to the companion Adam thought of the night he had dined as a guest of the wardroom. Landsmen could never understand how a captain could be a guest in his own command. Perhaps it was a ship's strength, like keel or timbers.

He closed his mind to everything but that same sense of warning, like a hand reaching out.

Tolan opened the screen door for him but dropped his eyes, and his thoughts or emotions remained hidden.

Bethune was waiting, facing the screen, as if he had

been in that stance since Troubridge had been sent to 'fetch' the commodore.

He was fully dressed, his shirt fresh against his waistcoat. He looked very calm; *not a hair out of place*, as Yovell would have said.

He gestured to a chair. Even that looked as if it had been arranged.

'Flags told you the latest intelligence, I take it?' He did not wait. 'My information is reliable. This fellow Carneiro has had contact with certain ship owners, would-be slavers if you like, as well as with powerful figures in business and politics.' His mouth twisted briefly. 'I daresay with *our* people, too.'

He waited while Tolan poured two glasses of wine.

'A local trading vessel sailed recently for Kingston, or so it was alleged. A man named Jacob, well known to the commodore, to all accounts.' He sipped the wine.

Adam did likewise but tasted nothing. He was hearing Troubridge's words at the conference, about who might carry the blame if the campaign misfired.

He saw Tolan standing by a hanging mirror and realized he was watching him. More like a voice than a pair of eyes. He carried messages for Bethune, anything he asked, but kept his mouth tight. Tolan had found out about the trader Jacob. It explained far more than his master's anger.

Bethune said, 'You *are* ready for sea, if need be?'

'By the dog watches, Sir Graham. I have passed the word.'

Bethune regarded him steadily. 'I did the right thing

to select you for flag captain.' He checked himself, as if he had gone too far. 'Do you have any proposals?'

So casually asked. The realization hit him like a fist. Bethune was desperate.

He said, 'Time is not on our side, Sir Graham.' He saw him clench his fist as if he could scarcely control his annoyance, or perhaps his anxiety. 'I think we should go directly to San José. If greed does not hold those vessels in port, then nothing will.' He saw Bethune stride to the stern windows and lean on the bench seat to peer out at the harbour. Across his bright epaulettes, he said, 'The reports of the weather are not good.' He did not turn, and Adam could almost feel the tension.

'It may be our only ally.' But he was thinking of *Athena*'s sailmaker, slotting his name. Cruikshank. A Dorset man. Some one must have mentioned it.

He said, 'I think we should take the *Villa de Bilbao* in company.' He waited, seeing the doubt, the disappointment perhaps. 'As the bait.'

Bethune nodded slowly, standing very upright, his neat hair touching the deckhead.

'We might just have the edge on them. The old equation, eh, Adam? Time, speed and distance?'

Adam wanted to leave, to begin something which he might regret for the rest of his life. Like being driven, inspired.

Bethune said quietly, 'I shall leave you to prepare things. I have every confidence. In the meantime, *I* shall deal with the commodore.'

As he reached the door, Bethune smiled for the first time.

'Good work, Adam.'

Standing by the hanging mirror, George Tolan gripped the back of a chair to control himself.

Bethune had said the same to him, that day when he had gone to meet the woman named Catherine.

The deserted house, the little servant who 'knew nothing', the bed where they had been together.

He smiled bitterly. *One betraying the other*.

He listened to all the new sounds. Like any ship. Or one ship he always remembered.

Athena was coming to life again.

14

Loyalty or Gratitude?

Captain Ian Munro gripped a mizzen stay and felt the wind transmitting its strength through every spar, from truck to keel. Even now, after countless watches at sea under most moods of weather, its power still excited him. He doubted if many of *Audacity*'s company would believe that.

He trained his telescope and waited for the bows to lift and steady, spray drifting over the deck like hail with the wind across the quarter. The other vessel was on the same bearing, her tan sails etched against the low banks of cloud. She was a large topsail schooner, no flag, her hull showing the marks and stains of hard usage.

Munro had ordered the usual preparations. *Beat to quarters and clear for action*. It was unlikely that any merchantman, slaver or not, would care to cross swords with a frigate. But from all he had learned and heard since joining Sir Graham Bethune's command, it was prudent not to take chances.

He could feel the sailing master's eyes on his back. The wind was getting stronger by the hour, but holding steady from the southeast. The glass had dropped, and the sea, although almost unbroken, had been building into long swells, stretching away from horizon to horizon.

He lowered the glass and wiped his eye with his sleeve. Main and mizzen courses had been taken in, forecourse and topsails reefed. He glanced at the big double wheel; he had put three helmsmen there to match the power of the rudder.

The sailing master was talking with his senior mate, who would be going across to the schooner with a boarding party, all experienced hands, with the two new midshipmen to assist and run errands. If the schooner proved to be a slaver, she would be held as a prize. No wonder the master's mate could grin about it. His own command, with a lion's share of slave bounty and prize money for good measure.

He ran his eye along the tilting deck to the boat-handling party, and the men who would be going over to the other vessel.

Audacity's first patrol on the station. It would make some of the other captains sit up and take notice of this old newcomer.

He said, 'Close enough. Fire the signal.'

The gun captain must have been watching and waiting. The dull bang of the shot was carried away by the wind.

He walked to the quarterdeck rail and said, 'No

risks, Mr Mowbray. Keep under our lee until you have everything in hand.'

'She's shortenin' sail, sir!'

Munro looked at the sailing master. 'Worried?'

He rubbed his chin. 'If there's a bad storm on the make, we should be able to work clear of it, or run ahead of a real blow. Lucky we hadn't entered the Windward Passage – less room to spread our wings there!'

Munro looked up at the clouds. Here and there he could still see a patch of blue, clear sky. *Now or never*.

'Heave to, if you please! Stand by to lower boats!'

Cutter and jolly boat, up and over the gangway and then as if by some miracle rising and plunging alongside, seamen scrambling down, the dull glare reflecting from cutlasses and muskets. Munro watched closely, remembering. He had been in boarding parties as a lieutenant, even as midshipman. The moment you left the ship was always the worst. Refuge, home, life itself. Afterwards, it was only the cut and thrust of combat you heard mentioned.

Some one breathed loudly, 'Oars out, sir! Both boats away!'

Canvas cracked and banged momentarily overhead as *Audacity* drifted out of command.

'Get the ship under way again! Man the braces! Resume course, nor' nor' west!'

When he looked again the two boats seemed already lost against the heaving water, like leaves on a mill race.

He walked to the compass box. *The worst part*.

* * *

Mowbray, master's mate, leaned back in the jolly boat's sternsheets and stared beyond the oarsmen and their steady, seemingly unhurried stroke. The boat felt heavy and cumbersome, with extra hands and weapons and the uncomfortable motion. Like running up a steep slope and down the other side, every man soaked in spray, trying not to peer astern at *Audacity*'s topsails.

He twisted round to look for the cutter, running almost abeam, with a boatswain's mate in charge. They had worked together before, and had enjoyed runs ashore in one port or another. They were professional, trusted sailors, who would always be back on board after a night they usually regretted.

Mowbray glanced at the two midshipmen huddled below the tiller. Officers one day, when they could make a Jack's life hell if the mood directed. When they walked their own quarterdecks, did they ever remember times like these, and the real sailors who had taught them?

He stared up at the schooner's poop. Close enough to see the scars and rough repairs. A hard-used vessel. Even the sails looked like patchwork.

The younger midshipman asked, '*Is* she a slaver, Mr Mowbray?'

Mowbray considered it, and wondered how or where this midshipman, Napier, had started off in life. But he never took his eyes from the other vessel, and a handful of figures clinging to the shrouds as if watching the two boats.

'Soon know. If we was lyin' downwind of 'er we'd

already be able to smell 'er. I've seen a few in me time, when it was all nice an' legal!'

The other midshipman muttered, '*All* the great empires were built on slavery . . .' He could not continue; his face looked green.

Mowbray snapped, 'Over the side. Don't spew in th' boat, damn you!'

He was too late.

The stroke oarsman lay back on his loom and rolled his eyes toward the clouds. '*Jesus.*'

David Napier swallowed and tried not to hear Boyce retching and vomiting over the gunwale.

The vessel loomed right over them now, so that the other sounds seemed muffled. Somewhere else. He knew without looking that the bowman had hurled his grapnel over the bulwark, and that somehow the oars were all suddenly inboard. Weapons had appeared, and he saw a seaman unwrapping the lock of his musket. The man's face was devoid of expression. As if it were a drill.

He felt for the dirk under his coat, remembering the fire and smoke of Algiers, Jago taking charge of a boat's crew for boarding one of the enemy ships. Voice flat and calm, eyes everywhere. And that other time when he had been on deck with the captain. *Keep by me, David.*

The crash of the shot was so close that he imagined for a second that one of the seamen's muskets had exploded prematurely.

Some one shouted, '*Cast off! Now*, for God's sake!'

Napier stared round, his heart pumping wildly.

Boyce had been shot. He could still hear his scream.

He stared down at the hand fastened around his wrist, and at Mowbray's face. His eyes, which seemed to steady him. It was then that he saw the blood on Mowbray's thigh and running across the bottom boards.

Mowbray spoke slowly and carefully, his grip never weakening, his gaze quite steady.

'I will be all right in a minute.' Somewhere in the background, another world, men were yelling and cursing. The cutter must have grappled alongside.

Mowbray stared at him as if making sure of something. Then he said, 'Lead them, Mister Napier. Lead them!'

Napier felt the boat riding against the hull on the swell. Somehow he was on his feet, the fine new dirk drawn and held above his head.

There was a voice, too. '*To me, Audacity! To me, lads!*'

The rest was drowned by an animal roar as the seamen sprang up the side, one of them pausing only to give his hand to the midshipman who had rallied them.

Napier clung to a halliard and stared around the unfamiliar deck. Men were being herded into groups, weapons kicked aside. *Audacity*'s boatswain's mate shouted, 'Put 'im *down*, Lacy, you've already scuppered the bugger!'

Napier looked over the side and saw Mowbray being helped into a sitting position. He was alive, and as he peered over the seaman's shoulder he saw him, and very slowly gave a mock salute.

Napier had to make three attempts to sheathe his dirk, and yet he was not aware of his hand shaking. Some one hurried past, but paused long enough to slap him on the shoulder.

Mowbray was being hoisted up and over the bulwark in a makeshift boatswain's chair, his face creased with pain.

He saw Napier and grinned weakly. 'To me, *Audacity*!' Then he fainted.

A burly seaman, with a bared cutlass thrust through his belt and wielding a boarding axe, yelled something to a group of the schooner's crew and glared wildly around at Napier. 'That showed 'em, by God!' He turned to hurry after the boatswain's mate, but halted as Napier said, 'Can you help Mr Boyce? He's been wounded!'

He remembered the unknown seaman's face for a long time afterwards. Boyce had somehow followed the others aboard and was squatting on a crate below the bulwark, one arm wrapped inside his coat, head bowed. Unable to move.

Abruptly, the seaman said, 'Don't you worry about the likes of 'im, sir, not after what you just done. 'E's not got a mark on 'im.' The boarding axe lifted a few inches. 'Not yet, anyways!' Then he was gone, with men he knew and trusted, faces he saw every time the hands were piped.

They were bundling a man in a blue coat away from the poop. Bearded, and contemptuous of those who held him. The ship's master.

The boatswain's mate said harshly, 'Won't say a

319

word, Mr Napier!' He saw Mowbray and exclaimed, 'You're with us again, Tom?' and grinned, with obvious relief that his friend had survived.

Mowbray breathed out heavily. 'Open the hatches. Man those swivels. Shoot any man who resists.' He was on his feet, using a musket like a crutch as he staggered with the ship's uneasy motion.

Napier saw the hatches being hauled away, recalling Mowbray's words when they had been pulling toward this schooner. It was still only partly real, everything blurred and out of focus. Then he caught the stench as the hatches fell aside, and the sound, like a solitary, wordless voice. A groan, more unreal still, and terrible.

Mowbray had his other arm around Napier's shoulders.

'Take a look, and remember what you see.' His grip tightened. 'I was proud of you back there, young Napier. Real proud. So were the lads.' He looked up suddenly and stared at the ship's master.

'Hear me. One word from you, *one word*, and you go below to join the "passengers"!'

Napier stared into the first hold. There were about thirty slaves. From the discarded manacles and the filth, there had obviously been many more. Crammed together, with food being thrown down through the bars as if to animals.

He felt his fingers tighten around the dirk. They were women. At a guess, all were young, some very young.

A seaman touched his sleeve. 'No closer, Mr Napier. They'd rip you to shreds.'

Napier felt a mug in his free hand. It must have come from somewhere . . .

He nearly choked, and some one called, 'Drop o' Nelson's blood! Do yer good!' They could even laugh about it.

He wanted to tell them. To share it. That he had been rendered senseless with tots of rum that day on *Unrivalled*'s orlop deck, when he had nearly lost his leg. But no voice came out.

There were more people now, and Napier heard profane greetings and wild laughter as another boat from *Audacity* surged alongside. It was the second master's mate; Napier could not recall his name, as if he had no control over his mind. Men swarming to halliards and braces, orders being yelled and obeyed by British Jack and slaver alike.

Mowbray was protesting as he was hoisted out over the side to be put in one of the boats, while his replacement was shouting and grinning down at him. 'Never fear, matey, I'll see you get yer share of the bounty money!' He pointed at Napier. 'Or *Mister Napier* 'ere will want to know why!'

It was only then that Napier realized he was being sent back to *Audacity*.

It was a choppy crossing, and the clouds warned of the coming storm. It was hard to think it through; and it was not the rum.

It seemed to take only half the time for the return journey. They said it always did . . . for the lucky ones.

The surgeon was waiting for Mowbray, and a

seaman who had broken his wrist when he had fallen from the slaver's shrouds while in pursuit of one of her sailors. Napier saw Midshipman Boyce, wild-eyed and sweating, being taken to the orlop, and heard him protesting, 'It's nothing! I was merely doing my duty!'

It only made it worse.

While *Audacity* heeled over and steadied on a fresh tack to weather the following storm, Captain Munro sent for him. Napier was not sure why, but, looking back, it was as if he wanted to discover something, perhaps to put in his report.

Instead he said, 'Mr Mowbray speaks very well of you.' He waited while his cabin steward poured a big mug of ginger beer. He even smiled when he saw Napier's slight frown as he watched the drink being poured. Like part of a memory.

Munro was called away, but said, 'Stay here and enjoy your ginger beer.' Then he turned to look back from the door, and added quietly, 'He'll be proud of you.'

The true reward.

Many of *Athena*'s ship's company had never been at sea in a real hurricane before, and those who had swore afterwards that it was their worst. At anchor, even in a safe harbour, the sudden shift of the wind's force and direction could drive a ship aground to become a total wreck even in the most experienced hands.

Adam Bolitho followed the rule and held *Athena* running ahead of the storm's path, with the wind and sea pounding across the starboard quarter, sails trimmed and reefs to a minimum. To most on board it was a world of chaos, rearing seas crashing against the hull with such strength that it felt as if she had indeed run ashore. Topmen fought their way aloft to obey the constant orders yelled from the quarterdeck; even Stirling had been seen to use a speaking-trumpet. They were blinded by spray, senses dulled by the endless battle with swollen cordage snared in blocks, or tearing apart under pressure with all the power and pain of a coachman's whip.

A smaller vessel would have run far ahead of the storm, or gone under. *Athena* seemed to brace herself and fight.

Helmsmen, four at a time, were lashed to the wheel, and no seaman ventured along the lee side of the main deck without a lifeline, or a trusted companion to share the risks.

Even the heavy guns seemed determined to break free. It was not unknown, and in one hurricane, a twenty-four pounder had snapped its breeching and run amok on the ship's lower deck, maiming anybody who got into its way.

Old Sam Petch the gunner had been ready. From ponderous carronade to lively nine-pounder, nothing broke adrift. When some one had praised him for his preparations he had answered scornfully, 'What did you expect, *matey*?'

On the fifth morning the sea was calmer, although still lively.

The sky was blue again, the last clouds speeding away like torn banners after a battle.

The galley fire was alight, and the air heavy with the smells of pitch and tar, new cordage, and rum.

Hammers and mallets were soon busy, and spare canvas was laid out to dry in the first sunlight, which some sailors had never expected to see again.

The storm was gone, probably curving northward by the Bahamas and out into the Atlantic.

Adam stood by the quarterdeck rail and sipped a scalding mug of coffee, which Bowles had somehow managed to make in the chaos of the cabin, his domain. He had remained aft throughout the storm, putting lashings on furniture and sending flasks of something lukewarm but strong by way of a messenger.

He had remarked on one occasion, 'In a sea fight I 'elps to look after the wounded. In a storm, I looks after meself!'

He saw Jago with a boatswain's mate climbing over the boat tier. All were firmly lashed in place and overflowing with sea water. In an hour or so they would be steaming in the heat.

Several of the hands had been injured, in falls, or having been hurled against guns by incoming waves.

If Daniel Yovell had been aboard he would have offered a prayer.

Adam rubbed his face with his palm. He could not remember when he had last had a shave.

He walked to the compass box and peered at the card. West by north. Only two men on the wheel now. He caught the eye of the first helmsman. The man licked his cracked lips and said, 'Glad we've got rid of that lot, sir!' Before, he would have said nothing, or averted his eyes.

Maybe that was as good as any prayer.

There was a strong plume of greasy smoke from the galley funnel now, and he felt his stomach contract. He should be starving, but the thought of food only sickened him.

He saw some seamen pause in their splicing and grin at each other. Jack could eat anything, any time. It was likely the cook's solid standby, skillygolee, oatmeal gruel with crushed and toasted ship's biscuit and great chunks of boiled meat. And another measure of rum. The purser would be anxiously watching every issue.

'Captain, sir?'

It was Tolan, freshly shaved and as smart as any marine, his eyes on the horizon.

'Sir Graham's compliments, sir, an' would you attend the cabin when you can.'

Adam felt the muscles of his back relax, for the first time in hours.

'Which means immediately, right?'

Tolan looked at him directly. 'I reckon so, sir.'

He followed him to the companion; a man you would never know, he thought.

A Royal Marine sentry brought his heels together and the first screen door opened soundlessly. There had been a sentry on guard in the vice-admiral's quarters throughout the storm. Would he have remained here if the ship had foundered? He shook himself free of the thoughts. He was more tired than he had believed.

It was the first time he had ever seen Bethune so disturbed and ill at ease. He took in the loose neck-cloth, and a stain of what looked like wine on one sleeve, like dried blood.

Bethune stared at him. 'Nothing to report?' Characteristically, he did not wait for an answer. 'Good, but I'm not a mind reader, you know!'

Adam realized for the first time that Troubridge was also present, on his knees beside one of Bethune's beautiful leather trunks. He did not look up.

Adam said quietly, 'Most of the running repairs are in hand, Sir Graham. I am sending both watches to breakfast. They've done well, very well.'

Bethune studied him, as if he were looking for another explanation.

He said, 'I've been like a caged animal down here! By God, I almost envied you working the ship, holding the people together!' He gave a short, humourless laugh. 'Never thought I'd hear myself say that. But when you're cooped up like this, well, you begin to believe anything!'

Adam's eyes moved around the main cabin. Furniture secured, the expensive desk covered with oilskin in case a heavy sea had smashed open a gunport.

Bethune did not know, or perhaps care, that other cabins and half of the wardroom had been removed during the long refit, when *Athena* had been transformed into a flagship and the space was required for her first admiral. He was hardly 'cooped up'.

Bethune snapped his fingers and a servant hurried to uncover a chair.

'What are our chances of making a rendezvous with
. . .' He snapped his fingers again and Troubridge
called from the open trunk, '*Villa de Bilbao*, Sir
Graham.'

Bethune leaned back slowly, as if the chair were
hurting him.

'Well, what *are* our chances, overall, I mean?'

'She's a sound ship, Sir Graham, and manned by
trained seamen. Volunteers. Pointer is in command,
and his second lieutenant from *Lotus*. Grimes was
with the original prize crew, and is more than capable.'

Bethune leaned over in the chair as if to see
Troubridge. 'Yes indeed, *Commander* Pointer as he is
now!' It sounded like an accusation.

Adam said, 'He is all but due, Sir Graham. It is not
an easy plan that we are about to execute.'

Bethune rubbed his chin. 'Pointer will enter San
José as if he is being pursued, by *Audacity*, or *Hostile*
if Captain Munro is off station due to the storm or
whatever. We shall be close by, should the slavers
attempt to break out.' The fingers had moved to one
arm of the chair, tapping a slow tattoo. '*Well?* What
are the chances of success, in your opinion?'

'I doubt if local shipping has been on the move in
San José's area. Bad coast, and the slavers are not
going to take unnecessary risks.' From a corner of his
eye he saw Troubridge's hand grip the edge of the
leather trunk. A caution. Or a prompt? 'Unless they've
already been warned, of course.'

Bethune did not rise to it.

'The weather is our ally, you said? That may be so . . . I'll not detain you, Adam. I've not forgotten what it's like to walk that deck with only my own wits to rely on.' He was almost jocular now. 'Duties permitting, sup with me this evening, eh?' He spoke to the cabin at large. 'Just the two of us.'

Adam left the cabin and climbed slowly to the quarterdeck.

The sky was already clearer, the horizon like burnished copper. And not another living thing in sight.

He glanced up through the shrouds and stays and the barely filling topsails, to the vice-admiral's flag at the fore.

As if it were yesterday, he could remember the stir Richard Bolitho had caused at the Admiralty and throughout the fleet when he had said that the days of the line of battle, the symbol of sea power, were numbered. Perhaps Bethune, sheltered for so many years behind those walls of Admiralty, was only just coming to see the strength of that argument. The Saintes, the Nile, and finally Trafalgar, had seen the last of the great squadrons, gun to gun at point-blank range. Lord Exmouth, still a frigate captain at heart, must have realized it at Algiers. Risk, courage, and Lady Luck, as Thomas Herrick called her, had been his true strength.

He thought of Bethune's words. *The weather is our ally. You said?* Doubts? Second thoughts? Suppose the mock attack failed, or the slavers had vanished? How resolute might he be then?

He looked up at the admiral's flag again, cracking out to a freak gust of wind.

Bethune knew it; so did Troubridge. If the plan misfired, the blame would only rest with one.

It was calm, even peaceful in the admiral's quarters later, when Adam returned. Storm lashings had all but vanished, and every piece of furniture shone in the glow of candles and lanterns.

Bethune was more his old self, elegant, assured, eager to make his guest comfortable and welcome.

'The beef will probably be like leather, Adam, but the wines are good enough to hide the cook's errors!'

Tolan and two other servants waited on table without bustle or noise. Adam relaxed very slowly. In two or three days' time *Athena* could be quivering to the crash and recoil of gunfire, and even in a hit-and-run skirmish there would be casualties. He thought of the small frigate *Audacity*, knowing the risk she might have to take, and all the similar risks he had known and shared since he had worn the King's coat.

Bethune said abruptly, 'Of course, Adam, I sometimes forget. How well do you know Lady Catherine?'

Adam met his eyes across the table. Troubridge's unspoken warning; Tolan's anger and something more, after his errand ashore in English Harbour.

He answered, 'She was very good to me when I needed help, and understanding.'

Bethune touched his lower lip with an empty glass. 'I heard something about that. And she wanted *you* to have Richard's Nile medal. I thought that was a fine thing to do. Had fate decided differently I would have relieved his squadron earlier. Fate indeed, Adam? Then I might have been the one to fall in battle.'

Adam tried not to listen to the thud of the tiller head, the clatter of blocks in a strengthening breeze. Stirling was there. He would call his captain if need be.

He said, 'We have all been close to death from time to time, Sir Graham.'

Bethune put down the glass sharply. 'That is not what I am saying. Lady Catherine is a fine person in every way. Brave and caring, as she showed every one when she was in an open boat with that wretched vessel's survivors. Anything might have happened. To her, I mean!' He waved one hand, lace spilling from the coat sleeve. 'To be truthful, I care for her very much.' He stared at him, his eyes reflecting the candle-light. 'Why am I telling you this? How may it concern you?' He shrugged. 'Perhaps because I feel I owe that much to you. Because of Sir Richard.'

Adam said quietly, 'Baron Sillitoe is somehow involved in the slave trade, directly or otherwise we cannot know. Lady Catherine feels indebted to him. He saved her life, protected her reputation.'

Bethune banged the table. 'Nobody knows that better than I do, dammit!' He calmed himself, the effort almost physical. 'But gratitude is never enough.'

He glanced round and snapped his fingers. 'Cognac, Tolan. Then leave us.'

Adam stared at the plates. He could still taste the

food, but did not recall eating anything, or if the beef had been like leather or otherwise.

Only the cognac seemed real. He said, 'Lady Catherine told you she was returning to England?'

'Eventually. I had hoped to see her when this so-called campaign is finished.' He regarded him steadily. 'The terms would be her own, but that she has always known. I would not betray her, be assured of that.'

Adam wondered if any one had ever seen or heard this Bethune, let alone shared something so significant, and so dangerous.

Bethune said, 'Walk from this cabin, and I will never mention this matter again. You are my flag captain – that must be enough, more than enough, some would say.' He tried to smile, but it would not come. 'But as a *friend*, tell me what you think.'

Adam thought he heard a door click. Maybe Tolan was listening, gauging his own future perhaps. Bethune's wife came of a rich and influential family. An affair would not be allowed to melt away so easily.

He heard himself say, 'I think she will have tried to warn Sillitoe, although I'd have thought that he of all people would be on his ready guard.'

'Warned him? Because I told her of the danger to her, if she remained in Antigua?'

'Loyalty reaches two ways, Sir Graham, as I have learned to my cost.'

Bethune was on his feet. 'Then I have put her in peril, is that what you are saying?' He came around the table, his coat sweeping his glass to the deck in fragments. 'Tell me, Adam – it's all I care about!'

331

Adam measured his words with care.

'If the ships are gone when we reach San José, no harm will have been done but to our reputations. Our pride.'

He felt Bethune's grip on his shoulder, heard one word. '*Mine!*'

He persisted, 'If not, we can put our plan into action. This man Carneiro will not risk being expelled from Cuba when he already has his eye on making Brazil separate from his own country. Independence or rebellion, what matters is at which end of the gun you are standing.'

Bethune let out a slow breath.

'Old head on young shoulders, Adam. I should have remembered.'

He swung away and slopped more cognac into unused tumblers.

When he faced him again his eyes were very bright, with alcohol, emotion or sheer excitement.

He thrust out his glass.

'To us, then! Captains all!'

Adam knew it was not something he would ever forget.

15

Reaching Out

The girl named Lowenna paused on the steeply slop-ing path that ran down from the narrow coastal road, and stared across Falmouth Bay. She had been warned about loose stones on this uneven track; in bad weather it could be treacherous.

She looked at the small, fan-shaped beach directly below her, which she had visited several times. It had become special to her, although she could not explain why. And always at this moment, with the tide on the turn, the sand hard and unmarked even by the rapa-cious gulls. Soon the tide would fall still further, and this small beach would join hands with the larger expanses around the immediate headland.

The breeze off the bay was cool, but she hardly felt it beneath the heavy cloak she had borrowed from Nancy.

She walked slowly down the remainder of the slope, and stepped on to a slab of rock which must have been washed from the cliff in some forgotten storm. It was perfectly shaped, like a giant doorstone.

She tucked some rebellious hair beneath the cloak's hood and gazed once more across the bay. It was almost noon, and opposite her St Anthony Head was partly hidden in mist, or spray blowing in from the sea.

A private place. She knew that if she looked back up the path the coastal road would be invisible, as would the stable boy who was minding the pony and Elizabeth's horse. She could almost feel the girl watching her. Curiosity, amusement, she still did not know her well enough to determine.

They had ridden three times together. This would be the fourth.

The pony, Jory, had been the model of behaviour; he had apparently been around as long as any one could remember. Elizabeth had remarked, 'Something bigger and a little more lively soon, Lowenna.' She was very much at home in the saddle, and knew it.

Lowenna sat down on a piece of rock and dragged off her boots. They were made of soft Spanish leather, and fitted her perfectly, and she wondered where Nancy had got them in the first place.

She stood slowly. Jory was gentle enough, but she could feel the effort of gripping him with her knees. She wondered what had made her do it, her legs bare astride the well-worn saddle.

Elizabeth had pronounced a side-saddle too dangerous. 'More so on these roads!'

Lowenna could imagine that, too. When a storm rolled into the bay they had told her that the road, no more than a track at the best of times, became impassable, and some parts had been washed away. She took the first steps on the hard, wet sand and watched the bubbles exploring her toes, the pressure of her feet changing the colour from gold to silver. It was cold, too, and she shivered.

She thought of the letter which had been brought to the Roxby house that morning, crumpled, stamped and counter-stamped. She had pressed it to her face and mouth. It even tasted of the sea, of Adam. It was not like watching the ships entering Falmouth, and Carrick Roads. Clinging to those few precious, desperate memories.

Adam had been *here*, with her. She had read it three times, but Nancy had said nothing, not even remarking on the fact that she had forsaken her breakfast before joining Elizabeth in the stable yard.

Like hearing his voice, seeing that little smile. Feeling his hands on her.

She cherished the memory of that last time together. Her fear, her anxiety, and then a wanton, uncontrollable desire which she had believed she would never experience.

He had written very little about the ship, or his relationship with his vice-admiral.

I would that I could deliver this letter myself, dearest Lowenna.

She staggered as her feet sank into a softer layer of sand.

When would he come back to England? She had to shut her ears to those who spoke of commissions extended at the whim of some politician or senior officer. It was still another world. So much to learn and understand.

She turned and looked up the beach and the fallen cliff beyond. She could see the boy's head over a slate wall, but nothing else.

What must she do? She felt it sweep over her again, like panic. *I cannot stay here forever, although Nancy makes it easy enough. I am still a stranger. Only my past is remembered.*

She thought of that last visit to London, to Montagu's lawyer. The will was being contested, and in any case . . . But while she had been there she had met Sir Gregory's oldest friend, Mark Fellowes, soon, it was said, to be honoured by the Prince Regent for a portrait he had completed. The subject had not been mentioned.

Fellowes had asked her if she would pose for him while she was in town. Natural enough, especially after all that Sir Gregory had taught her.

Elizabeth had touched on it unknowingly shortly after her return to Cornwall; she must have been giving it a good deal of thought. Like the discussions they had had about her sketches of mermaids. She had heard herself say, *when you pose you become a study, not a body.*

It had been with her ever since, when she allowed it to take her unaware.

The studio beside the Thames, like any other. Mark Fellowes and two or three associates. She could not even remember that clearly.

It was like the recurrence of a nightmare.

When she had started to disrobe, something had snapped within her. Like that moment when Adam and young Troubridge had burst into that other studio, and she had nearly killed the man who had tried to take her like a common whore.

I would have killed him . . .

She had run out of the room. Fellowes had written to her since, but she had not known how to reply.

I did not feel like a subject. I felt like a living woman.

She heard feet on the wet sand, and wondered what the girl would think if she really knew her thoughts.

'What is it?'

Elizabeth said, 'I don't like that man.'

Lowenna realized that there was another shadow moving below the path.

Nancy had introduced him once, following Bryan Ferguson's funeral, and she had seen him on the Roxby estate a few times. Harry Flinders was Roxby's steward, and at one time his senior bailiff, when 'the King of Cornwall' had been a magistrate here. Tall, strongly built, with the brisk and efficient manner of a soldier. But she had heard Francis, Nancy's coachman, who was ex-cavalry himself, observe on one occasion, 'Soldier, that one? We weren't *that* short of men, even when Boney was just across the Channel!' Obviously not popular. But why Elizabeth?

'Well, ladies, a bit off your usual promenade, ain't you?'

Lowenna smiled coolly. 'Keeping an eye on us, were you, Mr Flinders?'

About forty, maybe older. A man who took care of himself, and one with ambition.

She realized that Flinders was carrying her boots.

'I wouldn't leave these lying about, Miss Lowenna. Too many light-fingered folk around, even out here!' He laughed. 'You've a lot to learn, if I may say so.' He laughed again. 'Bare feet, too!'

Lowenna found another rock and sat. It was no longer a private place.

'I can manage, thank you.' She pulled on each boot slowly and deliberately, feeling the breeze on her legs, like being in a studio. The eyes. The anticipation.

'I'll walk you to the road.' He waved up to the stable boy. '*Jump*, lad! You're not here to dream!'

He half turned and winked. 'Though there's a lot to dream about, eh, Miss Lowenna?'

She walked past him, Adam's letter coming to her mind as if she had heard him speak. *I want you as my wife, my lover, my friend*.

Elizabeth pointed out to sea and said, 'Fishing boats coming back! Let's go and have a look at them!' She did not turn as Flinders heaved himself into his saddle and wheeled round in the road.

She repeated softly, 'I don't like that man. He watches.'

Lowenna touched her shoulder and felt her flinch.

She said quietly, 'Anything, Elizabeth – tell me first.'

They walked back to the road in silence.

* * *

The parish church of King Charles the Martyr was all but empty; it seemed as if everybody who had nothing else to do was down by the water, watching the fishing boats unload. Traders jostling with one another to catch the barker's eye, innkeepers and housewives looking for bargains as the fish were arranged in baskets along the jetty.

In the church it was quiet, timeless. Lowenna sat at the end of a pew, one hand on the prayer book shelf, recalling the day she had met Adam here; the sunlight was streaming through the great window above the high altar, exactly as it had been that day.

She glanced along the pews; there were three or four bowed heads in private prayer, or simply enjoying the solitude. A tiny woman in a smock was polishing the big marble font and its finely carved cover, neither of which looked in need of her care.

She heard a man's voice, like an echo, coming from behind one of the galleries, and Nancy Roxby's in answer. She had come to see the curate about something, and had asked Lowenna to join her.

Lowenna looked at the plaques and memorial inscriptions, the busts, and here and there a carved likeness of one of Falmouth's sons. Campaigns in foreign lands, sea battles and shipwrecks around the pitiless Cornish coastline: many a hero was remembered here. Nancy would be thinking of them, and her own family, her father and brothers, all those watching faces that lined the walls and stairwell of the old grey house.

On the way from the house she had said, 'I heard

you were down on your little beach again?' She had not waited for a reply, or a denial. 'Yes, Flinders told me. He doesn't miss very much, you know. Does a good job of work, honest, and reliable. Roxby chose him for those very reasons.'

Lowenna smiled. She always referred to her late husband as Roxby, never by his first name. As if his presence, even now, was too powerful to suppress. Because she still needed him.

Nancy had also confided her concern over the affairs of the two adjoining estates. Daniel Yovell had been a tower of strength and had helped Bryan Ferguson greatly in his ever demanding bookwork and dealings with tenants and farmers.

Nancy had closed the carriage partition then, and said, 'But I can't expect him to do everything, now that poor Bryan is no longer with us.'

She sensed that Yovell disliked working with Flinders. He had already showed his willingness to help here, in the church, where the Falmouth Sunday school was being extended to include day education, the first, she thought, in Cornwall.

Something would have to be done. Lawyers could not round up sheep, or arrange the cutting of slate for barns and walls.

She shifted her position in the hard pew; her body was very aware of its riding lessons. With distaste, she recalled Flinders' remark about her bare feet in the sand.

She tried to shut it from her thoughts. She was a visitor, with no right to criticize or interfere.

Her mind lingered on Adam's letter, and the long-ing that matched her own. Did one ever get used to it, and if one did, did one lose something, some inde-pendence, some essence of self?

'Ah, there you are, my dear!' Nancy came to the door of the pew and paused, looking around the church, at the shadows and the shimmering colours from the windows. 'You must meet the curate, Lowenna, when you have a moment. He will want to know you.' She touched her arm impulsively, like Adam, or a young girl again. 'Before Adam comes home.'

Lowenna stepped from the pew. *When he had touched her* . . .

'If only . . .' She stopped and reached out. 'What is it, Nancy? Is something wrong?'

Nancy shook her head, but seemed unable to speak. One of the isolated figures had stood up to leave a smaller chapel, where Lowenna had seen old flags and banners hanging. A man dressed in dark clothing, moving stiffly past a table laden with books. Only his hair stood out, grey, but in the occasional shaft of sunlight it looked nearly white.

He seemed to realize they were there, separated by the rows of empty pews, and the little cleaning woman by the font.

Nancy called out, and her voice rang in the dim air.

'Thomas!' She was almost sobbing. 'Thomas Herrick! It really *is* you!'

Herrick pushed past the last barrier and stared from one to the other before taking Nancy's hand in his and studying her, his cocked hat falling unheeded to the tiles. It was then that Lowenna saw that he had only one arm.

Nancy said softly, 'This is Thomas Herrick, my brother Richard's best friend, who became part of our lives a long, long time ago.' She watched as he lifted her hand to his lips, saw the face she remembered so well, aged and tanned like leather, but the eyes the same, blue and clear: the young lieutenant still there, looking out. She smiled. 'Rear-Admiral Herrick, as he now is.'

Herrick bowed to Lowenna as she was introduced, and said, 'To think that we might not have met! It must be fate.'

'We heard you were returning to Africa?' She hesitated. 'Have you finished with the sea, Thomas, is that it?'

Herrick released her hand, his features partly hidden by shadow.

'The sea is done with me, Lady Roxby.'

'Nancy, Thomas. There are no ranks or titles with us, here of all places.'

Herrick glanced at the nearest plaque. *Who fell in battle, for King and Country.* He said without bitterness, 'He was lucky.'

They walked together toward the big doors.

Lowenna thought: beyond those doors there will be a crowd, noise, like an enemy.

She walked beside the man who had been a rear-admiral, one of Adam's world. Her world, if she could seize it.

Herrick said, 'I went to the house. I was going to

342

ask Bryan Ferguson to drive me over to Fallowfield, to the inn. There would be friends there, I thought.' He winced; the pain of the amputation had not left him. 'I knew nothing about his death. It was like a door slamming when I heard. I was planning to go back to Plymouth . . . something made me come in here.' The clear blue eyes moved once more. 'Many memories linger in these walls . . . Nancy.'

'You should have come to us, Thomas.' Although her lips were smiling, she seemed close to tears. 'And The Old Hyperion is probably too full, even for a friend, with all these tradesmen and salesmen using the new road.'

The doors opened and two people entered the church, seeing nothing, and unaware of the moment.

'I shall call Francis.'

Herrick moved as if to stop her, but Lowenna said, 'Please, let her. I am a stranger here, but I have heard her speak of you many times, with much warmth.'

Herrick was looking down at her hand on his sleeve.

'You are a very beautiful girl.' Then he raised his chin a little. 'I am glad you are her friend.'

They walked slowly into the hard light, and Herrick shaded his eyes from the glare.

'Like being cast adrift.' He might have been talking to himself. 'All the ships, thousands of faces, good will, and hatred, gone. I knew it was coming. Have done for months, maybe years. But I could not accept it.'

He looked up as the bells began to chime. 'I was here when Richard was married, you know. John Allday

– you'll not know him,' he almost smiled, 'the rascal. He was there when Richard fell. Told me he was asking for me, even at the end.' He seemed to take a grip on himself. 'But then you'll know about the Bolitho legend?'

Lowenna put out her hand and said softly, 'I am going to marry Adam Bolitho. God willing, I may become part of that legend.'

Nancy paused at the foot of the steps, looking up at them.

'Ride with us, Thomas. There is plenty of room at the house.' She saw the stubbornness in the blue eyes. He, at least, would never change, and she was suddenly grateful for it.

'I can pay my way . . .' He turned as the coachman and a porter from the posting house, pushing a large black chest on a barrow, appeared around the corner of the church. It was probably all he possessed in the world, Nancy thought.

She said, 'And *pay* you will, *sir*!'

Francis had taken in the plain, heavy coat and unfashionable cocked hat. He was still a King's officer, no matter what. That was good enough for him.

Lowenna looked at the passing crowd, heard some one playing a violin, and another shouting his wares.

She would write of it all in her next letter to Adam.

She watched Nancy's face, her expression, but knew she would not be able to describe either.

It was sad; it was beautiful. And it might never have happened.

Francis lowered the step and held her gown clear

of the door. For a second their eyes met, and he murmured, 'Turned out a better day than I thought, Miss Lowenna.'

She was no longer a stranger.

Unis Allday walked across the inn yard and looked up at the sky. Not much cloud, but it was a hard blue, without warmth. She tugged her shawl across her shoulders and heard The Old Hyperion's sign swinging now, creaking in the breeze from Falmouth Bay. The nights were drawing in; there would not be much business tonight. But they could not complain, far from it. They would have to hire more staff if trade continued to grow. The new road, which she could see from her bedroom window stretching away across the fields, had brought more travellers than any one had expected.

Today there were still a few customers unwilling to leave, some pitching horseshoes for bets, others simply yarning; all nodded to her with a measure of respect as she passed. A few might try to take liberties with the woman of the house, but they only attempted it once with Unis.

She had heard one of the local traders who had called into The Old Hyperion for some of her apple pie reading extracts from the *Gazette* aloud for the benefit of some illiterate farm workers. It was the latest report from Africa, where two of the King's ships had been in action with slavers intent on running the blockade.

Unis had been married to a sailor long before she

had wed John Allday, and was no stranger to such news. But it worried her, more so now that Bryan Ferguson had died not far from this yard. The best of friends, although as her brother, the other John, had often remarked, he and Allday had always been like chalk and cheese.

When her John had been forced to quit the sea, after Sir Richard Bolitho had been killed, he had depended on Ferguson to keep the old links and memories intact. A man-of-war entering Falmouth would see John and his friend there on the jetty, taking in every detail, recalling all the names and places. Like the time when a frigate had anchored in the Roads when Allday had been watching from the jetty; the captain had seen him and sent a midshipman with a boat to collect him and take him to the ship like an honoured guest. She had never forgotten his face as he related the story, and the part when the young midshipman had called him 'sir'.

She saw Jack, the inn's latest recruit, hurrying across the yard to the cellar door.

He saw her and called, 'You said I was to put up another cask of ale if we needs one. A pin will do it!' He was about fourteen, and pleased with his authority.

'You're a good lad, Jack.' She knew from experience that if her husband knew about it he would try and do such tasks himself. A sword thrust in the chest had almost killed him. She had sworn that no more harm would come to that big, shambling figure. Clumsy, some might think. But he could fashion beautiful ship models with every spar and block in perfect miniature with those hard, scarred hands.

She brushed some flour from her bare elbow and smiled to herself. The same man had given her their little Kate. No longer so little . . .

Two more traders rode noisily from the yard, each waving his hat to the slightly built woman who had made this the most popular inn between Falmouth and Helston.

She thought about the girl Lowenna who was staying with Lady Roxby. Her John had met her after Bryan's death. Beautiful, he had called her, and she had heard him threaten to throw out two men who were the worse for drink, because they had tried to repeat some alleged scandal about her.

There was bound to be gossip; this business thrived on it. She saw the last horseshoe catch around its stake, heard laughter and the clink of money. Especially where men were concerned . . .

And they said Captain Adam was going to marry her. Her heart softened.

What that old house needs. She turned as she heard Allday's voice from the stable. *What we all need*.

Allday was standing, hands on hips, surveying the horses being led out for three of the departing visitors.

'That's all of 'em, Unis. I'll give a hand with the kitchen before the carter arrives.' He scowled. 'Not sorry to see the stern of that one!'

It was Harry Flinders, the Roxby steward, until recently a rare visitor to Fallowfield. Always polite and careful to show her every courtesy, but not popular with the local people.

He turned easily in the saddle and touched his hat.

'I've been telling my friends here that there's no finer hostelry on Falmouth Bay, no warmer welcome neither!' He grinned, his teeth very strong. Like the man. He looked directly at Allday. 'There was a French ship in Carrick Roads yesterday. I'd have thought you would have been across to see her. There was quite a crowd of old sea dogs.'

Allday said, 'The day I shakes 'ands with a Frog will be the first time, Mister Flinders.'

Flinders shook his head. 'The war's over and done for, man.'

Allday remained very calm. 'I knows that too. 'Cause Jacks like me won it, no other poxy reason. That's it an' all about it!'

The horses clattered out on to the road, Flinders raising his hat again, this time to the dark-haired girl, Nessa, who had become so much a part of their family after being disowned by her parents. Unis had already noticed that she ignored him.

He had better watch his step with our Nessa.

Allday must have read her thoughts. He was still brooding, and annoyed at himself for showing it to the one he loved beyond measure. 'Thinks every woman wets 'er bed over his good looks!'

Two ostlers turned to watch as Unis clutched Allday's arm and fell against him, shrieking with laughter.

Something they could share. Perhaps without knowing why.

Lowenna opened her eyes wide and lay very still; for
how long, or what had awakened her she did not know.
For a few moments she imagined she had overslept,
that it was morning, even though she knew it was
impossible.

Very slowly the big, high-ceilinged room took shape
above and around her; the house was completely silent.
So bright that it was a wonder she had been able to
fall asleep in the first place. The food and wine, and
the fascination of listening to the conversation had
worked well.

Something made her swing her legs over the bed
and walk to the windows. The moon seemed to fill
the sky, so that the stars were almost incidental.

She eased open one of the windows and felt the air
around her body, not cold, as she might have expected
at this time of year. She thought of Nancy's pleasure,
her unusual animation as she had spoken with, and
listened to, Thomas Herrick.

It seemed strange that a man who had seen and
done so much, and had indirectly been a part of the
Bolitho family's life should seem so reticent, even shy,
until Nancy had triggered off a name or memory which
then they both shared.

Through Montagu Lowenna had met several senior
officers, both naval and military, and had gained an
overall impression of supreme confidence, a quality
which usually became evident in the subsequent portrait.

Herrick was not like that. Modest to a point of humility, he spoke openly of his humble upbringing, and his own surprise when he had been awarded the King's commission, the one desire in his life which had never deserted him.

As the logs had burned low in the grate, he had talked of the ships he had served and known over the years, battles which he had described with the easy skill of a painter with a new canvas, without bluff or exaggeration, evoking them so clearly that she could see what he had seen, even hear it, like thunder in the hills. Names became faces; she had watched Herrick's eyes as he had recounted some experience where an admiral or a common seaman had taken over the stage at some point of his life. A storm at sea, the cheerful aftermath with the backbreaking work, and 'too much grog', as he had put it.

And Richard Bolitho was never far away, sometimes as if he had been there with them. *As I was with Adam. Walk with me . . .*

He spoke of their first service together, when Herrick had become his first lieutenant.

He had looked over at Nancy, and said, 'I was there, at the house, when your father brought out the old sword and gave it to Richard.' He had gazed at his empty sleeve, perhaps without seeing it, and said softly, 'There was no finer man on God's earth.' He had paused. 'I beg your pardon, ladies. Blame this good wine for my loose tongue.'

Nancy had waited for her moment. 'You are going back to Plymouth in a few days' time, Thomas?'

He had nodded, perhaps trying to face the reality of his immediate future. His life.

'I am to make a report for their lordships.' Again, the painful shrug. 'The slave trade, what steps remain to be taken. After that . . .'

Nancy picked up her glass and tasted some wine, and for a second Lowenna saw her as a young woman again. Choosing the words.

'You have seen some of the estate, Thomas, the Bolitho house and holdings. You must have been aware of the problems which daily arise, on the farms, with the livestock, to say nothing of what the new road will bring. *Is* bringing. Too many able men taken away to fight, too few returning to honest work on the land.'

'I have heard it mentioned often enough. I have been a sailor all my life, but I appreciate the difficulties.'

She had reached out impetuously and grasped his hand.

'Then stay with us, Thomas. Share it with us. Who better to prepare the way for Lowenna, and for Adam when he eventually comes home?'

Herrick had stared at her as if he had somehow misunderstood.

'But I have no training, no experience!'

Nancy had kept her hand on his. 'My father once said – I forget what roused him at the time – *any man who can command a King's ship, with his inbuilt sense of order, discipline and loyalty, should be well able to run the world!'*

Herrick had looked from her to Lowenna as if to reassure himself.

'I'd take no favours, m' lady, and not because I've run my course . . .'

Nancy had shaken her head. 'I despair of you sometimes! What do they say up north? Nothing for nothing and not much for a penny! Will you take it, Thomas? Join us?'

'If I failed you in some way . . .'

Nancy had stopped him. 'The folk around here do not forget. Many of them know and respect you. You have more than earned your right to live in peace.' She had hesitated. 'And to be amongst friends who care for you.'

Another bottle of wine had appeared. It was settled.

Lowenna opened the window wider and stared into the deeper shadows beyond the trees. The Old Glebe House lay in that direction. What would become of it, she wondered. Perhaps after Sir Gregory's will had been settled, the place would be torn down. Forgotten.

She shivered, and walked to the small table where roses stood in a vase.

She held them to her face and felt some moisture from the petals against her skin. Like her tears, when they had touched for the last time.

She saw her full reflection in the tall glass by the window. It would not be for the last time. Soon, sometime, Adam would be coming back. Like the ship and the mermaids. Coming back . . .

And together they would walk through the old house again. It would not be a dream.

Herrick had spoken of the Caribbean, names and

places, experiences which Adam would recognize, and in turn describe to her.

Very deliberately she faced the glass and pulled the ribbon of her gown, like watching a stranger as it fell around her feet. In the clear, glacier light she stood like a statue, her bare shoulders silvered as she reached out and took the roses, holding them to her breast.

How long she had been standing there she did not know; there was no sound or movement. She could have had the house to herself.

But it was as if there had been a crash of thunder, or some one had screamed a name. His name.

She knew she had pressed the roses against her body, that there was blood on her fingers, like that other time.

But she knew, and wanted to cry out.

It was not in the future. It was now. She touched her lips and tasted the blood.

It was now. And Adam was in peril.

She stared at the glass again, saw the hand move to touch her body.

'*Adam!*'

And she was afraid.

16

No Drums . . . No Quarter

'Ship cleared for action, sir. All pumps manned, boats lowered and towing astern.'

'Thank you, Mr Stirling. That was smartly done.' Adam unclenched each fist beneath his coat, aware for the first time of the force of his grip. The first lieutenant's tall figure was only a vague shape by the quarterdeck rail, his powerful voice formal, unperturbed, giving no hint of doubt or anxiety. Perhaps that was his strength.

Adam turned and stared into the darkness. *What I need*.

Despite the care and the supervision, every sound had seemed exaggerated while seamen and marines had crept between and above decks to prepare for battle if the need arose. Screens taken down to open the ship from bow to stern, unwanted messdeck clutter tossed overboard, each gun tackle checked and checked again, powder and shot laid in readiness. Touch, familiarity, the results of training, skill and some hard knocks along the way for old Jacks and new hands alike. Some one had dropped a handspike on the deck beside one of the long eighteen-pounders. Beyond the gently swaying hull nobody would hear it. But to the men on deck it sounded like a thunderclap.

Even the compass light, invisible from a few paces away, seemed to shine like a beacon, but reflected only in the eyes of the senior helmsman.

In his mind Adam could picture *Athena*'s slow progress, her course to the southwest, the sea empty. Their solitary consort, the frigate *Hostile*, was holding well up to windward, ready to dash down in support of her flagship if another vessel, friend or enemy, showed herself when dawn eventually broke.

Hours yet; they were still only halfway through the middle watch. It was uncanny to sense the people around him. Faces he had come to know, some better than others, always held at a distance. A captain had little choice.

Hard to believe there were over four hundred souls scattered around and beneath his feet, and each in his own fashion measuring the distance from the land which, hour by hour, was reaching out on either bow. The old hands swore they could smell it; the experienced ones like Fraser the sailing master and Mudge the boatswain perceived the hazards like marks on a chart.

Adam heard boots on the damp planking, a whispered word from Lieutenant Kirkland of the Royal Marines to one of his sergeants. Half of *Athena*'s marines had been sent over to the *Villa de Bilbao* as part of the attacking force. Kirkland was no doubt pondering what would happen if his superior, the debonair Captain Souter, failed to return from the proposed venture.

Adam took a few paces to the weather rail and back again. The slavers might already have quit San José; what would Bethune do then? And how, in such a crowded ship, could the vice-admiral manage to remain so distant? The optimism was no longer evident, and his manner was more abrupt, especially toward his young flag lieutenant.

He loosened his fingers, which had once more clenched into fists. It was a wild scheme, but all they had. He thought of their reunion with the prize ship and the frigate *Audacity*. A wild scheme, maybe, but so far time and weather had been on their side.

He wondered what *Audacity*'s captain was thinking as he waited for the first light of dawn. And young David Napier in his new role.

What he wanted, or was it for my own satisfaction?

His fingers brushed against the gold lace on his sleeve. It was his best coat, from the same tailor in Plymouth who had helped transform an eager boy into a King's officer.

He paced slowly along the deck, his feet avoiding tackles and ringbolts without conscious effort.

There would be no line of battle. No heavy ship-to-ship encounter like those other times.

Something his uncle had told him. 'They will want to see you, Adam. Their captain. To know you're there with them when the iron begins to fly.'

He touched the lace again and felt his jaw tighten. Pride or conceit? He could almost hear James Tyacke's voice. *And for what?*

He felt some one move past him and knew it was Jago.

'I never care for the waiting, Luke.'

Jago watched him in the darkness. *So he feels it too.* The ship rising above them, the clatter of blocks and rigging, the occasional crack of canvas in a gust of wind over the quarter. Like sailing a ghost ship into nowhere. But Jago used his freedom to come and go as he pleased to keep note of such things: the lines on the chart, the quiet discussions between the sailing master and his mates, and the captain. It would probably all blow over. Jago was sickened by the way he had seen slaves treated. But it was a fact of life. It was not a sailor's concern, nothing to die for. Or was it?

He thought of young Napier, somewhere up ahead in the little *Audacity*. He had done well, to all accounts, and he had only been aboard for a dog watch. He smiled to himself. Mister Napier indeed!

Adam called, 'Take over, Mr Stirling. I am going below for a while.'

He hesitated, and heard Stirling answer, 'I'll know where you are, sir.'

Adam turned on his heel.

'Come with me.'

Jago followed him to the companion way. The same ship, but so different. He should be used to it. How many fights? Sometimes all the ships and the people

seemed to overlap in his memory. The din and excitement of battle; and always the pain. There was never
time for fear. He grinned. The bloody officers saw to
that!

Adam walked past the guns, hearing the faint squeak
of breeching ropes as the hull tilted to wind and sea,
the water slapping beneath the sealed ports. Tiny, shuttered lanterns gave light to the lounging figures of the
waiting crews. The air was close and humid between
decks, and he saw that most of the men had already
stripped off their shirts, their bodies shining faintly in
the feeble lights like statuary.

Feet shuffled, and faces came into the glow as men
realized their captain was on one of his unheralded
rounds. Some wondered why he bothered, when his
word was the law which meant life or death to any
one he chose. And why he was wearing his dress
uniform when it would mark him out to any sniper if
the time came, as it had done for others, among them
his famous uncle, and Nelson himself.

A voice called, 'Think us'll fight, zur?'

Adam stopped. 'Fellow Cornishman, eh?'

The man showed his teeth in a broad grin. 'Helston,
zur, not too long a walk from your part o' God's county,
zur!'

Jago leaned forward to listen, to share it in some
way. Like that time at Algiers, when he had watched
his face after the fight, and had seen through and
beyond the thing they called courage.

Adam looked past the line of black breeches, the
powder and shot. Gone were the mess tables which

were normally fixed between each pair of guns. Everyday things, the hooks where a man could sling his hammock: overcrowded, and yet each man an individual.

Now there was no war, and the enemy was unfamiliar. But to the ordinary Jack, it made no difference when the guns were run out.

Jago thought of the men put ashore, unwanted in peace. He had seen plenty of them on pier and jetty, watching the ships, and 'swinging the lamp' with each mug of ale.

Did they remember, he wondered, how they had cursed the navy and the masters who walked the quarterdeck in their fine uniforms?

Adam said quietly, 'I think we *shall* fight. The enemy flies no flag, nor does he uphold any cause except greed and tyranny over the helpless. So when the time comes, think well on that!'

The man from Helston called after them, 'Us Cornish lads'll show 'em, Cap'n!'

There was a burst of cheering, joined by seamen at the guns on the opposite side, few of whom could have heard what their captain had said.

A midshipman dodged around the guns until he had caught Adam's eye.

'Beg pardon, sir, but Sir Graham sends his compliments, and would you join him aft?'

'Thank you, Mr Manners. I'll come directly.' A young, eager face. Uplifted, as if he had just been told something inspiring.

Jago walked with him to the main companion.

Beyond the small lights, the ship was still in darkness. Waiting.

He realized that Bolitho had turned to face him, as if they were quite alone, the ship deserted.

'Is that all it takes, Luke? These men don't even know what we are doing here, or why some will die, as surely they will!'

Jago stood his ground, knowing it was important, for both of them.

'You spoke fair, Cap'n. Somebody's got to do it, an' if it wasn't us it would be some other poor Jack. That's the way it goes, an' nothing'll ever change it!'

He stared down as Adam grasped his arm, and for an instant thought he had at last gone too far.

But Adam let his hand fall to his side, and said, 'So let's be about it, eh?' As if another voice had spoken.

The ship was ready. Choice did not come into it.

Lieutenant Francis Troubridge winced as his shin scraped against a cask propped by a hatch coaming to catch the unwary. He had heard the first lieutenant giving orders for every available barrel or bucket to be filled with sea water in case of fire. Even the empty boat tier had been lined with canvas, and more water pumped into it as a precaution.

He had mentioned it to Petch, the gunner. Had it been light enough to see his weathered face, he might have discovered amusement there. Or pity. Old Petch, who had been at sea all his life, since the age of nine it was rumoured, had been present at several major battles, and had been a gun captain in the *Bellerophon* at Trafalgar, in the thick of it.

Petch would be down there in the main magazine now, slopping about in his old felt slippers, *so as not to make a spark or two*, as he often said. One spark would be enough; the whole ship could be blasted apart.

'Them buggers might 'ave furnaces goin' when we gets there.' He had shaken his grey head. ''Eated shot – can be very nasty, sir.'

Troubridge had already served in a ship of the line, the *Superb*, under the famous Captain Keats. He had never forgotten the first time they had cleared for action, the exhilaration, nerves tingling, as if he were being caught and carried on a tide race. Men running to their stations, commands barked from every side, the squeal of calls, but above all the urgent, insistent rattle of the drums beating to quarters.

Petch and some of the others had experienced it many times, seen the faces of messmates and gun crews, seamen and marines, all welded into a single force, like a weapon. Troubridge had been only a midshipman in the *Superb*, but he had never forgotten the thrill and indescribable awe of that moment.

He reached the quarterdeck and strode aft to the poop.

This was so very different. Unreal. The ship thrusting into a sea without stars or horizon. Figures pushing past, voices hushed, breathing like old men, groping at cordage and cold metal, often urged on by hard hands and whispered threats.

'This way, sir.' Bowles, the cabin servant, loomed from nowhere and plucked at his sleeve.

Troubridge groped his way into the cabin and peered around. Two twelve-pounders shared this space where the captain's private quarters had been. The screens were gone; the place where they had talked together, shared a drink or spoken occasionally of home, was now just an extension of the hull. He thought of the portrait he had seen here, the living face he had seen when he and Bolitho had burst into that tawdry studio in London. The lovely body chained and helpless, awaiting her fate. He saw Bowles move toward him and guessed he had spoken her name aloud. *Andromeda*.

Would Bolitho be thinking of her at this very moment? Wondering, groping for hope, when all he had before him was duty and obedience?

Bowles said in a matter-of-fact tone, 'I'm going down to the sick bay shortly, sir. Make meself useful, maybe. Anythin' I can fetch you afore I shove off?'

Troubridge shook his head. If he took a drink now, he might not be able to stop.

Aloud he said, 'It's not like going into action at all, is it?'

Bowles seemed to relax. He had his measure. It always helped.

'I 'eard Mr Fraser tellin' some one of a battle 'e was in a while back, with the Dons it was that time, when it took all day to close with the enemy. Imagine, *all day*, the Spanish tops'ls crawling up an' over the sea like they was enjoyin' it!'

362

Another shape came out of the darkness. '*Sir Graham, John!*' He heard a gulp, and, 'Sorry, sir, didn't see you 'ere!'

It helped to rally Troubridge more than the unseen speaker would ever know.

Bethune strode past, ducking beneath the deckhead beams, his voice sharp, impatient.

'I've just sent for the captain.'

Bowles said, 'He's on the lower gun deck, Sir Graham. I sent word . . .'

Bethune said something under his breath as the deck swayed over, through an invisible trough. Troubridge heard glass clink against the admiral's buttons, and thought he could smell cognac.

He said, 'The wind's holding, Sir Graham. At this rate we should make our landfall as estimated.'

Bethune snapped, 'When I want advice I shall *ask* for it, Flags! And when I want the captain I do not expect to have to go searching for him!'

Troubridge listened to spray pattering across the skylight. Perhaps the wind was getting up, or changing? That would throw all their careful plans into disarray.

He imagined the anchorage, as it was marked on the chart, as it was described by the sailing master and, of all people, George Crawford the surgeon, who had visited San José in his first ship. It was little enough, but sailors had survived on less.

Troubridge was calm again. It had given him time. This was a mood in which he had never seen Bethune before. A hardness which defied his normally easy nature.

Bethune was saying curtly, 'I'm not sure about *Audacity*, and Captain Munro. It is asking rather a lot of him. Young, impetuous . . .' He turned as voices came from the quarterdeck.

Troubridge remembered the room at the Admiralty, the paintings of ships in battle. A time when Bethune had been young, and probably impetuous himself.

Bethune said, 'Ah, Adam, just a word about a few points. In the chart room, I think.'

Composed and apparently relaxed, another change.

Troubridge touched the curved hanger at his side.

He was suddenly reminded of Bethune's previous flag lieutenant. They had hardly spoken but for the formalities of handing over the appointment. Angry, resentful; looking back it was hard to determine. He had been too startled by his own unexpected advance up the ladder.

But the outgoing flag lieutenant had noticed the well-shaped and balanced hanger, which had been a gift from Troubridge's father when he had been commissioned, it seemed a lifetime ago. Long forgotten and dismissed from his mind, his parting remark now rang clearly in Troubridge's memory.

'You'll not need that while you serve Sir Graham Bethune, my young friend! I doubt you'll draw close enough to a real enemy!'

He hesitated, the muffled shipboard noises and occasional shadowy movements very stark and real. Something unknown and different was gnawing at him. He recognized it as fear.

The chart room seemed to be filled with people,

under unshuttered lights almost blinding after the stuffy darkness. Fraser the sailing master and Harper, his senior mate, Vincent the signals midshipman, stiff-faced with concentration as he scribbled some notes, probably for the first lieutenant. Two boatswain's mates and Tarrant, the third lieutenant, who appeared to be cleaning a telescope.

They all faded away as Bethune leaned both hands on the table and stared at the uppermost chart. Fraser watched impassively. Nobody, not even an admiral, could fault his tidy calculations and clearly printed notes.

'Show me.'

Fraser's big brass dividers touched the chart and the neat, converging lines of their course. The points of the dividers stopped above the nearest line of latitude. 'San José, Sir Graham.' His eyes flickered briefly to Bethune's profile, but gave nothing away. 'Two hours if the wind holds.'

Troubridge found that he was gripping the hanger and pressing it against his hip as if to steady himself. Two hours, the sailing master had said. The little frigate *Audacity* would begin her mock attack. He wanted to say something, to wipe his eyes in the stinging glare.

Two hours. On the chart the land still looked many miles distant.

Some one said, 'Captain's coming, sir.'

Troubridge realized for the first time that Bethune's personal servant was also present, in a corner by the chart rack, his eyes shaded by his hat, his mouth a tight line. A man who showed little emotion at any time. Efficient, discreet, probably closer to Bethune than any of them.

Shutters squeaked and then closed again. Troubridge saw the captain framed against the door and the after-guard's musket rack, now empty. He had known Bolitho for so short a time, only since Bethune had requested his appointment as his flag captain. Commanded would be nearer the truth.

There was never any doubt about it. He had heard one of the old clerks remark, 'It's not what you know in Admiralty, it's *who* you know!' Troubridge looked at Bolitho now. A face he would always remember. Dark eyes, sometimes withdrawn, sometimes hostile, but without the arrogance he had seen and found in many. He recalled Bethune's comment about *Audacity*'s young captain: 'impetuous'. Perhaps that, too, but not one to sacrifice the men he commanded, and led.

He started as Bethune remarked, 'When you are with us, Flags, I want to clarify a few final points.'

Some one chuckled, and Adam Bolitho smiled directly at him, and said, 'Waiting is often the worst part, and that is all but over.' He looked at the chart as if his mind was momentarily somewhere else. 'I recall reading an account of the opening engagement at Trafalgar. A young lieutenant wrote of it to his parents: *here began the din of war*.' They watched his hand as it touched the chart by Fraser's dividers. 'So let *us* begin . . .'

Dugald Fraser thought afterwards it was something he would record in his log.

* * *

Even though most of *Audacity*'s seamen and marines had been standing to throughout the night, or snatching brief moments to doze at their stations, the crash of her bow-chaser came as a shock. Some ran to the shrouds or climbed the gangways above the tethered guns as if expecting to see something; others, the more experienced hands, glanced at their companions as if to confirm what they already knew.

It was not just another exercise or drill; the plan outlined by the captain through his officers was real. It was now.

A few gulls, early scavengers which had glided down to meet the ship, wheeled angrily away, their screams following the echo of the first shot. They had doubtless flown out from the land. They were that close.

A gun captain pressed his hands on the breech of his twelve-pounder and muttered, 'That's right, tell the whole bloody world what we're about!'

The air was warm, his shirt clinging to his skin, but the gun was like ice. He heard somebody laugh nearby and added, 'Not much longer, my old beauty!'

On the quarterdeck with one hand loosely touching the rail, *Audacity*'s captain watched the sky. The first hint of a new day; some one less experienced would scarcely have noticed it. In no time now they would see their heavy companion, and all caution would be tossed aside. The real game was about to begin.

He stared along the length of his ship, seeing the waiting gun crews, the sanded decks, the charges ready to be tamped home down each muzzle. Yet there was only darkness. He prided himself that he knew every scar and seam, the faces of the men who would lead, and others who would leap into a gap if those first men fell.

His first lieutenant was beside him; other figures were close by, messengers and boatswain's mates ready to pipe and carry every command to the point of need. Of strength; and it would all come from aft, from their captain.

He could hear the sailing master murmuring to one of his men. He would be missing his senior mate, Mowbray, who had been wounded in the schooner's capture. He was down in the sick bay and the surgeon had already told Munro of his attempts to quit his cot and go on deck where he belonged.

He looked up at the spiralling masthead and felt his lips go dry. He could see the maintop, the black web of shrouds and ratlines. His best lookouts were in their precarious perches, watching, waiting to be the first to sight the heavy barque.

He thought of the officer who was in charge of the *Villa de Bilbao*, Roger Pointer, who had been with Captain Adam Bolitho at the commodore's meeting. He wiped his face. It seemed so long ago, and yet . . .

'*Deck there!*'

Faces peered up, and Munro heard the first lieutenant say, 'Peters is first again! A bet to be settled, I think!'

There were chuckles, too.

The lookout called, '*Larboard bow, sir!*'

That was all, but again Munro felt a shaft of pride. There were not many ships, large or small, where quarterdeck and forecastle maintained so close a liaison.

He felt a hand touch his elbow and said quietly, 'I see it, Philip.'

Like a pale ghost, a curling patch of mist, then stronger as a gust of wind lifted the big ensign up and clear of the gaff, and close to it the metal of a block caught the first ray of daylight.

Dawn. Almost . . .

'Another gun, Philip. Some may still be asleep!'

The gun captain was ready. The bang was louder, and the echo drawn out, as if feeling the land.

It would carry on the wind, and men would be running to identify the ship being chased into their sanctuary.

Pointer and his men would be on their own once *Audacity* was forced to withdraw. Renegades, pirates, or slavers, it made little difference when the iron began to fly.

Munro tried to empty his mind of everything but the picture of the final approach, and how it would look to San José's defenders. How it *must* look. *Audacity* was fast and agile. But she was no ship of the line like *Athena*. He thought of the rendezvous, and his own responsibility. The big prize was strangely transformed, with the huge insignia of a crucifix which *Athena*'s sailmaker and crew had managed to make stitched to her great foresail. Even a good lookout saw only what he expected to see. It might help convince the eyes ashore that the ship being chased by a naval patrol was indeed one of their brotherhood.

But if not . . .

He half turned as a light exploded high in the air before drifting down like a falling star. A rocket or flare of some kind.

He wanted to clear his throat but stopped himself with effort. The light was gone just as suddenly. He saw the chart again in his mind, hidden behind that headland where the first invaders had thrown up their defences.

'Sou' west by west, sir!'

One of the helmsmen reached up for a spoke, and Munro realized for the first time that he could see him.

'Very well. Loose t' gallants and have the guns loaded when you are ready, Philip.'

The first lieutenant looked at him, his face still in deep shadow.

'Double-shotted, sir?'

Munro saw the new midshipman, Napier, hurry past, another ensign draped over his shoulder.

He had already been in a major attack, at Algiers. Some were saying it would be the last fleet battle for all time.

Munro looked across the larboard bow and saw the prize. How could any ship so large have remained invisible until now?

He called, 'Watch your step, Mr Napier. It will be warm work today!'

Napier paused, his dirk slapping against his thigh.

370

Two more shots crashed across the dark water, the flashes like orange tongues. The *Villa de Bilbao* was playing her part, firing back at her attacker.

He heard himself murmur, 'And you do the same, Captain.'

Some one was shouting his name and he turned to go.

Like hearing a voice, or feeling a hand on his shoulder. It made no sense. But he was not afraid.

But . . . He shook himself and hurried to the call, the new flag dragging at his shoulder.

In the first light, its red cross looked like blood.

Adam Bolitho climbed on to the tightly packed hammock nettings and waited for Midshipman Vincent to hand the big signals telescope up to him. Only two hours or so since they had gathered in the chart room and tried to seek out any possible flaws in today's attack. Now it was as if a vast curtain had been rolled aside, with only a dark purple line to divide sea from sky.

He half listened to the faint shouts of command, the clatter of blocks as men threw their weight on the braces to swing the yards still further and contain the wind.

With great care he held the telescope steady, his forearm resting on hammocks stowed with particular attention, creating a barrier to withstand a musket ball or deadly splinter. If you were lucky.

He waited for the ship to lean over on the new tack and saw the land spreading away on either bow, some still lost in haze or shadow, other areas keen and bright in the first sunlight. The sea, too, was shark-blue again, the depths varying in shade like fresh paint on a canvas.

He held his breath as he saw the two other ships, the barque with every sail set, changing colour even as he watched as the morning light found her and opened up her side. Almost in line and close astern, small and graceful by comparison, the frigate appeared to be touching her.

There were more flashes, the report almost lost in shipboard sounds and the hiss of spray along the weather side.

The glass moved again and he saw the low, craggy headland, and some tiny islets directly ahead, caught in *Athena*'s mesh of rigging. There were soundings on the chart, although any experienced sailor would give that part of the bay a wide berth. But somebody had discovered this place, had taken all the risks. He blinked to clear his eye. And some had paid dearly for it, he thought.

He tried to contain his impatience while the hull plunged heavily in an offshore swell. Then he found it again: the old fortifications, and a lower stretch of land where a slipway and some storehouses were said to be located. People, too, some of whom would be waiting and watching from the headland, and the other end of the bay where the deep moorings lay.

He saw *Audacity*'s low hull lengthening as she changed tack yet again, her gunports a checkered line beneath her flapping canvas. He could almost hear the yards turning to refill the sails, see men scampering up the shrouds in response to more commands. All in his mind; he had heard those sounds so often that they were part of himself, his very life.

Something made him twist round to look behind him. He saw Bethune with Troubridge at his side, pointing at the land, stabbing the air with one finger to emphasize something. Perhaps his purpose was faltering, considering the aftermath if the slave ships were already gone, and the whole operation wasted. There would be enemies who would use it against him quickly enough.

He gripped the glass again. Bethune had changed since the discussion in the chart room, and was wearing a long, dark coat with a caped collar, as if he might have worn for riding in poor weather. He remembered that Tolan had been carrying it over his arm while they were examining the chart and comparing notes with the sailing master.

Beneath his own coat his body felt hot and clammy. He glanced down at his gold lace. A ready target for any marksman, they said. Was that what Bethune thought?

Somebody said, 'Wind's easin' off, sir.'

He heard Stirling's blunt response. 'It's the land. Look at the pendant, man!'

Adam trained the glass once more. The others were turning now across *Athena*'s jib boom, sails rippling in confusion as they headed toward the final approach.

There was more gunfire, a different bearing this time. The masthead lookouts would be reporting any change of play as soon as they saw anything.

He turned his head slightly and heard more shots, heavier this time. If any fell near the *Villa de Bilbao* they would know that the ruse had failed. He felt his jaw tighten as what seemed tiny feathers of spray floated past *Audacity*'s stern. Close to, they would be bursting columns as tall as the frigate's counter.

He touched his coat again and saw the shop in his mind, and the boy's surprise, his pleasure.

He shifted the glass very slightly on the hammocks, and could almost feel Vincent's irritation.

He forced himself to remain quite still, moving the glass only slightly when the hull dipped over toward the brightening water.

He remembered it suddenly, as if some one had spoken of it to remind him. When he had been a child, so young he could not put a date or time to it.

He had been lying in some long grass, and his mother had been with him. There had been a line of tall trees along the edge of a nearby farm where he had sometimes done little jobs to earn some money, or be allowed to ride in one of the wagons with their huge horses.

He had seen some small clouds rising and twisting above those same trees. Up and down, never getting any closer. Somebody had laughed at his anxious questions, and then his mother had said, 'It's the time of year, Adam – they are only insects. Thousands of

374

them. You mustn't worry so much!'

He spoke over his shoulder. 'Fetch the first lieutenant, Mr Vincent.' He wanted to control the rasp in his voice. 'Jump to it!'

Not insects this time. He lowered the telescope and dabbed his eye with his wrist. They were tiny balls of smoke. He could imagine the urgency, the crude bellows, the fuel in the ovens changing from red to white around the shot for those hidden guns.

'Take care, David.' He had spoken aloud. 'For God's sake, be careful!'

'You called for me, sir?'

Adam clambered down to the deck and saw Stirling's eyes move briefly to the stains on his breeches.

'They're heating shot. They must have sighted us earlier than we thought.'

Stirling almost shrugged. 'Or been warned, sir.'

Adam swung round as a seaman shouted, '*Audacity*'s been hit!' He was shaking his fist in the air, as if he could see every detail.

Adam raised the heavy telescope again and watched as *Audacity*'s fore topmast tilted toward her bows, and then, as the rigging snapped, gathered speed down and over the side like a broken wing.

At best it would slow her down. At worst . . . In his mind he could still see the clouds of insects above the line of trees.

He said, 'We must signal *Audacity* to withdraw, Sir Graham. They're heating shot at this moment.' He saw Bethune's face and knew it was pointless.

Bethune brushed something from his heavy riding coat.

'They would know at once what we are doing. The *Villa de Bilbao* would have no time to come about. No chance at all!'

Troubridge said something but Adam did not hear what it was, only Bethune's sharp reply. 'When I say so and not before!'

Adam shaded his eyes and watched the *Audacity*, shortening once more as she tacked past an outthrust shoulder of rocks. There were more shots, but no sign of another hit or near miss. But once in the wider part of the channel she would be within range of the main battery. He did not trust himself to look at Bethune. It was his decision; his word would be upheld. It was his responsibility. He looked again at the frigate, smaller now as she sailed into the span of the channel. *And it was my suggestion.*

Bethune said, 'You may load and run out, Captain Bolitho. Make a signal to *Hostile*. *Prepare for battle*.'

The halliards squeaked again and the signal broke from the yard. As planned.

Adam walked to the quarterdeck rail, his hands clenched beneath his coat.

He heard the sullen bang of a heavier weapon and saw the land slowly falling back to reveal the bay and the anchorage, still partly covered in mist. Or smoke.

He watched *Audacity*'s shape lengthening again, her graceful line marred by the missing topmast. Men would be up forward, hacking the mast and cordage away, and the sodden canvas, too, before it acted like a sea anchor and dragged the hull round and across those guns.

Captain Munro would know and maybe blame himself.

The guns fired together. It was already too late.

17

The Reckoning

Vice-Admiral Sir Graham Bethune walked to the companion ladder and shaded his eyes to stare at the land. The rugged hills were touched with a bright copper glow, like the sea. He groped for one of the guns to steady himself as the deck tilted and the helm went over. The metal was no longer cold. It might have just been fired.

The lookout's voice pealed out again.

'*One ship under way, sir!*'

Bethune snapped, 'Find out what the fool has seen, will you?'

Adam called, 'Go aloft, Mr Evelyn, and take a glass.'

It was hard to keep his tone level and unhurried.

Evelyn was the sixth lieutenant, *Athena*'s most junior officer. But there was nothing wrong with his sharp intelligence or his eyesight.

A vessel big enough for the lookout to see at this

distance could mean one thing only. The alarm had gone out. Any experienced slaver would rather risk a clash with the ships converging on the bay than meekly surrender. Once in open water there was always a chance of escape.

He forced himself to remain calm. In control. He had even remembered the lieutenant's name.

Evelyn must have chased up the ratlines like a monkey. His voice carried easily above the wind and sea.

'*Two* ships making sail, sir!' A brief pause, probably to discuss it with the lookout. One of Stirling's best, whatever Bethune thought.

He watched a tiny hump of land far across the starboard bow. Like a basking whale. But too dangerous to ignore.

He breathed out slowly as one of the leadsmen in the chains began to heave his line up and over his head, as if he were oblivious to the ship at his back and everything else.

The heavy lead soared away and splashed into the water well ahead of *Athena*'s massive bows.

Aft came the cry: '*No bottom, sir!*'

Adam had taken chances in the past, and could admit it. He had seen his ship's entire shadow on the seabed once, and known he had been within a fathom of losing his command, and his life.

The leadsman was already coiling his line, his fingers automatically feeling and separating the distinguishing marks of leather, knots and bunting. An experienced leadsman could tell one from another in his sleep.

'*Deck, there!*' Evelyn again, his voice shrill with effort. One of the gun's crew nearby grinned at his mate.

Adam waited, thankful that sailors could still share a private joke, danger or not.

Evelyn shouted, 'One small vessel, sir. The first one is a barque!'

Bethune dabbed his mouth with a handkerchief. 'They'll all be scattering if we let 'em!'

The leadsman, unperturbed, yelled, '*By th' mark ten!*'

Adam saw the sailing master peer at his notes. Sixty feet under the keel.

Bethune said, 'We must anchor if it shelves.' He turned, caught off guard as two more shots echoed across the water. 'We'll engage them after they try to break out!'

'*An' deep sixteen!*'

Fraser glanced at his master's mate and blew out his cheeks.

Adam pictured *Athena*'s shadow as she moved slowly into deeper water. He stared along the starboard gangway and saw Lieutenant Barclay beside one of the crouching carronades. Doubtless listening to every sounding, ready to drop anchor at a few seconds' notice.

Another face fixed in his mind, when he had thought he would never become a part of this ship.

There was a chorus of groans and shouts. *Audacity* had been hit again; her whole foremast lay over the side. And there was smoke.

380

Adam climbed into the shrouds and tried to shade his eyes from the coppery glare. He saw the barque which had up-anchored, turning bat-like past some other moored craft. But he kept his eyes on the frigate, knowing she had been hit by heated shot, how badly he could not determine.

He heard Bethune call, 'Where's Tolan? I want him here!'

The leadsman's voice was unimpressed. '*No bottom, sir!*'

'So there you are, man!' Bethune's face shone with sweat as he began to unfasten his heavy coat. He stared at Tolan's telescope. '*What?*'

Tolan looked past him at the nearest strip of land. There were tiny figures running along a beach, like spectators at some terrible contest.

He answered flatly, 'It's the schooner, Sir Graham. Jacob's boat.'

His eyes were cold as he watched the words strike home.

'Are you certain? It could be any vessel in this damned place!'

'*I* took your message, Sir Graham.' He raised the telescope again. Poised and steady, as if he had done it all his life.

Jago stood near him, his face grim. 'The errand you was on?'

Tolan nodded. 'I'll lay odds she's aboard that schooner right now!'

No name was mentioned. Adam stared at the admiral. There was no need. Not the ordered routine

381

of English Harbour, or London. It was here, a place where few of his men had ever visited. Where a ship was dying, and her people with her.

Somebody had brought the crippled *Audacity* under command. Her remaining canvas was coming about, filling to a wind across her quarter. But there was smoke, pale like steam as *Audacity*'s men fought to douse the smouldering fire from one of the shots.

Bethune exclaimed, 'Make a signal to *Hostile* . . .' His voice all but trailed away. 'It's no use, is it?'

Adam watched the smoke. Bethune had ordered *Hostile* to stand away to the north, ready to run down on any slaver who managed to escape Pointer's eventual attack on the moorings.

Catherine might or might not be aboard the little schooner. Jacob was apparently well known for his dealings with the navy and felons alike. But somehow he knew she was here at San José, because of Bethune, and the man who had always protected her. Sillitoe.

Adam forced himself to use the big signals telescope again, to take time with each thought and reaction, and all the while his body seemed to shake with anger, and with hatred.

Audacity had been hit yet again, and was drifting with the wind, smoke rising above her maincourse like a cloud.

He said, 'I intend to engage the shore battery, Sir Graham. Commander Pointer will soon be in position.' He did not look at Jago as he added, 'Remember Algiers. Boat action!'

He heard the snap of commands, Jago calling out names abruptly. Like that last time when Lord Exmouth's fleet had broken all the rules by choosing to fight against sited and entrenched guns. When every ship was a target.

He waited, knowing his last reserve would snap if Bethune overruled him. But Bethune was standing by the compass box, for another moment unaware of the helmsmen, and the gun crews on either side of the quarterdeck. Boatswain's mates, midshipmen, and the remaining section of Royal Marines. He could have been completely alone.

When he spoke, his voice was barely audible. 'Signal *Hostile* to close on *Flag*.' Then he did look directly at his flag captain. 'Lay a course to weather the headland. We will engage.'

Adam heard the order run through the waiting seamen and marines with the speed of light. He saw Bethune peel off his coat and toss it to his servant. Most of all, he remembered Bethune's eyes, his expression. Like a stranger. An enemy.

The heavy coat lay on the deck where it had fallen. Tolan had hurried after Jago, while men snatched up weapons from the open arms chests.

Jago asked harshly, 'You a volunteer?'

Tolan nodded, and said something he did not hear. But Jago looked past him and up to the rail by the poop ladder.

Adam saw him and lifted one hand in salute. Something only they had come to understand.

There was a dull explosion, the searing hiss of spark

and flame in the bay. A ship had blown up. Twenty-eight years old, like her captain. Finished.

We will engage.

The leadsman called out from the chains, 'No bottom, sir!'

Adam loosened his collar and touched the silk stocking she had given him, which he had wound around his neck.

Stirling shouted, 'Ready, sir!' His eyes were on *Athena*'s captain, not the vice-admiral.

Adam tightened his grip and heard her voice.

Walk with me. The rest had been a dream.

'Steady she goes, sir! West sou' west!' The senior helmsman peered up as the canvas cracked when the wind fell away, and the land moved out to shield them.

Adam had climbed on to the nettings again, his eye smarting in the reflected glare. The water in the bay was like burnished metal, as if the seabed were on fire. There was smoke, too, from *Audacity*'s burning hull or from the hidden guns ashore. He was conscious only of the ship's slow, unwavering advance; the people hurrying about her decks or working high aloft on the yards and rigging seemed merely incidental, as if *Athena* was her own mistress.

There was more activity amongst the moored ships. Patches of sail had appeared, but many of the slavers' seamen were probably ashore. Unless they had been expecting some form of action . . .

He tore his eyes away to watch Jago and two boats' crews running aft to haul their craft alongside.

He jumped down to the deck again and called, 'Bring her up a point!'

He strode to the rail and stared along the full length of the ship. Every gun loaded, its crew grouped around it, some peering at the nearest land as it glided past above the starboard gangway. All the tackles were fully manned, with extra hands from the opposite side for the first, perhaps vital show of force. If Pointer was unable to get his men into position the slavers might still escape, and their attack would be futile. Far worse, it might cost the life of every man who fell into the enemy's hands.

Enemy . . . They *were* the enemy. Flags no longer counted for anything.

Then he saw *Audacity*, or what remained of her. Almost on her beam, and surrounded by burned flotsam and a spreading carpet of ash. One boat was nearby, the oars moving very slowly as it pulled past and among the wreckage. A few figures were clinging to broken spars and a half-burned hatch cover, others drifted beyond all aid or hope. The end of a ship. Something against which he should be hardened.

He was not.

There was silence on *Athena*'s upper deck. Men stood by their guns and at the braces and halliards, and gazed at the burned-out ship. One of their own. There were no words for it.

'*Boats*, starboard bow, sir!'

Adam wiped his face and stared beyond the bow. The small schooner had either hove to, or her steering had gone. She was beam on, some half mile beyond

Audacity's remains. The boats were almost hidden by *Athena*'s beakhead and jib, but there was no room for doubt. He saw the glint of steel, and the tiny flash of a pistol or musket.

Perhaps the trader named Jacob was trying to get away, detach himself from any blame or retaliation.

He saw Stirling by the massive trunk of the main-mast, arms folded as he watched the guns, and the spread of pale canvas towering overhead. Two midshipmen waited with him, ready to pass a message or carry an order without losing a second. One of them could have been David.

A sharp glance aft and he saw Bethune standing by some nettings, Troubridge beside him.

Adam watched the land again, a small, rounded hill with an isolated clump of trees straying down one side, like scattered fugitives.

He cupped one hand to his mouth. There was no point in reporting to Bethune what he must already know. *He who will not risk*. He shut his mind to it.

'Open the ports to starboard!' He made himself count the seconds as the port lids squeaked open from bow to stern along both gun decks.

Where he had walked with Jago, and had spoken with these same men, and the one who came from Helston, from 'God's county'. And they had cheered him.

Only hours ago. This very day.

The ports on the lee side would remain closed until it was time to bring the other broadside to bear.

He looked up and into the bay. If they ever reached that far.

Midshipman Manners shouted, 'Listen! Listen, sir!' His youthful face was filled with disbelief. He took off his hat and waved it with wild excitement. '*Huzza! Huzza!*'

Vincent snapped, 'Silence on deck there!' But even he seemed at a loss.

Adam heard it. Faint at first, then carried on the offshore breeze it blended into a wave of cheering.

Dugald Fraser said, 'Cheerin' *us*! And I thought I'd seen all there was to see!'

Adam swallowed hard and saw some of the small figures in the water twisting round to watch *Athena*'s slow approach. Maybe the first time any of them had found time to look for her.

He said, 'Run out, Mr Stirling!'

The decks quivered as every gun squeaked up to its open port, men throwing all their strength and weight on the tackles to haul their massive charges into the sunlight.

Adam leaned on the quarterdeck rail, although he did not recall having moved. He did not need a glass. Here was the headland, the white buildings he had seen through the signals telescope, drifting smoke in blotches against the sky, insects no longer. A brief glance at the tilting compass card, seeing the helmsman's fist opening and closing around a spoke, as if beating time to something.

He heard a shot, perhaps two, and looked up as a ball punched a hole through the main topgallant sail.

He saw Stirling's arm shoot out, like a man controlling an excited horse. 'Steady, lads!' His eyes must have moved along every gun, while down in the semi-darkness of the lower gun deck they would all be listening, waiting for the signal from aft.

Adam stared at the land again and felt the silence like something physical.

'*On the uproll!*' There was no sense in calling a target. At this range they could not miss.

He felt the deck tilt as the wind refilled the sails and pictured *Athena*'s double line of teeth lifting to maximum elevation.

'*Fire!*'

The effect was devastating as every gun along the ship's starboard side roared out as one, each hurling itself inboard on its tackles, the crews yelling and gasping as smoke funnelled through the open ports. Dazed by the tremendous broadside, men were already sponging out and preparing to reload even before the combined thunder had died, and still the echo thrown from the land lingered above and around them. Adam held his hand across his mouth, his mind blurred by the power of the guns. It was as if *Athena* lay side by side with an enemy in some invisible line of battle, while below decks in the gloom and whirling smoke it must have felt as if the ship had run aground.

He peered up at the sails and to the masthead pendant, still whipping out toward the larboard bow, when all else was partly hidden by smoke.

He saw gun captains standing by their crews, one fist and then another raised and ready. It was as if everything else was moving, while *Athena* remained as before.

The big barque which had been the first one to make sail lay across the larboard bow, on a converging tack, desperate now to clear the headland and reach open water.

He held up his arm and saw Stirling acknowledge him. Men, their bodies shining with sweat, were running across to await the next command.

'Open the ports!'

Stirling swung round as the forgotten leadsman shouted, '*By th' mark five!*' Just thirty feet under the keel. Adam found a second to wonder how the seaman could think and concentrate on the line snaking through his fingers while the ship, his world, reeled about him.

'*Run out!*' Easier for the depleted crews as the deck heeled in their favour to another flurry of wind.

Adam took a telescope from a master's mate and trained it abeam. One of the long buildings and a crude-looking pier had taken most of the broadside, and one entire wall had collapsed in the old fortifications, leaving a gap like missing teeth.

He saw Fitzroy, the fourth lieutenant, walking unhurriedly along the eighteen-pounders under his charge. He might have been alone in a country lane.

'As you bear! Lay for the foremast! On the uproll!'

Just seconds. To some an eternity; then, '*Fire!*'

The water was hidden by smoke, the air cringing to the irregular crash of shot as each gun captain gauged the moment before jerking his firing lanyard.

The barque had been badly hit, and her fore and main topmasts seemed to bow to each other as the double-shotted broadside smashed through them.

Some one yelled out, 'Not just slaves this time, you bastard!'

As if he saw only a single enemy. Perhaps he was right.

Adam gripped the rail as he felt the deck jerk under his feet. And then another, deep in the lower hull. Heated shot or not; they would soon know.

He tried to keep his mind clear of everything but the shifting panorama across and beyond *Athena*'s beakhead, with Bethune's flag casting a shadow above the taut jib.

The pumps were going, and there was water in every kind of cask if the worst happened.

A flurry of shots, from the barque or one of the drifting boats nearby. A seaman running to join the boatswain's men at the braces seemed to falter, and look around as if something had caught his attention. Then he fell, his face shot away.

Another figure ran toward him but stopped when a petty officer shouted to him.

Clough, *Athena*'s carpenter, was hurrying forward with his own crew, his face intent, the true professional. Few ever considered that when a King's ship left port, her carpenter had to be ready for anything from repairing, even building some kind of boat, to dealing with every seam and plank above or below deck.

A hand seized his arm, and for an instant Adam believed he had been hit by some invisible marksman.

But it was Bethune, staring through the drifting smoke, his eyes reddened by strain and something more. Desperation.

'Yonder, Adam – is that the schooner?'

Adam heard some one cry out, and saw two marines dragging a limp figure clear of the starboard gangway.

He saw the little schooner, some boats apparently trying to grapple alongside. Two other boats were moving toward her, the oars rising and falling like wings, the best Jago could get at such short notice. Adam licked his lips, recalling his curt order.

Boat action. All Jago would need. *And for what?*

'Aye, sir. She's out of command.' He stared at the land again, measuring it. Watching the changing colours in the bay, very aware of Fraser and his mates, and Stirling's motionless figure by the guns.

And all the others he could not see, who obeyed because they had no choice. Because there was none.

'I intend to come about directly, Sir Graham, and rake their defences as we leave.Without those guns to support them they'll crack, and Commander Pointer will get his chance. Until then . . .' He winced as a seaman fell from the mainyard and hit the deck, his face staring at the copper sky.

'*Sir!*' It was Kirkland, the lieutenant of Royal Marines; surprised, shocked, it was beyond either.

Adam strode to the nettings and climbed on to them. He felt cordage cutting his knee where his breeches had been torn open. It was madness. There was more blood by a stanchion, where another man had been cut down. Yet all he could hold in his reeling mind was a picture of Bowles, and his horror when he had seen his captain donning his best uniform before beating to quarters.

The smoke was thinner down on the low foreshore, and he could see some upended boats near the water close to a rough road or track. No fifes or drums, no commands to bark out the pace or the dressing, but the scarlet coats and white crossbelts of *Athena*'s Royal Marines marched in perfect order, Captain Souter in the lead, hatless and with a bandage around his head, but with all the style of a barracks parade.

There were flames at the top of the bay: a ship ablaze, or Pointer's own signal of success.

'Stand by to come about!'

He heard the leadsman's cry. '*Deep four!*' No doubt wondering if any one heard or cared with iron beating into the hull, and men dying.

The sailing master had heard well enough.

'Christ, she'll be sailing on wet grass in a minute!' *Athena* drew eighteen feet.

Men were running to the braces, while somewhere high overhead axes were slashing away broken cordage and sails torn apart by haphazard shots from the land and from the barque, which had taken the full brunt of *Athena*'s vengeful broadside. For revenge it was. Adam looked at Bethune's face. There was no deception now. If anything, it was despair.

He looked at the marching figures on the land, joined now by others, sailors from other ships of English Harbour, redcoats from the garrison. He had heard Bethune's servant speak of them, an English county regiment. Not what they had been expecting when they had left home.

He measured the distance again, and gauged the wind. It had to be now.

He heard more shots hammering into the hull, men shouting, saw the tell-tale smoke seeping from one of the hatch gratings. The gun crews were poised with handspikes ready, slow matches in their tubs in case the flintlocks should fail at the moment of action.

Small scenes stood out and gripped his attention, even though every fibre was screaming for him to begin what might be his last moments in this, the only world he truly understood. A midshipman writing busily on his slate, as if it was all that mattered. Bethune shaking his head as Troubridge tried to offer him the heavy coat again, perhaps because of a tall splinter which had been levered from the deck like a quill a few yards from where he was standing.

Adam knew Stirling was watching him, judging the moment, and the remaining time for *Athena*, his ship, to come about.

He walked swiftly to the rail and touched the sailing master's arm, but did not take his eyes from the upper yards and the masthead pendant.

'Remember what you said to me when I came to *Athena*? That she was a fine sailer even close to the wind?'

He saw Fraser stare at him, and then nod. 'Good as any frigate, sir!' Determination, and perhaps relief that his captain had not cracked under the strain.

'*Stand by to come about!*' He saw Bethune walk across the deck, his eyes on the nearest land, the ground and hillside still smoking from their first broadside.

'Aim for the battery.' He leaned on the rail. 'Put the helm down!'

The spokes were spinning round; the helmsmen needed no urging.

'Helm a-lee, sir!'

Some one had loosened the awning across the empty boat tier, and some of the released water was surging across the deck where seamen were already forming a bucket chain.

'*Off tacks and sheets!*'

Still turning into the wind, a few boats pulling away as if they imagined they were the new target.

Adam felt the deck tilting, the land sliding past, the rounded hill suddenly standing like a marker on the opposite bow. The yards were as tightly braced as they could bear, the canvas almost aback as the ship came slowly into the wind. Small things stood out. The hole punched in the topsail had spread across the full breadth of canvas; torn rigging trailed down toward the deck like dead creeper. Then the tip of the headland itself, some crumbling fortifications clearly etched now against the sky. And directly beyond it, like water piled in a great dam, was the open sea.

'*Steady as you go!*'

He could see a tiny pyramid of sail, like pale shells in the strengthening sunlight as the frigate *Hostile* hurried to obey *Athena*'s last signal, to close on the flagship.

He saw Bethune by the poop ladder, leaning across an unmanned swivel gun to stare at the small schooner. He wondered what Jago would think when he saw *Athena* sail past, heading once more for open water.

'East by north, sir!'

He saw Fraser watching him from the compass box. He knew. It was as close to the wind as *Athena* would come. Perhaps even better than he had promised.

Each gun captain was ready. Here a handspike moved to adjust the muzzle's elevation, or a tackle squeaked to train a gun a fraction more, until the eye over the breech was satisfied.

'*Ready*, sir!' That was Stirling again. The ship had come about and was on the opposite tack. The drills and careful selection of seamen known for their skill and reliability, in all weathers and in the face of death itself, had been his main concern, a first lieutenant's role, ship of the line or little sixth-rate like *Audacity*.

Adam knew that Bethune had joined him. Perhaps already trying to gauge the final outcome, perhaps the blame when the repercussions began, as they surely would. Renegades or not, this was Cuba, Spanish territory. Face would have to be saved, until the next time.

Bethune watched Adam raise his hand over his head.

He said, 'After this, Adam. I have to know.' His eyes were steady, even calm. '*I must know!*'

Adam saw the nearest gun captain testing his trigger line. It was taut. To him, nothing else mattered. He was right. Leave questions to others.

His arm sliced down. '*Fire!*'

It took even longer for the dust and smoke to settle. The hillside looked much as before the broadside, but merged now with the fallen walls and rooftops where the battery had been sited to command the approaches.

'Reload, sir?'

Adam shaded his eyes to stare along the foreshore, where he could just discern the scarlet coats of the marines. They would wait to ensure there was no further resistance while the slavers were seized by Pointer's prize crews, or scuttled where they lay.

'I think you should see this, sir.' It was Troubridge, pale and tight-lipped. But somehow more mature, confident.

Adam trained the glass on the bearing Troubridge was indicating. Faces leaped into focus, vignettes of excitement, and pain. And pride. The sailor's lot.

He saw the little schooner, boats still tied or drifting alongside. His fingers tightened on the warm metal. *And a flag.* A smaller version of the one which *Athena* had flown since leaving English Harbour.

Jago had done it. As they had arranged. So he must be safe. He looked across the bay where they had seen the last of *Audacity*. If only . . .

'I propose to anchor directly, Sir Graham.' For a moment he thought he had not heard, but Bethune said, 'Do so. I shall see that your part in this affair does not pass unnoticed.'

He knew Troubridge was watching, perhaps realizing for the first time that he knew his admiral better than he had thought.

Bethune said quietly, 'I should like to go across, Adam.'

He was not demanding. If anything, he was pleading.

It was like being on the outside of something. Orders were being shouted or relayed by the piercing twitter of Spithead Nightingales. Men stood back from their guns, while others clung to halliards and braces, the ship under command while they peered around, seeking special friends, or staring at the damage.

Bowles hurried past with a list of names, men who had been killed or were in the orlop being treated, or dying.

No great action this time, but the price was always too high.

Some were cheering, letting go, the blues and whites of officers and warrant ranks mixing with all the others. Some were looking aft, at the quarterdeck where their lives could be changed or ended without question or blame.

Bethune said, 'I must go below. Let me know when . . .' He did not end it.

He would find no peace or escape there. The admiral's quarters would still be cleared for action, like his own and the whole ship. He thought of her portrait. Waiting.

It was as if some one else had spoken. He said, 'I think you should stay a while, Sir Graham.' He glanced at the faces below the quarterdeck rail. 'They look to you. Trust, obedience, I'm never sure.'

Troubridge joined him by the ladder, and watched as Bethune made his way to the main deck and walked along the line of guns. Hesitant at first, the sailors jostled around him, some reaching out as if to touch him, others laughing and calling his name.

Adam was glad he could not see his face.

He knew people were waiting to see him: Stirling about casualties, and rearranging the watch bills, filling the gaps. The surgeon with his bill. Men to be buried. Repairs were already being carried out; sailors could not waste much time on regrets and tears.

But for a few moments longer . . . *They look to you.*

Troubridge said, 'When you need a lieutenant, I'd be obliged if you'd bear me in mind.'

Adam turned, his eyes cold. But it passed as quickly.

He touched his sleeve and said, 'I shall never see my own flag up there, my friend.' He saw Stirling looming through the seamen and strode to meet him. To escape.

Troubridge smiled. *I would serve you in any capacity!*

One hour later, with a different leadsman in the chains, *Athena* turned slowly into the wind again, and dropped anchor.

Her remaining boats were being warped alongside, crews called or pushed to the tackles for hoisting them inboard. The aftermath of battle. Any battle. Men putting their ship in order. Ready to fight if need be, to face a storm, to survive. There was a smell of rum in the air but there had been no time to open the spirit store. Hoarding rum was an offence, but today men drank to each other, and to absent friends whom they would never see again.

Stirling strode aft and touched his hat. 'Boat's ready, sir. The second cutter.' It sounded like an apology, but Adam doubted if Bethune would even notice. He glanced at the flag at the foremast truck. Perhaps *Athena* would never see an admiral's barge being hoisted aboard.

'Very well. Man the side.' He wondered if anything would or could move this unbreakable man. He saw smoke on the wind, but it was the galley funnel, the first priority after a fight. But the thought of food made him feel light-headed.

He followed Stirling to the entry port where a small squad of Royal Marines were already paraded and being inspected by their lieutenant. Two boatswain's mates waited with their silver calls to pipe Bethune into the boat.

While *Athena* swung to her cable the land remained invisible to the assembled side party. There was only the sea, bright now, almost blinding in the reflected glare.

Adam saw *Hostile* making her final approach, and even without a glass he could see her people clinging to shrouds and high on the yards. Here, Vincent was ready with his signals party, unsmiling as he watched flags being pulled from their locker.

Perhaps it was better, safer, to be like Vincent, or the lieutenant of marines. Or Stirling, secure in his strength and his loneliness, with only the ship to sustain him.

''Ere he comes, boys!'

That was the sailor named Grundy, who had once

served under Bethune when he had been a captain. Whom he had pretended to remember, even recognize, when he had hoisted his flag over *Athena*. Another lie . . .

Grundy raised a cheer which was taken up by others, working on repairs and hoisting new cordage aloft for the sailmaker's crew. The cheers were soon quelled by the master-at-arms.

And here was Bethune, brushing aside any one who attempted to assist him through the entry port. He looked strained, but nodded to the Royal Marines, some of whom carried the stains and scars of the morning. Adam saw that his uniform was perfect by comparison. As if, like that first day, he had just stepped aboard.

He said, 'I should like you to accompany me, Captain Bolitho.'

Clipped and formal.

Adam was deeply moved. Another lie, and he was unprepared for it. He climbed down into the cutter, Lieutenant Evelyn standing in the sternsheets to receive him.

Above the boat he heard the slap of muskets, and the trill of calls as Bethune climbed down to join him.

'Out oars! Give way together!'

Adam touched the thwart where a stray musket ball had scored its mark. The faces of the oarsmen, ones he had believed he would never know, watched the stroke, the blades dipping and rising together, the tension and the fear already draining away.

And all at once the schooner was looming over them. More faces he recognized, even some of Captain

Souter's landing party, their scarlet coats at odds with the others, and some he assumed were the schooner's own men. Bethune clambered up the side, hardly waiting for the bowman to hook on.

And here was Jago, teeth bared in a grin as he seized Adam's hands and pulled him aboard.

He said, 'Made it as fast as I could, Cap'n! Them bastards boarded the schooner. It was touch an' go. I wanted to send the gig, but—'

He turned as Bethune said, 'Where is she?'

Adam realized that two of the marines were guarding a tall man who, like Bethune, appeared unmarked by the events Jago had described.

Somehow he knew it was Sillitoe, the central figure whose name had featured in most of Bethune's despatches.

Captain Souter said, 'In the cabin, Sir Graham. There was nothing we could do.'

Adam said, 'Let me . . .' but Bethune pushed past him. Only for a few seconds he stared over the side toward the same sloping headland.

'*Why?*'

Jago said quietly, 'We'd just got aboard, y' see, Cap'n. They started shootin', so did we. Then I see her comin' on deck. I think she saw the ship.' He gazed over the water, remembering. '*Our* ship.'

Adam heard something fall, the movement of boats alongside. And Bethune's voice.

Jago shook his head. 'There was blood, but she seemed to be smiling.' He shook himself. 'I ain't sure, Cap'n.'

Adam took his arm, like those other times. 'Try to remember, Luke. What she said.'

Jago looked at him fully, his unshaven features suddenly calm.

'She said, "It's Richard!"' He looked away, toward the sea. 'Then she fell.'

Bethune had reappeared on the littered deck. He looked around, but seemed to see nothing.

Then he became aware of Adam, and said brokenly, 'I've lost her, Adam. Lost her . . .'

Sillitoe said, with great contempt, 'She was never yours to lose, damn your bloody eyes!'

Captain Souter snapped, 'Take that man across to *Athena*, Corporal, in irons if you see fit!'

Adam saw that Bethune was carrying a green shawl, and heard him murmur, 'She was always fond of this colour.'

He walked to the bulwark and stood staring down at the cutter.

'I want her taken to English Harbour, Adam. She was happy there, I believe.' He seemed to realize for the first time that Jago was beside him.

He said, 'I'll take the cutter. You stay with the flag captain.'

Jago watched the boat pull clear of the side, frowning at the stroke.

Then he said, 'I'll 'ave the gig ready when you says the word, Cap'n.'

Adam looked at him and saw that Tolan, Bethune's loyal servant, was still on board, and recalled that they had ignored one another.

Then he saw Jago's face.

'What is it?'

Jago pushed through some seamen and leaned over the gunwale again. *Athena*'s gig was tugging at her painter, two injured sailors squatting on the bottom boards as if nothing had happened.

'Where did you find him?' He could scarcely form the words.

'The bloody Royals got him, would you believe.' He could not control his pleasure, but it was far more than that.

Adam stared at the slight figure propped in the sternsheets, partly covered by a jacket, the white collar patches very clear in the sun's glare. His legs were bare, and he could see the same savage scar, as if it had just happened.

Jago said, 'There was two middies when they found 'em. But the other one was dead. It seems that young David swam with him to the shore after *Audacity* went down.'

Adam saw the boy looking up at him, saw him smile, and the two seamen turning to share the moment.

Jago was saying, 'He's a bit weak. But he's through the worst of it.'

'What did you tell him?' He thought of Bethune's anguish, and the woman who lay in the cabin below their feet.

Jago smiled freely for the first time.

'I told him you would be takin' him home, Cap'n.'

Soon he would be that captain again. But now, the words would not come.

Jago had found two mugs from somewhere, and put one in Adam's hand.

He glanced over at *Athena*'s loosely brailed topsails, and something flashing from her poop, catching the sun.

Then he looked at Adam, and was glad. 'Not a bad old ship in some ways, eh, Cap'n?'

A man of war.